C0069 60206

D1186668

The
Strawberry
Field Girls

Karen Dickson lives in Dorset and used to work at her local branch of WHSmith, where she was fondly known as The Book Lady. *The Strawberry Field Girls* is her fourth novel.

Also by Karen Dickson:

The Shop Girl's Soldier
The Dressmaker's Secret
A Songbird in Wartime

The Strawberry Field Girls

KAREN DICKSON

**SIMON &
SCHUSTER**

London · New York · Sydney · Toronto · New Delhi

First published in Great Britain by Simon & Schuster UK Ltd, 2022

Copyright © Karen Dickson, 2022

The right of Karen Dickson to be identified as author
of this work has been asserted in accordance with the
Copyright, Designs and Patents Act, 1988.

1 3 5 7 9 10 8 6 4 2

Simon & Schuster UK Ltd
1st Floor
222 Gray's Inn Road
London WC1X 8HB

Simon & Schuster Australia, Sydney
Simon & Schuster India, New Delhi

www.simonandschuster.co.uk
www.simonandschuster.com.au
www.simonandschuster.co.in

A CIP catalogue record for this book
is available from the British Library

Hardback ISBN: 978-1-3985-0367-0
eBook ISBN: 978-1-3985-0368-7
Audio ISBN: 978-1-3985-1706-6

This book is a work of fiction. Names, characters, places and incidents are either
a product of the author's imagination or are used fictitiously. Any resemblance
to actual people living or dead, events or locales is entirely coincidental.

Typeset in Bembo by M Rules
Printed and Bound in the UK using 100% Renewable
Electricity at CPI Group (UK) Ltd

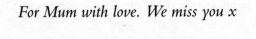

For Mum with love. We miss you x

The
Strawberry
Field Girls

CHAPTER ONE

1913

'Leah, Daisy. It's half past four. Time to get up.'

At the sound of her mother's voice, 16-year-old Leah Hopwood groaned and rolled onto her back. She stared up at the ceiling in the murky, pre-dawn light. From the lane below came the creak of wagon wheels and the slam of a cottage door. She sighed and nudged her 14-year-old sister. 'Come on, Daisy. Get up.'

Mumbling incoherently, Daisy rolled over, dragging the bedcovers with her. The gush of cold air on her exposed legs along with the rattle of the stove lid in the kitchen below was enough to spur Leah into action.

'Get up,' she said, giving Daisy's shoulder a shake. 'You can't afford to be late. Neither of us can.' She climbed out of bed and dressed quickly by the light of the pale dawn filtering through the thin curtains. Favouring their late father, William, Leah was tall and willowy with dark blonde hair and blue eyes while Daisy, three inches shorter with wavy, light brown hair and hazel eyes, resembled their mother.

As Leah twisted her hair into plaits, she couldn't help her gaze straying to the spot on the landing where Freddie's bed had once stood. She swallowed the lump in her throat. It had been four years since the diphtheria epidemic that swept through the tiny hamlet of Strawbridge had claimed the lives of so many. Leah's father, older brother and two younger sisters had all succumbed to the disease. Her strong, dependable father had been the first to slip away, followed by Freddie, three days later, dying on the eve of his sixteenth birthday. Mary and Sarah, just eight and five years old respectively, had passed away within hours of each other a few days later.

Forcing herself not to dwell on how noisy and happy the early summer mornings had once been with all five Hopwood children boisterously preparing for a long day in the strawberry fields, Leah hurried down the stairs.

The parlour was sparsely furnished. A single lead-paned window looked out onto the lane and the strawberry fields beyond. A large fireplace took up one end of the room, a brass coal scuttle standing beside the empty grate. Upon the mantelpiece, in pride of place, stood a framed photograph of Leah's parents, William and Hannah. It had been taken shortly after their wedding twenty-one years earlier. Beside it, between a pair of brass candlesticks, stood a photograph of the five Hopwood children taken two years before the epidemic.

Leah remembered the day it was taken as if it were

yesterday. It had been on a rare trip in Southampton. Dressed in their Sunday best, they'd dined at the Crown Hotel before visiting a photographer's studio close to the Bargate on Above Bar and there had been great excitement when the photograph had arrived in the morning post some three weeks later.

The sofa stood under the window, its faded upholstery hidden by a red and white crocheted blanket. Pushed up against the inside wall was the dropleaf table and four chairs. An oval mirror hung on the wall above it. On scuffed wooden floorboards were several handmade rugs. Above a small writing desk hung a watercolour depicting Salisbury Cathedral, its spire shrouded in mist, with the water mead-ows in the foreground. As usual, Leah paused to admire it. Her father had been inordinately fond of the painting, which he had bought off a market stall on a long-ago trip to Salisbury before he and Hannah were married. He had always promised to take them all to see the cathedral, a promise he could now no longer keep, and so the painting had garnered a certain poignancy for Leah.

Feeling the familiar tightening of her throat, she swallowed quickly and hurried into the warm, steam-filled kitchen where her mother stood at the stove stirring the porridge.

'Morning, Mum.'

'Morning, love,' Hannah replied, smiling at Leah over her shoulder. 'Is Daisy up?' Lifting the heavy-bottomed pan from the heat, she placed it on the metal trivet in the centre of the table.

'She was just stirring,' Leah said, pulling out a chair and sitting down.

'It was a mild night,' her mother said with a quick glance at the clock on the wall above the table. 'With a bit of luck, we've seen the last of the frost.'

'Let's hope so,' Leah said, ladling porridge into the waiting bowls. It was warm in the kitchen. Droplets of condensation ran down the misted-up window that looked out on to the back garden and the privy they shared with their neighbours. Theirs was the middle cottage in a row of three. The cottages that made up the hamlet of Strawbridge were grouped in twos or threes, sixteen in all, spread out between the Glyn Arms public house, the vicarage and St Luke's church.

Beyond the shared privy was a large chicken run and a flourishing vegetable patch, bordered by a hawthorn hedge, beyond which were the grounds of Streawberige House, home to the wealthy Whitworth family.

Blowing on her porridge to cool it, Leah looked up as footsteps sounded on the stairs and Daisy came bounding into the kitchen, her dark hair flying around her face. She dragged out a chair, its legs scrapping noisily on the slate floor, and was about to sit down when there was a knock at the back door.

'Who can that be?' Hannah wondered out loud. Setting the brown ceramic teapot on the table, she wiped her plump hands on her apron and opened the door.

'Morning, Mrs Hopwood.' The young man standing on

the threshold grinned cheerfully. He had a shock of black hair and olive skin that crinkled around his eyes when he smiled. 'I brought you something for your supper,' he beamed, holding up a brace of pheasants. 'And a posy for the lovely Leah.'

'You'll be for it if Mr Whitworth's gamekeeper catches you poaching, Joshua Mullens,' Hannah scolded, the smile in her eyes belying her stern tone. 'Come on in.' She stood aside and opened the door wider. 'There's porridge in the pot if you're hungry.'

'Starving, I am,' Joshua said. He handed Hannah the pheasants, pausing to remove his dirty boots on the mat before entering the kitchen. 'Morning, Leah, Daisy,' he said with a mock bow as Hannah took the pheasants to hang in the pantry. 'Flowers for the prettiest girl in Strawbridge,' he said, presenting Leah with a posy of early summer wild flowers.

She blushed. 'You're a fool, Joshua Mullens,' she chided him, but she couldn't help smiling as went into the pantry to find an empty jam jar to put them in.

'Will you tell me if you'll accompany me to the picker's ball, Leah?' he asked, as she placed the jam jar on the table and dished him up a generous helping of porridge. 'Or will you keep me in my agony of torment until I die of a broken heart?'

'You're silly,' Leah smiled, but her mirth was not reflected in her dark blue eyes. She was flattered by his attentions. Who wouldn't be? He was very handsome but ... She hesitated, reluctant to hurt his feelings. He was a good man, a little wild but his unruly ways hid a generous heart and, usually, she would have jumped at the chance to attend the ball with him . . .

'Oh, come on, Leah,' Joshua said, interrupting her rambling thoughts. 'Won't you put me out of my misery?' he cajoled, dousing his porridge in milk. His grin broadened. He paused and looked up at her, one eyebrow raised quizzically. 'You're not holding out for a better offer, are you?' he teased.

Leah felt the colour rise in her cheeks and quickly averted her gaze.

'I haven't decided whether I'm going to the ball,' she mumbled.

'What are you talking about?' Daisy scoffed in amazement. 'It's the highlight of the year. No one misses the Pickers' Ball, least of all you.'

'Who's missing the ball?' Hannah asked, coming in from the garden with five fresh eggs in her apron which she placed in a bowl on the table. She looked at Leah questioningly.

'You don't mean that?' Joshua said in a wounded tone. 'You always go.' His thick, black brows knitted together across his sculptured nose. 'With me. Why's this year any different?' he asked suspiciously.

'No reason,' Leah replied. Pushing back her chair, she began to clear the table, conscious of Joshua's wounded gaze following her about the kitchen.

How could she explain to Joshua that she was hoping

someone else would invite her to the ball? She felt wretched just thinking about it, but . . . She plunged her arms into the soapy water. She could feel Joshua's gaze burning into her back. Daisy was telling him something, but she could tell by his non-committal grunts that he wasn't really listening. But despite her discomfort, she couldn't deny the tingle of pleasure that raced up her spine at the thought that she'd see *him* again, very soon.

His name was Harry. She'd noticed him the day the strawberry picking season started. He wasn't from Strawbridge or the surrounding area so she'd assumed he must be one of the many 'Joe Pickers' who made their way over from Southampton every morning to work on the various strawberry farms around the likes of Hedge End, Botley, Sarisbury and Curdridge.

He was tall and well-built, with fair hair and pale blue eyes. Within days of working in the fields she had watched in veiled amusement as his face and forearms bloomed an angry shade of crimson before turning a deep shade of honey-brown.

On that first day she'd been packing straw around the base of the vulnerable young plants. It was backbreaking work and as she'd straightened up, rubbing the base of her spine in an effort to relieve the ache in her back, she'd happened to glance up at him. He was standing on the back of the cart, on a mound of straw, tossing clumps of it to the ground with his pitchfork. As she caught his eye, he'd smiled a smile so infectious, she couldn't help but grin back at him. After that, she'd watched him surreptitiously, inwardly smiling as she caught him looking over at her each time she glanced his way. Over the days that followed their smiles had progressed to brief exchanges when they happened to meet when emptying their baskets, or queuing for a drink of water at the trough. After a while she began to notice, whether by accident or design, he was usually working close to her. Now, two weeks had passed and she was certain he was working up the courage to invite her to go walking with him.

'Will you join us for supper this evening, Joshua?' Hannah asked, interrupting Leah's daydreaming as she bustled past to empty the teapot in the slop bucket.

'I'm afraid I can't, Mrs Hopwood,' Joshua replied, sounding disappointed to be missing an opportunity to spend time with Leah. 'I'm collecting the new curate from the station.'

'Well, you know you're welcome anytime,' Hannah assured him with a warm smile.

'Thanks Mrs H,' Joshua grinned. He wiped his mouth on his sleeve and pushed back his chair. 'I'd better get off. Thanks for the breakfast.'

'Thank you for the pheasants,' Hannah countered, walking him to the backdoor. 'Give my love to your nan.'

'Will do, Mrs H. See you, Daisy.' His expression softened. 'I'll see you later, Leah?' he ventured, hopefully.

Leah nodded. 'Thanks for the flowers,' she said, as an afterthought, as she dried her hands on a tea towel. Joshua nodded. He looked as though he wanted to say something else but decided against it. Instead, he raised his hand in a jaunty salute and with a quick 'goodbye', ducked out of the back door and disappeared around the side of the privy.

'You shouldn't string the poor lad along,' Hannah said sternly, rounding on her eldest daughter. 'If you don't want to go to the ball with him, you should tell him so.'

'I'm not stringing him along, Mum,' Leah contradicted her. 'I just haven't made up my mind whether I want to go with him.'

'I'd go to the ball with Joshua,' Daisy said, picking up a tea towel with which to dry the dishes. She gave a wistful sigh. 'If only he'd ask me.'

'Daisy,' her mother admonished her. 'You're too young to be thinking about boys in that sort of way.'

'You were fourteen when you started courting Dad,' she retorted stoutly.

'I was almost fifteen,' her mother replied with a smile. 'Your time will come,' she said, giving Daisy's shoulder a quick pat. 'But I do believe Joshua's heart belongs wholly to our Leah.'

They were interrupted by the chiming of the church clock.

'It's a quarter past five,' Hannah said briskly, clapping her reddened, workworn hands. 'Come along, girls. You need to get a move on, or you'll both be late for work.'

Draping her shawl around her shoulders, Leah followed Daisy hurriedly out of the door, almost colliding with her neighbour, Dora Webb, in her haste.

'Oh!' Dora exclaimed, taking a step backwards. 'You are ready. I was about to knock for you. I dare not be late again.'

'Well, you won't be,' Leah assured her cheerfully, tucking her arm through her friend's.

'Good,' Dora smiled, wearily. 'I can't afford to have my wages docked. What with my father's doctor's bills, it'll be hard enough making the rent this month as it is.' She put her hand in front of her mouth, stifling a yawn.

'Bad night?' Leah asked as they crossed the lane, dodging the horse-drawn carts lining up along the verge in readiness to ferry the first of the day's harvest to the railway station.

'I hardly slept a wink,' sighed Dora. 'Dad's head kept him awake most of the night.'

'Poor you,' Leah said, with sympathy as they joined the queue to clock in and collect their baskets from Beatrice Turner, the overseer's wife. 'I expect he's in a filthy temper, then?'

Dora rolled her eyes. 'The worst. He threw his porridge all up the wall this morning. I hope he's calmed down by the time your mum goes in later.'

'You know Mum won't take any nonsense from him,' chuckled Leah.

'I don't know what I'd do without your mum, Leah,' Dora said, welling up.

'Hey, come on,' Leah said, giving Dora's arm a squeeze. 'You're exhausted, Dor. Why don't you come round to ours for your tea tonight? Have an hour off?'

Smiling wistfully, Dora shook her head. 'It's nice of you,

Leah but it's not fair for me to leave Dad on his own too often. He gets so lonely stuck in the house by himself while I'm at work as it is.'

'Mum says it's his own fault. If he hadn't driven all his friends away with his bad moods, he wouldn't be on his own all the time,' Daisy said, scanning the fields which were, despite the early hour, already teeming with pickers. Leah nudged her roughly and shot her a warning glare. 'What?' Daisy scowled. 'It's true.'

'Your mum's not wrong,' Dora said glumly. 'He doesn't mean it, though. He just gets so frustrated, you see?'

'It can't be easy for him,' Leah sympathized. She shot her sister another warning look, though Daisy had only spoken the truth. In Leah's opinion, the man who had once been her father's closest friend had become a bad-tempered, ill-mannered boor who treated his daughter like a slave. Many were the nights she and Daisy had lain in bed listening to the ruckus going on next door as he shouted and ranted at her.

'Good morning, girls.' Leah's train of thought was interrupted by the cheerful voice of Beatrice Turner as they reached the front of the queue.

'It looks like we're in for a fine day,' Beatrice remarked, smiling as she ticked their names off her list.

In her early fifties, she was an attractive woman with greying auburn hair and bright green eyes. She'd moved into the cottage adjacent to Leah's two years earlier when she married Mathew Turner, and had become good friends with Leah and Daisy's mother.

'Help yourselves to a basket,' she said, indicating the fast-depleting mountain of wicker baskets off to the side.

'Thank you, Mrs Turner.' Leah glanced over her shoulder. 'Is Alice not here yet?'

'She should be along any minute,' responded Beatrice, her gaze shifting to the bend in the lane. 'Ah, here she comes now,' she said, as a young woman rounded the bend on a bicycle.

Leah followed her gaze, grinning at the sight of her friend peddling furiously up the lane. The skirt of her green-sprigged dress billowed out at the sides and one hand clamped her straw hat to her head, while the other clutched the handlebars as she precariously steered her way between the ruts on the road.

'Hello, Alice,' Leah called out with a wave of her hand. Cautiously releasing her grip on her hat, Alice waved back, the bike wobbling precariously as she braked hard, and rolled to a halt outside the pub.

'Leah.' Daisy patted Leah's arm. 'I can see Lizzie and Nora. I'm going over to pick with them.'

'Okay,' Leah replied absently, as she waited for Alice to prop her bicycle against the pub's grey-stone wall and hurry across the lane towards them.

'Sorry I'm late, Grandma' she panted, her cheeks pink with exertion. 'I got stuck behind Farmer Troke's cows on the ox drove.' She brushed a strand of chestnut brown hair from her damp forehead and smiled at Beatrice. 'Mother said to remind you about supper tomorrow.'

'Thank you, Alice. I certainly hadn't forgotten.' Beatrice smiled. 'You'd better get along now,' she said to the three girls, turning her attention to the group of women coming up behind them.

'See you later, Grandma,' Alice said as she leaned over to plant a kiss on the older woman's soft cheek. 'How are you both?' she asked Leah and Dora as they made their way along the rows of strawberry plants. The ground was soft underfoot from the recent rain and the air smelled earthy and fresh. 'How's your dad, Dora?'

Dora shrugged. 'Not too good.'

'Oh, poor you,' Alice sympathized. 'You know, I wouldn't mind sitting with him for a while, if you wanted to go into the village to do some shopping or something.'

'It's kind of you to offer, Alice,' replied Dora, 'but you know how funny he can be about people coming in. He only just tolerates Leah's mum. Your mum's a diamond for putting up with him, Leah.'

But Leah wasn't listening. Oblivious to Dora and Alice's knowing smiles, her gaze was focused on the tall, well-built young man with a shock of fair hair, ambling towards the empty crates that were stacked at the end of each row. He paused and, as if aware of Leah's gaze, glanced over at her and grinned. His cheeks were flushed and his tanned forehead glistened with perspiration. Leah smiled back. Harry's smile made her pulse race in a way that Joshua's never had.

CHAPTER TWO

The whistle blew, signalling the midday meal break.

'We've done well,' Leah said, getting to her feet and brushing soil from her fingertips as she surveyed the baskets, brimming with ripe strawberries destined for Cole's jam factory in Bermondsey. 'That's two baskets each already. We'll be able to get off early if we keep up the pace.'

Alice sat back on her heels and wiped her brow with the back of her hand. Her shoulders ached and she had a painful spasm in her thigh muscle but despite her discomfort, she much preferred the time she spent working in the strawberry fields alongside her friends, than being cooped up in the school room teaching 11-year-old twins Clementine and Eloise Hampton-Sinclair their lessons.

'Ooh, I've got cramp,' Dora moaned ruefully, massaging the back of her calf as she stood up.

'Me, too,' sympathized Alice, getting gingerly to her feet. She held on to Leah and put pressure on her leg. 'Oh, it doesn't feel too bad now I'm up.'

'Try walking on it,' Leah suggested to Dora, who was bent over rubbing her calf muscles. 'That usually helps.'

'It'll go in a minute,' Dora said, wincing as she hobbled alongside her two friends to the end of the row. As they took turns emptying their baskets into the crates, Leah gripped Dora's arm.

'There's Harry,' she whispered, inclining her head in his direction. As if conscious of her gaze, Harry looked up from where he was emptying his basket a few rows along, and grinned. 'You go on,' Leah urged Dora, her voice low. 'I'll see you after dinner.'

Alice and Dora exchanged smiles and, after emptying their harvest into an almost full-to-the brim crate, they continued up towards the lane, turning every now and then to glance back over their shoulders.

'Aren't you coming?' Daisy asked her sister, coming up to empty her basket.

'In a few minutes,' Leah said, watching Harry avidly as he made his way over the rough grass towards her. Daisy gave her a knowing grin.

'I think he likes you,' she whispered, tipping her basket into the crate. 'I've noticed him watching you.' She set her basket on the grass and wiped her hands on her smock. 'I'll see you at home.'

Leah nodded, but her attention was on Harry. Ever since she'd begun to blossom around the age of fourteen, she'd never been short of male admirers but, apart from Joshua, no one had ever piqued her interest, until now.

'Hello, Leah.' Harry said. He stood barely two feet from her, roses of colour blossoming on his cheeks as he shuffled awkwardly from foot to foot.

'Hello, Harry,' she replied, her benign smile belying the way her heart was pounding. Harry was like no one she'd ever met before. The fact that he spoke as though he had a plum in his mouth had intrigued her, and she couldn't help but wonder why someone who was clearly so well brought up would spend their summer picking fruit.

'Um,' Harry stammered, whipping off his hat. He fixed his gaze on the caps of his dusty shoes, fiddling nervously with the brim of his hat.

'Yes?' Leah prompted him, waiting expectantly. She found his shyness endearing and it was another thing that intrigued her about him, causing her to assume that he'd led something of a sheltered life. He shuffled his feet again as he cast his gaze around the rapidly emptying fields.

'I was wondering,' he said, sounding slightly breathless. 'Whether you might like to go walking with me tomorrow afternoon?' he blurted out, adding, almost apologetically, 'If you're not busy, of course.'

'I'm not busy,' Leah replied, flushing with pleasure. 'And I would very much like to go walking. Thank you.'

'Oh, right,' Harry stammered, seemingly both surprised and relieved by her answer. 'Thank you.' he set his hat back on his head and rubbed his hands on his trousers. 'Super. Right, well, I'll call for you tomorrow afternoon. Shall we say half past two?'

'That would be perfect,' replied Leah. 'I live at Sunnynook Cottage.'

She was about to turn and point it out to him when, to her delight, Harry nodded and said, 'Yes, I know.'

A silence fell between them, broken a moment later by Leah. 'I'd better go. My mother will be expecting me in for my dinner.'

'Of course,' Harry said, with an apologetic smile. 'I'm sorry to keep you. I'll see you later.'

'Yes.' Breathing deeply to calm her rapidly beating heart, Leah turned and hurried across the uneven ground to the lane.

'So, did he ask you out?' demanded Daisy the moment Leah set foot in the cottage.

'He might have,' Leah teased, going into the scullery to wash her hands.

'I hope you're going to tell Joshua you're going walking with another boy,' her mother called after her.

In the cool, dim scullery, Leah silently rolled her eyes. She'd had fun with Joshua, she admitted to herself, drying her hands on the towel hanging on the hook behind the door. They'd always been friends, playing together as children, running barefoot through the fields and woods in the carefree days before diphtheria raged through the district.

As she grew older, it had been partly his wild, unconventional lifestyle as well as the air of the exotic that had attracted her. At the time, the aura of danger and mystery that surrounded him had excited her. Joshua neither knew nor cared who his father was. He'd been brought up by his great-grandma, Pearl, after his mother had absconded one night when he was a baby. As Romany gypsies, they were often viewed with suspicion, althoughnone of the locals were averse to calling on Pearl when they were in need of a herbal remedy or wished to have their fortunes read. And many a family had been grateful to Joshua for the odd rabbit or pheasant to supplement the pot during the lean winter months.

But now her feelings for Joshua had paled in comparison to the excitement she felt at the prospect of seeing Harry. There was seldom a moment during the day that he didn't occupy her thoughts. Thinking about him now, her stomach gave a little flip and she was smiling as she emerged from the pantry.

'You look like the cat that got the cream,' her mother remarked, drily.

'Harry has invited me to go walking with him tomorrow afternoon,' Leah told her, taking her place at the table and helping herself to a slice of bread and a hunk of cheese.

'He talks very posh,' Daisy said.

'Don't speak with your mouth full,' Hannah reprimanded her. Turning to Leah she said sombrely, while pouring the tea. 'Perhaps his family have fallen on hard times. It happens.' She set the teapot down and fell silent. Leah reached across and patted her mother's hand, knowing she was thinking of their father. To add to the aching void left by the loss of her father and older brother, their fortunes had taken a definite downturn with the loss of the two main breadwinners.

'Just don't go getting too fond of this boy, Leah,' her mother went on. 'If he's not from around here, he'll be going back to where he came from come the end of the summer. Just bear that in mind. You don't want to end up with a broken heart.'

'We're just going walking, Mum,' Leah assured her with a casual toss of her plaits as she cut herself another chunk of cheese. *September was months away*, she mused with an inward smile. The whole summer stretched before her, tantalising with its possibilities. She was determined to enjoy every moment she got to spend with Harry, for as long as she could.

CHAPTER THREE

Sitting in the cold church the next morning, Leah could hardly contain her impatience. Unable to concentrate on Reverend Aldridge's long-winded sermon, she let her gaze wander. The church had been built in 1867 by Isaac Whitworth's grandfather for his tenants and could seat a congregation of up to a hundred. The pulpit was set up high and could be reached by a curved, dark-wood staircase. Behind the altar hung a large board. On one side was the Lord's Prayer, on the other, the Ten Commandments, all written in gold.

Here and there, ornate memorial plaques commemorating various members of the Whitworth family adorned the smooth grey-stone walls. The windows were stained glass. Made by a master glazier from London, they depicted detailed accounts of well-known biblical stories.

The newly arrived curate, Samuel Roberts, sat beneath a simple wooden cross to the right of the pulpit. He was quite good-looking, Leah noted, though her view of him, sitting to the left of the pulpit, was partially obscured by Isaac and Frances Whitworth. They sat close together in the Whitworth family pew, as still as statues and ramrod straight. It was rare to see Frances in church. She made no secret of the fact she despised spending time in Strawbridge, preferring to remain at their London home instead of accompanying her husband to his country estate, and Leah could only assume it was to carry out her duty in welcoming the new curate that had brought her here today.

Sitting between her mother and Daisy in a pew close to the middle of the church, Leah had caught sight of Joshua and Pearl, slipping into their usual pew at the back. Beatrice and Mathew Turner, the church warden, sat behind the Whitworths. Bored, Leah stifled an impatient sigh. She wished Dora was here. At least they could smile at each other during the hymns. But Dora seldom attended church. Between work and taking care of her father, the poor girl was run ragged. Sundays was when she caught up with the household chores or her sleep.

A stirring amongst the congregation drew Leah's attention back to the pulpit. Reverend Aldridge was winding down and ten minutes later they were spilling out into the mild spring sunshine. As she walked down the winding cinder path with her mother and sister, Leah noticed Frances Whitworth pause beside a row of gravestones surrounded by a low iron railing. The Whitworth family plot was dominated by a large, weathered stone tomb, covered in lichen, the inscription barely legible. It was surrounded by several other gravestones. The three stones in front of where Frances now stood were well-kept and clean. Leah had grown up reading the inscriptions and she knew the words by heart.

CELESTIA LOUISE WHITWORTH
INFANT DAUGHTER OF ISAAC AND FRANCES
BORN 24TH MARCH 1890
DIED 1ST APRIL 1890

DAVID ISAAC
SON OF ISAAC AND FRANCES WHITWORTH
BORN 15 JUNE 1892
DIED 3RD JANUARY 1893

FLORENCE EMMA
BORN SLEEPING 16TH MARCH 1894

Frances had left Strawbridge soon after the funeral of her third child and, though Isaac spent most of the summer at Streawberige House in order to oversee the strawberry harvest, she never accompanied him. It was common knowledge that Frances hated Strawbridge. And who could blame her, Leah mused, averting her gaze from the woman's grief, when the place had brought her so much unhappiness.

The grave where Leah's father, brother Freddie and two little sisters rested was close by, beneath a large yew tree, and all thoughts of the Whitworth family fled as Leah gazed down at the family grave, waiting as her mother laid a small posy on the daisy-covered mound, as she did every Sunday. Hannah took a shaky breath and gave the headstone a quick pat.

'Sleep well, my precious loves,' she said softly, wiping away a surreptitious tear. 'Till we see you again.'

Leah slipped her arm through her mother's and Daisy did the same on the other side. They passed through the lychgate and started up the lane. They hadn't gone very far when they heard Beatrice Turner calling after them and they paused, waiting for her to catch up.

'What do you think of the new curate?' Beatrice asked, one hand on her chest as she caught her breath. Her quick pace had brought a rosy hue to her weathered cheeks.

'He's very handsome,' Daisy responded with a sigh that made her mother and Beatrice laugh.

'He is that,' Beatrice agreed with a smile. 'I reckon our little congregation will swell considerably once word gets out.' She was interrupted by a shout.

'Leah! Wait up.' At the sound of Joshua's voice, Leah stopped and raised her eyes heavenward. Her mother shot her a warning look. With an inaudible sigh, Leah plastered a smile on her face and turned to face him.

'You didn't stop and say hello,' he said, accusingly.

'Sorry, we're in a bit of a hurry,' she responded

apologetically, glancing over her shoulder at her mother for confirmation.

'Reverend Aldridge did go on a bit,' Hannah said with a wry smile.

'I have to confess,' Beatrice said, clutching her hat as a brisk gust swept down the lane in a flurry of dead leaves and dust. 'I was beginning to worry more about my partridge drying out in the oven than I was about my immortal soul.'

The two women laughed again.

'Would you and Nanny Pearl like to join us for dinner, Joshua?' asked Hannah. Leah's heart sank. She didn't relish the thought of having to make polite conversation across the dinner table with Joshua while she was thinking about her walk later with Harry, so it was a relief when Joshua shook his head.

'Thanks Mrs H, but Nan's got a bit of a headache so I'm taking her home.'

'All right, love. Give her our best, won't you?'

'I will, Mrs H. Ta.' He locked eyes with Leah. 'I'm going fishing later if you'd like to come?' he said, hopefully.

'I'm sorry. I'm busy this afternoon,' Leah replied, suppressing a twinge of guilt as Joshua's face fell.

'Right.' He shoved his hands in his pockets, his usual self-assuredness replaced by awkwardness. 'I'll see you tomorrow, then.' He recovered enough to tell Hannah, 'If I'm lucky, I'll drop some trout round later.'

'Oi!' Beatrice said in mock alarm. 'You'll get caught one of these days and then you'll be in hot water.'

'Old gamekeeper Ryall's got to catch me first,' Joshua said, but his laugh sounded hollow.

Shoulders slumped, he headed back towards the church where Pearl was waiting by the lychgate, a tiny figure dressed all in black.

'You mustn't string the poor lad along, Leah,' Hannah said sternly, as they reached the row of cottages. 'It isn't fair.'

'I know,' Leah sighed. 'I *will* tell him.'

'Don't leave it too long. Better he hears it from you, than from someone else.' She gave Leah a knowing look. Strawbridge was a small place. Nothing remained a secret for long.

'I'll see you later, Hannah,' Beatrice interrupted, as they came to a halt outside her front door.

'Sorry, Bea.' Hannah patted her friend's arm. 'Pop round for a cup of tea later, if you like. Say about three?'

'Thanks,' smiled Beatrice. 'I will. Mathew will be going over to the church about then, anyway, to get ready for Evensong.' She said goodbye and disappeared indoors as Hannah pushed open her own front door and ushered her girls inside.

'What time are you going walking with Harry?' Hannah asked Leah as she hung up her shawl.

'Half past two.'

'We'd better get on with the dinner then,' her mother smiled. 'You won't want to keep the young man waiting.'

Leah glanced at the clock. It had just gone a quarter to twelve. 'There's plenty of time yet,' she said, a trifle impatiently, following her mother into the kitchen.

'Just be careful, love,' Hannah said, opening the oven door and peering in at the stew simmering in the pot. 'You don't know anything about this lad.'

'I will, Mum,' promised Leah, sniffing the air apprecia- tively. 'Hmm, that smells so good.'

'I'm so hungry,' Daisy complained, dragging out a chair. 'I honestly thought my stomach was going to grumble in church. How embarrassing would that have been in front of that nice new curate. Didn't you think he was rather gor- geous, Leah?'

'He was all right,' replied Leah non-committedly. In truth, her head had been so full of Harry, she'd barely noticed him.

'Rather too good-looking, I'd say,' Hannah added, head- ing upstairs to change out of her Sunday best. 'I expect he'll break a few hearts before he's done.'

At promptly half past two Harry knocked on the cottage door. Having been watching for him from the upstairs window for the past ten minutes, Leah took her time answer- ing it. After all, it wouldn't do to appear too keen. Feeling giddy with excitement, she checked her reflection in the mirror. She'd taken time with her appearance and knew she looked good. She was wearing her pink, rose-sprigged dress and had brushed her dark blonde hair until it shone, falling in a shimmering curtain to her waist.

Aware that her mother and Daisy were watching her with ill-concealed amusement, Leah took a deep breath and opened the door.

'Good afternoon, Harry.'

Harry's mouth fell open and he fiddled nervously with his tie, momentarily lost for words. 'Good afternoon, Leah,' he blurted, finally finding his voice. 'You look lovely,' he stammered.

'Thank you,' Leah replied, smiling at the effect she was obviously having on him. Of course, he'd only ever seen her in her coarse work dress with her hair in plaits. 'Would you like to come in for a minute?'

Harry swallowed nervously, his Adam's apple bobbing in his throat as he stepped into the dim parlour.

'Mum,' Leah said with a flourish. 'This is Harry . . .' She paused, her brows knitting together in a small frown.

'White,' Harry replied quickly. 'Harry White.'

Leah smiled. 'Harry White, may I introduce my mother, Mrs Hopwood, and my sister, Daisy.'

'Good afternoon, Harry,' Hannah smiled, laying aside her mending. 'It's very nice to meet you.'

'Good afternoon, Mrs Hopwood,' Harry said politely. 'Good afternoon, Miss Daisy.' He nodded at Daisy, who was curled up on the sofa, an upturned book on her lap, all pretence at reading abandoned as she regarded the visitor with open curiosity.

'Have we met before?' Hannah asked, frowning. 'You look familiar, though Leah tells me you're not from around here?'

'No, ma'am, I don't believe we have.' Harry flushed. 'I'm a Londoner. This is my first visit to Hampshire.'

'London?' Leah looked at him in surprised dismay as she

realized just how little really she knew about him. Harry raised a questioning eyebrow, seemingly puzzled by her surprise and she shrugged. 'I assumed you came in from Southampton, that's all.'

'I'm London born and bred,' he grinned.

'Well, it's a pleasure to meet you, Harry,' Hannah smiled. 'Have a nice walk.' She glanced through the open doorway. 'It looks as though it'll stay fine for you.'

Leah adjusted her hat and they started off down the lane. For a while they walked in companionable silence. They were close, but not touching, and Leah felt his nearness in every fibre of her being. Her heart was beating so loudly, she thought he must hear it. *Coming from London, he was obviously far more worldly than she was,* she mused, a frisson of excitement coursing up her spine. She'd never gone further than Southampton. She hoped he wouldn't find her dull company after the young ladies of London.

'Whereabouts in London are you from?' she asked him, as they walked past the church, keen, suddenly, to know more about this handsome stranger who'd captured her interest.

'Richmond,' Harry replied, glancing upwards as the church clock chimed the quarter hour, sending a cloud of rooks clamouring into the sky. 'Perhaps we might follow this path?' he suggested quickly, indicating a narrow footpath running adjacent to the church yard.

Leah had been about to enquire whether he had family back in London but, realizing Harry appeared eager to deflect any further questions about his private life, she simply nodded. She knew enough of London to know Richmond was an area of affluence. If Harry's family had fallen on hard times he would, understandably, be reluctant to talk about his life there.

'It follows the stream to the pond,' she said instead. 'It's a pleasant walk, if it's not too muddy.'

The relief at the change of subject was evident on Harry's face as they set off along the path, but she couldn't help asking, 'Will you be returning to Richmond when the strawberry harvest is over?'

'It depends,' Harry replied with a quick grin.

'On what?' Leah asked, boldly.

'On whether or not there's a reason for me to stay,' replied Harry, his cheeks reddening.

Hiding her smile, Leah turned her gaze to the crystal-clear stream tinkling musically over the smooth pebbles.

'What about yourself?' Harry asked, sounding genuinely interested. 'Have you always lived round here?'

'I'm Strawbridge born and bred. My father's family have been tenants of the Whitworths since the mid-eighteen-hundreds. My dad passed away four years ago.'

'I'm sorry to hear that,' Harry said soberly, his expression of sympathy deepening as Leah told him about her siblings, and how the epidemic had swept through the hamlet.

'That's how Dora's father ended up bed-ridden. He got sick not long after my father. He recovered, only to suffer the stroke which left him paralysed. It's such a burden for Dora to bear but, bless her, she does it cheerfully enough.' She eyed Harry curiously. 'So, do you have family?'

'Wow!' Harry exclaimed, appearing not to hear Leah's question as they rounded a bend in the path where the stream spilled into a large pond, surrounded by thick foliage. 'How idyllic,' he said, clearly impressed.

'It's my favourite place,' Leah told him, pleased by his reaction. She gazed across the tranquil waters. Sunlight played on the smooth surface that reflected the surrounding trees and bushes. A pair of swans emerged from the rushes, their brood of six grey-brown signets gliding gracefully behind. A wisp of smoke rose above the trees from where Pearl's caravan was situated on the edge of Isaac Whitworth's orchard.

'We used to play here all the time when we were children,' Leah told Harry. Misty-eyed, she motioned to a length of frayed rope dangling over the water, suspended from the branch of a sturdy oak. 'My brother Freddie made that swing the summer before he died. It was such a magical summer.'

'I was never allowed to do anything like that,' Harry replied, eying the rope swing with wistful envy. 'My mother is a bit over protective, shall we say?' He grinned ruefully. 'I spent most of my time indoors with my tutor. I was seldom allowed to venture outside unless it was to accompany Mother on an errand.'

'It sounds a very lonely life,' Leah remarked.

Harry pulled a face. 'It was.'

Golden buttercups brushed the hem of Leah's skirt as she led the way up the sloping bank. Fluffy white clouds drifted slowly across the sky. Fish darted amongst the pebbles, flashing silver as they caught the light. The sun was warm.

Shrugging off his jacket, Harry spread it on the soft grass and invited Leah to sit down. Rolling up his sleeves, he pointed out a long-legged heron standing motionless in the shadows.

'I bet there're loads of trout in there.'

'Ha, yes, there are,' Leah grinned, taking off her hat and laying it aside. 'But they all belong to our landlord, Isaac Whitworth and, as you see,' she said, pointing to a crudely written sign tacked to a nearby tree trunk, 'no fishing is allowed. Although there are those who're willing to take the risk,' she laughed, thinking of Joshua and his penchant for poaching.

'The land's been in Isaac's family for generations,' she went on. 'There's been a settlement here, of sorts, since Roman times and strawberries have been grown around this area for hundreds of years.' She gave Harry a sideways glance, wondering if she was boring him, but he was staring at her with rapt attention. 'My father told me that our little hamlet used to be called Streawberige, like Isaac Whitworth's house. I expect you've seen the great big gates as you come down the lane?' Harry nodded. 'Well, apparently, it's an old English name for strawberry. Over time the name evolved to became Strawbridge.' She grinned. 'Much easier on the tongue.'

'Interesting,' Harry said, abruptly getting to his feet. 'Shall we walk on a bit?'

'Oh,' Leah said, taken by surprise. 'All right, if you like.' She held out a hand and Harry pulled her to her feet.

'If we follow the path, it will take us all the way to Botley,' Leah said, puzzled by Harry's strange behaviour. She hoped he didn't think she was trying to show off by telling him the history of Strawbridge.

'That sounds pleasant,' Harry agreed, bending down to retrieve Leah's hat.

'Thank you,' responded Leah, taking the hat from Harry. They skirted the pond and continued along the footpath. Nettles brushed Leah's skirt, butterflies flitting along in front of them. To her relief, Harry appeared totally at ease again, perfectly content to listen to Leah's chatter as she acquainted him with Strawbridge and its inhabitants.

The afternoon flew by and Leah was disappointed when, standing on a small rise overlooking the fields of sun-ripened strawberries, she heard the church clock chiming half past four.

'I'm afraid we'd better be heading back,' she said, reluctantly. 'I have chores to do before Evensong.'

They walked back slowly, both keen to delay the moment of their parting as long as possible. All too soon, it seemed to Leah, they were standing outside her front door.

'Shall I call for you next Sunday?' Harry asked, hopefully.

'I would like that very much,' Leah replied. The thought crossed her mind to invite him in to join the family for tea, but she decided against it. She didn't want to appear too eager. If Harry was disappointed, he didn't show it.

'I shall look forward to it,' he said as he turned to leave.

Smiling, Leah slipped into the house. Her mother and Daisy were hovering in the kitchen doorway, eager to hear all about it. Needing a moment to compose herself and allow her racing heart to calm, Leah turned her back on her family. She took her time taking off her hat and hanging it up.

'Well?' Hannah prompted, wiping her hands on a tea towel. 'Did you have a nice time?'

'It was very nice, thank you,' Leah said, turning to smile at her mother. She could hardly contain her excitement. 'He's asked me to go walking again next Sunday.'

'Now you have to tell Joshua,' Hannah said, seriously. 'It's only fair, if you're going to be seeing Harry again.'

'I will,' Leah agreed, with a sigh. 'Though I'm not looking forward to it.'

'He's a big boy, Leah,' her mother comforted her. 'Being disappointed in love is a fact of life. He'll get over it.'

'I know.' Leah bit her lip. 'It still doesn't make it easy though, does it?'

'No.' Hannah gave her a hug. 'Just bear in mind that Harry is a migrant worker. There's every likelihood he'll go back home after the harvest.'

'I don't want to think about that just yet,' Leah said, pursing her lips. 'But whatever happens with Harry, it's confirmed what I've always supposed. Joshua isn't the man for me.'

CHAPTER FOUR

Leah and Alice were sitting in Alice's grandmother's sunny kitchen. It was the first weekend in June and the weather had been warm and sultry all week. A bee crawled amongst the African violets on the windowsill and a warm breeze wafted in through the open back door. From outside came the contented cluck of chickens and the heady fragrance of honeysuckle and jasmine.

'Are you sure I can't help with the dishes before I go?' Leah asked, getting up to leave.

'You're all right, thanks love,' Beatrice said, coming in the back door with a bucket of clean water. 'There's not much. Alice and I will do it. You get off home.'

'If you're certain?'

'I am,' Beatrice assured her.

'Thank you again for the invitation to tea. We've had a good natter, haven't we, Alice?'

'We have indeed,' Alice replied, with a grin. 'I'll be heading home soon myself.'

'I'll see you next Saturday,' Leah said over her shoulder as she left by way of the back door. 'Have a good week and don't let those twins get you down.'

'Would you mind doing me a favour before you go?' Beatrice asked once Leah had left and she and Alice were tackling the dishes.

'Of course not.' Alice hung the tea towel over the range to dry and smoothed down her skirt. 'What can I do for you?'

'Your grandfather has got a meeting with Reverend Aldridge at half past five and he's forgotten the accounts ledger. Would you run it over to him? He's probably forgotten he brought it home to go through the figures last night and will most likely be in the vestry looking for it.'

'I'll go now,' Alice said.

'Thank you. Are you sure you can spare the time? I know James can be a bit stuffy about punctuality at meal times.'

'Five minutes won't make much difference, Grandma, and we don't tend to dine until six on Saturdays, anyway.'

She put on her hat and left by the front door. For the moment the lane was quiet, though Alice knew from experience the tranquillity would not last. Drunken brawls outside the Glyn Arms on a Saturday evening were not uncommon.

The sun was still high above the trees, bathing the fields in its dusty golden light. Humming quietly to herself, she walked through the lychgate and into the shady churchyard. She found the heavy oak door ajar. It creaked loudly as she pushed it and stepped into the cool, dim church. The air smelled of beeswax polish and the cloying scent of the lilies adorning the alter. Dust motes danced in the hazy sunshine streaming through the stained-glass windows. Her footsteps echoing noisily on the stone floor, she crossed the narthex and into the nave.

'Grandfather?' She poked her head around the vestry door, inhaling the musty tang of old books and damp. Seeing her step-grandfather bent over and rummaging in a drawer, she smiled. 'Are these what you're looking for?' she said, holding up the ledgers.

Mathew Turner looked up, frowning. In his early fif-ties, he was a handsome man and Alice could see why her grandmother had fallen for him. He let out a long sigh of irritation.

'I've spent the last fifteen minutes hunting for those,' he said in exasperation, running his hand through his hair as he got to his feet. Thick and dark, it was streaked with grey, as was his neatly trimmed beard. 'Of course, I took them home with me the other day to work on them after supper.' He took the accounts book from her, shaking his head in mock despair. 'Don't get old, Alice, love,' he smiled.

'You're hardly that old, Grandfather,' Alice laughed. 'Will you be a while? I don't mind waiting. It would be nice to walk back together.'

'You run along, love,' Mathew replied, shaking his head. 'I'm waiting for Reverend Aldridge. We're going over the figures together. Have a good week.'

'I'll try,' grimaced Alice, not relishing another five days stuck in the schoolroom with the Hampton-Sinclair twins. She kissed his cheek. 'I'll see you next Saturday.'

The late afternoon sunlight shone through the trees, dappling the daisy-strewn grass. Alice's shoes crunched on the cinder path as she followed it between the rows of gravestones. It was eerily quiet. Even the birdsong seemed muted and the squeak of a gate on rusty hinges sounded inordinately loud. Expecting to see Reverend Aldridge's portly frame, she was surprised to see a tall, rather good-looking young man come loping through the gap in the privet hedge. He was holding a sheet of paper in one hand and appeared to be talking to himself. He glanced up, stopping short in surprise at the sight of Alice.

'Oh, I beg your pardon,' he said, blushing slightly. 'I didn't expect anyone to be about.' He indicated the sheet of paper. 'I'm working on my sermon for tomorrow.'

'I'm sorry if I startled you,' Alice apologized with a smile. He really was devilishly handsome, she thought. He looked to be in his early twenties, and was at least six feet tall with unruly dark-brown hair and eyes the colour of ripe cobnuts. He was dressed all in black, a white clerical collar at his throat. 'Please, don't let me disturb you.'

'No need to apologize,' he smiled amiably. 'I could do with a break. I'm the new curate by the way. Samuel Roberts. Were you in church last week? I'm sure I'd have remembered you.'

Alice smiled and shook her head. 'No, I confess I wasn't.

I'm Alice Russell. I live over in Hedge End so I'm only in Strawbridge on Saturdays.' She inclined her head towards the church. 'I just popped in to see my grandfather. He's the church warden.'

'Ah, yes, Mathew Turner.' Samuel grinned. 'From what I gather, Reverend Aldridge would be lost without him.'

'He does seem to rely on him quite heavily,' agreed Alice. 'And how are you finding Strawbridge, so far?'

Samuel's grin broadened. 'It's quiet. I had requested I be allowed to complete my curacy in one of Southampton's more deprived areas.' He shrugged. 'But I was sent here instead.'

'I'm sure there's lots of good you can do here,' Alice assured him. 'Most families hereabouts are poor. The winter months in particular can be very difficult.'

They were interrupted by the crunch of footsteps and the portly figure of Reverend Walter Aldridge appeared between the yew trees.

'Ah, Samuel, practising for tomorrow, I see,' he said, nodding at the paper in Samuel's hands. 'Excellent, excellent. Miss Russell.' He nodded at Alice. 'Good afternoon.'

'Good afternoon, Reverend,' smiled Alice. 'Are you well?'

'Exceptionally well, my dear,' Walter replied jovially. 'I've just been having my daily constitutional.' He patted his rotund belly. 'Well, well, I've got a meeting with Mathew in a few minutes so I'd better wash up. I'll see you at supper, Samuel.' He tipped his hat. 'Miss Russell.'

'Goodbye, Reverend,' Alice responded as Walter turned and headed for the vicarage. 'Well, I shall leave you to your sermon-making,' she said pleasantly. 'It was nice meeting you, Reverend.'

'Likewise, Miss Russell. I do hope our paths cross again.'

'I find myself thinking about him all the time,' Alice confided to Leah and Dora the following Saturday morning as they picked along a row of mature strawberry plants. The yield was high and they were already well on their way to fulfilling their quotas.

If the yield continued at this level, Dora mused, only half listening to what Alice was saying, she'd have enough this week to pay off a large chunk of the doctor's bill, and perhaps a little extra to spend on herself. Despite her best efforts with needle and thread, both her dresses were almost beyond repair.

'I know what you mean, Alice,' Leah was saying, her hand bumping Dora's as they both reached for the same strawberry. Leah laughed. 'You take it, Dor,' she said, wiping her brow with the back of her arm. It was hot, thirsty work. She could feel the sweat trickling down her spine and it wasn't yet ten o'clock. She sat back on her heels. 'I think about Harry all the time, too,' she said, lowering her voice and glancing round to see if he was within earshot. He wasn't. She'd spotted him earlier on the far side of the next field earlier.

'I have so little to occupy my mind during the week,' Alice lamented. 'It's no wonder I spend my time daydreaming.' And it was true. While her charges, Clementine and Eloise, were bent over their books, she would find her gaze drifting to the window where, instead of seeing the clouds scudding across the sky, or the cows grazing on the distant hill, she saw the Reverend Samuel Roberts' face. As she pictured the way the skin crinkled around his eyes when he smiled, her pulse raced in a way she'd never experienced before.

'He's probably a lot different to the men your aunt keeps introducing you to,' Dora remarked, idly.

'Well,' Alice bit her lip thoughtfully. 'They're all very well-connected young men, and all perfectly pleasant, of course, but . . .' She broke off, blushing.

'They're also perfectly dull,' finished Leah with a grin.

'Yes,' Alice smiled. 'Quite.' She sat back on her heels, brushing aside a strand of chestnut-brown hair that had adhered itself to her damp forehead. 'Reverend Roberts seems so much more interesting. I'd really like to have a proper conversation with him. I'm sure we'd have much to talk about.'

'You may have your wish granted,' Leah whispered to Alice later that afternoon as she returned from emptying her basket.

'What do you mean?' queried Alice with a puzzled frown.

Leah grinned. 'I heard your grandmother saying that she'd invited Revered Aldridge and a certain young curate to supper this evening.'

'Really?' Alice's eyes widened. 'She has?'

Laughing, Leah nodded. 'I think you should wangle yourself an invitation, don't you?'

'That won't be a problem,' Alice grinned back, her dark eyes sparkling. 'Grandma loves it when I stay over. I'll ask one of the boys to get a message to my mother.'

Beatrice was delighted when Alice announced that she had decided to spend the night at her grandparents'.

'And it's rather fortuitous that you should pick tonight to stay, Alice,' said Beatrice, as she scrubbed and sliced potatoes. 'Your Grandfather has invited Reverend Aldridge and young Roberts to join us for supper.'

'Oh, really?' Alice said, feigning surprise.

'It will be nice for Reverend Roberts to have someone closer to his age to talk to,' said Beatrice with a knowing smile. 'I'm sure you'll both find Grandfather and Reverend Aldridge's church talk very dull.' She put the potatoes in a pan and covered them with cold water. 'He's certainly set some hearts racing since he's been here,' she continued as she added salt to the water and set the pan on the hob to boil. 'He's not been in the village a fortnight but your grandfather says he's been inundated with invitations to supper. Mrs Hurst is quite put out, I must say.' She turned to Alice, wiping her hands on her apron. 'Did Leah tell you how full the church was last Sunday? Filled to the rafters, it was. They must have come from all over the district. Preening and strutting like peacocks, they were.' She clicked her tongue in distaste. 'The poor man didn't know where to look.'

Alice floured the table in readiness for rolling out the pastry for the dessert, listening to her grandmother's chatter

41

with growing disquiet. While it came as no big surprise that such an attractive young man would attract much female attention, she couldn't help feeling slightly disappointed. She was pretty enough, she supposed, with her wavy, chestnut-brown hair and chocolate-brown eyes, but she couldn't be described as a beauty, like Leah. If Samuel was constantly surrounded by pretty girls vying for his attention, it was unlikely he'd even remember their brief encounter in the churchyard. With a quiet sigh, she laid the pastry over a dish of stewed dried apples and began to crimp the edges. She heard footsteps outside and glanced up to see her grandfather pass the window.

'Something smells good,' Mathew said, sniffing the air appreciatively as he sat down to take off his boots. 'Will you be staying for supper, Alice?'

'I will.'

'Ah,' Mathew said, laying his boots aside and reaching for the slippers Beatrice had put by the range to warm. 'You'll be good company for young Roberts. He was asking after you, earlier.' Seeming not to notice Alice's flush of pleasure, he pulled his pipe from his jacket pocket and lit it. 'He seems a nice enough young man,' he said, leaning back in his chair and puffing contentedly. 'Brimming with ideas. Walter likes him. He's even talking about retiring next spring once Roberts is ordained.'

'I believe Reverend Roberts was hoping for a more urban parish,' Alice said as she laid the table.

'People can be just as poor in the country as they are in

the towns,' remarked Mathew drily. 'I think he'll find he's able to fulfil his need for social justice and reform right here in Strawbridge. Most families in this parish don't have two ha'pennies to rub together once the strawberry harvest is over.'

'That's what I told him.' Alice nodded soberly as she straightened the tablecloth. 'I know Dora's already worrying about what she'll do after September. Hopefully she'll get taken on at the drysalters again.'

'Whitworth should do more to help Stephen,' Mathew said, shaking his head in disgust. 'And all his other tenants affected by the epidemic. That's a just cause young Roberts can get his teeth into.' He waved his pipe in the air to make his point.

There was a knock and the sound of the rattle of the latch, followed by Reverend Aldridge's voice calling 'Hello, there,' as Mathew rose from his chair.

'Come in, Reverends, come on in,' he cried heartily, stepping into the parlour to greet them. Relieving them of their hats, he ushered them into the kitchen.

'You've met my granddaughter, Alice,' Mathew said, addressing Samuel.

'Yes, sir,' Samuel said with a warm smile that set Alice's pulse racing. 'I have had the pleasure. Good evening, Alice. It's nice to see you again.' He nodded at Beatrice, who was hunched over the sink draining the vegetables, enveloped in a cloud of swirling steam. 'Mrs Turner. Good evening.'

'Good evening to you both, Reverends,' she replied,

turning round to smile at the two men. 'Do sit down. Supper will be ready in a moment.'

As the men settled themselves round the table, Alice fetched the plates warming on the range and passed them to her grandmother.

'Mrs Hurst was glad of an evening off,' Walter said, smiling in anticipation of the roasted rabbit, boiled potatoes and fresh garden vegetables Beatrice was dishing up. 'She'd arranged to attend a recital with her sister so now they have time to enjoy a meal out beforehand.'

'That will be nice treat for her,' Beatrice said, placing a plate of food in front of the portly vicar.

'That looks delicious, Mrs Turner,' Walter beamed.

Quietly pleased that she'd been left the seat opposite Samuel, Alice pulled up her chair. While her grandfather and Reverend Aldridge conversed about church matters, Alice probed Samuel's interest in books and music, and was delighted to find their tastes were similar on many topics.

'Has it always been your ambition to go into the church, Reverend Roberts?' she ventured during a brief lull in the conversation.

'It's Samuel, please.' His lazy smile sent a tingle down her spine. 'My father was a vicar and so it was always rather assumed that I would follow in his footsteps.'

'He must be pleased,' Beatrice said, stacking the dirty plates.

'Unfortunately, I lost both my parents in a boating accident some years ago.'

'Oh, I'm so sorry to hear that,' said Beatrice, looking genuinely moved.

'I'm sorry, too,' said Alice quietly. Samuel acknowledged her sympathy with a smile.

'Thank you. I do miss them, of course, but the passage of time has eased the pain somewhat.'

Beatrice got up from the table and began to gather up the dirty dishes. 'If everybody's finished, I'll fetch the apple pie.' Alice started to get up to help her, but Beatrice motioned for her to stay seated. 'You stay and chat,' she said, smiling at her granddaughter over her shoulder before disappearing in to the scullery to fetch the dessert.

CHAPTER FIVE

'Alice, wait.' Leah's shoes crunched on the path as she hurried to catch up with her friend. 'How did it go, last night?' she whispered. She slipped her arm through Alice's, then grinned. 'Very well, I reckon, if your smile is anything to go by.'

'It was a pleasant evening,' Alice replied, teasingly. It was starting to drizzle and she pulled her shawl up over her hair.

'And?' Leah said impatiently. 'What's he like? To talk to?'

'Interesting,' replied Alice after a moment's thought. 'It seems the Reverend and I have similar tastes in books and music. We both share an enjoyment of the theatre and museums. His great-uncle was acquainted with my late Grandfather Copperfield.'

Leah nodded. Alice made no secret of her aristocratic relatives, or that the latter part of her childhood had been so vastly different to Leah's. Her wealthy aunt Eleanor, whom Leah had met once or twice, seemed a pleasant, warm-hearted woman who appeared to enjoy nothing more than treating her niece to the best of all that London had to offer. But, Leah mused happily, for all Alice's advantages, she was as down-to-earth as they come, and a good friend.

'He is also brimming with compassion for those less fortunate than ourselves,' Alice continued. 'Which I think is a very worthwhile trait, in a vicar.'

'Not to mention he's extremely good looking,' Leah added with a grin.

'Far better looking than a man of the cloth has the right to be,' a voice whispered in her ear. Leah turned to find herself face to face with the vicars' housekeeper.

'Good morning, Mrs Hurst,' the girls said politely, blushing with mortification that their hushed conversation had been overheard.

'It's utterly ridiculous.' Mrs Hurst pursed her pale lips. She was a thin, angular woman in her mid-forties with greying dark hair she wore in a tight bun and small, piercing blue eyes that missed nothing. Despite the prefix to her name, she had never been married.

'I've lost count of the young ladies that keep turning up at the vicarage on one silly pretence or another,' she muttered, scowling as she glanced up at the sombre sky. A raindrop hit her in the eye and she blinked, shaking her head. 'Some silly girl even accosted me at the station yesterday, wanting to know if Reverend Roberts was attached. I sent her away with a flea in her ear, I can tell you.' She sniffed and, adjusting her goatskin gloves, stalked towards the church, leaving Leah and Alice shaking with laughter in her wake.

'I hope she doesn't think I'm a silly, empty-headed girl, because I fancy the curate,' Alice giggled as they dashed along the path and up the steps out of the heavy rain.

'Dora had a bit of a time of it again last night,' Leah said as they made their way down the aisle, breathing in the smell of damp cloth. Candlelight danced up the grey walls and flickered on the scuffed flagstones. 'I could hear her dad shouting and throwing things until well into the night.'

Alice shook her head in dismay. 'Poor thing. Perhaps I'll call round and see her before I go home. It might cheer her up to see a friendly face. Do you want to come?'

Leah smiled. 'I would,' she whispered as they slipped into an empty pew. 'If I wasn't meeting Harry.'

From her vantage point in the pew across the aisle from the Whitworths, Alice had a clear view of Samuel sitting on the smaller of the two high-backed throne-like chairs set to one side of the altar.

The organist began to play and the congregation rose to sing the first hymn. Samuel's address was short, witty and thought-provoking, delivered with humour and, while he engaged with the entire congregation, Alice was pleased to notice how often his dark gaze sought her out. As they stood for the blessing, she gave herself a mental shake. With just about every girl in the district vying for Samuel's attention, did she really have a chance of capturing the young curate's heart?

*

Dora draped the last pillow case over the wooden clothes horse and sighed. Her back ached and her hands were red raw from scrubbing. She leaned against the table, breathing in the strong scent of carbolic soap.

She hated Sundays, being stuck indoors with her father all day. Immediately she was flooded with guilt. It wasn't his fault. Of course, he became frustrated at times and, on occasion, that frustration might boil over into rage.

She closed her eyes, the memory of the night before as fresh in her mind as the bruise on her arm.

She'd been late getting his supper. The afternoon had been fine and warm, and, excited that she'd almost done half again of her daily quota, Dora had asked Beatrice Turner if she might work on, as several of the pickers were doing. It had been gone six by the time she returned to the cottage, smiling at the thought of the extra wages in her pocket and how she might treat them both. She'd known what sort of mood he was in the minute she'd opened the door. Despite Leah's mum having been in to make him a cup of tea and help him to use the chamber pot, he'd railed at Dora the moment she walked in. She remembered how she'd shrunk back against the doorframe in shame, acutely aware that his shouting and cursing could be heard next door, if not halfway down the lane.

As usual he appeared immune to her tears and her apologies had fallen on stony ground as he'd continued to bellow and curse while she hurried to heat up the leftover stew.

His mood had proceeded to deteriorate throughout the

evening. Anything within arm's reach was thrown at the walls. When Dora tried to calm him down, he'd gripped her arm so tightly his fingers had left a large purple bruise.

He'd finally fallen asleep around eleven o'clock but it had been gone midnight by the time Dora had finished cleaning the cottage and dragged herself wearily up the stairs to bed.

She heard her father calling her now, and her heart sank.

'Coming, Dad.' She dried her hands and went into the front room.

'I can't get comfortable,' Stephen whined, pouting like a petulant child. 'You need to sort out my pillows.'

'All right, Dad.' Dora leaned him forward and, with one hand supporting her father's weight, she arranged the pillows behind him. 'Is that better?' she asked, easing him back gently.

'It'll do, I suppose,' he grunted ungratefully. He closed his eyes, his large hands resting on the top of the bedclothes, and exhaled loudly.

Dora sighed. Boredom was the biggest curse of the bedridden. Stephen had never been much of a reader but since his stroke, the concentration required to read even a page or two caused him insufferable headaches. If he was in an amiable mood, Dora would read to him, as he found the melodious sound of her voice soothing, even if he was unable to concentrate on the words. Their choice of reading material was limited as books were a scarce commodity in their house. On more than one occasion Alice had offered to lend Stephen something from her stepfather's extensive library but Dora's father had declined, rather ungraciously, to Dora's embarrassment.

She crossed to the rain-spattered window. People were walking back from church, no doubt discussing the upcoming ball. The highlight of the year, the Strawberry Pickers' Ball was all anyone was talking about at the moment.

Not that she would know, Dora thought wryly. She had never been asked – and no wonder, she mused ruefully, staring at her face reflected in the glass. She was conscious that her looks were what might be deemed 'plain'. 'Unremarkable' was how she had once heard an elderly aunt describe her features, an observation Dora didn't dispute. She only had to glance in the mirror to acknowledge the fact her face was too round, her blue eyes too close together, her mouth too wide, and her nose too long. Her hair was fair and long, but thin, reaching almost to her waist. She wore it plaited and wound around her head for convenience.

That same maiden aunt had proclaimed Dora as 'unmarriable' and she was inclined to believe the woman was right. Even if she were lucky enough to attract a potential husband, it would take a special sort of man who'd be willing to take on her father.

It grieved her deeply that her father, once such a well-liked and respected member of the community, had, over time, alienated even his closest friends. Any sympathy he might once have garnered had long since been eroded by disgust for his temper and the abysmal way in which he treated his daughter.

It was probably just as well she was unlikely to be invited to the ball, Dora thought, moving away from the window as a gust of wind shook the frame. She had nothing suitable to wear and even with the extra money she'd earned this week, it wouldn't stretch to a dress suitable to wear to a ball.

'Why don't I read to you for a while, Dad?' she suggested, going over to the small shelf that housed their meagre collection of books. 'What about *Martin Chuzzlewit*? You like that one?'

Despite the continual downpour, Leah and Alice were deep in conversation as they left the churchyard, both wondering whether it was socially acceptable in a small place like Strawbridge for a lady to ask a man to the ball.

Hearing Alice's name being called, Leah glanced over her shoulder.

'I think our curate wants a word,' she said, nudging Alice in the ribs. Both girls turned as Samuel came hurrying down the path after them, shielded from the rain by a large, black umbrella.

'I'll see you at home, Alice,' Beatrice smiled. 'Leah?' Beatrice raised an eyebrow. Taking the hint, Leah bade Alice a quick goodbye, and hurried to catch up with her mother and Daisy.

'I was hoping I might get a chance to talk to you,' Samuel said, looking slightly nervous as he held the umbrella over Alice's head. 'It has been brought to my attention several times this morning, that the village ball is just two weeks hence and, as I'm aware I shall probably not see you again before next weekend, I was wondering whether, if you're not already spoken for, you'd consider accompanying me?'

'I would very much like to go to the ball,' smiled Alice. 'Thank you.'

'Right, thank you.' Samuel's grin broadened as he exhaled in relief. 'Perhaps I might call on you next Sunday, and introduce myself to your parents?'

'That would be nice. Shall we say four o'clock? You could stay for tea if you liked?'

'I shall look forward to it.'

'Reverend Roberts,' Walter Aldridge called across the rain-lashed churchyard. 'Mrs Beale would like a word.'

'Duty calls,' Samuel said, giving Alice a rueful grin. 'Until next weekend, then.'

'Yes. Goodbye, Samuel.'

Already planning in her head to ask her mother to make her a new dress to wear to the ball, Alice hurried after her grandmother. She had accompanied her grandfather to the ball the previous year when Beatrice had been taken ill, and had thoroughly enjoyed herself. The idea that she would be attending on the arm of the district's newest eligible bachelor sent a tingle of excitement coursing down her spine and she couldn't help but feel rather smug.

As she let herself in the front door of Nettlebed Cottage, shaking rain water from her clothes, her thoughts turned to Dora. As soon as the midday meal was over and she'd helped Beatrice wash up, she flung her still-damp shawl around her shoulders and hurried round to the Webbs. Thankfully, the rain had eased and patches of blue sky were visible amidst the grey as she stood on the doorstep waiting for Dora to answer her knock.

'Oh, hello, Alice,' Dora said wearily. She looked pale and wan. 'Come in.' She stood back to allow Alice into the dingy parlour where Stephen's loud snores reverberated off the walls. 'He's just nodded off,' Dora said, the relief evident in her tired voice. 'Let's go through to the kitchen.'

Holding her breath against the all-pervading smell of stale sweat and human excrement, Alice followed Dora into the back room. The laundry draped in front of the range gave off a damp smell and Alice noticed patches of black mould blooming in the corners of the ceiling.

'Sorry about the mess.' Dora moved the clothes horse slightly to allow Alice to pull out a chair. She opened the back door, letting in the cool breeze.. Water dripped from the eaves and raindrops glistened on the grass where the chickens were scratching for worms.

'You look exhausted,' Alice said, her brow crinkling in concern as Dora busied herself making tea.

'I'm all right,' replied Dora with a smile that didn't meet her eyes. 'Just tired.' She set the teapot and two mugs between them and sat down, resting her elbows on the tabletop. 'I'm afraid we're out of milk,' she apologized, stopping short of explaining that her father had knocked the milk jug from her hand in a rage when she'd attempted to pour some in his bedtime cocoa.

'It's fine as it comes,' Alice assured her.

She stayed an hour. She refrained from mentioning the ball, knowing that Dora wasn't going. Instead, they talked about the strawberry harvest and laughed about some of the more eccentric characters they worked with.

Stephen woke up just as Alice was getting ready to leave.

'What's she doing here?' he snarled at his daughter, shooting Alice a filthy look. 'Come to have a gawp at the cripple, have you?'

'Mr Webb, I assure you . . .' Alice stammered, her cheeks turning puce with mortification.

'Get out!' Stephen bellowed, his angry eyes searching for something to throw.

'Dad,' pleaded Dora. 'Alice is my guest.'

'We don't want people here,' he repeated, spittle frothing on his thin, dry lips. 'Go on, get out.'

Alice looked at Dora in alarm, wondering whether she should leave her friend alone when her father was in such a belligerent mood. Reading the question in Alice's eyes, Dora gave a subtle shake of her head.

'Thank you for coming, Alice,' she said, with forced joviality as she ushered her friend towards the door.

'Will you be all right?' Alice whispered, once she was out on the street. Dora nodded quickly.

'I'll see you tomorrow,' she said, all but slamming the door in Alice's face. Feeling helpless and dreadfully sad for her friend, Alice turned away. Stephen's demented ranting followed her as she passed by Leah's cottage, to her grandparents'. His voice was still ringing in her ears even after she'd stepped inside.

She closed the door and leaned against it, her heart thumping.

'Are you all right, dear?' Beatrice looked up from her knitting. She was sitting on the armchair closest to the empty hearth. A lamp burned on the small table beside her. Mathew sat at his writing desk, reading a book. He put it down and took of his glasses.

'You do look a little shook up,' he said, rubbing the bridge of his nose with his forefinger.

'Mr Webb woke up as I was leaving,' Alice said, unwinding her shawl and hanging it up. 'He got a bit upset.'

'That poor girl.' Beatrice shook her head in dismay.

'She's a heavy cross to bear,' Mathew agreed, putting his glasses back on. 'Such a shame he's grown so bitter. He was always such a likeable man. He'd have done anything for anyone.'

'I feel so sorry for her,' Alice said, glancing at the mantlepiece clock. 'Shall I make some tea before I go?'

'That would be lovely, Alice,' Beatrice smiled. 'Thank you.'

Beatrice laid her knitting on her lap and watched her eldest grandchild disappear into the kitchen. She shared her daughter Lily's relief that Alice had inherited nothing of her late father's corrupt nature. Beatrice had never known Jez Elkin but he'd sounded a nasty piece of work and she didn't doubt her daughter when she'd said his passing had gone largely unlamented. It had brought her great sorrow to learn how the daughter she had been forced to give up when she was just a few days old had ended up with the likes of Jez and his wicked mother, Doris. The thought often crossed her mind that it was just as well the evil cow was dead and buried, or by golly, she'd have done away with the old baggage herself.

At least she could take comfort in the fact that her Lily was now happily remarried. James was a good man who clearly adored his wife and children. And it was obvious to everyone who knew him that he couldn't be fonder of Alice if she were his own flesh and blood.

'What are you thinking, Grandma?' Alice asked, coming in with the tea tray. 'You look miles away.'

'I'm just thinking how blessed I am,' Beatrice smiled, picking up her needles again as Alice set the tray on the low table and poured the tea.

'Oh,' she said, as she passed Beatrice her cup. 'I forgot to tell you. We had a letter from my Uncle Charlie. He's going to be a father at the grand old age of forty-two.'

'That's excellent news,' smiled Beatrice. 'Charlie is a good man. He deserves all the happiness in the world. I couldn't be more pleased for him.'

CHAPTER SIX

A pale, watery sun had emerged from the clouds by the time Leah and Harry made their way down the lane towards their favourite spot by the pond. Swallows dipped and dived in the warm air, snapping at the insects that had emerged after the rain. The swans were nestled on the far side of the water, the signets tucked safely under their mother's wing. Rooks squabbled high up in the trees and blue-green dragonflies skimmed the shimmering surface.

Harry draped his jacket on the damp ground and they sat down. The old rope swing creaked gently in the light breeze that rustled the trees.

Leah leaned back on her hands, tilting her chin to the sun. This was the third Sunday in a row Harry had invited her to go walking. During the week they took every opportunity they could to snatch a few precious moments together and people were beginning to notice. She exhaled slowly, knowing she'd have to speak to Joshua soon. She should have done so already. She knew she was being cowardly to keep delaying the moment and making excuses every time she saw him. He wasn't a fool. She could tell by the look in his eyes that he knew something was up.

'What are you thinking?' Harry asked. Leah smiled at him. 'Nothing important.'

'Good,' replied Harry. 'Because there's something I'd like to ask you.'

'Oh, yes?' Leah sat up straighter. 'And what might that be?'

Harry cleared his throat. 'I'd be very honoured if you'd accompany me to the Pickers' Ball,' he said, hopefully.

'I'd love to,' Leah said, almost giddy with relief. She'd been certain he would ask her but with only two weeks to go, she had been getting a little panicky. Alice had already offered to lend her one of her dresses. Having a friend whose mother was a dressmaker was a huge advantage as far as Leah was concerned and she was not so proud that she would turn down the offer of a dress that, only last season, had been the height of fashion.

'I've been trying to pluck up the courage to ask you all week,' Harry grinned.

Leah laughed. 'And I've been waiting all week for you to do so.'

'Well, I'm glad that's settled, then.' Harry entwined his fingers with hers and cleared his throat. 'It will be my first Pickers' Ball.'

'You'll enjoy it,' Leah said. The touch of his skin on her hand was almost mesmerising and she had to force herself to concentrate on what she was saying. 'Mr Whitworth pays for everything. There's a whole roasted hog on a spit and an endless supply of ale and cider.' She grimaced. 'There's usually a fight or two towards the end of the night.' She didn't add that her usual dance partner, Joshua, was normally in the thick of it.

'Sounds like a fun evening.'

'Oh, it is,' Leah assured him. 'And although Mr Whitworth foots the bill, he never comes.' An idle thought struck her. 'I must say, I'm surprised to see Mrs Whitworth is still here,' she said, chewing her bottom lip thoughtfully. 'I know she's not fond of the place, but then, you wouldn't know the history, being a newcomer.'

Hannah hammered on the door of Woodpecker Cottage. At the sight of Dora's pale, weary face, her heart went out to the girl.

'Hello, Dora, love. I'm here to see your dad. Is he awake?'

Without waiting for a reply, she squeezed by her, and marched straight over to where Stephen lay propped up against the pillows.

'Now listen here, Stephen Webb,' she said sternly, before he had chance to utter a word. 'I've been listening to you ranting and raving all afternoon and I'm heartily sick of it.' She stood with her hands on her ample hips and glared at him. 'You treat this poor girl of yours like a skivvy and it's got to stop. Your Susannah must be turning in her grave, she'd be that ashamed of you,' she blazed. Slumped against his pillows, Stephen stared at her mutely.

'Right,' Hannah continued, her tone softening. 'Dora, you go round to ours. Daisy's there and I'm expecting Leah back shortly. You can stay and have your tea with us. It's all right,' she added, catching the look of uncertainty Dora threw her father. 'Your dad will be fine about it, won't you?' Stephen gave a reluctant nod of his head. Shooting Hannah a grateful smile, Dora scuttled out of the door.

'Now, you listen,' Hannah said, turning back to Stephen once she'd gone. 'Dora's going to enjoy an hour or so at ours. I'll be over in a bit to bring you some supper. Do you need the chamber pot before I go?'

'No!' Stephen snorted. He waved his arm, brushing her away like an annoying insect.

'If you need anything, just holler,' she said, with a wry smile. 'We'll hear you.' She paused in the doorway, glancing back at him over her shoulder. 'And you mind what I say, Stephen, start treating Dora better, or you'll have me to answer to.'

'It won't hurt him to stew in his own juices for a while,' she said to Dora a few seconds later as she stepped into her own parlour. 'He can't treat you like that, love. Yes, life has dealt him a cruel blow but he's alive, which is more than can be said for many.' Her face clouded as her gaze drifted to the framed photographs on the mantelpiece. 'My William wouldn't recognize the man your dad is now.' Dora hung her head as tears pricked her eyelids.

'Don't get upset, love.' Hannah pulled the girl into her

embrace. 'I know it's difficult for him but that doesn't excuse his behaviour. You're dutybound to look after him, but he should still have a bit of gratitude and treat you with respect. Now,' she said, glancing up at the clouds gathering overhead. 'Why don't you girls go out and collect the eggs and when Leah gets back, we'll have a game of Snakes and Ladders?'

Leah arrived home half an hour later, brimming with excitement.

'Harry has invited me to the ball.' Clutching a cushion to her chest, she waltzed around the parlour. 'Oh, I'm so excited and Alice has the perfect dress for me, too. It's midnight-blue velvet. She says it will complement my eyes.'

'I'm very happy for you,' her mother remarked drily. 'Have you thought to tell poor Joshua?'

Leah sighed loudly. 'No, I haven't. But I will. I'll see him tomorrow and tell him then.' She caught her mother's gaze. 'I will. I promise.'

'I'm glad he asked you at last,' Dora said, with only a trace of envy. 'He's a nice-looking chap.'

'He's hinted that he may stay in Strawbridge for the winter,' she confided to Dora as they set the board game out on the parlour table.

'I hope he does, as you're so keen on him,' Dora said wisely.

'I'd be devastated if he left.' Leah's smile dimmed. She grasped Dora's hands in hers. 'Oh, I hope he stays. I really do.'

'Perhaps you should invite your young man to have tea

with us next Sunday,' suggested Hannah. 'Once you've spoken to Joshua.'

Leah gave her mother an impatient grimace. 'I'll speak to him, Mum. Don't nag.'

Alice wheeled her bicycle around the back of the large red-brick Victorian villa. She could hear the voices of her four younger half-siblings drifting from the bottom of the garden. Smiling, she rested her bicycle against the coal bunker and entered the airy kitchen

'Mother, I'm home,' she called out, taking off her hat and laying it on the scuffed oak table. A sleek marmalade-coloured cat eyed her sleepily from the window seat. Herbs hung drying on a rack suspended from the high ceiling and the grey-slate floor was scattered with brightly-coloured handwoven rugs.

'Hello, Alice.' Her mother wafted into the kitchen, the skirt of her blue dress rustling as she picked up the plate of burnt toast and tossed it out the back door on to the lawn where it was immediately set upon by some squabbling crows. 'Did you have a good time?'

'I did,' replied Alice. 'The new curate, Reverend Roberts, was invited too.'

'Oh, yes?' Lily said, regarding her daughter quizzically. 'And?'

'And,' said Alice, her cheeks flushing slightly, 'he has invited me to the Pickers' Ball. Will you make me a dress? I know you're busy with commissions and I would attempt to make one myself but you know I have neither your talent nor patience for dressmaking.'

Lily smiled. 'I'm sure that between us we can come up with something. In fact, I had some new patterns arrive this very morning. One of which, I believe, will be perfect for you.'

'Thank you.' Alice hugged her mother warmly. At thirty-seven, her mother was still an attractive woman, she mused, watching her bustling about the kitchen. Wisps of dark, auburn hair had fallen loose from her chignon, softly framing her face.

'Ah, Alice, you're home.' James Russell came striding into the kitchen, rubbing his hands. He was a tall man of slender build, fair-haired and blue-eyed. His thin, blond moustache gave him an appearance of sternness which belied his amiable nature.

'Hello, Father,' Alice greeted him fondly. 'I was just telling Mother, I've been invited to the Pickers' Ball by the new curate.'

'A curate, hm?' frowned James. 'I'd rather you went with a man of the cloth than some of those picker louts.'

'They're not all louts, Father,' protested Alice. She knew her stepfather didn't wholly approve of her spending her Saturdays working in the fields alongside what he termed 'the rougher elements' of society. 'Most of the men working in the fields are decent, hardworking folk. Just because someone has very little money, doesn't mean they're not good people,' she chided him.

'That's not what I'm saying, Alice,' James replied good-humouredly. 'But I should feel more at ease knowing you are out with a curate, than some Joe Picker who hails from the rougher side of town.'

Alice and her mother exchanged glances. Though James was aware of the hardships his wife and stepdaughter had endured in the past, it was seldom alluded to. And while Alice had very little recollection of her life before moving to Weymouth as a young girl, as she had explained to Samuel, she was certain her compassion for those less fortunate than herself stemmed from the snippets of conversation she'd heard between her mother and grandmother.

She knew her mother occasionally suffered nightmares about the past. She'd heard her call out in the night, then she would hear the soft, comforting voice of her stepfather, calming her down, reassuring her that Jez was gone, and could never hurt her, or Alice, again.

CHAPTER SEVEN

'Leah! Leah, wait!'

Leah's stomach muscles clenched and she let out an anxious sigh. She couldn't put Joshua off another minute. She'd been avoiding him for days but now, with just over a week to go until the ball, she could do so no longer.

'Morning, Joshua,' she said, plastering a smile on her face. In spite of everything, she was fond of him and was determined to let him down as gently as she could.

'I'll leave you to it,' Dora said, giving her a sympathetic smile. 'Come on, Daisy.' She gave the younger girl a nudge. 'Your sister and Joshua need to talk.'

Leah waited as Joshua ran up to her, his handsome face marred by confusion. 'What's going on?' he asked in a low voice. 'Whenever I call by your house, you're always out. You've been ignoring me at work.' He managed an anxious smile. 'If I didn't know any better, I'd think you were avoiding me.'

When Leah didn't respond his smile faltered. 'Come on, Leah. If it's something I've done . . . ?'

'It's nothing you've done,' Leah sighed. 'You're a good friend, but . . .' Conscious of the streams of people threading their way passed them, Leah moved to the edge of the road. Joshua followed her, a worried frown creasing his brow.

'I've been invited to the ball by someone else.' There, she'd said it. Despite Joshua's obvious bewilderment, she felt only relief.

'What? Who? Who are you going with?'

'Does it matter?' She started walking quickly.

'Yes, it matters!' he said loudly. Shoving his hands deep in his trouser pockets, his long stride caught up with her easily. 'I want to know who'd be so bold as to ask you when everyone knows you're my girl.'

'I'm not your girl,' Leah responded with an exasperated air.

'We have an understanding,' he persisted. He frowned as his confidence appeared to falter. 'Haven't we?'

'I'm sorry, Joshua. I should have been honest with you,' Leah said, slightly remorseful in light of Joshua's obvious hurt. 'I like you as a friend. Nothing more.'

'I see.' Joshua pursed his lips. 'So, are you going to tell me who he is, then?'

'Harry,' replied Leah quietly.

'Harry?' Joshua frowned. He stopped walking. 'You can't mean Henry Whitworth?'

'Henry Whitworth?' Leah repeated, regarding Joshua with a puzzled frown. 'Who's he when he's at home? No, Harry,' she said, her expression softening. 'Harry White.'

'Harry White?' snorted Joshua with a mocking grin. 'That

might be what he's calling himself but his name's Henry Whitworth. He's old Whitworth's son.'

'Don't be ridiculous,' Leah scoffed. 'Where did you hear such nonsense? Mr Whitworth doesn't have a son.'

'I'm telling you, Leah, it's true. He's recently finished at Eton and is spending the summer working the fields before the old man trains him up to take over the business. Why do you think Isaac's missus is here? Because she can't bear to let her precious boy out of her sight, that's why.'

'Why would he pretend to be someone else then?' Leah replied 'Why would he lie?'

Joshua shrugged. Leah was about to stalk off but something in his expression caused her to hesitate. 'How do you know this?' she asked in a small voice.

'I overheard old Whitworth talking to Mathew Turner,' Joshua replied matter-of-factly.

Leah swallowed. She felt sick. Angry tears burned her throat. 'It can't be true. Harry wouldn't lie to me.'

'Why don't you ask him?' Joshua said with a shrug. He inclined his head towards the pub. Leah followed his gaze, her heart skipping a beat as she spotted Harry talking to one of the landlord's boys.

'I shall do just that,' she retorted, with a determined thrust of her chin. Certain that this was just some malicious ploy of Joshua's to get her to change her mind about accepting Harry's invitation to the ball, she dodged between the horse-drawn carts and crossed the lane, clenching and unclenching her fists in agitation.

'Leah.' The way Harry's face lit up at the sight of her, sent her heart racing. He had such an open, honest face, how could she even think he would set out to deceive her? He shook the pub landlord's son's hand. 'Thanks, Seth. I'll be in touch.'

'Morning, Miss Hopwood.' Seth Merrifield, a big, burly lad of eighteen, gave Leah a wide grin and touched the brim of his cap.

'Good morning, Seth.' Seth was the middle child of five, all strapping lads who took after their publican father, Reuben.

'Is everything all right, Leah?' Harry frowned, as Seth disappeared round the side of the pub. 'You look troubled.'

'There's something I need to ask you,' Leah replied. 'I'm sure it's not true but, it's just … Joshua says you're Isaac Whitworth's son.' She smiled, fully expecting him to burst into laughter at the absolute absurdity of her remark. Instead, his cheeks turned the colour of beetroots and she realized straight away that what Joshua had told her was true.

'Why would you lie about who you are?' she asked, shock and disbelief forming a leaden lump in her chest.

'I didn't lie,' Harry replied, flustered. 'I didn't tell you because … well, because I wanted you to like me for who I am, not because of my family name.'

'Did you think it was funny? Letting me witter on about the history of Strawbridge when you probably know it better than I do?' Leah demanded, angrily. 'Did you enjoy making a fool out of me?'

'No!' Harry looked shocked and hurt but Leah didn't care. She wanted to hurt him, as much as he'd hurt her.

'I didn't just pretend to be interested,' he pleaded. 'My mother has never spoken about this place. She hates it here. I've never known anything about my heritage, or the history of Strawbridge.' He paused for breath, and held out his hands. 'Leah, please,' he said, his eyes imploring her to listen. 'I wanted to tell you, I promise, and I was going to, after the ball. I'd hoped that by then you'd like me enough that it wouldn't matter who I was.'

'I suppose all your mates know?' said Leah, crossly, fighting back tears of anger and disappointment. 'Did you have a good laugh at my expense?'

'Of course not!' Harry shook his head, clearly appalled at the very idea. 'Only Mathew Turner knows my identity and my father swore him to secrecy. It was one of the conditions in agreeing to work for him, that I was treated just like everyone else.' He frowned. 'I don't know how Joshua found out.'

'Oh,' Leah gave a mirthless laugh. 'Nothing much gets by him.' Her voice trembled and she took a deep breath to steady it. 'Was I just a dalliance?' she asked. 'An amusement to pass the time until you go back to London?'

'Leah, don't do this,' Harry pleaded. 'I know you're upset, and I'm sorry. I never meant to hurt you.'

'Well, you have.' Leah choked back a sob. She'd fallen hard for Harry and to find out that he wasn't who she thought was a bitter pill to swallow. 'You'll have to find yourself another dance partner for the ball,' she said, a tremor to her voice.

'You don't mean that?' Harry's face clouded. 'Leah, I've said I'm sorry. What more can I do?'

'I can't trust you,' Leah said. 'I don't want to see you again.'

Blinking back tears, she turned on her heel and ran across the lane, almost colliding with a pony and cart in her haste.

'Watch it, miss,' the driver shouted, shaking his head.

Leah took no notice. The tears were spilling down her face and she wiped them away angrily with the back of her hand. Harry, or rather, Henry, Whitworth wasn't worth her tears. She heard him call after her, but she ignored him.

'Everything all right, love?' Beatrice asked as Leah went to sign on and collect her basket.

'Yes, thank you,' she replied curtly. She snatched up a basket and stumbled across the field in search of Dora.

'What's the matter?' Dora looked up in alarm. 'You look like you've seen a ghost,' she said, getting to her feet and taking Leah by the elbow. 'Sit down in case you faint. I'll get you some water.'

'I'm fine,' Leah replied weakly, but Dora was already hurrying off to the water butt. She sank to her knees and buried her face in her hands. What a fool she was. She should have had some inkling that Harry was not all he claimed to be, surely. The way he spoke should have been a dead giveaway. And the way he was so vague about himself. She was such an idiot. How he must have been laughing at her behind her back.

Well, that was that, she thought with a shaky breath. It was over.

*

'Here, drink this.' Dora appeared at her side with the water dipper. Leah took a sip of the tepid water and grimaced, wiping her lips with the back of her hand.

'Tell me what's happened,' Dora cajoled her gently.

'It's Harry,' Leah said with a rueful smile. 'He's only Mr Whitworth's son, isn't he?'

'Really?' Dora's eyebrows rose in surprise. 'Mr Whitworth has a son? Gosh! That's a turn up. When did he tell you that?'

Leah shook her head. 'He didn't. Joshua told me.'

Dora's expression turned sceptical. 'You can't trust everything Joshua says, you know. You've just broken his heart. Of course, he's going to try and change your mind. Much as I like Joshua, I wouldn't put it past him to make up something like that.'

Leah shook her head. 'It's true,' she said, bleakly. 'Harry confirmed it.'

'I see.' Dora sat back on her heels, and picked up her basket, resting it on her lap.

'I'm not seeing him again.'

Dora nodded her understanding. It was a courtship that could never go anywhere. There was no chance Mr Whitworth would allow his only son to marry one of his tenants. She reached for Leah's hand and gave it a squeeze. 'I'm sorry, Leah. I know how fond you are of him.'

Not trusting herself to speak, Leah could only nod.

'Oi!' A woman's voice hollered down the rows of strawberry plants. 'Who's got the water dipper?'

'Sorry, Sally, I've got it here,' Dora called back, getting

swiftly to her feet. 'I'll bring it back.' She rolled her eyes at Leah who managed a weak smile in return, and trudged over to the water butt.

'You're supposed to take your drink here,' the woman snapped, snatching the dipper out of Dora's hand.

'My friend felt unwell,' Dora retorted, not intimidated by the woman's surly manner in the slightest. 'She needed a drink.'

'Yeah, well tell her to get off her backside and get it herself next time,' the woman snarled, plunging the metal ladle deep into the barrel.

Several times over the course of the day, Leah caught Harry looking over at her and she quickly averted her gaze. He looked so lost that she had to fight the urge to run over to him and tell him everything was all right. All was forgiven. Instead, she tried to force all thoughts of him from her mind. Despite her best efforts, her heart felt leaden as she made her way home late that afternoon. She could barely concentrate on Dora's constant chatter. Never usually a garrulous person, she knew her friend was only prattling on in order to take Leah's mind off Harry, and she gave her a grateful smile as they parted ways outside the cottages.

'Did you have any idea Harry is Isaac Whitworth's son?' Leah asked her mother the moment she walked through the door.

Hannah looked up from her mending in surprise. 'Isaac has a son?' She shook her head. 'No, of course not but now you mention it,' she pursed her lips thoughtfully, 'he does have a look of Isaac about him, when he was a younger man.' Setting her work basket aside, she got to her feet. 'Has he just told you that himself?'

'Oh, he didn't tell me,' Leah said bitterly. 'It was Joshua who told me. Oh, I'm such an idiot,' she lamented, falling into the nearest chair and staring into the empty fireplace dejectedly. 'He must have thought it a right joke,' she fumed. 'All the while he was playing the attentive beau, I bet he was laughing inside.'

'Now, Leah,' her mother chided her. 'You don't know that. Have you asked him about it?'

'Of course. I confronted him. He said he wanted me to like him for himself and not for who he is.'

'Well, I can see his point. The Whitworth name is a powerful one. Perhaps he just wanted to be himself for a while, and not just old Whitworth's son.'

'That's what he said,' replied Leah sullenly.

'Does anyone else know?'

Leah shrugged. 'Just Mr Turner, apparently.'

'There you are then. He didn't deliberately set out to deceive you. He just didn't want to be treated differently.'

The door opened and Daisy burst into the room, her cheeks pink. 'Joshua says Harry is Mr Whitworth's son!' she exclaimed, her face agog. 'Is it true?'

Leah scowled at her. 'Yes.'

'Goodness! You're going to the ball with Mr Whitworth's son. How romantic,' she beamed. 'It's like Cinderella. You might end up marrying him,' she teased.

'I'm not going to the ball with him,' Leah snapped.

'Daisy, leave your sister alone,' Hannah warned her younger daughter. 'She's a bit out of sorts.'

That was an understatement. Leah frowned, her gaze focused on the empty hearth. She heard a flock of geese honk raucously as they flew over the cottage and the clock on the mantelpiece started to whir as it got ready to chime the quarter hour.

She felt hollow inside, bereft. She really liked Harry and, though it was early days, she had even allowed herself to fantasize about a future with him. But those dreams lay trampled in the dust now. It had been cruel of him to lead her on. Frances and Isaac Whitworth would never have accepted her, one of their tenants, and no doubt already had some wealthy debutante picked out as a prospective bride for their precious son. The thought brought tears of jealousy to Leah's eyes and she wiped them away with an angry swipe of her hand.

She listened to her mother and Daisy clattering about the kitchen as they prepared the evening meal, talking in hushed voices. About her no doubt, and what a fool she had been. It was so unfair, she fumed inwardly. Just when she finally met someone she really liked and could envisage a future with, fate had intervened.

'Supper's ready.' Hannah appeared in the doorway, hands on her hips.

'I'm not very hungry,' Leah said, dully.

'That's as may be,' said her mother, her eyes clouding in sympathy. 'But you need to eat. Come on. You'll feel better once you've got something inside you.' Leah rolled her eyes. Her shattered heart was one ailment her mother's home cooking wouldn't cure.

Oh, why did he have to be a Whitworth? she groaned, getting up from the chair and going into the kitchen. It just wasn't fair.

CHAPTER EIGHT

It was the evening before Midsummer's Eve. Even though it was gone nine o'clock, the sun was as bright and warm as it had been at midday. The surrounding trees resonated with birdsong and from far away in the distance came the shrill whistle of a train.

The strawberry fields were teeming with pickers. The long, lighter evenings were perfect for picking and there were very few who could afford to turn down the extra wages.

Leah eased herself back onto her haunches. She'd been out in the fields since five o'clock that morning and she was exhausted. She welcomed the tiredness. It meant she was too tired to think about Harry, or to dwell on the fact that she was missing the Pickers Ball the following evening.

She had been disappointed, but not surprised, to discover that, much to her sister Daisy's chagrin, Joshua had asked Dora to go to the ball with him. In spite of her own misery, Leah had been mildly amused to find that her sister had been harbouring a secret hope that he might invite her. Instead,

Daisy was going with Leonard Merrifield, the youngest of publican Rueben's five boys.

Leah got to her feet, brushing soil from her finger tips. Picking up her basket, full to the brim with the vibrant red strawberries, she made her way to the stack of crates at the far end of the row. Careful so as not to bruise the fruit, she emptied her basket into an almost empty crate, and was about to start back down the row, intending to fill one more basket before calling it a night, when she caught sight of Harry. He appeared to be heading her way, his expression one of abject misery.

In spite of her daily resolve to have nothing to do with him, her traitorous heart skipped a beat as her breath caught in her throat. She glanced about for a way of escape, but there was none. Over the past fortnight, she had been careful to avoid him and, seemingly respectful of her wishes, he had kept his distance. But she could see from the determined thrust of his jaw that he was intent on speaking to her now. Her empty basket hanging at her side, Leah braced herself to face him.

'Can we talk?' Harry said, in a strangled voice.

Leah glanced about her. No one seemed to be paying them any attention. She shrugged, her steely glare giving lie to her tumultuous emotions.

'Not here. Please,' Harry implored. 'I shan't keep you long.'

Leah nodded and they walked in silence passed the rows of strawberry plants towards a fallen tree trunk. The neighbouring trees cast long shadows across the ground where rabbits were enjoying the fresh stalks of grass in the relative safety of the hedgerows.

Brushing lichen and moss from the ancient tree trunk, Leah smoothed down her skirt and sat down.

'What is it you want to say?' she asked coolly, setting her basket on the ground beside her feet.

'That I miss you and I'm sorry. I know I should have been honest with you. I should have trusted you.'

'You made a fool of me,' Leah said, but her tone lacked any anger.

'I didn't mean to,' Harry assured her, his gaze sorrowful.

'It doesn't matter now, anyway,' Leah said, with weary resignation. 'If I'd known who you were from the start, I would have kept my distance. I wouldn't have accepted your invitation to go walking.'

'Why not?' Harry frowned, puzzled.

'Because you are a Whitworth!' exclaimed Leah in exasperated. 'Your parents would never allow you to court one of their tenants. You must realize that?'

'My parents be blowed!' Harry said with an uncharacteristic flash of anger. 'Please reconsider, Leah. I would still like you to go to the ball with me.'

'I don't want to get hurt.'

Harry opened his mouth to object but she stopped him with a shake of her head. 'What is it you want from me, Harry? A summer of romance and then you return to London in the autumn without a backward glance?'

'No!' Harry objected, looking wounded.

'I'm serious about you, Leah. I know we haven't known each other very long but,' he smiled sheepishly. 'I can't explain it, but I'm happy when I'm with you and downright miserable when I'm not.'

Leah was quiet for a moment. 'What about your parents?' she asked, doubtfully.

'Father is always telling me I need to grow up.' He allowed himself a tentative smile. 'I'll handle my parents, Leah.'

Leah bit her lip as her pride wrestled with her emotions. She sighed. 'Very well,' she said, slightly embarrassed at having capitulated so easily. 'I will go to the ball with you. But no more secrets, Harry – or should I call you Henry, now?'

He pulled a face. 'Oh, please don't. Only my relations call me Henry.'

'Very well, Harry,' Leah said, grinned in spite of herself. 'But I mean it. No secrets. Promise.'

'I promise,' smiled Harry.

They walked back along the edge of the field, but despite Harry's amiable chatter, Leah couldn't ignore the flutter of unease in her stomach. For no matter how determined Harry might be, she was in no doubt that Isaac and Frances Whitworth would be appalled that their son was taking one of their own tenants to the ball.

It was almost ten o'clock by the time she let herself into the cottage, only to find the parlour in a state of disarray and Dora standing in the middle of the mess, clad in only her shift.

'We're making Dora a dress to wear to the ball,' Daisy said, handing the pinking shears to Hannah, who nodded in confirmation, her mouth full of pins.

'That's pretty.' Leah fingered the cream and navy-blue material. 'Where did you get this?'

'It used to be mine,' her mother said, removing the pins and jabbing them into a pin cushion. 'I wore it when your father and I first started courting. It's a bit old fashioned but it will look better once we've added a few trimmings.'

'Your mum's ever so kind,' Dora said, her arms wrapped around her bust self-consciously. 'I was going to tell Joshua I couldn't go with him because I didn't have anything to wear but your mum told me not to be so silly.' Her eyes sparkled with tears.

'And why shouldn't you go to the ball?' Hannah said sternly, getting to her feet. 'With everything you do for your dad, you deserve some fun. Arms up, now.'

Dora obeyed and Hannah slipped the dress over her head. 'The length is all right,' she said, smoothing down the skirt before stepping back to appraise her handiwork. 'I think I'll add a velvet trim down the bodice and along the cuffs,' she said. 'All right, let's have it off again.'

'Are you sure you don't mind me going with Joshua?' Dora asked Leah, as she reached for her clothes.

'I don't mind at all,' Leah assured her. 'And anyway, Harry and I have made up. I am going to the ball after all.'

Dora and Daisy looked at Leah in surprise.

'Why?' asked Daisy, using a discarded length of velvet

ribbon to tie back her hair. 'I mean, it's great that you're going to the ball, but I thought you'd sworn off Harry for good.'

'So did I,' Hannah frowned. 'What made you change your mind?'

'We had a good talk.' Leah explained.

Her mother regarded Leah with concern. 'Just be careful, love. You do know it can't go anywhere, don't you?' she said gently. 'I don't want to see you get hurt, Leah, so make sure you don't fall too hard.'

'It's too late for that, Mum. And I'm sure the Whitworths will have Harry on the first train home as soon as they see us at the ball together.' Her brave attempt at a smile failed, and Hannah's heart went out to her.

'Oh, sweetheart,' she said, giving Leah a hug. 'Just enjoy the ball and don't worry too much about the future,' she advised, brushing a strand of hair from Leah's eyes.

Leah nodded. She was worried that Harry's parents might even forbid him from attending the ball once they knew who he was going with but she kept that thought to herself and, while Hannah was sewing the ribbon on to Dora's dress, she went into the kitchen to make them all a mug of cocoa.

'I'm pleased things seem better at home since I had that word with your dad,' Hannah said as she and Dora sipped their cocoa a short while later. They were sitting round the kitchen table, the door open to the night breeze. The altered dress was hanging on the back of the parlour door, ready to be pressed in the morning.

'It's certainly been easier,' Dora nodded, cradling her mug in her hands. 'That sleeping draught that Pearl gave me seems to be helping. He's sleeping through the night now so he isn't as tired and bad-tempered. Though he does still have his moments.' She smiled ruefully, remembering the vile expletives her father had thrown her way after she'd told him she was popping next door for half an hour. Thankfully, the sleeping draught had kicked in quite soon afterwards, and she had been able to leave the house slightly less guilt-ridden. She'd popped back twice in the hour and a half she'd been gone and had been relieved to find him sleeping like a baby.

'I think you're a saint,' Leah said, filled with admiration for her friend. 'I couldn't do what you do.'

'You would if you had to,' Hannah told her. 'Now, drink up, girls. You'll have a late night tomorrow.'

CHAPTER NINE

'Be careful, Leah!' Daisy screeched, snatching her cream and green-sprigged gown from the floor and clutching it to her chest as she glared at her sister. 'You trod on my dress.'

'You shouldn't leave it on the floor, then,' Leah retorted under her breath as she turned this way and that in front of the mirror.

'Will you give me a hand, Leah?' Dora asked, contorting herself into all sorts of positions in order to reach the buttons down her back.

'Of course,' Leah replied. 'Just give me a minute while I find my shoes.'

'They're under the bed,' Daisy said. 'Where you left them. Oh,' she wailed. 'Where is my hair ribbon?'

'I saw it somewhere. On the bed, I think,' Leah said, hurrying to help Dora with her buttons. 'It was kind of Mrs White to sit with your dad tonight,' she said, her nimble fingers making quick work of the fiddly little buttons.

'Yes. I think she's a little apprehensive. He wasn't happy

about me going out and he let us both know it,' replied Dora ruefully. 'I hope he'll be all right.'

'Don't spoil your evening worrying about your dad, Dor,' Leah said, going to stand in front of her. 'You look lovely, by the way. Joshua is a very lucky man.'

'Oh, get away with you,' Dora blushed, but she looked pleased.

'Girls,' Hannah called up the stairs. 'Alice is here.'

Leah stepped out onto the landing just as Alice was coming up the stairs, bathed in the dusty sunlight streaming through the landing window.

'You look lovely, Alice,' Leah said, feeling a twinge of envy as she took in the dark maroon silk gown that hugged her friend's neat figure. She had pinned up her lustrous dark hair in an elegant style that emphasized her slender neck. 'It's a beautiful dress.'

'Thank you,' Alice said, graciously. 'Having a dressmaker for a mother has its advantages.'

'Alice!' Dora shrieked, catching sight of Alice on the landing. 'You look so pretty.'

'Thank you, Dora. So do you.' Moving aside a crumpled work dress, Alice sat down on the bed. 'Daisy, you look so grown up. I like your hair like that.'

'Do you?' Daisy beamed, using her fingers to fluff up the dark ringlets that framed her tanned face. 'The uncomfortable night sleeping with my hair tied up in rags was worth it then.'

*

'I'm leaving now, girls,' Hannah called up the stairs a short while later. 'I'll see you there.'

'I hope Mum will be all right,' Leah said, watching from the window as her mother emerged from the house and set off down the lane, a covered basket over her arm. 'It's the first time she's attended the ball since Dad died.'

'She's only going to help,' Daisy pointed out.

'Yes, but it might still bring back painful memories for her.'

'Do you remember how we used to love watching her get ready to go the ball?' said Daisy, smiling at the memory. 'She always looked so pretty. I was always sure Mum and Dad must be the most handsome couple there.'

'I was always jealous that Freddie got to go and we didn't,' Leah remembered, with a bittersweet smile. Despite the four-year age difference, she'd been close to her older brother and, though time had dimmed the agony of grief, there were days, like now, when she felt his loss more keenly.

'I used to pretend Freddie was my brother sometimes,' Dora blurted out, blushing as the three girls turned to her in surprise. 'It's lonely being an only child and Freddie was always so nice to me. I suppose I was jealous of your large family.'

'And now it's just the three of us,' Daisy said, sadly.

'Hey, come on, Daisy, love,' Leah chided her sister. 'Now's not the time to get all maudlin. We've got a ball to go to.' She leaned out of the window and looked down the lane. 'Where are those young men? I hope they're not going to be late.'

*

Samuel and Harry arrived a few minutes later. The two men nodded cordially.

'You must be Harry?' Samuel said, thrusting out his hand. 'Samuel Roberts.'

'Ah, the new curate,' Harry said, giving the proffered hand a hearty shake. 'Harry Whitworth.' He waited for the young reverend to make the connection but Samuel didn't comment. Harry exhaled in relief. Once they'd overcome their surprise that, firstly, Isaac Whitworth had a son he'd never mentioned and, secondly, that his son was the likable, amiable Harry, most people, pickers and villagers alike, had taken the revelation in their stride. Only a handful of the men who'd worked alongside him in the fields appeared to have taken the deception to heart and it bothered him that men he'd called friends, now either ignored him or treated him with scorn.

His train of thought was interrupted by Samuel. 'I have to admit,' the curate said, 'I am somewhat nervous,'

'Me too,' Harry grinned as he rapped on the door. From inside came the sound of nervous giggling and scampering feet. The door flew open and Leah stood in the doorway, framed by Alice, Dora and Daisy.

'Leah,' Harry said, blinking in awe at the sight of Leah in her ballgown, her hair piled extravagantly on top of her head, tendrils falling attractively around her flushed face. 'You're beautiful,' he breathed.

'Well, thank you,' Leah grinned.

'So are you, Alice,' Samuel said. 'All you ladies look particularly lovely this evening.'

Dora's gaze searched the lane anxiously. It was teeming with people heading for the hall and her heart beat painfully against her ribcage.

'Joshua will be here in a minute,' Leah assured her. 'His timekeeping is notoriously erratic. We'll wait with you.'

'No, there's no need. As you say, I'm sure he'll be here shortly.' Dora smiled, surreptitiously crossing her fingers behind her back.

'Leonard's not here yet, either,' Daisy said, 'So I'll wait with you, Dor. You lot go on, if you like.'

Leah and Alice exchanged glances.

'We'll wait,' Leah announced firmly. Harry and Samuel shuffled their feet as they waited in uncomfortable silence, listening to the snippets of conversation from the people passing by.

Mathew and Beatrice emerged, arm in arm from the next-door cottage.

'Good evening, ladies, Reverend. Good evening, Harry.'

'Evening Mr Turner, Mrs Turner.' Samuel and Harry nodded politely.

'We're just waiting for two more of our party,' Alice explained to her grandparents.

'Oh, here he comes now,' Dora said with a rush of relief as Joshua strode into view. She smiled, her round cheeks flushing with colour.

'Hello, sorry I'm late, Dora,' he apologized. He smiled but his eyes were on Leah. He nodded to Samuel but barely acknowledged Harry's presence.

'Ah, here comes Leonard.' Daisy pushed her way out into the lane. 'I thought you'd changed your mind,' she teased, grabbing hold of his arm. Leonard blushed to the roots of his mouse-brown hair and shrugged. Like all Reuben Merryfield's boys he was stocky, with rugged features. With Daisy clinging to his arm, they started up the lane.

'Shall we?' Samuel offered Alice his arm. Harry did like-wise and the two couples set off. Dora looked uncertainly at Joshua. He was watching Leah walking arm in arm with Harry, his expression mutinous.

Leah glanced back over her shoulder, and smiled. 'Come on, you two.'

'I suppose we'd better catch them up,' Joshua said, offering Dora his arm. 'You'd like to stay with your friends. I presume?' he said, a trifle impatiently as she hesitated.

'Oh, yes, of course,' she agreed quickly. Flustered, she slipped her arm through his. Walking beside him along the sun-kissed lane she felt slightly light-headed. He smelled of woodsmoke and, could it be whiskey? She suppressed a tremor of excitement at the thought of everyone seeing her on Joshua's arm.

The church hall, built on the site of an eleventh-century tithe barn, was situated at the very edge of Isaac Whitworth's land, and was as far away from the church as it was possible to be whilst still being considered part of Strawbridge. Its ancient oak doors were propped wide open by two large hay bales. It was midsummer's eve and the sun was still high in an unblemished sky.

Smoke billowed from the nearby firepit and the aroma of roasting pig filled the air.

Two lean, middle-aged men, wearing brightly coloured neckerchiefs, hats pulled low over their eyes, were tuning their instruments. A third played a quick ditty on a mouth organ, the notes drifting away on the balmy air. Couples milled around, the men holding jugs of cider aloft, talking and laughing. The Pickers' Ball was the highlight of the summer season.

Hannah came out of the hall, tucking a strand of hair behind her ear.

'Hello, girls,' she said, smiling. 'You all look lovely, and accompanied by such dapper looking gentlemen,' she teased. 'Help yourself to something to drink. There's plenty of cider, ale and lemonade in the hall.'

'Is Pearl well?' Dora asked Joshua, as they carried their glasses over to where some bales of hay had been placed as makeshift seats.

'Very,' Joshua said, sipping his ale, while watching Leah over the rim of his glass.

'She made a sleeping draught for my father,' Dora explained, in an attempt to draw her partner's attention back to herself. 'It seems to work.'

'I wouldn't put too much store by the old girl's potions,' Joshua said drily.

Dora coloured. She didn't have Leah or Alice's easy manner when it came to talking to people, even those she'd known her whole life, like Joshua. Sitting beside him on the prickly bale of hay, it was as if her mind had completely emptied itself of every intelligent thought. *How dull he must think me after Leah's lively chatter,* she mused miserably, watching Leah emerge from the hall, her hand resting on Harry's arm.

Leah caught Dora's eye and gave a small wave.

'Dora looks a bit lost,' she said to Harry in a low voice. 'Shall we go over and sit with her?'

'If you like,' Harry agreed affably, taking a sip of his cider.

'Alice, we're going to go and sit with Dora and Joshua.'

'We'll come with you,' Alice said. 'You don't mind, do you, Samuel?'

'Of course not.'

'Mind if we join you?' Leah asked Dora, deliberately keeping her gaze averted away from Joshua. Without waiting for a reply, she tucked her skirt beneath her and sat down, pulling Harry down beside her. 'This lemonade is delicious,' she said, taking a sip. 'It has just the right amount of sweetness.'

She could feel Joshua's gaze on her. She'd noticed him watching her, and she felt annoyed on Dora's behalf. This was supposed to be a special evening for her friend. She did hope Joshua wasn't going to spoil it for her by being an idiot. She risked a sideways glance at him as he downed the rest of his pint.

'Anyone for another?' he asked, holding up his glass.

Samuel and Harry, still only partway through their first mug, shook their heads.

'Suit yourselves,' he said. Glowering at Harry, he pushed himself off the hay bale and headed for the hall.

'Are you enjoying yourself, Dora?'

'I'm having a lovely time,' replied Dora, rather unconvincingly, Leah thought.

'Don't let him drink too much. You know how he can be when he's had a skinful.'

Dora nodded, looking worried. 'Maybe you should keep Harry away from him,' she suggested. 'It's only provoking him seeing the two of you together.' She flashed Leah a deprecating smile. 'I realize now that he only asked me in the hope it would make you jealous.'

Leah was about to reply when she caught sight of Isaac Whitworth striding towards the hall and her heart sank. Tall and debonair, there was no denying he was a handsome man, with his mane of silver hair and the healthy tan of a man who spent much of his time in outdoor pursuits.

He moved amongst his workers and tenants, nodding greetings... Beside her, Leah felt Harry stiffen.

'What's he doing here?' he muttered. 'I thought you said he never came to the ball.'

'He doesn't, usually,' Leah whispered back.

Isaac stopped to have a word with Mathew Turner. Though his head was bent towards Mathew, his piercing blue-eyed gaze scanned the milling throng, coming to rest on Harry. His smile broadened.

'Damn! He's spotted me.'

Leah felt herself grow hot as Harry's father excused himself and strode towards them purposefully.

'Good evening, ladies,' he smiled, rather wolfishly, Leah

thought. 'Please, there's no need to stand on ceremony,' he said, as the three girls rose quickly to their feet. 'Perhaps you'd care to introduce me to your friends, Henry? I believe you all now know that Harry, as he likes to call himself, is my son?'

'Yes, sir,' they said in unison.

Harry cleared his throat nervously, his Adam's apple bobbing up and down.

'Of course, father. Leah Hopwood, Dora Webb, Alice . . . ?'

'Russell, sir,' Alice finished. 'Alice Russell. Beatrice Turner is my grandmother.'

'Ah, yes, of course. A delightful woman.' He turned his smile on Leah. 'I knew your father, Miss Hopwood. He was a good man.'

Leah nodded. 'Thank you, sir.'

'And the Reverend Roberts, I know, already of course.'

'Good evening, Mr Whitworth.'

'Good evening, Reverend,' Isaac responded with a nod. 'An excellent sermon last week.' He stroked his beard. 'Very thought provoking.'

'That was my intention, sir.'

'Well, I shan't intrude on your evening.' He smiled round at the girls. 'Ladies, I believe the dancing is about to start.'

As if on cue the musical trio struck up a jaunty tune.

'Shall we?' Samuel asked, offering Alice his hand.

'I'd love to,' she replied. 'It's been so long since I last danced.'

'I must warn you,' grinned Samuel. 'I have two left feet.'

'Don't worry,' laughed Alice. 'So have I.'

Harry held out his hand to Leah and they followed Alice and Samuel.

'Your father seems nice,' Leah said, as Harry took her in his arms. 'I've never spoken to him before. I've always been a bit in awe of him, I suppose.'

'He's nice enough, as fathers go.' He shrugged. 'We're not close. I didn't see much of him growing up. I was a sickly child and I spent much of my childhood confined to the nursery. He spent much of his time here, while Mother preferred to remain in London. She would never allow me to accompany him. She hates it here.'

'Strawbridge has brought your mother a lot of sadness,' Leah replied, as realization dawned. 'Is that why she's here now? Because of you?'

'Yes. I'm a grown man, yet she still treats me like a child,' he replied, a slight bitterness to his tone. 'She's always been overprotective of me. She didn't even want to send me away to school but my father insisted. I saw even less of him then, of course.' His eyes clouded. 'I believe I'm something of a disappointment to my father.'

Leah gave him a sympathetic smile as they both glanced over to where Isaac was chatting amiably to a group of his workers, the same men who had taken against Harry in recent days.

'They'll come round,' Leah said, feeling Harry tensed.

'I hope so but you know what people can be like.'

Leah nodded. She did know. Especially in a small place like

Strawbridge. Her scalp prickled with shame as she recalled her own reaction to Harry's identity. Just this evening she'd noticed a few funny looks aimed her way. There would be those who'd say she was having aspirations above her station, but, *so what if she was?* she thought with a flash of defiance. She liked Harry. And she was certain he liked her,

but whether their courtship would survive beyond the end of the summer remained to be seen.

'What are you thinking?' Harry asked, his brow creasing. 'You look worried.'

Leah smiled, and shook her head. She wasn't going to spoil her favourite evening of the year fretting over the future.

'Nothing at all,' she said, as the music came to an end. They drew apart and clapped, before the trio began the next number.

His hand resting gently against the small of her back, Joshua walked Dora back to the makeshift seat. She thanked him and sat down, reaching for her glass of warm lemonade. Her cheeks were red and her face glistened with perspiration, sweat trickling down her spine. She sipped her drink, watching Joshua heading for the hall. She watched him through the wide doorway, as he laughed and joked with a couple of the Merrifield boys. Their father, Reuben, was chatting to Isaac Whitworth, both men holding jugs of cider.

She set her glass aside and turned her attention to the dancing, smiling at the sight of Daisy, dwarfed by the burly Leonard. Mr and Mrs Tuner spun gracefully by. Mrs Turner was laughing, her head thrown back. Strands of greying auburn hair had come loose from their pins, tumbling girlishly down her back. Alice and the curate stood on the periphery of the dancers, their heads together, talking animatedly. At the sight of Leah whirling by in Harry's arms, Dora's body shuddered with an envious sigh.

All the while she had been dancing with Joshua, she hadn't failed to notice how his eyes had followed Leah. Several times Dora had tried to initiate a conversation, wracking her brain for something interesting or witty to say, but he'd either not heard her over the music or had simply ignored her. She'd finally given up. It had been a blessing when the music came to an end and Joshua walked her back to her seat.

She watched Leah now, dark-blonde hair flying as she smiled up at Harry in that beguiling way she had. There were more than a handful of men watching from the side lines who couldn't tear their gaze away. Even as a little girl, Leah had attracted attention.

'Those looks will get that girl into trouble one day,' Dora's mother had been fond of saying.

Dora sighed again. She loved Leah like a sister and was generous enough not to begrudge her her pretty face but, just once, she'd like a young man to look at her that way. The way Harry Whitworth was gazing so adoringly at Leah, or the way the new curate looked at Alice.

'You all right, love?' Hannah came bustling over, her expression one of concern. 'You not dancing?'

'Joshua's gone to fetch a drink.'

Hannah shook her head. 'He's a one, is that Joshua,' she said, sitting down beside Dora. She was fond of the girl, had known her since she was barely hours old. She was only a few months younger than her Leah. 'Heart of gold he has, but he does sail a bit too close to the wind for my liking. And he can be a devil when he's got the drink inside him.' Hannah watched the dancing for a while. *Leah was certainly the belle of the ball*, she mused with maternal pride.

Hannah and Dora weren't the only ones watching Leah dance. Leaning against the bar nursing a pint of cider, Isaac Whitworth had the perfect view of the dancefloor. He stroked his beard absentmindedly, his piercing blue gaze on Leah, pink-cheeked and animated as she whirled and spun across the grass, skirts flying. He had understood immediately why Henry was so smitten with the girl. She was a beauty all right, with her flawless complexion and honey-blonde hair.

Perhaps Henry was more like him than he'd realized, he grinned. Have your fun with the local lasses then marry one of your own, that had been his own father's advice. Isaac had done just that and Henry appeared to be doing the same. He frowned slightly, regretting the rift between them. Perhaps if Frances hadn't insisted on mollycoddling him as she had, terrified lest he catch so much as a trifling cold, and had allowed him to accompany Isaac on his annual trips to Hampshire, things might have been different. The gap between them had only widened after Henry went away to Eton. Isaac was never in residence at their Richmond home during the summer holidays. They were virtual strangers to each other now.

The musicians finished their set to a burst of appreciative applause and Isaac kept his gaze trained on Harry as he led Leah to a bench in the shade of a nearby silver beech. He saw a couple of lads walk over to them, and he stiffened. He hadn't agreed with his son's idea to keep his identity a secret, and he worried that he'd made life more difficult for himself by the deception.

As he watched, he saw Harry frown, and half rise from his seat, gesturing with his hands in an appeasing manner. Isaac put down his glass, ready to wade in if needed but, to his surprise, the two men let out a guffaw. One of them slapped Harry on the back and Isaac relaxed. Picking up his pint, he took a long swallow. The musicians crowded in beside him, elbowing each other aside as they made their way to the bar.

'Three pints of cider coming up, lads,' Reuben's hearty voice rang out behind him. 'You've certainly earned it.'

'See,' Leah told Harry as Alice and Samuel made their way across the dry grass to join them. 'If the Jones brothers are willing to accept you, then you won't have any problems with any of the others. Give it few days and no one will care that you're the boss's son. You work just as hard as anyone.'

'Joshua doesn't like me,' Harry said, his gaze following Joshua as he joined Dora and Hannah on the hay bale. As if feeling Harry's eyes on him, he looked their way, glowering.

'Ignore him,' said Leah. 'He's just jealous. He's taken me

to the ball for three years in a row and he assumed I'd be going with him again this year. His pride's dented, that's all.'

'I hope Dora's all right,' Alice murmured. 'She does look a bit lost.'

'Poor Dora,' Leah commiserated. 'She doesn't look like she's having a very good time, does she?'

'That's because Joshua keeps staring after you,' Harry remarked, somewhat peevishly.

'I tried to call round to visit Mr Webb several times,' Samuel interjected, biting his lip in consternation. 'But I'm afraid he wasn't very welcoming.'

'He's a miserable old so and so,' retorted Leah unsympathetically. 'He used to be so nice, too. Him and my dad were best of friends.' She shrugged. 'He just feels sorry for himself all the time now. He makes Dora's life hell, the selfish old git.'

'It's Dora I feel sorry for,' Alice said, keeping her voice low. 'It can't be much fun for her.'

Dora was feeling very fed up. It was gone ten o'clock and the western sky had turned the colour of ripe damsons, streaked with vibrant crimson and orange. A gentle breeze stirred the trees and an owl hooted nearby. The evening she had looked forward to all week had turned into a disappointment. As the night wore on it had become increasingly clear that Joshua wasn't at all interested in her, and the more he drank, the more distracted he became. Dora had spent most of the evening talking to her neighbours, Beatrice and Hannah, while Joshua slumped at the bar, staring morosely at Leah.

She stifled a yawn, feeling tears of self-pity pricking at her eyelids. The musicians were packing up and people were saying their goodbyes.

'Do you want to walk back with us?' Alice asked her, casting a look of concern towards Joshua, who now sat hunched nearby, nursing an empty cider jug.

Dora looked over to where Hannah and Beatrice and some of the other women were tidying up.

'They'll be a while yet,' Alice said. 'Grandma told me to go on home. Daisy's already gone.'

Dora stood up and bade Joshua goodnight. He barely glanced up. She linked arms with Alice and they set off along the lane. Leah and Harry followed a few steps behind. Isaac Whitworth had left some times ago and the windows of Streawberige House blazed with light. The moon was a pearly-white sphere suspended above the treeline and the velvet-blue sky sparkled with stars.

A gentle breeze stirred the hedgerows. Somewhere close by a fox barked, followed by the piercing squeal of its prey. As they neared the row of cottages, Dora squeezed Alice's arm in alarm. The door to Woodpecker Cottage was open, lamplight pooling on to the front step. Mrs White stood in the doorway, wringing her hands in agitation.

'Dad!' Letting go of Alice's arm, Dora picked up her skirts and ran the last few yards. 'What is it?' she cried. 'What's happened?'

'Oh Dora,' Mrs White wailed as Dora pushed her way past her and into the cottage. 'He's gone mad!'

Dora glanced round wildly, taking in the scene. Daisy was pressed against the wall, her face white, her hands to her mouth, her shocked gaze on Leonard, who had hold of Stephen by the arms and was attempting to calm him down.

She crossed to her father's bedside. Something crunched beneath her feet. She looked down in dismay at the bits of broken china littering the floor. 'Oh, Dad,' she cried. 'That was Mum's favourite. It was a wedding present, remember?'

She nodded at Leonard. 'Thank you. I can manage him now.' After a moment's hesitation, he reluctantly let go of Stephen's arms and went to stand next to Daisy.

Stephen buried his face against Dora's shoulder and burst into noisy sobs. 'I'm sorry. I'm sorry. I don't know why I behave like this.' He looked up, his face twisted in a mixture of revulsion and self-pity. 'I don't mean it, Dora.'

Dora hugged him. 'I know, Dad,' she whispered. 'I know.' She straightened up, locking eyes with Leonard, who nodded.

'You know where I am if you need me,' he said. Dora managed a weary smile. She walked them to the door where Alice, Leah, Samuel and Harry stood looking in, their expressions anxious.

'He went berserk,' Mrs White said to Dora, gathering her things as she prepared to leave. 'I made him a cup of tea, and he started calling me the most awful names under the sun and throwing everything he could get his hands on. Your poor mother must be turning in her grave.' She shook her head in disgust.

'I'm so sorry, Mrs White,' Dora apologized, her cheeks puce with mortification. 'He can't help himself sometimes.'

'He should be in an institution, if you ask me,' Mrs White snorted as she marched off down the lane.

'Do you want us to stay?' Leah asked softly, casting a nervous glance in Stephen's direction.

'I'm happy to stay and talk to him,' Samuel offered. 'Perhaps I can calm him down if he starts again.'

'He'll be all right now,' Dora told them. 'But thanks.' She smiled at her friends. 'I appreciate your concern.'

'Are you sure?' Leah laid a comforting hand on Dora's arm. Her friend nodded.

'He'll be quiet as a lamb now,' she said, ruefully, knowing the pattern from old. Filled with remorse, Stephen would spend the next day or two being as nice as pie, then something would set him off and the whole process would start again. Dora sighed as she shut the door. It was very wearying.

CHAPTER TEN

Joshua rounded the side of the cottage just as Dora was emptying the bowl of dirty washing-up water onto the garden. The morning had dawned overcast and cool, the dark clouds a perfect reflection of her mood.

'I've come to say sorry,' he said, without preamble. 'My behaviour towards you yesterday was unforgivable. I've brought you this.' He held out a freshly skinned rabbit.

Still holding the washing bowl in her hands, Dora regarded him coolly. Ignoring the rabbit, she said, 'If you didn't want to take me to the ball, why did you ask me?'

Joshua hung his head, shamefaced.

'I didn't realize seeing Leah with Whitworth would affect me so much,' he said, running a hand through his thick, unruly hair. 'I was unfair to you, and I'm sorry.'

Dora sighed and looked away. An awkward silence fell between them, broken only by the peal of the church bells, summoning the faithful to the morning service.

'Get a move on, Leah.' At the sound of Hannah's voice,

they both glanced towards the upstairs window of the cottage next door but, if Leah replied, neither of them heard it.

'It's all right, Joshua,' Dora said at length, as the door of Sunnynook Cottage banged shut and voices sounded in the lane. 'I know how you feel about Leah. I wasn't expecting anything from you. I just wanted to enjoy myself and forget about things for a bit.'

'I know. And I'm sorry.' He held up the rabbit. 'Forgive me?'

Dora couldn't help but grin at his expression of remorse. 'I suppose so.' She took the rabbit from him. 'Thank you. Father will enjoy this.'

'I'd better go,' Joshua said, wiping his hands on his trousers. 'Nanny Pearl will be hopping mad if we're late for church.'

Dora watched him go with mixed feelings. She'd known Joshua all her life and, while she was fond of him, she knew it would take someone very special to make him forget Leah, and that clearly wasn't to be herself.

She carried the rabbit into the kitchen and laid it on the table, reaching for a knife. She'd get a stew on the go and then tackle the mountain of laundry, she decided, feeling decidedly cheered at the thought of having a delicious gamey meal to look forward to later.

'I really enjoyed myself last night,' Samuel said, as he and Alice strolled along the lane. 'I do hope your friend is all right?'

'I saw Dora briefly this morning before I left for church,'

Alice told him. 'Apparently Joshua went round first thing this morning with a peace offering.'

'And her father?'

'Things are calmer.'

Samuel nodded. 'Perhaps I should offer to sit with him occasionally, let Dora have an evening off.'

'That's very kind of you, but I think that's what started the whole thing off last night. Mr Webb seems to get aggressive whenever someone else sits with him. It's as if he's intent on punishing Dora for daring to go out and enjoy herself. The only person he seems to tolerate is Mrs Hopwood.'

'Dora must find it very difficult.' Samuel's expression brightened. 'Ah, look, it's Harry and your friend, Leah.'

'So, it is.' Alice waved at the couple sitting on the banks of the pond. 'How nice.'

'Alice, Reverend,' Leah waved back and patted the blanket spread on the grass. 'Come and join us.'

'Hasn't it turned into a perfect afternoon?' said Alice sitting down beside her friend.

'Perfect,' Leah agreed, leaning back on her elbows. The sun was warm on her face and she closed her eyes, listening to Harry and Samuel as they discussed some cricket match.

'I have to say,' Alice whispered in Leah's ear, 'I find cricket a very dull sport indeed. My stepfather is very fond of it, however, and plays for the village team.'

'What a marvellous idea, Alice,' Samuel said, breaking off his conversation with Harry mid-sentence. Both Alice and Leah sat up.

'What is?' asked Alice, puzzled.

'A local cricket team. You know the lads, Harry. You can get them to organize a couple of teams. We could have matches on a Sunday afternoon.'

'It's a good idea,' Harry said, a little doubtfully. 'Though I'm not sure I'm the man to recruit a team.'

'Nonsense,' Leah scolded him. 'Everyone will be fine, you'll see.' She turned to Samuel. 'I think a cricket team for Strawbridge is a great idea. Your grandad would be up for it, wouldn't he, Alice?'

They were interrupted by the gruff bark of a dog just beyond the clearing. The undergrowth rustled and a scruffy-looking white and black mongrel dog emerged, nose to the ground and wagging its long, thin tail. He was followed by a small, wizened old woman with snow-white hair scraped into a bun and covered by a colourful silk scarf. She wore an ankle-length plain black skirt and a white blouse, with a black knitted shawl slung loosely around her bony shoulders. Over one arm, she carried a basket full of what looked like bits of leaves and twigs.

Intent on burying its snout amongst the rushes lining the water's edge, the dog ignored the four young people sprawled out on the blanket, but the old woman paused.

'Hello, Miss Leah,' she said, flashing her few remaining teeth. Her beady blue eyes settled on Harry. 'Master Whitworth, Reverend.' Samuel nodded and returned her greeting. As did Harry, though he couldn't help feeling slightly discomforted by the old woman's stare.

'Hello, Pearl,' Leah said. She sat up straighter. 'Alice, this is Joshua's great-grandmother, Pearl. I don't believe you've met?'

'I've seen you in church a few times, dearie,' Pearl said in her thin raspy voice. 'You're Mathew Turner's granddaughter.'

'I am,' Alice smiled. 'Alice Russell. I'm pleased to meet you.'

Pearl returned her smile. There was something warm and engaging about the old woman's gaze that instantly put Alice at her ease.

'You must come and take tea in my caravan one afternoon,' Pearl said to Alice. 'I'll do you a reading.'

'I don't think so,' Samuel said quickly, adding, 'It's all nonsense, Alice, you know that.' Alice blushed and gave him a look. But instead of looking upset, Pearl merely smiled.

'Enjoy the rest of your afternoon,' she said. 'Come along, Bear.' The dog came instantly to her side, and they set off along the track that would take them back towards the grounds of Streawberige House.

'That was a bit rude of the Reverend,' Leah murmured to Alice. 'Pearl's harmless enough and her predictions usually come true.' Raising her voice, she said, 'Pearl warned Fred Moffett his wife was going to break her ankle last week, and she did.'

Samuel rolled his eyes good-naturedly and got to his feet. 'I need to be getting back. I've got to prepare for Evensong.' He looked at Alice. 'Will you come? I'll see you safely home afterwards.'

Alice blushed. 'Actually, I had already planned to stay,' she said with a shy smile. 'My grandfather has already offered to see me home.'

'Tell him there's no need,' Samuel grinned as he helped her up. 'It will be my pleasure.'

'We may as well start back, too,' Leah said, much to Harry's obvious dismay. 'You're welcome to join my family for tea, Harry?' she added, brushing bits of grass from her skirt. 'It's only leftovers from dinner, but you're more than welcome.'

Having just been contemplating the prospect of another long, boring evening making small talk with his parents, Harry jumped at the invitation.

'Mum will be pleased,' Leah said, as the foursome made their way down the track to the lane. 'She's keen to know you better.'

'I'll see you at six, then,' Samuel said as he and Alice parted company outside her grandparents' cottage.

'Yes, see you then.' Saying goodbye to Leah and Harry, Alice hurried indoors. Her grandmother was kneeling in front of the dresser. The bottom drawer was open and Beatrice was studying what looked to Alice like a photograph. She was so absorbed that she failed to notice Alice until she was startled by her cheery 'Hello, Grandma.'

'Goodness, Alice,' Beatrice puffed. 'You made me jump.' Hastily shoving the photograph beneath a pile of folded table cloths, Beatrice shut the drawer and got to her feet.

Her smile didn't quite meet her eyes as she turned to face her granddaughter.

'Did you have a pleasant afternoon?' she asked, her cheeks glowing pink.

'Yes, thank you,' replied Alice, frowning. 'Is everything all right?'

'Yes, of course.' Beatrice assured her, waving away her concern. 'I was just having a bit of a sort out. Now,' she flapped, hurrying into the kitchen. 'I'd better make a start on the tea if we're to be ready in time for Evensong.'

'It's a pleasure to have you, Harry,' Hannah said, refilling Harry's tea cup. 'I knew your father as a young man. He and your grandparents always spent their summers in Strawbridge.' She set the teapot on the trivet and sat down; her gaze misty with memories of yesteryear. 'I remember the year your grandparents decided to spend Christmas at Streawberige House. It was your aunty Miranda's sixteenth birthday, as I recall, so your father must have been about eighteen? They held a ball. I was just a girl but I can still remember all the comings and goings. My friends and I used to loiter outside the gates and watch all the grand carriages arriving.' Hannah's smile broadened. 'Later, some of us bolder kids snuck in to the grounds and peered in the windows.' Her eyes sparkled at the memory. 'The house had been transformed into a magical wonderland,' she said, her voice echoing the awe she'd felt on that long-ago Christmas. 'All the beautiful ladies in their ball gowns, lights twinkling everywhere and the tree! Oh, my goodness, none of us had ever seen such a thing. It touched the ceiling of the main hall.'

'I don't suppose any of you were invited?' Daisy remarked drily, helping herself to another slice of bread.

Hannah chuckled. 'Certainly not. The groundsman's dog gave us away, the little rascal, and we were sent packing with a good telling off and the threat of being arrested for trespassing. Don't look so appalled, Harry,' she added, patting his arm. 'The next morning platters of leftover food were delivered to the church so we had a good feast after the morning service.'

'I imagine that was the cook's doing rather than my grandfather's,' Harry said ruefully. 'I never thought my grandfather a particularly charitable soul.' Hannah raised an eyebrow but said nothing. She wasn't about to disparage the boy's family to his face.

While Hannah and Daisy cleared the table and washed up, Leah and Harry went out into the garden. Dora was just coming out of the privy and Leah's heart went out to her. Her friend looked worn out.

'Have you had a nice day?' she asked, coming over. There were dark shadows under her eyes and her hair looked lank and greasy.

'It's been good,' Leah replied. 'How's your dad been today?'

Dora shrugged. 'He's full of remorse, as always.' Her eyes swam with tears. 'It's not his fault,' she said, her shoulders slumping despondently. 'He can't help it.'

Leah nodded, though her expression was more sceptical

than sympathetic. Like most of her neighbours, she had lost all respect for Stephen Webb.

The church bells began to ring. 'Why don't you come to Evensong with us?' she suggested. 'Your dad will be all right on his own for half an hour or so.'

For a moment Dora looked tempted by the prospect of a few minutes peace and quiet but she shook her head. 'I promised I'd read to him. It calms his nerves.' She managed a smile. 'I'll see you in the morning. Bye, Harry. Nice to see you.'

'I feel so sorry for her,' Leah said, as Dora disappeared indoors.

'So do I,' Harry said. 'I wish there was something we could do.'

CHAPTER ELEVEN

Alice glanced at the clock. It was a quarter to three. The room was silent but for the rhythmic ticking and the scratch of pen on paper. The twins, Clementine and Eloise, were bent diligently over their desks. Dappled sunshine danced across the wooden floor boards as the boughs of the sturdy oak creaked and sighed in the breeze.

It had been a long week, the monotony of the school room broken only by the occasional walk round the grounds, and Alice was looking forward to the morning when she would return to Strawbridge. She swallowed, aware that the colour was rising in her cheeks, as it did each time she happened to think of Samuel, which was often.

The strength of her feelings for the young curate had surprised her. She'd always considered herself to be a calm, rational sort of person, not one given to wild emotions or passionate desires, yet since knowing Samuel, her stomach had been in a perpetual state of turmoil. She found she couldn't concentrate on anything before she realized that she was thinking about him again. Several times during the past week one or other of the girls had had to repeatedly call Alice's name quite forcefully before she had become aware of them, and it troubled her deeply. She was not one for such unprofessionalism.

Again, her gaze strayed to the ticking clock. Barely five minutes had passed. The knock at the door startled her.

'Come in.'

Expecting Mrs Maskell, the housekeeper, she was surprised by the unexpected entrance of her pupils' mother.

'Mama!' the girls chorused in unison, sliding out from behind their desks to fling themselves at their mother.

'Hello, darlings!' Monica Hampton-Sinclair cried in her shrill voice, embracing her daughters warmly.

'Mrs Hampton-Sinclair,' Alice said, flustered by the sudden appearance of her employer. She rose to her feet. 'I'm sorry. I understood you would be in London for another fortnight?'

Standing with her arms around her daughters, Monica smiled across at Alice. She was an attractive woman in her mid-thirties, with dark, wavey hair and green eyes.

'We have only just arrived,' Monica said, a little breathlessly, glancing at the clock. 'You may dismiss the girls, Alice. I'd like to speak to you. Girls, your father is waiting for you in the drawing room.'

'Papa,' called Clementine and Eloise, scampering off like exuberant puppies and almost falling over each other as they fought to be the first through the doorway.

Alice swallowed anxiously, alarmed suddenly that tales of her distractions had somehow reached Mrs Hampton-Sinclair's ears.

'Girls, girls!' Monica went to the door to implore her daughters to behave in a seemlier manner. 'They are so excitable,' she said, as she came back into the room. Taking a moment to glance at Clementine's workbook, she carefully moved it aside and perched on the edge of the desk. Alice remained standing, her heart thumping against her ribcage.

'I'm afraid I have some news, Alice,' Monica said. She crossed her dainty ankles, momentarily distracted by the caw of a magpie in the tree outside.

'Mr Hampton-Sinclair has been offered a position abroad. Kenya. He will be leaving to take up his new post at the end of next month. I shall accompany him of course. The girls, however, will remain in England. My husband and I will be looking at suitable schools over the coming weeks and I believe it will be at least a year before I will see Clementine and Eloise again.' Here Monica's voice trembled and she paused in order to collect herself. Taking a shaky breath, she continued, 'I want to spend as much time with them as I can before we leave. Therefore, we have decided to return to London with them tomorrow, so your services will no longer be required. You will, of course, be paid up until the end of the month and, it goes without saying, that I shall furnish you with an excellent reference.'

'Thank you, Mrs Hampton-Sinclair,' Alice said, feeling

slightly dazed. Just like that, she was unemployed? The days teaching the twins had been mind-numbingly dull but at least it was a job, an income. She was just grateful her family didn't rely on her wages, like Leah and Dora's did.

'I wish you and your husband all the best,' Alice said, as Monica accompanied her down the sweeping staircase. 'And don't worry about the girls. I'm sure they'll soon settle at their new school.'

Monica patted Alice's arm. 'Thank you, dear. I'm sure they will,' she agreed, sounding doubtful.

'I shall have your reference ready for you before we leave tomorrow,' Monica promised as she saw her out the side door. 'I shall get one of the maids to deliver it. Now,' she smiled, pausing outside the drawing room, 'you'll want to say goodbye to the girls before you go.'

As she walked down the winding driveway a short time later, Alice wondered whether the rest of the staff would be losing their jobs, too and her heart went out to them. She knew Molly, the little kitchen maid, was supporting her widowed mother and four younger siblings on her wages. She hoped she'd be able to find another job quickly.

It was a balmy mid-summer afternoon. Birds warbled in the hedgerows and the azure sky was streaked with feathery white clouds. As she walked down the main street through the village, she saw her sister, Martha, emerging from the butcher's shop.

'Martha, wait,' she called, hurrying to catch up with her beneath the red and white striped awning.

'You're home early,' Martha said, batting at the flies that swarmed the glassy-eyed rabbits hanging in the window.

'I've been let go,' Alice said, taking the wicker basket from her sister's arm.

'What?' Martha's mouth fell open in surprise. 'You got the sack?'

'Not exactly,' Alice laughed. As they followed the road passed the village school, she explained what had happened.

'Poor girls,' commiserated Martha. 'I wouldn't like to be sent away to school. It must be pretty grim.'

'I'm sure they'll choose carefully,' replied Alice, more for her own assurance than Martha's. She didn't like to think of Clementine and Eloise homesick and miserable. A year was a very long time to be away from one's family.

'Speaking of schools,' she said, turning to Martha. 'How did you get on in your test?'

'I got full marks,' Martha replied modestly.

'Well done,' grinned Alice. 'I expected nothing less.'

'Father is hoping I'll win a scholarship to go to high school,' she told Alice solemnly.

'You're certainly bright enough. And, if you want to be a doctor, you'll need a higher grade school education to get in to medical school.'

'Cousin Benjamin said men don't like clever women and no one will want to marry me if I become a doctor,' she said with a snort.

'Benji's just teasing you,' Alice told her. 'I'm sure there are lots of men who like clever women,' she said, remembering the witty conversations she had with Samuel.

'Well, I don't intend to marry anyway.'

'You'll change your mind when you're older,' smiled Alice. As they neared the house, she heard the sound of children playing. Jimmy, Caroline and little Jonathan were chasing round the front garden.

'Hello, Alice, hello, Martha,' they called out. 'Come and play with us.'

'In a minute,' Martha called back. 'I've got to start on the supper. Where's mother?'

'In her workroom,' Caroline replied, swinging 4-year-old Jonathan round by his arms. 'She has a fitting.'

Alice followed Martha into the cool hallway. The grandfather clock ticked loudly, its pendulum swinging rhythmically. Alice smiled, remembering how, as a child, she had loved sitting on the black and white tiled floor watching the pendulum and waiting for the hour to strike, the clock's deep, melodious chimes seeming to rumble all the way through her body.

'Alice, what a pleasant surprise,' her stepfather said, emerged from the drawing room.

'I'm afraid I've been let go,' she replied, slightly apprehensively. James frowned.

'Oh? What happened?'

'They're emigrating to Africa. Mr Hampton-Sinclair has been posted to Kenya. The girls are being sent to boarding school.'

James stroked his beard. 'Oh, dear. That's unfortunate. I can ask around, see if there are any other local families in need of a governess?'

'Thank you, Father.' Alice followed him into the kitchen where Martha was preparing the pork chops for the oven.

'I believe those apples are to be made into a sauce,' he said, motioning the bag of green fruit on the table.

'I'll do that,' Alice offered. 'You go and play with the others,' she told Martha.

'Oh, really? Thank you. I promised Johnny and Jimmy I'd help them build a fort.' Whipping off her apron, Martha dashed out of the back door, yelling for her siblings.

'She may be almost twelve but she's still a child at heart,' James smiled, looking out the window.

'She did very well in her test, she tells me,' Alice said, taking the paring knife from the cutlery drawer.

'She's a very clever girl,' her stepfather replied, helping himself to a glass of water. 'She deserves to follow her dreams.' He sipped his water, his gaze on Alice. 'Are you seeing that curate of yours this weekend?' he asked.

'I'm hoping so,' Alice blushed. 'We're meant to be going for a walk on Sunday afternoon.'

'He appears to be a decent chap, and Mathew seems to like him. Perhaps you should invite him over for a meal one evening. Check with your mother first, of course.'

'Thank you. I'd like that,' Alice said, putting the pan of apples on the stove to simmer.

*

'To be honest, I'm not sure I want to take another position as governess,' Alice said, later that evening as the family gathered around the dining table.

'Oh? Had you something else in mind?' her mother asked as their eyes met across the table.

'As I've said before,' her stepfather interrupted. 'I'm quite prepared to pay for you to attend a secretarial course. More and more businesses these days are employing female secretaries.'

'What I'd really like to do, Father, is work full time in the strawberry fields. Just until the end of the summer,' she added quickly, catching his look of dismay. 'I can look at starting a secretarial course in the autumn.'

'I can't understand why you want to spend your days picking fruit, Alice,' James frowned, wiping his lips on his napkin. 'You're a bright young woman. You'd be wasted in the strawberry fields.' He turned to his wife. 'What do you think, Lily?'

'I have no objections,' Lily replied. 'As long as you're not taking the work from someone who really needs it, Alice.'

'I wouldn't be,' Alice told her seriously. 'Most of the pickers who come down from London go on to the bigger farms over the other side of Botley where the pay is better. Grandfather was saying just the other week how it's been such a bumper crop this year, they're in desperate need of more pickers.' She looked at her stepfather hopefully.

'Johnny, don't chew with your mouth open,' James said, giving his youngest son a disapproving glare. He shrugged in resignation. 'If it's just for the summer, I suppose it will be all right.'

'Thank you, Father,' Alice beamed, relishing the thought of spending her days out in the fresh air instead of a stuffy school room. It would also mean that, with luck, she would get to see more of Samuel.

CHAPTER TWELVE

Dora sat back on her heels and wiped her brow with her sleeve. It was mid-August and swelteringly hot. Perspiration trickled down her spine and the rough material of her dress chafed under her armpits. She glanced over to where Alice and Leah were laughing together, and experienced a twinge of envy which she quickly quenched with a deep breath.

In the time the three girls had been working together six days a week, their friendship had deepened considerably. When life at home became almost too much to bear, there was no one Dora would want by her side other than Leah and Alice. They didn't mind if she wanted a good moan, or to cry on their shoulders. She knew without a doubt that they were there for her through thick and thin, as she was for them. Though for Alice and Leah, life appeared pretty good right now.

Alice's romance with the young curate seemed to be moving along very nicely. He had been invited round for afternoon tea on several occasions and had, by all accounts, made a good impression on both of Alice's parents. Her stepfather, in particular, had found something of a kindred spirit in Samuel and the two men had spent many pleasant hours discussing theology and the merits and failings of the education system.

Leah, too, appeared to be blissfully happy with her Harry, though she was understandably anxious as the passing weeks brought their inevitable separation ever closer.

'Dora, I was just telling Leah that there's a concert on Saturday evening,' Alice said, getting to her feet and dusting soil from her skirt. There had been no rain for days and the soil was bone-hard. The strawberry plants were wilting in the heat and the pickers' children had been tasked with running up and down the rows with buckets of water, a gruelling job beneath the unrelenting summer sun.

'Do you fancy it?'

Dora's brow furrowed and she pursed her lips. 'I'm not sure I can afford a concert ticket,' she said, a slight sarcastic edge to her voice.

'Oh, sorry, how silly of me,' Alice quickly apologized. 'It's free. Well, free to us, anyway. Father has been given some complimentary tickets. He and mother have a previous engagement so he suggested we might like to go.'

'What about Reverend Aldridge's prayer evening?' Dora asked. 'Don't you usually go to that on Saturday evenings?'

'I'm quite happy to miss it,' Alice grinned. 'I only go because Samuel is obliged to attend and it means I get to spend the evening with him.'

'I can't leave Father,' Dora said, inspecting her dirty finger nails.

'I'm sure Mum will look in on him,' Leah assured her. 'Please say you'll come. It will be such a treat for the three of us to have an evening out.'

'If you're sure Aunty Hannah won't mind?'

'Of course, she won't,' Leah said airily as Dora smiled. A concert would be a welcome distraction from her daily worries and cares. She couldn't remember the last time she'd been into Southampton.

'Then, yes,' she grinned. 'Thank you. I would love to go.'

'Great. The show starts at seven so I suggest we catch the four-forty train. That way we can have supper first.'

Dora nodded. She'd have to take the train fare out of the rent money but, with luck, she could work late every evening that week to make it back up.

By Saturday evening the hot weather broke. Dark storm clouds had been gathering all day, and thunder was rumbling in the distance by the time the girls boarded the train at Botley.

The concert was being held in the Congregational church hall in The Avenue in Southampton. The tall trees swayed in the stiff breeze and the first drops of rain began to fall as the girls alighted the tram and hurried across the wide street, holding tightly on to their hats.

They had arrived in plenty of time yet the hall was nearly full, voices rising and falling as chair legs scraped along the

wooden floor. At the front of the room a woman was playing a piano.

Managing to find three seats together in the middle of the
room, they sat down and Leah removed her gloves. They
smelled slightly of vinegar, a lingering reminder of the fish
supper they'd shared at a tiny café in Above Bar.

'It's very well attended,' Alice remarked behind her hand,
as the mayor of Southampton and his wife made their way
down the aisle to the row of seats reserved for them at
the front.

'It is for the *Titanic* widows and orphan's fund,' Leah
reminded her. 'The local dignitaries will want to be seen to
support it.' Suddenly she blanched. 'Oh, no!'

'What?' Alice asked as she and Dora craned their necks to
follow Leah's gaze.

'It's the Whitworths,' Leah hissed, shrinking down in her
seat and hoping they wouldn't notice her. Though Harry
had tried to downplay his mother's reaction to the news
that her son was courting one of his father's tenants, she
was astute enough to realize that, in Frances Whitworth's
eyes, she would never be an acceptable choice for her son.
She watched Isaac guide his wife down the aisle, his hand
resting lightly on her back. Their seats were in the row
second from the front. *So, the Whitworths weren't grand enough
to warrant one of the reserved seats then*, she mused with grim
satisfaction. She was grateful that Harry seemed nothing
like his parents, though she couldn't help the niggle of
anxiety when she thought that come mid-September he'd

likely be returning to London and a life of which Leah could never be a part of.

'I thought Mrs Whitworth had gone back to London?' whispered Alice, shuffling in her seat to get a better look at Frances, who was gazing about her with a look of abject disdain.

'She had,' Leah replied, wondering why Harry hadn't mentioned his mother's return. 'She must have come down specifically for this concert.'

'She doesn't look impressed,' Dora noted. While Frances had initially been viewed with sympathy after the loss of her babies, her continued lack of connection with her husband's tenants and blatant disinterest in their lives had led to an apathy in the hamlet. Unlike the wives of many wealthy landowners, she never sent gifts of food when there was a new baby, or a death in a family. She was respected as Isaac's wife, not because of anything she had done in her own right.

'Not posh enough for her, I shouldn't wonder,' Leah said, wrinkling her nose. 'I expect she's more used to the theatres of the West End.'

It was raining hard now, she could hear it drumming on the roof, and the smell of wet cloth filled the hall as more and more people arrived, rain water forming puddles on the scuffed floorboards.

The rest of the dignitaries arrived, members of the *Titanic* Enquiry Commission and the fundraising committee. A hush fell over the room and the concert began.

The music was a mixture of joyful, lively tunes that had

the audience tapping their feet and clapping along, and melancholy melodies which had the ladies weeping into their handkerchiefs. Tears streamed unchecked down Leah's cheeks as her thoughts turned to her father and Freddie, and her little sisters. Though they hadn't perished on the *Titanic*, the emotional impact of the music meant she felt their loss just as keenly. Sitting beside her, Dora squeezed her hand and gave her a wan smile.

All three girls were feeling emotionally drained by the time the curtain came down.

They were jostled along by the crowd surging for the doors, and out into the fresh air. The rain had eased but for a fine drizzle that danced in the glow of the streetlamps. A sudden squall blew a flurry of fallen leaves along the gutter and tugged at their skirts, almost whipping their hats from their heads.

'I really must buy some hat pins,' Alice grumbled, snatching hold of her hat just as it was about to take off. Another young lady wasn't so lucky, and her loud wail rended the air as her hat was swept along the gutter, pursued by her gentleman escort.

'See that lady over there,' Leah pointed to a solemn-looking young woman standing on the periphery of the milling crowd. 'She worked as a stewardess on the *Titanic*. I recognize her from her photograph in the newspaper.'

'Poor thing,' Dora murmured sympathetically. 'I can't imagine how terrifying it must have been for those poor people.'

'It doesn't bear thinking about,' agreed Alice with a shudder.

'You can't live round here and not be affected,' Leah said, her gaze straying to the *Titanic* Disaster Fund posters pasted on to the walls of the hall. 'Almost all of us knows a family who lost loved ones.'

'Excuse us, ladies,' said a familiar voice and Leah paled as she found herself face to face with Isaac and Frances Whitworth. She saw the flicker of recognition in his expression. 'Miss Hopwood, good evening,' he said, touching the brim of his hat. 'Miss Russell, Miss Webb, I trust you enjoyed the concert?' he asked as Frances stood mutely by his side, regarding Leah with a stony expression.

'Yes, sir,' the girls replied.

'Excellent, excellent.' Isaac gave a little bow. 'Have a safe journey home.' Taking Frances' arm, he guided her towards one of the cars parked alongside the kerb. As he reached down to open the passenger seat door, she glanced back over her shoulder.

'That's her, isn't it?' Leah heard her say in a loud stage whisper. 'The Hopwood girl?'

Isaac's reply was lost in the rumble of an approaching tram. Leah followed her friends aboard and handed the inspector her ticket. By the time she was seated, the Whitworths' car had gone. She settled back in her seat, and tried to concentrate on Alice and Dora's conversation but she couldn't shake the image of Frances Whitworth from her mind. She would never forget the expression on the woman's face, and it sent a cold shiver down her spine. It was a look of complete repugnance.

'Henry, I'd like a word, please. In my study.'

Holding back a sigh of irritation, Harry paused at the foot of the stairs. He had hoped to slip out of the house unnoticed by his parents.

'I was just on my way,' he said, buttoning up his jacket.

'I shan't keep you long,' Isaac promised drily, holding open the door to his well-appointed study.

'Is everything all right between you and Mother?' Harry asked, with a frown as he took one of the two wing-backed chairs on either side of the empty fireplace. He had sensed the strained atmosphere over dinner but had assumed his parents had had a tiff. Perhaps his father wanted to tell him his mother was heading back to the city and wished him, Harry, to accompany her. Well, he would refuse, again.

'Relations between your mother and I are fine, Henry,' Isaac chuckled. 'I'm afraid it's your relationship with the Hopwood girl your mother and, to some extent myself, are concerned about.'

'Her name is Leah,' Harry said through gritted teeth, 'not the Hopwood girl.'

Isaac nodded in acknowledgment as he took the chair on the opposite side of the marble fire place. He leaned forward, his elbows resting on his knees and smiled at his son.

'I understand your attraction to this girl, Henry, believe

me,' he said, giving his son a conspiratorial wink. 'She's a pretty girl. If I were thirty years younger . . .'

'God, you're disgusting!' Henry blurted angrily, jumping to his feet. 'If you've called me in here to tell me to stay away from her, then you're wasting your breath, Father.'

'All right, all right.' Isaac held up his hands in a placatory manner. 'That was boorish of me and I apologize.' He indicated the empty chair. 'Please?'

After a moment's hesitation, Harry did as he asked. He fixed his mutinous gaze on the painting hanging above the fireplace, a vivid depiction of the Battle of Waterloo.

Isaac sat back in his chair, his fingers pressed together under his chin, and regarded his son thoughtfully.

'I know you probably fancy yourself to be in love with this girl,' he said slowly, 'But I can assure you it's nothing but infatuation.' He chuckled. 'When I was your age, I dallied with several young ladies of the parish, but it was always with the understanding that I would marry a young lady of similar social standing to myself.' He flexed his fingers. 'Your mother is determined to take you back to London on the next train.'

'I prefer to stay here, Father,' retorted Harry coolly. 'I am not a child.'

'You are not yet of age,' Isaac reminded him mildly. 'And under my roof you are subject to my rules.'

'Then I shall leave,' Harry declared, getting abruptly to his feet. 'I shall find accommodation locally and you may pay me the going wage to work in your fields.'

'Don't be ridiculous!' his father exploded with a mirth-less laugh. 'Your mother would crucify me.' He ran hand through his hair. 'Sit down, for goodness's sake.'

'I prefer to stand, thank you.'

Isaac sighed, getting to his feet. 'I don't want to quarrel with you, Henry.' Standing with his back to the fireplace, he gazed out of the bay window. The squally weather from the day before had cleared, leaving blue skies and a gentle breeze in its wake. He watched a red squirrel scampering across the lawn and disappear up a sycamore tree.

'All I'm saying is,' he continued, drawing his gaze away from the view and back to his son. 'Don't go making rash promises you'll regret.' Harry opened his mouth to speak but Isaac raised his hand. 'Let me finish,' he said sternly. 'The season ends in four weeks' time and you will be returning to Richmond. I will brook no argument on that score. Enjoy your time with this girl, if you must. You're young, you deserve a bit of fun. Lord knows your mother has mollycod-dled you long enough. So, like I said, have your fun, then, go home and find yourself a more suitable girl.'

'More suitable?' Harry's expression hardened. 'You're such a snob, Father. Even if I do return to London with you, my feelings for Leah will remain unchanged. I love her, Father, and one day, I would like to marry her, if she'll have me.'

'Marry her?' Isaac snorted with laughter. 'Are you insane, boy? I hope you haven't mentioned marriage to the Hopwood girl.' Harry's mouth tightened and Isaac sighed. 'You cannot marry without my permission until you are twenty-one. By

130

then you will feel completely different. It's unfair, cruel even, to give Miss Hopwood false hope.'

'I shall not change my mind,' Harry insisted, clenching his fists in frustration. 'I love her.'

'Come on, Henry.' Sighing deeply, Isaac walked over to his son and laid his hand on his shoulder. 'I don't always agree with your mother, but in this instance she may have a point. Perhaps it's better for you to return home. Once you're back in London, you'll soon forget about this girl.'

'The way I feel about Leah isn't some passing fancy, Father,' Harry retorted. 'You can tell Mother I shall not be returning with her and I'll thank you both to keep out of my affairs,' he added, striding purposefully from the room.

CHAPTER THIRTEEN

Hannah was washing the kitchen floor when the knock came. She put her scrubbing brush down beside the bucket of scummy water and rose stiffly to her feet, wincing at the painful twinge in her right knee. Drying her hands on her pinny, she hurried into the parlour where dusty sunlight streamed in through the window and opened the door.

'Mr Whitworth,' she said, not wholly surprised to find her landlord standing on her doorstep. 'Good morning.'

'Good morning, Mrs Hopwood,' Isaac said politely, removing his hat. 'May I come in?'

'I had a feeling you'd be calling round sooner or later,' Hannah said, standing aside to let him pass.

Leah had returned from her walk on Sunday in tears. Apparently, there had been some sort of altercation between Harry and his parents over his relationship with Leah in which Harry had refused point blank to return home with his mother as she'd insisted. Hannah had been sweeping her doorstep yesterday when Frances had gone by in the carriage on her way to the station. As she'd driven by, she'd turned her head slightly and Hannah had felt a stab of sympathy for the woman. She had looked so alone, bereft even, but then she'd caught sight of Hannah and her expression had hardened. In that brief exchange, Hannah's sympathy melted beneath the heat of Frances' venomous glare.

'Have a seat,' Hannah said now to Isaac, indicating the couch under the window. 'I'll put the kettle on.'

'There's no need to stand on ceremony,' Isaac said, following her through to the kitchen. 'I'm happy to sit in the kitchen.' He stepped over the bucket, careful not to walk on the wet slate, and pulled out a chair.

'Suit yourself.' Hannah filled the kettle and set it on the range. 'I take it you're here to talk about our children?' Hands on hips, she regarded him with a wry smile.

'Look, Hannah,' Isaac said, looking slightly uncomfortable. 'I've got nothing against your girl ...'

'But you don't think she's suitable for your Harry?' Hannah smiled. 'They've known each other barely four months. Isn't it a bit premature to be worrying?'

'As far as I'm concerned, yes,' Isaac agreed, as Hannah poured boiling water into the teapot. 'After all, we'll be heading back to London in just under a month. With such a distance between them it's likely they'll forget all about each other by next spring.' He sighed. 'It's Frances who's fretting. Before she left she asked me to have a word.'

Hannah sat across the table from him, her workworn

hands curled around her mug. She blew on the surface of her milky tea and smiled.

'There was a time when you were hellbent on marrying a local girl yourself,' she reminded him drily.

'Ah, yes,' Isaac nodded. 'How is your cousin? I heard she married a tanner over Northam way.'

'Jessie is very well, thank you for asking,' Hannah relied. 'She and Malcolm will have been married, what, twenty-nine, thirty years? Last I heard she was expecting her fifth grandchild.'

'I'm glad she's lived a good life,' Isaac said, taking a sip of his tea. Hannah regarded him closely. *Was that regret in his eyes?* she wondered.

'She deserved it. You broke her heart when you called off the engagement.'

Isaac had the grace to look shamefaced. 'I treated her abysmally,' he admitted. 'I should never have allowed our relationship to progress as far as it did. Which is why I want to save your Leah from suffering the same heartache.'

Hannah regarded him thoughtfully over the rim of her mug. 'If your father hadn't threatened to cut you off, would you have married Jessie?'

'My father simply reminded me of my duty.'

'He threatened to cut you off.'

Isaac shrugged. 'Be that as it may, I had a duty to my family and Henry will understand that he, too, must put duty before his own desires.'

'Perhaps the son is made of sterner stuff than the father,' said Hannah tartly.

Isaac smiled. 'I doubt it.' He drained his mug. 'Well, I've said my piece so I must be on my way. Thank you for the tea. It's been good catching up,' he said. He stood up and gazed round the kitchen. 'I sometimes miss all this,' he said, with a wistful smile. 'William's older brothers, they were good friends of mine. It's a shame we lost touch when they left Strawbridge. Are they well?'

'As far as I know,' Hannah said, walking him to the door. 'I haven't seen them since the funerals.' Isaac nodded.

'If you'll have a word with your girl,' he said, pausing in the doorway.

'Leah's never been one to take much notice of what I say,' she replied wryly. 'She will do what she wants. However, as you say, Harry will be going home soon and only time will tell if they're feelings are strong enough to survive the separation.'

'As soon as he's back home, among his own people, he'll forget all about these silly fancies.' Isaac snorted. He touched the brim of his hat. 'Good day, Hannah,' he said, his amiable manner dissipating like dew under a hot sun. 'I assure you Henry shall come to his senses.'

Leah arched her back, easing the tension from the base of her spine and, happening to glance towards the cottages, was startled to see Isaac Whitworth leaving her own. Shielding her eyes against the sun, she followed him as he strode up the lane in the direction of Streawberige House. From the way he held himself, he didn't look happy.

'Did I see Mr Whitworth coming out of your cottage?' Dora asked, with a frown. 'I wonder what he wanted.'

'I have a very good idea,' Leah muttered bitterly. Some of the other women had noticed Isaac leaving her cottage too. *That would feed the gossips*, she thought bitterly. She'd already been warned by a few of the older women that she was building herself up for a fall.

Picking up her basket, she walked over to the crates. Glancing across the row, she noticed Harry, too, was watching his father's progress up the lane. His lips were pursed, and his brow furrowed. Leah caught his eye and he smiled, nodding at her encouragingly. *The gossips be blowed*, thought Leah, smiling back. They didn't know Harry like she did. She let out an impatient sigh. She couldn't wait until the midday whistle so she could ask her mother what Isaac had wanted, though as she'd told Dora, she had no doubt it was to warn her away from his precious son.

The rest of the morning dragged. As soon as the whistle blew, Leah left her basket and, without waiting for Alice and Dora, ran across the lane to the cottage.

'Mum, Mum!' she called, running into the house. 'I saw Mr Whitworth leaving. What did he say?'

'Calm down, love,' Hannah said, her soothing manner taking the edge off Leah's anxiety. 'I expect you know what he came to say?'

'He wants me to stay away from Harry,' Leah replied miserably.

'Of course, we knew the Whitworths weren't going to

be thrilled with the idea of Harry walking out with you,' her mother said, handing Leah a mug of tea. 'But I told Mr Whitworth in no uncertain terms that I won't interfere. All I will say, love—' She broke off as Daisy came in, her face flushed with the heat.

'Is everything all right?' the young girl asked, picking up on the atmosphere.

'Everything's fine, Daisy,' Hannah said. 'Go and wash up. Dinner's on the table.' Turning back to Leah, she continued,

'As I was saying, Harry will be returning to London soon, so just bear that in mind.'

Leah nodded, her mother's words only serving to increase her feeling of wretchedness.

CHAPTER FOURTEEN

Leah tried all afternoon to catch a few minutes alone with Harry and her chance came later that evening, when she saw him heading to the water trough. She hurried over to join him.

His expression was grim. He filled the ladle and handed it to her. 'I expect your mother told you the purpose of my father's visit?'

Leah drank deeply, and nodded. She filled the ladle again and handed it to Harry.

'I shan't let him put me off, Leah,' Harry said softly, his gaze locking on hers. She nodded, not entirely convinced. She wanted to trust him, but she was sure Isaac Whitworth could be quite convincing, and once Harry was back in London under his parents' influence, she couldn't help but wonder if his resolve would be strong enough to withstand their objections.

'I shall miss you when you return to London,' she blurted out.

Harry splashed water over his face and smiled ruefully. 'I'm dreading it,' he said softly. 'But I shall write every day, I promise.' He tilted her chin so she was looking up at him. 'Cheer up. Spring will be here soon enough and we'll be together again.'

'You might forget all about me,' Leah said, earnestly.

'Forget about you?' repeated Harry, incredulous. 'As if I could.'

Someone coughed nearby and Leah looked up to see Mathew Turner watching them.

'I'd better get back to work,' she said, reluctantly.

'Wait.' Harry grabbed her wrist. 'Meet me by the pond later? About nine?'

'I will,' Leah promised, hurrying back to her row.

Harry was waiting for her in the moon-dappled clearing when she arrived just before nine o'clock. He spread his jacket on the dew-damp grass, and Leah leaned against him as they watched the rising moon cast its silvery path across the surface of the pond.

'It's so beautiful,' Leah whispered, the reflected moonlight shimmering as a gentle breeze ruffled the water.

Harry rolled onto his side, studying her face in the light of the moon. 'I wish I could stay like this forever,' he said, running his thumb softly across her cheek.

'I feel the same,' Leah sighed, entwining her fingers in his. In spite of her smile, she felt hollow inside. Their time together was growing short and despite Harry's protestations to the contrary, she was worried that once he returned to London's high society, mingling with girls he'd grown up with, he would forget all about her.

A creature squeaked in the twilight and a twig snapped nearby, making them both jerk upright as a figure emerged from the shadowy undergrowth.

'Joshua!' Leah exclaimed as the figure emerged into the moonlight. 'You startled us.'

'Sorry,' Joshua muttered, scowling at the sight of Leah and Harry together on the grassy bank. From his hands dangled two freshly killed rabbits.

'I could have you arrested for poaching,' Harry said mildly, leaning back on his elbow.

'But you won't,' retorted Joshua, disparagingly. 'And anyway, I just spotted your gamekeeper helping himself to a brace of pheasants on the far side of the brook.'

Harry shrugged. 'I believe Mr Ryall has asked you to beat at Father's shoot in November?'

'That he has,' Joshua said, coming closer. His teeth gleamed white in the moonlight. 'Will you be down for it?' he asked nonchalantly, thinking that once Harry was out of the way, he might stand another chance with Leah.

Leah looked at Harry, her gaze hopeful. 'You never mentioned you might be back in November,' she said but her excitement was quickly dashed when Harry shook his head.

'I'm not included in the invitation. Select friends and acquaintances only. No doubt Mother has one of her boring soirees or card parties lined up for me to attend instead.'

And being paraded before all the eligible young ladies, added Leah silently, scowling at the thought. She sat up straight, watching the moon dancing on the pond, conscious of Joshua's gaze resting on her. Harry coughed and, to his relief, Joshua appeared to catch the hint.

'Enjoy the rest of your evening,' he said sullenly, disappearing back into the undergrowth. They could hear him crashing through the bushes, whistling loudly.

'He's got a lot of nerve, I must say,' Harry remarked.

'He's not a bad person,' Leah said. 'It's only him and Pearl. You can't blame him for supplementing his wages with a bit of meat for the pot. He's not the only one.'

'It's no better than stealing, though, is it?' Harry objected.

'Have you ever been hungry, Harry?' Leah asked, narrowing her eyes. 'Really hungry?'

'Well, no, of course not.'

'I didn't think so. Once the strawberry picking season ends, if we can't find jobs for the winter, we don't eat. It's people like Joshua who keep a lot of families in Strawbridge from starvation. I do think Cuthbert Ryall's got a bit of a cheek, though. He gets paid a fair wage all year round and he's got no extra mouths to feed. Greedy bugger.'

'Have you got work lined up over the winter?' Harry asked, wishing he could take Leah back to London with him and thinking how much she'd love the bright lights of the Christmas season. He imagined taking her up West to see a show, or shopping in the big department stores with their gaily decorated windows, and ice skating in Richmond Park.

'I'll go back to the drysalters again if they'll take me.' She pulled a face. 'It's horrible. I hate it there. The dye stains my hands and the chemicals make me cough. It's a lot longer day, as well, as it's an hour's walk each way.'

Harry traced his finger along her jaw. 'I wish you didn't have to do it,' he said softly. 'I have an allowance. Let me help you.'

Leah drew away, her expression stern. 'No, Harry. Can you not see how that would look to people? They'd think you were paying me for favours.'

'Who cares what people think?' protested Harry.

'I do. I care.' Leah arched her back, thrusting her chin out in defiance. She was nothing if not proud.

'I'm sorry. I didn't mean to offend you. It's just, well, I know we haven't known each other very long but I'm very fond of you, Leah. In fact, I'm falling in love with you. I wish I was in a position to take care of you.' He looked so woebegone that Leah couldn't help but laugh.

'Just knowing you feel that way about me is enough for now,' Leah said, tilting her face towards his. Harry smiled. Gently cupping her chin in his hands, he brought his lips to hers. Leah closed her eyes and let herself be lost in the wonder of their first kiss.

CHAPTER FIFTEEN

'What if Pearl reads something awful in my tea leaves?' Dora muttered nervously, brushing soil from a large plump strawberry before putting it in her basket. It was early September and the strawberry yield was beginning to wane. Many of the seasonal workers had already left to find other work. A cool breeze swept across the fields and the trees were turning from green to red and gold.

'I'm sure she won't,' Leah replied airily. 'Oh, come on, Dor. It'll be fun.'

'Samuel wouldn't like it,' Alice said, brushing a loose strand of hair from her eyes. 'You know how he feels about such things.'

'Oh, Alice,' Leah chided her with a grin. 'You're not married to him yet.'

'Leah!' Alice gave her a friendly slap on the arm. 'Are you saying I'm too subservient?' she laughed.

'I'm saying you're besotted with our young curate,' Leah grinned. 'And it's obvious he feels the same. I shouldn't be surprised if you're engaged before the year is out.'

'I think you'll make a good vicar's wife,' Dora teased. 'He's already got you teaching Sunday School as it is.'

'Only while Miss Cridge is recovering from her broken ankle,' Alice pointed out but she was smiling. She and Samuel had been courting officially since the Pickers' Ball in June, but she felt as though she had known him for years. They had so much in common that they never ran out of conversation and it was clear from the frequently issued supper invitations that both her parents were very fond of him.

'Well, Pearl will be able to tell you if you're cut out to be a vicar's wife or not,' insisted Leah. 'Please? Harry leaves in ten days' time. I need to know if he's going to stay true to me.'

'Surely everything Pearl says should be taken with a pinch of salt anyway,' said Alice with a sceptical smile.

'No,' Dora interjected earnestly. 'She told Martha Timmins she'd be married within the year and she was.'

'Coincidence,' laughed Alice.

'Oh, ye of little faith,' Leah said. 'Come with me and you'll see. I bet Pearl tells you you'll be married within the year too.'

'Within the year?' Alice smiled. 'I doubt it.'

'People don't bother with long engagements around here,' Dora reminded her, as the whistle blew. The nights were drawing in and they seldom worked beyond four or five o'clock these days.

'Katie Miller met and married her husband within three months,' she continued as they carried their baskets to the crates. 'They're blissfully happy and expecting their third child.'

'Please say you'll come, both of you,' Leah begged. 'I don't want to go on my own.'

'Oh, all right. It'll be a bit of fun, I suppose,' Alice capitulated. 'What time? We'll need to be home before dark.'

'Shall we say seven o'clock?' suggested Leah. 'That way we'll have finished our chores and you'll have plenty of time to get back home before it's dark.'

'All right. Seven should be fine,' Alice said, emptying her basket into the crate. 'Dora, will you be able to get someone to sit with your dad?'

'Will your mum look in on him, do you think?' Dora asked, turning to Leah.

'Of course she will,' Leah assured her. 'We won't be long, anyway. Oh, there's Harry. I'll see you both later.' She hurried off to where Harry was helping to load the last of the day's crates on to the cart waiting to take them to the station.

'I hope Pearl tells her what she wants to hear,' Dora said as she and Alice made their way across the field to the lane.

'Oh, she will,' Alice said with a knowing smile. 'That's how she earns her money.'

'Are you going out again?' Stephen glowered at Dora over the rim of his teacup. 'You're always going out and leaving me on my own. You clearly don't care that I'm stuck here all day by myself. Do you know how boring it is, lying here all day with no one to talk to?' he whined, sounding like a petulant child.

Dora took a deep breath, forcing down the feelings of guilt.

'I'm sorry, Dad but I shan't be long,' she promised, leaning over to kiss his bristled cheek. 'Aunty Hannah's going to look in on you, but I've left the broom handle within reach. If you need anything just bang on the wall. and she'll be straight round.'

Stephen didn't reply. Dora sighed. Ignoring his mutinous glare, she glanced around the cramped room. She'd fed him his supper and helped him use the chamber pot, which she'd already washed out and replaced under the bed. She lit the lamp and placed a book and the newspaper next to his bed, knowing he'd bother with neither. *He'd rather lie there ruminating on how hard done by he was*, she mused, with a rare flash of irritation. She'd done her best by him and, as Leah and Alice were always saying, she was entitled to something of a life for herself. Another half an hour or so on his own wouldn't hurt.

Grabbing her shawl from the hook behind her door, she draped it around her shoulders and lifted the latch, emerging from her cottage to find Leah and Alice waiting for her in the lane. They caught each other's eyes and giggled nervously.

It was still light as they linked arms and walked down the lane. The bank of clouds in the western sky were tinged crimson and orange but there was a noticeable chill in the air.

'Autumn's definitely on its way,' Alice said, as they negotiated the rough track towards the pond. The brook tinkled musically over pebbles and rocks, and a cool breeze sighed through the trees as they left the well-worn pathway to follow a narrow footpath, half-hidden by brambles and nettles that wound through the undergrowth.

Pearl's caravan was situated at the far end of the Whitworths' orchard and soon Alice spotted the tell-tale curl of smoke drifting up through the trees. The thick foliage gave way to smooth, manicured lawns.

'Impressive,' said Alice, shielding her eyes from the sun as she gazed across the sloping lawns towards the red-brick façade of Streawberige House. French windows opened onto a sun-drenched terrace, complete with table and chairs. It was deserted, as were the gardens with their pretty shrubs and flowerbeds, rockeries and water-spouting stone cherubs.

Alice turned to Leah in awe. 'Harry stands to inherit all this?'

'Yes,' Leah swallowed. Lying in her bed at night, she occasionally allowed herself to fantasize that she might, one day, be mistress of all this, but then she'd scold herself for being ridiculous. Isaac Whitworth would disinherit Harry before he'd see the likes of Leah mistress of his ancestral home. If she and Harry were to have a future, as he promised, it would have to be somewhere other than Strawbridge.

'It's so peaceful,' Dora sighed just as the tranquillity was shattered by a gruff bark. They turned their gaze across the lawn to the orchard where Pearl's ancient caravan nestled amongst the apple and pear trees. Bear, Pearl's black-and-white dog, stood in the shadows, nose quivering as he kept a beady eye on the three girls. Pearl was stooped over a small campfire, stirring something in a black pot. Without glancing in the girls' direction, she straightened up and called out, 'Are you going to come on over or do you intend to skulk in the bushes all night? I don't bite.'

The girls exchanged nervous glances. 'He doesn't either.' Pearl muttered something to the dog who lay down, resting his nose on his paws but keeping his gaze trained on the visitors.

Giggling like anxious schoolgirls, with Leah leading the way, the three girls made their way across the lawn. The trees were laden with ripening fruit. Pearl motioned to a basket of apples on the grass at the foot of a nearby tree.

'Early windfalls,' she said. 'Help yourself.'

After a brief hesitation, they each took an apple. The wind sighed through the branches, sending a shiver up Dora's spine as she bit into the sweet fruit.

Pearl poked at the coals with a stick and motioned for the three girls to sit. There were four straight-back chairs grouped close to the fire, as if Pearl had been expecting them. On the grass beside one of the chairs was a basket of green cob nuts and one containing large fir cones. Pearl picked one up and threw it on the flames where it hissed and popped in the heat, filling the smoky air with its spicy scent.

'I expect you're wanting me to read your tea leaves?' she said, regarding the three girls with her sharp gaze. Leah nodded, and swallowed, as nerves dried her throat.

'Yes, please, Pearl,' croaked Dora.

'I'd better put the water on then.' Pearl grinned, showing

her few remaining teeth. The girls watched, mesmerized as she hung a soot-blackened kettle over the fire beside the pot, from which wafted the most delicious aroma, and sat down to wait for the water to boil.

The dog ambled over to his mistress and flopped at her feet. Pearl reached down to fondle his shaggy head.

'Is Joshua not here?' Leah broke the silence, relieved that there appeared to be no sign of him at the camp for, surely, if he'd been in the caravan, he would have come out to say hello.

'He's away to the railway station,' Pearl said, sitting back up and tugging her shawl tighter around the thin shoulders. She glanced up at the colourful sky. 'There won't be too many more evenings I can sit out like this,' she said by way of conversation. 'The damp seeps into my bones.' She rubbed her elbow as if to emphasize the point. Leah glanced nervously at the kettle. Steam rose from its spout, curling into the cool evening air. Her palms were sweaty and her heart was racing. She really hoped Pearl could give her something to cling on to. She was dreading the winter without Harry and was prepared to hold on to any shred of hope, however tenuous. Spring seemed so far away.

'Here we are,' Pearl said, getting stiffly to her feet as the water began to boil furiously. 'You, girl.' She pointed a bony finger at Leah. 'Fetch some cups and saucers and the tea caddy.' Shooting a nervous glance at Alice, who merely shrugged, Leah hurried over to the caravan and slowly climbed the wooden steps.

'Be quick about it,' Pearl called after her.

Leah pushed aside the floral curtain. Though she had been inside Pearl's caravan many times over the years, she never failed to be awed by the opulent interior. The wooden roof was inlaid with gold panels and the floor was a patchwork of different coloured tiles. The polished walnut surfaces gleamed like bronze. On top of a chest of drawers stood a cluster of framed photographs of a beautiful but sullen-looking woman, Joshua's mother, displayed proudly. Pearl's bed was at the far end of the caravan, about waist height, and half-hidden by gaily painted doors. There was a padded bench to one side where Joshua slept opposite the small, cast-iron stove. Taking three cups from the hooks on the dresser, Leah found the tin tea caddy and saucers on the shelf below, and hurried back outside, careful not to trip down the steps.

'The water's boiled,' Pearl remarked, relieving her of the crockery and the tea. Dora reached out and squeezed Leah's hand nervously. An owl hooted in a nearby pear tree, making them all jump. They looked at each other and giggled. It seemed a bit surreal, sitting around a campfire outside Pearl's caravan, listening to the birds warbling in the trees and the crackle and pop of the flames as the old woman spooned tea leaves into the three cups.

They held their breath while Pearl poured boiling water over the tea leaves and handed round the cups of steaming hot tea.

'Think about what you want to know,' she said, returning to her seat. She reached down to stroke the dog. He whined softly and nuzzled Pearl's gnarled fingers.

Will Harry and I marry? Leah whispered inaudibly, closing her eyes in concentration as if by just thinking it, she would make it happen.

I just want someone to love me, Dora sighed, grimacing as she took a sip of the strong, bitter liquid.

Is my future with Samuel? wondered Alice, fighting the urge to laugh. What on earth would Samuel say if he could see her now? At best he'd think her ridiculous, at worst he'd be annoyed as he was so vehemently against such things. Clairvoyants and mediums were evil, as far as he was concerned, and Alice knew he would have no truck with Pearl's predictions. Despite the fact that Pearl attended church faithfully every Sunday, and Reverend Aldridge viewed her fortune-telling as a bit of harmless fun, she knew Samuel regarded her with suspicion.

'When you've got only a mouthful of tea left,' Pearl said, breaking the long silence in which the only sounds had been birdsong, the sigh of the wind through the trees and the occasional thud of an apple hitting the ground. 'Take your cup in your left hand and swirl it three times, from left to right.'

Solemnly, the three girls did as they were told.

'Now, turn your cup upside down and place it on your saucer.' Not daring to look at each other, the girls complied.

The sky over Streawberige House was a fiery red streaked with gold. A flock of geese flew overhead, honking loudly, causing Bear to lift his head and growl softly.

'Right,' Pearl said, suddenly brisk and business-like. 'Turn them back up.' They did so, peering into the mess of damp leaves at the bottom. Dora looked up. Pearl nodded at her. 'I'll read yours first.' She took Dora's cup in her trembling hands, her brow crinkled in studious concentration. Dora held her breath. Pearl's thin lips widened into a smile.

'I see a tall, dark, handsome stranger,' she intoned. Alice spluttered and Dora giggled. Pearl glared at them.

'Sorry,' they mumbled, suitably chastened.

'I see troubles and sadness on your horizon,' Pearl continued seriously, causing Dora to shrink back in alarm.

'What sort of trouble?' she asked in a small voice.

Pearl shook her head. 'I can only reveal what the leaves tell me,' she intoned mysteriously. 'But I see a long and happy marriage in your future.'

'Oh,' Dora's expression brightened. 'Thank you.'

Pearl snorted. Handing Dora back her cup, she reached for Leah's.

She seemed to stare into Leah's cup for such a long time that she began to grow uncomfortable. 'What do you think she can see?' she mouthed to Dora, who shrugged. The three girls exchanged nervous glances. Pearl's features revealed nothing, and her sudden grunt of alarm startled them all.

'I'm sorry,' she said, almost throwing Leah's cup back at her as she struggled to her feet. Bear whined and tucked his tail between his legs as he flattened himself against Pearl's skirts. 'I can do no more readings tonight.'

'What did you see?' Leah cried, staring into the bottom of her cup in alarm. 'Please, you must tell me?'

'Nothing!' Pearl snapped, averting her troubled gaze. 'I saw nothing. Go home!' Pearl said loudly, waving them away with her hand as she hobbled towards the caravan steps. 'Go on, away with you.' She hauled herself up the steps, leaving the three girls staring after her in shock.

'Wait, we haven't paid,' Leah called after her.

'No charge,' Pearl called back as she ducked through the curtain.

'Well! What on earth was that about?' Alice gave a nervous laugh. Pearl's behaviour had unnerved them all.

'She saw something terrible in my tea leaves,' Leah said, anxiously. Her face was white in the encroaching darkness.

'Don't be silly,' Alice tried to reassure her, linking her arm through Leah's. 'I reckon she couldn't think of anything to say and she could hardly tell you that you were going to meet a tall, dark, handsome stranger when everyone knows you're walking out with Harry who's as fair as they come.'

Leah managed a wan smile. 'You were right, Dora,' she said, as they made their way across the lawn back towards the track. 'We should never have come.'

'It's all a lot of nonsense, anyway,' Dora said, linking Leah's other arm. 'Where on earth am I going to meet a handsome stranger?' She gave a self-deprecating laugh.

'Don't let what Pearl said worry you, Leah,' Alice said. 'As you said earlier, it's only a bit of fun. A fairground attraction. It doesn't mean anything.'

Leah nodded, but her stomach was in turmoil. She knew

something bad was going to happen, she just didn't know what, or when.

Pearl watched the girls cross the lawn. She was shaking and her heart was racing so hard she was afraid it might fail. She couldn't articulate what she had seen at the bottom of Leah's cup, even if she'd wanted to. In Leah's tea leaves she'd seen a complex future that involved Alice and her husband, the young curate, and even her own beloved great-grandson, Joshua. She couldn't fathom it. But, before that, she had seen such a darkness lurking on the horizon. A blackness that seemed to emanate from the jaws of Hell.

She felt her throat close and she lay down on the bed, her faithful dog pressed against her. She could feel the soft beat of his heart against her side. Slowly her own rapidly beating heart began to calm and she fell into a troubled sleep filled with frightening images that kept her tossing and turning until dawn.

CHAPTER SIXTEEN

'What do you think she meant?' Leah asked Alice as they each selected an empty basket and picked their way over the damp earth to one of the few rows of plants still yielding strawberries.

In the two days since her visit to Pearl's caravan, Leah was finding it difficult coming to terms with the old woman's strange behaviour. Both Harry and Hannah had laughed off her worries, but try as she might, Leah couldn't shake off the sense that something terrible was about to befall her and Harry. It made her dread his imminent departure all the more.

'I don't think she meant anything,' said Alice, level-headed as always. 'I still think she realized she couldn't feed you the same line she'd fed Dora, and she got into a flap.'

'But she must have seen something,' persisted Leah as they settled themselves on the ground. The hedgerows were shrouded with spiderwebs, their gossamer thin strands shimmering in the early morning sun that was breaking through the thin mist. 'Her reaction was so extreme.'

'Samuel said we were silly to go in the first place,' Alice said with a sigh, her cheeks reddening slightly as she recalled his dismay when she'd admitted to having gone to see the old woman. 'He told me I was wrong to encourage you in such folly.'

'You didn't,' Leah retorted, sitting back on her heels in dismay. 'It was my idea.'

'That's what I told him.' Alice frowned. 'I'm afraid we had a bit of a disagreement about it.'

'I suppose being a man of the cloth, Reverend Roberts can't be seen to condone such things,' Dora remarked, with a worried expression. 'I do hope he isn't still cross with you?'

'He did apologize,' Alice smiled. 'I just hope he doesn't say anything to Pearl.'

'I still believe Pearl saw something awful about me and Harry,' Leah said morosely, reaching beneath a clump of leaves for a particularly large strawberry. 'Something she felt she couldn't tell me.'

'Don't take it too seriously,' Dora told her kindly, sliding her arm across Leah's shoulders. 'I don't believe a word she said. Like Alice said, she likely couldn't think of anything else to say so she feigned some nonsense about not being able to see anything more to get us to leave. I bet if you confronted her, she'd admit to it, too.'

Leah sighed. 'I wish I could believe that,' she said, 'But, to be honest, I've had a queer feeling in my gut for a while now. I don't think me and Harry are going to last.' Her blue eyes swam with tears.

'Oh, Leah,' Dora said, pulling her into a bear hug. 'It's obvious how much he adores you. He's not going to let convention stop him doing what he wants. Look how popular he is with the lads. He's one of them more than he is a Whitworth. He'll do what he feels is right, I'm sure of it. Didn't he tell Reverend Roberts he's besotted with her, Alice?'

'He did,' Alice confirmed, sitting back on her heels. 'If I were you, I'd take no notice of Pearl's weird outburst and just enjoy what time you have left with Harry before he goes back to London.'

'You're right, I suppose,' Leah acknowledged with a sigh. 'I just can't shake this horrible foreboding.'

'She's spooked you, that's all,' Dora said firmly. 'Don't let the ramblings of a silly old woman spoil your peace of mind.'

Leah nodded, blinking back her tears. She was so grateful for Alice and Dora's friendship. She was going to need them more than ever over the long winter months without Harry. She could only hope and pray that he'd be true to his word and return in the spring.

'Alice!' came a voice.

Alice whirled round to see Samuel hurrying up the lane towards her, his hat in his hands, his long, black robes flowing.

'Ladies,' Samuel nodded to Leah and Dora, who smiled and returned his greeting. 'Alice, may I speak with you for a moment, if you're not in a hurry to get home?'

'I'm not in any particular hurry,' replied Alice.

'Shall we walk?' He offered her his arm.

'We'll see you tomorrow,' Leah said.

'Yes, see you tomorrow, Leah, bye, Dora.'

'You received my roses,' Samuel said, as they walked in the direction of the church.

'I did,' Alice smiled. 'It was a lovely gesture but unnecessary.'

'I behaved like a pompous idiot,' Samuel insisted. 'Can you forgive me?'

'I already have,' Alice assured him, squeezing his arm. Samuel stroked her bare fingers. Noticing the dirt beneath her nails, she experienced a twinge of embarrassment but Samuel either hadn't noticed or clearly didn't mind.

They ducked beneath the lychgate. The churchyard was deserted and their footsteps sounded loud as they crunched along the cinder path that wound between the yew trees. The slanting rays of autumn sunshine bathed the gravestones in pale, buttery light and sparkled on the stained-glass windows.

Samuel opened the gate in the privet hedge, its rusty hinges squeaking in protest, and stood back to allow Alice into the vicarage garden.

A smoky-grey cat emerged from the shrubbery to wind itself around Alice's ankles. She stooped down to scratch the top of its head.

'That's Walter's cat, Humphrey,' Samuel told her, his lip curling in distaste.

'You're not a cat lover?' asked Alice, straightening up.

'Not really. He sheds all over my cassock.' Samuel indicated a rustic wooden bench overlooking the small fishpond. The cat leapt up onto the arm of the bench, its golden-eyed gaze fixed avidly on a vivid orange fish wallowing in the shadows. 'Walter dotes on him, of course, as does Mrs Hurst. I suppose he does keep the vermin under control,' he added, somewhat begrudgingly.

Using his hand, he swept the bench free of fallen leaves and Alice sat down. Despite the lateness of the season, it was still possible to sit outside in relative comfort. A lone black-bird trilled in the branches of a nearby beech tree and the slowly setting sun had painted the sky a vivid array of colours.

'Have you given any thought to what employment you're going to look for after next week?' Samuel asked, once Mrs Hurst had brought them mugs of hot cocoa and a plate of her homemade biscuits.

Alice licked chocolate from her upper lip. 'Father is encouraging me to enrol on a secretarial course.' She sighed, not relishing the prospect of returning to the school room. 'I haven't quite got round to filling out the form.'

'What would you say if I told you Walter and I are looking to employ a secretary? Might you be interested?'

'What, me?' said Alice, surprised. 'Working for you and Reverend Aldridge?'

'You wouldn't need to bother with a course. It's simple bookkeeping and correspondence, that's all.'

'I didn't know you were looking for a secretary? When did this come about?'

'To be fair, Walter's been talking about it since I arrived.

Neither of us is very good at correspondence or paperwork. You'd be paid a fair wage.' He named the sum and Alice raised her brows in surprise.

'That sounds very generous,' she said.

'Your hours would be half past eight until five o'clock,' Samuel said. Taking her mug from her hand, he set it on the floor beside his own and, taking both her hands in his, he looked Alice straight in the eye. 'Please say you'll accept.'

'It's a very tempting offer.'

'Then, do you accept?' Samuel asked again, hopefully.

'I believe I'd be silly not to.' Her smile faded as she frowned. 'Does Reverend Aldridge not want to interview me?'

'It was he who suggested you for the job. Your grandfather has vouched for your character, which is all the reference we need.' He grinned. 'I think you're exactly the right person to sort out the chaos in the office and, more importantly, it means I shall get to see you every day.'

Alice laughed. 'That's a bonus I can't argue with. When would you like me to start?'

'As soon as possible. Tomorrow?' he asked hopefully.

'I'd like to finish the week in the fields, if I may. Shall we say Monday?'

'Monday it is, then. I shall look forward to having you around. Perhaps I can even persuade you to help me with my sermon.'

'I wouldn't go that far,' Alice said with a smile. She felt a lightness in her spirit, knowing that, for the foreseeable future at least, she would be gainfully employed.

'Shall we go and break the good news to Walter?' Samuel said, standing up and drawing Alice to her feet. 'And perhaps you'd like to stay for supper? We could discuss the terms of your employment over Mrs Hurst's pork casserole.'

'That sounds delicious. I'll need to send word to my parents that I'll be staying in Strawbridge overnight though?'

'I shall get one of the neighbours' lads to take a message. Your grandparents won't mind you staying with them?'

'Oh, no,' Alice assured him. 'Grandma loves having me stay. I was thinking of bringing Martha and the children over on Sunday. Perhaps have a picnic at the pond before the weather turns too cold.'

'Marvellous idea,' Samuel agreed. 'I shall enjoy spending time with your siblings. They're delightful.' He offered Alice his arm. 'Shall we?'

Slipping her hand through the crook of his elbow, she smiled at him and they made their way down the steps to the vicarage.

CHAPTER SEVENTEEN

A bitter wind was blowing as Leah and Dora emerged from the drysalters on Millbank Street. Pulling their woollen scarves over their hair, they hurried down the street, the damp, smoky night air filling their lungs as the icy wind scoured their cheeks. The streetlamps hissed and droplets of ice swirled in the pools of sickly yellow light pooling on the damp pavement.

The streets were teeming with horse-drawn traffic and pedestrians. Smoke billowed from the surrounding factories, obliterating any sliver of moonlight that might have penetrated the thick bank of cloud cover.

Leah coughed. The fumes from the dye stung the back of her throat. She could smell the damp rising off the River Itchen as they approached the ferry. Snippets of conversation carried on the frosty night air but the majority of people queueing for the ferry were, like Dora and herself, too exhausted to do much more than put one foot in front of the other, the minds of the fortunate ones contemplating the warm hearth and hearty supper that awaited them after a long day in the factories.

Leah's stomach rumbled and she coughed again. She hated her job at the drysalters. Not only was it worse than she'd remembered, the factory was a good hour and a half walk, morning and night. She left home before sun-up and never arrived home until gone seven. It was a dismal existence and she often felt that it was only Harry's letters that kept her spirits up. She tugged the collar of her coat up around her neck, the chill wind blowing off the waters seeming to seep right into her bones.

She paid the ferryman and stepped aboard, Dora close behind her. Breathing in a lungful of tangy, briny air, she managed to find a space on one of the narrow wooden benches, and sat down, shuffling up so Dora could squeeze on beside her.

'I wonder if there'll be a letter from Harry today,' she murmured, as the ferry began to pull away from the shore. Lanterns bobbed on the mud flats, the muffled voices of the mudlarks rising and falling on the wind as they scoured the exposed mudbanks for anything left behind by the ebbing tide that might be worth a penny or two.

'I haven't heard from him in almost a week.' Leah stamped her cold feet. A fine mist drifted off the water, carrying the reek of rotting fish and damp.

'I'm sure there will be,' Dora assured her, rubbing her hands together. Despite her woollen gloves, her fingertips were tingling with the cold. She shivered. It was only early

November but the weather was turning colder by the day and the newspapers were forecasting a severe winter. She just hoped that if they got snow, it wouldn't be bad enough to block the roads. She desperately needed her wages and if she couldn't get in to work, she wouldn't get paid. The foreman had made that clear enough times.

'Hey, Dor, move over.' Leah instantly recognized the stringent tones of Sally Shaw, a woman they'd worked with in the fields over the summer. Despite the lack of space, she somehow managed to squeeze her ample bottom on the edge of the seat. 'You've got a room going begging, haven't you?'

Recoiling at the stench of the woman's rancid breath, Dora nodded. Since her father's stroke, his bedroom, the larger of the two, had remained empty.

'Would you consider renting it out?' Sally went on. The ferry rolled slightly and she almost toppled over, grabbing hold of the guard rope in order to retain her balance.

'Are you needing a place to stay?' Dora asked hesitantly, casting Leah a sideways glance. Much as the extra money would be welcome, she didn't fancy living under the same roof as Sally.

'Oh, no,' Sally laughed. 'It's not for me. It's for my cousin Barbara and her lad. He's got himself a job in Botley, something with the railway and they're in need of lodgings close by.'

'Why can't they stay with you?' asked Leah, regarding the older woman suspiciously.

'In my pokey cottage?' Sally looked incredulous. 'We're

packed in like sardines as it is, besides,' she added, a little smugly. 'I've got myself a new man, haven't I? He won't want my cousin and her kid cramping his style.'

'How much?' Dora asked.

Sally shrugged. 'They're able to pay the going rate. Barbara's late husband left her comfortably off and, as I say, the lad's got himself a good job with the railway company.'

'I'd certainly be interested,' Dora heard herself say, as the wind whistled around her ears. 'I'd have to talk it over with my dad though. When were they wanting to move in?'

'He starts his new job Monday week so they'll be arriving next Saturday. They've booked a couple of nights at the Railway Arms so, shall we say the Monday, if your dad agrees?'

'I'll speak to him tonight, and let you know tomorrow,' Dora promised, getting unsteadily to her feet as the ferry bumped against the jetty.

'I hope Sally's cousin isn't much like her,' Leah remarked as they started the long walk home. It was almost pitch black but there was quite a crowd of them heading back to the villages and hamlets on the outskirts of the city. Several of the men had brought lanterns but, even so, it was hard going and both girls were relieved when they spotted the lights of Strawbridge twinkling through the trees. Dora was rehearsing in her head what she would say to her father to persuade him to agree to taking in lodgers, while Leah was hoping and praying that she'd find a letter from Harry waiting for her.

*

'I won't have strangers in my house!' Stephen roared, his face turning a dark shade of crimson.

Dora shrank back from his anger, her heart racing as she wracked her brains to think of some way to make him see sense. In her head she was already spending the extra money. Her father needed some new shirts and she, herself, could do with a new pair of shoes. Her old ones were worn through and let the water in when it rained. With careful planning she might even be able to put a bit aside for Christmas. But all her plans would come to nothing if she couldn't convince her father to take in Sally's cousin.

'Dad, please,' she tried again, close to tears. She was exhausted after a twelve-hour shift on her feet and the last thing she wanted, or needed, was an argument. 'They're willing to pay decent money. It'll see us through the winter, especially if it snows and I can't get into work.'

'I said no!' Stephen shouted, clenching his fists. 'Just because I'm a useless cripple doesn't mean you can do as you please. This is still my house. You're not mistress of it yet,' he sneered nastily.

Finding it difficult to swallow for the lump in her throat, and fighting back the tears, Dora pulled on her coat.

'Where are you going?' her father barked.

Unable to speak, Dora just shook her head and yanked open the door. Letting it bang shut behind her, she turned and knocked at Leah's door. It was opened almost immediately.

'Come on in, Dor,' Leah said, standing aside to let her pass. 'We heard the commotion.'

Choking back a sob, Dora stumbled inside.

'Are you all right, love?' Hannah asked from the kitchen doorway. 'Come in here. It's warmer. You look half starved to death.

'Sit down, love,' Hannah led Dora to the chair nearest the fire. 'Now, what's all the fuss about this time? Is it your dad?' she asked, her face creased in sympathy. 'Is it to do with these lodgers Leah's told me about?'

Dora nodded. 'I know it'll be an imposition but the extra money will come in so handy.'

Hannah sighed. 'That man,' she said, shaking her head. 'It's not right. You work your fingers to the bone looking after him. He's nothing but a selfish old goat. I'm sorry, Dora. I know he's your dad, but it's the truth.' She started to untie her apron. 'Right, I'm going round to give the old misery a piece of my mind. You can have your supper with us and he can flipping well stew in his own juices. Daisy, lay an extra place for Dora. Leah, butter another couple of slices of bread. I'll be back in a tick.'

'From what I could hear, he didn't sound keen on the idea?' Leah remarked, once her mother had left.

Dora shook her head. 'He went mad.' She shook her head in frustration. 'You'd think he'd welcome the extra money. It'd make his life a lot easier too, not just mine.' Leah handed her a mug of tea and she wrapped her chilled fingers around it gratefully. Seeing her friend's woebegone expression, Dora felt a pang of guilt. Chiding herself for being so selfish she asked, 'Did you get a letter?'

Leah shook her head. 'Something's wrong,' she said, her lips pursed with anxiety. 'Harry never goes more than a day or two without writing.' She looked at Dora with large, worried eyes. 'He was attending a ball last weekend. Do you think he might have met someone there? Someone his mother deemed more suitable?'

'Certainly not,' replied Dora with feeling. 'A blind man can see how much Harry adores you. He's neither so fickle that he'd go off with the first pretty girl who batted her eyelids at him, nor so cowardly as to not tell you, if he did.'

'That's what me and Mum keep telling her,' Daisy piped up, setting a plate and cutlery in front of Dora. 'There could be any number of explanations.' She glanced at her sister. Seeing that she was in no mood to do anything but stare broodingly into space, she went into the pantry to fetch the bread and the butter dish.

'Exactly,' Dora agreed cheerfully, forcefully putting her own worries aside in order to cheer up her friend. 'Letters go astray all the time. Likely one will arrive soon.'

'I hope so,' muttered Leah, unconvinced. 'I've just got such a bad feeling in my stomach. Perhaps this is the reason why Pearl had her funny episode.'

'Oh, don't start on that again,' Daisy laughed, emerging from the pantry. 'That's the only reason you're fretting about Harry, because of what that silly old woman said – or didn't say, as it happens.' She caught Dora's eye. 'Tell her, Dora. She's worrying unnecessarily.'

'I'm sure Daisy's right, Leah,' Dora affirmed. 'I'll bet you anything you'll get a letter tomorrow and you'll feel silly for getting yourself in such a state.'

Leah gave her a wan smile. 'I hope you're right.'

The back door flew open and Hannah blew in on a squall of icy rain. 'Right, your dad's agreed to you taking your lodgers on a three-month trial,' she said, unwinding her shawl and draping it over a chair to dry. 'He's sorry for the fuss he made and he says you're to stay here as long as you like and enjoy yourself. Now.' She rubbed her cold hands. 'Where's that tea, Daisy? That wind's gone right through to my bones.'

'I don't know how you do it, Aunty Hannah,' Dora laughed, giddy with relief.

'I just give him what-for,' Hannah replied with a wry smile. 'Easier for me to do, I suppose, than his daughter. I said you'd take him some dinner when you go back. There's more than enough to go around.'

CHAPTER EIGHTEEN

A cold wind howled along the station platform. It was the middle Saturday in November and Botley railway station was bustling. The sky was grey and overcast and there was the threat of rain in the damp air.

'It's been lovely seeing you, Alice,' Violet Upshall said as she embraced her goddaughter warmly.

'And you, Aunty Violet,' Alice replied, returning the hug.

'I'm so pleased you were able to have some time off so we could spend it together,' Violet smiled. 'You know how fond I am of you. I'm fond of you all, of course. Your sisters and brothers are adorable, but you, Alice, will always hold a special place in my heart.'

Alice laughed. Violet was her mother's dearest friend and had been a huge support to her during the difficult times in Alice's early childhood. Now in her late fifties, she was still a striking woman. She looked very arresting in her dove-grey hat and coat which she wore over a rich, plum-coloured velvet dress, the hem just resting on the tips of her black shoes.

Since she'd started working at the vicarage, and with the nights drawing in, Alice had started boarding with her grandparents. It was an arrangement that worked well but she would have been disappointed to miss Violet's visit, so she had been pleasantly surprised and pleased when Reverend Aldridge had encouraged her to take a few days off.

Now Violet regarded Alice fondly with eyes the colour of a wintery sea. 'Give my regards to that nice curate of yours, won't you?'

'I will,' promised Alice. As they drew apart, she wondered why Violet had never married, but the thought was snuffed out by the shrill whistle of the approaching train.

'I shall write to let you know I'm home,' Violet said, giving Alice's mother a final hug. 'Look after yourself, Lily and, God willing, I shall see you both at Christmas.'

'I shall look forward to it,' Alice's mother said, wiping away a tear as she straightened her hat. Though there was an almost twenty-year age-gap between the two women, there was no one Lily was closer to than Violet, apart from her half-sister Eleanor. Even her husband, James, didn't know half of what Lily had endured as a young girl. Things that, without Violet's help and support, she could not have borne, and it was always a wrench to say goodbye when her visits came to an end.

The train roared into the station in a cloud of hissing steam and the squeal of brakes.

'Goodbye, my dears,' Violet called, clutching her hat as she hurried to board, moving against the flow of disembarking passengers.

'Travel safe, Violet,' Lily called after her, smiling through her tears. 'I hate goodbyes,' she sniffed, blowing her nose.

'She'll be back before you know it,' Alice assured her mother. 'It's only five weeks until Christmas.' She was aware of this because she'd been kept busy at the vicarage for the past few weeks helping the two reverends put together their programme for Advent.

The whistle blew and the train started to move slowly alongside the platform.

'Goodbye, my dears. Goodbye,' Violet called, waving from the window.

'Goodbye, Violet. Godspeed.' Lily waved back, keeping pace with the train until it began to pick up speed. Suddenly, as the swirling steam and smoke began to dissipate, she caught sight of a figure on the platform that struck terror into her heart. *Jez?* She stood still, her heart racing. She tried to swallow but her mouth was dry.

'What is it, Mother?' she heard Alice ask. She clutched her arm, clearly alarmed. 'You've gone as white as a sheet.'

'I . . . Nothing.' Lily scanned the crowd. Whoever she saw had disappeared, swallowed up by the throng of disembarked passengers heading for the exit. She shook her head, chiding herself for her foolishness. Jez had been dead for fifteen years, and even if, by some queer trick of fate, he'd lived, he'd be in his forties now. The person she thought she'd seen was a young man in his late teens.

'I'm just tired,' she said, in reply to Alice's concern. She smiled as her heart rate slowly returned to normal. 'Let's get going. I'm a bit behind with my commissions what with Violet being here. It won't do to let my ladies down just before Christmas.'

'If I was any good with a needle, I'd offer to give you a hand,' joked Alice, as they hurried down the station steps, pleased to see the colour returning to her mother's cheeks.

'I know you would, my dear,' Lily smiled, patting her daughter's gloved hand. 'You help me in so many other ways and . . .' The words died on her lips as she came to an abrupt halt. She stood as if frozen to the pavement, staring at the queue of passengers waiting to board one of the three omnibuses lining the street opposite the station.

'Mother?' Alice frowned, and followed the direction of her mother's gaze, unable to fathom what she'd seen to cause her such upset. Her gaze came to rest on a woman at the back of the queue. She was wearing a dark coat and hat and appeared to be staring straight at Alice and her mother. The woman said something to the tall young man at her side and, leaving her baggage in his care, turned and walked towards them.

'Well, well,' she said as she approached, giving them a mocking smile. 'If it isn't Lily Elkin. I thought it was you I saw on the platform.' She looked Lily up and down disparagingly.

Alice gave her mother a sideways glance, relieved to see that in the time it had taken the woman to walk from the bus queue to the station steps, Lily appeared to have regained her composure. She regarded the woman coolly.

'Hello, Barbie-Jean, but it's Lily Russel now. I remarried.'

'So did I,' Barbie-Jean said, with a toss of her head. 'I'm a widow, now.'

'I'm sorry to hear that,' Lily said with genuine sympathy. She regarded the other woman with a critical eye. The years hadn't been kind to the woman who'd done nothing but add to Lily's misery. Lily worked out that she must be somewhere in her mid-thirties, only a couple of years younger than herself, yet she appeared decades older, and she could certainly afford to shed a few pounds. The buttons of her stylish black coat strained across her broad hips, but despite the extra weight, Lily could see a semblance of the pretty girl she had once been.

'You must be Alice?' Barbie-Jean said. 'I don't expect you remember me, do you? I'm your Aunty Barbie-Jean?'

'Not really,' replied Alice, with a shiver of revulsion. She'd heard enough about her childhood to know that her father's mistress had caused her mother untold shame and embarrassment, moving into the marital home after the death of Alice's paternal grandmother.

'Perhaps not.' Barbie-Jean shrugged. 'You were only a kid.' She smiled, displaying uneven teeth. 'Anyway, I've got a surprise for you, Alice. Nate!' she called over her shoulder. 'Come here.'

Alice heard her mother's rapid intake of breath as the tall, dark-haired young man left the omnibus queue and ambled towards them, and frowned, wondering what Barbie-Jean meant. Beside her, her mother stiffened.

'I saw him on the platform,' she said quietly, her brows knitting together in confusion. 'I thought . . .'

'That he was Jez come back from the dead?' Barbie-Jean laughed. 'I'm not surprised. He's the spit of him, isn't he?' Before Lily could respond, the woman had turned back to Alice. 'Alice, meet your half-brother, Nate Gardener.'

'What?' Alice looked to Lily for confirmation.

'Oh, he took my late husband's name,' Barbie-Jean smirked. 'Didn't want the poor lad to have Jez's reputation following him around like a bad smell all his life.'

'I beg your pardon, Mother? My half-sister?' Nate's puzzled gaze moved between his mother and Alice. He was a good-looking boy, there was no denying the fact, but then, so had his father been. Lily could see the similarities between Alice and Barbie-Jean's boy.

'But how— ?' she started to ask but Barbie-Jean interrupted her.

'I discovered I was pregnant just after Jez got arrested. I know Nate looks older, but he's only fifteen. He's mature for his age.'

'I'll be sixteen in February,' Nathan retorted, drawing himself to his full height. He flashed Alice a friendly smile. 'Pleased to meet you, half-sister.'

'Likewise,' Alice said, good manners prevailing after a brief hesitation. and it crossed Lily's mind to wonder whether, like her daughter, Nate had inherited Jez's colouring and features, but nothing of his unpleasant character. She supposed that would remain to be seen.

'Well, it's been nice catching up,' Barbie-Jean said, her tone implying that it had been anything but. 'But we must be going.'

'I hope we meet again, soon,' Nate said, grinning at Alice over his shoulder as his mother ushered him away.

'I hope not,' Alice murmured, echoing her mother's thoughts but any such hopes that that would be the last they saw of Barbie-Jean and her son were dashed when they heard them pay the fare for Strawbridge. Boarding the omnibus behind them, Lily and Alice exchanged glances.

'I wonder if they're Dora's lodgers?' Alice whispered as they paid their fare.

'Oh, no,' Lily blanched as she followed Alice down the aisle. 'I pity Dora if that's the case.'

Keeping her gaze averted, Lily made her way to the back of the bus where she found two empty seats and sat down. Alice followed. As she passed the seats where Nate sat beside his mother, she inadvertently found herself meeting his gaze. He grinned. Taken by surprise, she almost returned his smile but managed to stop herself in time. Turning her face away, she hurried to join her mother. Half-brother or not, she wanted nothing to do with Nate Gardener.

Dora glanced out of the bedroom window for the fourth time in twenty minutes. She was feeling nervous. Wiping her sweaty palms on her apron, she gazed round the room for the umpteenth time, inspecting every detail. The previous week Mathew Turner had taken her to Southampton in his cart where she'd spent some of her hard-earned cash on a second-hand iron bedstead for the master bedroom and two thin mattresses, one of which she kept propped up behind the pantry door. She'd spent the past few days scrubbing and cleaning the two upstairs rooms until they were spotless. The bedding had been freshly laundered and aired, and the rugs beaten. She'd even washed the curtains.

Leaning her elbows on the wide sill, she peered down at the lane below. A cold wind blew across the barren fields, rattling the glass in its frame.

She yawned. She'd been up since before dawn. Her father had, mercifully, passed the night relatively peacefully and there had been no soiled bedding to add to her workload that morning. She'd helped him shave and had managed to cajole him into a clean shirt. She just hoped he'd curb his tongue when the new lodgers arrived. She'd invested a lot in this venture and she could ill afford to have them change their mind because of any unpleasantness from her father.

The sound of hooves drew her from her wanderings and she hurried downstairs as the omnibus rumbled passed the cottage.

'They'll be here in a few minutes,' she told her father, smoothing down her apron and patting her hair as she gave the parlour a final, critical glance. There was a slight smell of ammonia emanating from the chamber pot under the bed which she'd forgotten to empty it but that couldn't be helped.

There wasn't time to do it now. The omnibus stopped outside the Glyn Arms. Sally Shaw's cousin and her boy would be at the door within minutes. She stood in the centre of the room, her eyes on the door, listening to the racing thud of her heartbeat.

Even though she was expecting it, the knock startled her. Wiping her clammy palms on her apron, she hurried to the door, opening it to find a thickset woman in a dark coat and hat standing on the threshold. Beside her stood a tall young man with wavy, dark hair and eyes so dark they were almost black.

'Dora Webb?' the woman asked, sounding slightly out of breath. She was pink-cheeked from the wind and her eyes were watering. 'Blimey, that wind goes right through you, doesn't it?' she chuckled, dabbing her streaming eyes with a handkerchief before thrusting out a black-gloved hand. 'How do you do? I'm Mrs Gardener and this is my son, Nate. I believe you're expecting us?'

'Yes,' Dora nodded, shaking the proffered hand. 'Pleased to meet you, Mrs Gardener, Nate. Please, do come in.' She stood aside to allow the woman to squeeze past her into the parlour. Taking off his cap, Nate ducked his head to avoid hitting it on the lintel. He must be at least six foot tall, Dora mused, craning her neck to look up at him.

'You must be Mr Webb, then?' the woman said, standing in the middle of the room and looking at Stephen curiously. 'Sally never mentioned your old man was a cripple.'

'Er, yes,' Dora said, hurriedly, before her father could

respond. 'Father, these are our lodgers. Mrs Gardener and her son, Nate. Mrs Gardener, Nate, my father, Stephen Webb.'

'Pleasure to meet you, sir,' Nate said. He dropped the bags on the floor with a thump, making Dora jump.

Stephen gave a curt nod. 'Morning.'

'If you'll follow me, I'll show you to your rooms,' Dora said, leading the way upstairs.

'Here we are. Mrs Gardener, you're in here.' she pushed open the door to what had once been her parents' bedroom, 'And Nate, you're just next door in here.'

'Thank you, miss,' Nate grinned.

Dora found herself grinning back. 'I hope you'll be comfortable.' Standing in the doorway, she surveyed the single bed pushed under the window, with its dark blue eiderdown. There was a small chest of drawers, a washstand and a small, wooden chair drawn close to the window.

'Have you come from far?' she said as she turned to leave.

'London,' Mrs Gardener replied, fluffing up her blonde hair. She looked even heavier without her coat. Her green woollen dress clung to all the wrong places.

'I'll leave you to settle in.' Dora said. 'I'll make some tea. I'm sure you're parched after your journey.'

'Wait!' Nate called after her. She paused on the top step and eyed him nervously, wondering what he could have found fault with so quickly.

'There are only two bedrooms,' he said, frowning.

'Yes.' Confused, Dora nodded.

'Where do you sleep?'

Dora gave a shrill laugh. 'Oh, don't worry about me. I'll be quite comfortable on a mattress in the kitchen.'

'No.' Nate shook his head. 'I'm afraid I can't allow that. I won't sleep in a bed while you sleep on the kitchen floor.'

Dora stared at him. 'It's all right, really,' she insisted. 'I'll be close to my dad if he needs me during the night.'

'No, I'm sorry. I'll sleep in the kitchen. I mean it.'

For a moment they stared at each other. Dora exhaled. 'Are you sure?'

'I am,' Nate replied. 'I'll keep my things in Mum's room and sleep in the kitchen at night. You can have your room back.'

Dora smiled. 'Thank you. That's very kind of you.'

Nate shrugged. 'My stepfather was a chivalrous man. I try to live up to his example.'

His dark eyes seemed to bore into her soul and she blushed.

'I'd better make that tea,' she said, breaking eye contact and hurrying down the stairs.

In the kitchen she could hear Mrs Gardener moving around her room upstairs, slamming drawers and opening and shutting the wardrobe doors, and she couldn't help but wonder what the next few weeks might bring. It was going to be a new experience for them both, sharing a house with total strangers.

'They seem nice,' she said, keeping her voice low as she handed her father his tea.

'As long as they don't bother me, I can tolerate them, I suppose,' he replied, ungraciously.

Dora sighed. His reaction was probably the best she could hope for, but she was going to have her work cut out from now on, she could see it.

CHAPTER NINETEEN

'It's been almost six weeks with no word,' Leah lamented. She wrapped her cold hands round her mug of hot cocoa but made no move to drink it.

'Nothing at all?' Dora asked, her brows raised.

'Nothing,' Leah repeated, close to tears.

The bell above the door jangled and both girls looked up as Alice blew in on a gust of icy wind, her arms laden with parcels. Spotting her friends in the far corner of the café, she attempted a wave but thought better of it, threading her way between the tables towards them instead.

'Goodness it's cold,' she said, dumping her parcels on the floor and rubbing her gloved hands together in an attempt to thaw her frozen fingers. Her cheeks were pink with cold and the tip of her nose glowed. 'I wouldn't be surprised if we don't get snow before the day's out.'

'Preferably not before we get home,' Dora remarked anxiously, her gaze straying to the steamed-up window through which she could just make out the blurred shapes of passers-by.

It was the second Saturday in December and the girls had come in to Southampton. Ostensibly the trip was to do a bit of Christmas shopping, but in reality, Dora and Alice were hoping to cheer Leah up.

Despite writing numerous letters, she'd heard nothing from Harry for weeks and she was desolate. Even her mother had run out of excuses as to why she might not have heard from him.

Leah had been hopeful that she might have had a chance to speak to Harry's father when he returned to Streawberige House for his shooting weekend but, to her disappointment, it had been cancelled at the last minute. According to the vicarage's housekeeper, Mrs Hurst, who was on friendly terms with the Whitworths' housekeeper, one of Isaac's acquaintances had just inherited a lodge in the wilds of Scotland and the lure of hunting stags rather than pheasants had, apparently, been too strong to resist.

She was convinced Harry had met a girl and had fallen in love. What other plausible reason could there be for his silence? She felt sick just thinking about it.

'I think I should go and see Pearl,' she said as Alice pulled out a chair.

'Whatever for?' frowned Dora. Leah waited while the waitress hurried over to take Alice's order before replying.

'I'm going to ask her what she saw in my tea leaves that day. She must have seen something awful to make her react that way. I need to know whether it was another woman so I know whether I'm wasting my time pining for Harry.'

'I don't think Harry going off with another girl would have caused such a violent reaction from Pearl,' Alice said, peeling off her gloves and laying them beside her plate. 'I still believe it was a charade on her part because she couldn't think up anything we'd believe.'

'Pearl tells fortunes for a living, Alice,' Leah said cuttingly. 'She's not going to run out of yarns to spin us, is she? No.' Leah shook her head. 'She saw something horrific and I need to know if it's got something to do with Harry and why I haven't heard from him.'

'There's bound to be a rational explanation,' Alice said, consolingly.

'What explanation can there be?' Leah snapped. She leaned back in her chair, her toasted teacake untouched on her plate.

Alice shrugged her shoulders. 'I don't know, Leah,' she said, lamely. 'But I refuse to believe he would just cut you off like with no word. The Harry we know wouldn't behave that way.'

'But do we know him?' Leah countered dully. 'I mean, he pretended to be someone he wasn't. Perhaps everything else has been a pretence, too.'

'Don't be silly,' chided Dora. 'Of course, it wasn't. Anyone could see how fond Harry is of you.'

'Then, perhaps,' Leah sighed. 'But he's home now, back with the girls he used to know. I know his mother will be throwing him into the path of every eligible young lady she knows.'

'Oh, Leah,' Alice laughed. 'I'm sure he's not that fickle.'

'It's all right for you,' pouted Leah. 'Your romance is going along swimmingly.'

Alice blushed. 'Samuel and I are very fond of each other,' she admitted, her smile reflected in her eyes. She lowered her gaze, studying the red and white checked table cloth. 'We have discussed marriage,' she said, quietly.

'What!' Dora squeaked. 'Oh, my, how exciting. Do you think he'll propose soon?'

'I believe he intends speaking to my stepfather very soon.'

'Oh, Alice! I'm so pleased for you.' Dora gave Alice's hand a squeeze. 'You're so perfect for each other.' She grinned. 'What did I tell you? I said you'd be engaged by the end of the year and it looks as though I'm right.'

'I'm happy for you, Alice,' Leah said, mustering a smile. 'I am, honestly,' she insisted in the face of Alice's and Dora's expressions of sympathy. The last thing she wanted was her friends' pity. She took a bite of her crumpet. It had gone cold, pools of melted butter congealing on the plate, and tasted like sawdust on her tongue.

'How are your lodgers?' she asked Dora, in an attempt to stop brooding.

Dora set down her mug. 'To be honest, it's better than I expected. Mrs Gardener keeps herself to herself. She only comes down for her meals.'

'And Nate?' Alice asked, casually. She was determined to have nothing to do with her half-brother, despite living next door to him, but often, when catching sight of him in the back garden, chopping wood for the fire or digging potatoes for the evening meal, she couldn't deny her curiosity got the better of her, though she refrained from asking after him in deference to her mother. Knowing that Jez had fathered another child whilst still married to Lily was just another humiliation for her poor mother to bear.

'He's a real gentleman,' Dora said, her face lighting up as she described how Nate insisted on helping with most of the heavy work about the house. 'I sometimes forget he's only fifteen,' she said, picking at the crumbs on her plate. 'He comes across as so much older. He's brilliant with Dad, too. The two of them spend a lot of time together. He even gets up at night to see to him.' She smiled at her two friends. 'Dad's so much calmer.'

'Just be careful,' warned Alice. 'From what I've learned about Jez, Nate could be a charmer, just like he was. Don't let yourself be taken in by him.'

'He might not necessarily take after your father, Alice,' Dora retorted, slightly annoyed. 'I'm sure you are nothing like him.'

'Yes, that's as may be, but I had my mother as a guiding influence in my life. Who has Nate got?' She pulled a face. 'From what little my mother's told me, Barbie-Jean doesn't seem like much of a role model.'

'Nate had a strong relationship with his stepfather, I believe.' Dora thrust out her chin in defiance. 'I know you're suspicious of him,' she said, in a placatory tone. 'But I like having him around. He's certainly lightened my load and I can afford occasional treats like this.' She waved her hand to encompass the bustling tearoom.

'We'd better get a move on if we're to make the matinee,' Leah said, draining her mug. She wasn't in the mood for the pantomime but she was hoping two hours of *The Babes in the Woods* might relieve her misery for a while. And she would certainly make plans to pay Pearl another visit in the next day or so. She was determined not to rest until she got to the bottom of the old woman's strange behaviour. Especially if it gave her a clue as to why she hadn't heard a word from Harry in such a long time.

By the time the girls emerged from the theatre some three hours later, it was starting to snow. Seagulls screeched in a monochrome sky. They stopped at a vendor on their way to the station and bought a bag of roasted chestnuts to share on the journey home. The Salvation Army band were playing outside the entrance and they all dug into their purses for a handful of coins which they dropped into the bucket as they ran up the steps and into the cavernous building, their breath billowing in front of their faces. They boarded the train just in time, and settled down in their seats, munching the hot chestnuts and laughing over the performance, which they'd all enjoyed immensely.

Leah had to admit, she was feeling much better. The pantomime had brought the light relief she needed and, by the time the train pulled into Botley station half an hour later, she was feeling much more optimistic about the future.

They emerged on to the bitterly cold street. The light from the streetlamps was all but obliterated by the swirling snow and, once they left the village behind, they were walking blind. Arm in arm, they made their way along the familiar lane, the thickly packed snow making the journey that much more arduous. Dora's boots were leaking, soaking her stockings as her toes slowly turned numb. The relief was tangible as they trudged passed a lone cottage, the first of the spaced-out dwellings that made up the hamlet of Strawbridge. Cracks in the curtains cast slivers of lamplight on to the freshly fallen snow, causing the three girls to quicken their pace in the knowledge they were almost home.

'Are you expecting visitors, Dora?' Alice asked as they passed the dark, silent church. Dora shook her head at the sight of the pony and trap tethered outside her cottage.

'It must be someone visiting the Gardeners.'

'Well, I'll see you both tomorrow at church,' Alice said, rearranging the packages in her arms as she attempted to open her grandparents' door.

'I'll come if I can,' Dora said. 'Nate's quite good about keeping Dad company on a Sunday morning, and I do enjoy Reverend Robert's sermons.'

'I'll be there,' Leah replied, 'Then in the afternoon I'm going to see Pearl.'

'Are you sure that's a good idea?' Alice asked in concern.

'I won't rest until I know what she saw,' Leah insisted.

Alice shrugged. 'It's your life.' They were interrupted by the lifting of the latch.

'You girls will catch your death standing out here yakking,' Alice's grandfather said, opening the door and grinning at them through the swirling snow. 'Bea's got a pan of mulled cider warming on the stove. You're all welcome to come in and have a glass.'

'Thank you, Mr Turner,' Dora replied, 'But I'd better get home. I've left Dad long enough.'

'Me, too, Mr Turner,' agreed Leah. 'But thanks, anyway.'

They said their goodbyes and hurried to their respective cottages.

Dora pushed open the door to find a strange man sitting in the parlour. He was tall and thin, with oiled greying-brown hair combed neatly across his balding pate, and a pencil-thin moustache.

'Miss Webb?' he said, getting swiftly to his feet. 'Good evening.' He thrust out his hand. He had bony wrists that protruded from the cuffs of his white shirt. 'Dominic Lyle. I'm a lawyer.'

'It's exciting news, Dora,' Stephen said, more animated than Dora could remember seeing him for a long time. 'Tell her, Mr Lyle.'

The lawyer cleared his throat. 'Perhaps you'd like to sit down,' he said, indicating an empty chair. Feeling quite bewildered and not a little bemused, Dora took off her coat and hat and sat. She folded her hands in her lap, trying not to wince at the pain in her frozen feet as they began to thaw.

'Miss Webb,' Dominic began, 'I represent the firm of Cavanagh & Kingsley. We are handling the estate of a Mr

Benjamin Baker and it is our belief that you and your father,' he paused to nod at Stephen, 'may be his only living relatives.'

'Do you see what that means, Dora?' her father said, excitedly. 'We could be in for some money.'

'It is true. There is an inheritance,' Dominic said. 'We're not sure of the exact amount but it could be substantial.'

Dora turned to her father, stunned.

'We'll be set for life, Dor,' he said. 'No more working in that factory or Whitworth's strawberry fields for you. You'll be able to stay at home and take care of me properly.' In his excitement, he failed to notice the look of alarm that flittered across his daughter's face at the thought of being stuck in the house all day.

'When is this likely to be confirmed?' Dora asked, frowning.

'Depending on how long the estate takes to go through probate, we could be talking as soon as late February, early March. Of course, nothing is guaranteed.'

'What do you mean?' demanded Stephen, the smile slipping from his face.

'Well,' Dominic shrugged. 'There's always the possibility that we could discover another, more recent will, or our enquiries might uncover other relatives. And I'm afraid we shan't know the amount until the creditors have been satisfied.'

'You have to be cautious, I understand,' Stephen nodded. 'But, as far as you can see, will the money be ours?'

'If things remain as they are now, then yes, I believe you, Mr Webb, will be the sole beneficiary of Benjamin Baker's estate.'

Dora's father let out a triumphant yell. 'Dora, bring the brandy. I believe this calls for a celebration. Mr Lyle, you'll join me, of course.'

'I have a long, cold ride ahead of me so a drop of brandy would be most welcome. Thank you,' said Dominic gratefully, as Dora got up to fetch the bottle from the pantry.

Her heart was racing as she contemplated what a large sum of money might mean.

Nate was sitting at the kitchen table poring over some paperwork. He looked up, his brow creased. 'Are you all right? You look troubled.'

'You heard what the lawyer said?' she asked, slightly uneasy as she recalled Alice's warning to beware of Nate.

'I did,' he replied apologetically. 'I'm sorry. I didn't mean to eavesdrop.'

Dora shook her head. 'No need to apologize.' She took a deep breath to steady her racing pulse. 'We're having a drop of brandy. Would you like to join us?'

'Thank you, but I'd better get on with this.' He smiled. 'You go and enjoy your celebration.'

She fetched the bottle of brandy from the pantry and was about to return to the parlour when Nate caught her arm. She whirled round, startled, the touch of his hand sending a shockwave up her spine. If Nate had experienced something similar, he didn't show it and she hastily composed herself.

'Just be careful how much to let on to my mother about this,' he said in a low voice. They both looked up as the floorboards overhead creaked loudly. 'She can be very . . .

manipulating.' He gave her a knowing look, and Dora nodded her understanding.

'Come on, Dor!' Her father bellowed from the parlour. 'Where the heck's that brandy?'

'Coming, Dad.' Flashing Nate a rueful smile, Dora hurried into the other room where she spent the next hour listening to Stephen and Dominic toasting the Webbs' upcoming change in fortune.

CHAPTER TWENTY

Leah could feel the sweat trickling beneath her thick woollen underwear, despite the frigid air. It had continued snowing heavily during the night and she was finding her journey hard going. She paused to catch her breath and take in the stillness of the whitewashed landscape. The only sound was her ragged breathing and the groan of the wind in the snow-laden trees.

She could see Pearl's caravan nestled amongst the gnarled branches of the empty fruit trees, grey smoke curving upwards from the stovepipe. Taking a deep breath, she ploughed her way through the thick snow towards where Joshua was sitting on a low stool outside the caravan, cleaning his traps. He looked up as she approached, his brows arched in surprise.

'Leah.'

'Hello, Joshua. I'm looking for Pearl. Is she here?'

'Nan!' Joshua shouted, getting slowly to his feet. 'Leah's here to see you.' He kept his gaze focused on Leah's face as they walked towards the steps. 'You keeping well?'

'Yes, thank you' She regarded him thoughtfully. 'You haven't been round in a while?'

Joshua shrugged. 'Well, you know, been busy.'

The caravan door opened and Pearl peered out, squinting against the brightness of the sunlight bouncing off the snow. She was so bundled up as to appear shapeless. Only her shrivelled face was visible amongst the woollen layers.

'What do you want, dearie?' she asked, without preamble.

'I need you to tell me what you saw in my tea leaves,' Leah said. 'Please.'

Pearl shook her head. One gloved hand gripped the doorframe, the other clasped a whittled beechwood walking stick.

'Sometimes it's best to not know what the future holds,' she said, studiously avoiding Leah's gaze.

'That's rich,' Leah chuckled sarcastically. 'When you make your living out of foretelling the future.'

'Oi,' Joshua shot Leah a look. 'Speak to my nan with respect.'

'I just want to know what you saw, that's all,' Leah said, calmly. 'You saw something that startled you, and I think it had to do with me and Harry. I haven't heard from him in weeks. Has he met someone else, is that it?' The words caught in the throat and she looked away, not wanting Joshua to witness her distress.

Pearl sighed. 'What I saw was like nothing I've seen before,' she said. 'Something dark and . . . evil.'

Leah stared at her in bewilderment. 'But what has that to do with me and Harry?'

'Don't count on a future with Harry, that's all I'll say,' Pearl said.

Leah's heart sank. 'What do you mean?' She noticed the old woman's hands were shaking. 'Doesn't he love me anymore?'

Pearl regarded Leah kindly. 'Dearie, his love for you burns as strong as it ever did.'

'Then, why?' Leah asked, confused.

'I've revealed too much,' Pearl cried in a tremulous voice. 'I can say no more. Go now.'

'No, wait! Please! What do you mean? If Harry loves me, why hasn't he written?' She put one foot on the bottom step, meaning to follow Pearl into the caravan, so determined was she get an answer that made sense. 'Why do you say we can't have a future?'

Pearl shook her head, and began backing away. Tears spilled from her rheumy-blue eyes and wend their way down the crevices of her age-worn cheeks.

'Go!' she cried again, turning away. 'Go!'

'Come on, Leah.' Joshua grabbed Leah's arm and pulled her away. 'She needs to rest.'

'Why won't she tell me what she saw?' Leah hissed.

'Look,' Joshua sighed, running a hand through his dark hair. He wore only a pair of trousers and a navy hand-knitted jumper, seemingly impervious to the biting cold. 'All I know is Nan's been agitated ever since that day you three girls came here. She hardly ever reads tea leaves anymore and when I ask her why, she says the same as she told you, that sometimes it's better not to know what's ahead.'

'But why?' Leah persisted. 'What did she see that was so bad?'

'Like she said,' Joshua shrugged. 'Something dark and evil.'

Leah pulled a face. For the first time she wondered if Alice might be right and Pearl's so-called fortune telling was just a carnival side-show designed to con gullible folk out of their hard-earned money.

'You want to keep an eye on your nan,' she said. 'I think she might be having some sort of a breakdown.'

'Nan?' scoffed Joshua. 'She's as fit as a fiddle and as bright as a new pin.' He shook his head. 'There's nothing wrong with her.' He glanced up at the darkening sky. 'There's another storm brewing. Would you like me to see you home?'

Leah shook her head. 'Thanks, Joshua but I'll be fine. There's plenty of daylight left yet. And I want to call in and see Dora. Tell her that all of Strawbridge is abuzz with news of her dad's good fortune.'

'What's that then?' frowned Joshua.

'Oh, you weren't in church this morning, were you? Well, apparently Mr Webb is the sole beneficiary to some chap's estate. Just think,' she grinned. 'Our Dor is going to be rich.'

'That's a turn up for the books,' Joshua grinned back. 'Good luck to her, that's all I can say. There's no one deserves it more than she does.'

Leah was still pondering Pearl's odd behaviour as she made her way past her own cottage to rap on Dora's front door. Hearing no answer, she lifted the latch and peeped inside.

'Hello, Mr Webb, it's just me, Leah.'

'Come on in,' Stephen called cheerfully. Stepping into the warm parlour, Leah was taken aback to see the woman sitting on the chair beside Stephen's bed.

'Oh, hello,' she stammered, realizing from Dora's rather unflattering description, that this must be Mrs Gardener, the lodger. 'I was hoping to see Dora.'

'She's in the kitchen,' Stephen said, just as Dora appeared in the doorway, wiping her hands on her apron.

'Hello, Leah, come on through. The tea's just brewing.'

As soon as Leah stepped foot in the kitchen, Dora grabbed her hand and dragged her out into the back garden.

'What's going on?' Leah asked, wrapping her arms around her body to ward off the cold. A raw wind was blowing off the fields and she was glad she hadn't had time to take her coat off. It was perishingly cold and Dora had nothing but the thin woollen shawl she'd grabbed from the back of a chair as she'd bundled Leah outside. No wonder she was shaking like a leaf.

'I think Mrs Gardener's got her eye on Dad's inheritance,' Dora said, through chattering teeth. 'Nate warned me to keep it quiet where his mother was concerned, but Dad's been shouting it out to all and sundry. He was calling out to folk on their way to church this morning, for goodness' sake. And obviously Mrs Gardener realized something was up last night, what with the lawyer being here and him and Dad drinking and carousing half the night.'

Leah frowned. 'Has she sat with him before?'

'Never. This is the first time.' Dora scowled. 'And I find her sudden interest in him a little concerning.'

'You're right to be suspicious,' Leah agreed. 'From the little Alice has told us, it sounds as though our Mrs Gardener is a piece of work. I'd watch her if I were you, Dor. If she gets her claws into your dad's inheritance, you might never get rid of her.'

'Surely Dad wouldn't be so foolish,' Dora countered. 'I mean, she's not bad looking, but still?'

Leah pulled a face. 'She'd be prettier if she lost a bit of weight, I suppose and . . .well, I can see how your dad might be flattered.'

Dora groaned. 'Oh, Leah, don't say that. I don't think I'd particularly like her for a stepmother.'

'I wouldn't worry about that just yet,' Leah grinned, giving Dora's arm a squeeze. 'Hopefully your dad's got his head screwed on the right way and isn't about to let himself be swayed by a pretty face.' She shivered. 'The tea's probably stewed by now, and you're turning blue, so let's go in before you catch your death.'

That evening Leah wrote again to Harry. Trying not to let her anger, worry and frustration spill onto the page, she kept her words light, telling him about the pantomime and Dora's unexpected news, and the snowstorm. She paused, her pen hovering above the page. The kitchen was warm and cosy but she could hear the wind shrieking under the eaves and howling down the chimney. Rain lashed the windowpane.

With luck by morning the snow would have been washed away, making it possible for her to get to work. Not only could she ill afford to lose a day's wages, the thought of being cooped up at home all day brooding was too much to contemplate.

She finished her letter by asking Harry about his plans for Christmas and, for what it might be worth, asking him to pass her regards on to his parents. Her mother came into the kitchen just as she was licking the envelope, ready for posting during her lunchbreak the following day.

'You ready for your cocoa?' Hannah asked. She was in her nightgown, a plaid shawl draped around her shoulders.

'Yes, please,' Leah replied with a yawn. She stretched her arms above her head, watching her mother moving about the kitchen. 'Mum, do you think Pearl really can see the future?'

Hannah turned, the open tin of cocoa powder in her hand. 'No, I don't,' she said firmly. 'Nearly all of us round here have had our fortunes told by Pearl at one time or another and for every one that appears to come true, there's half a dozen that don't.' She turned back to the stove, and stirred the pan of milk. 'I'd take anything she tells you with a pinch of salt, love.'

'She said she saw something evil.'

'If you listen to Reverend Roberts, the whole business of fortune-telling is evil.' She fetched three mugs from the dresser and set them on the table. 'Whatever she's told you, I wouldn't worry about it. I know you're hurting over your Harry, and I don't know what the lad's playing at, I really don't. I thought he had more gumption than his old man, but it seems I was wrong. I'd give him until Christmas, and if you haven't heard anything by then, well, I reckon you know where you stand.'

Leah sighed. 'You're right, Mum. I was afraid this would happen. That's why I didn't want to get involved in the first place once I knew who he was.' Her voice broke and Hannah put an arm round her.

'Come on, love. You're young. You'll get over him.'

Leah nodded, unconvinced. She fished in her pocket for her handkerchief and blew her nose.

'Let's take our drinks in the other room,' Hannah said, filling the mugs with steaming hot cocoa. 'We can have a quick game of cards before we go up.'

As Leah got up to follow her mother into the parlour, Hannah put down the mugs and gave her a hug. 'You'll be all right, love,' she said, brushing a strand of fair hair from Leah's eyes. 'I know you will.'

CHAPTER TWENTY-ONE

The sky glittered with stars as the congregation spilled out of the church amidst choruses of 'Merry Christmas.'

'Merry Christmas,' Alice said softly, slipping her gloved hand through the crook of Samuel's arm.

'Merry Christmas, my love.'

The midnight air was crisp and cold and the soles of their shoes crunched on the frozen ground. Frost glistened in the pale moonlight as their breath clouded in the frigid air.

Walking ahead were Alice's parents, and her sister, Martha. Violet, who had come to spend Christmas with the family, had volunteered to stay home and mind the younger children. They had been in a heightened state of excitement all evening and it was only when their father had threatened them with the prospect of a lump of coal in their stockings on Christmas morning that they had finally settled down and gone to sleep, well over an hour later than their usual bedtime.

'It's been a pleasant, if exhausting day,' Samuel said with a grin.

'My brothers can be rather boisterous,' Alice agreed wryly. 'It was kind of you to spend so much time playing with them.'

'I enjoyed myself,' Samuel said earnestly. 'They're good boys. Exuberant, but so they should be at that age.'

'They're growing up so fast,' sighed Alice. 'I can't believe Johnny will be starting school after Christmas.'

'I'm glad you're so fond of children,' Samuel teased. 'I'm envisioning a house full of them.'

Alice blushed. 'I would like perhaps three or four,' she replied demurely.

'Oh, Alice,' Samuel said, coming to an abrupt halt. 'There is something I must ask you. Something important.' He took her hand from his arm and gently tugged off her glove. She shivered as the cold air touched her skin. Samuel glanced down the street. Alice followed his gaze. Her mother was laughing at something Martha had said. As if aware of Alice's gaze, Lily glanced back over her shoulder, and stopped walking. Martha and James turned to look. James smiled and took Lily's hand. After a moment, Lily turned away and followed him up the garden path. Martha stared a few seconds longer until a word from her father sent her scuttling indoors.

Alice licked her lips and tried to swallow. She knew Samuel had been to speak to her stepfather the previous week. Her siblings were notoriously bad at keeping secrets and had been giggling about the visit all evening, finally spilling the beans during supper.

Ever since Alice had been waiting with expectation. Both

Leah and Dora were convinced Samuel would propose over Christmas – 'so romantic', Dora had sighed – and it would seem her dear friends were to be correct.

She held her breath. Her heart was beating so loudly she was sure Samuel must be able to hear it.

'Alice,' he said again, his voice rising an octave or two. He coughed and cleared his throat. 'I know we've only been courting for six months but I'm as sure as I've ever been about anything in my life. You are the woman I wish to spend the rest of my life with.' He paused. With his free hand he reached into his pocket and took out a small velvet box. 'Alice, if you can bear to spend your life yoked to a lowly vicar, would you do me the great honour of becoming my wife?'

'Yes,' Alice cried, excitement tingling down her spine as Samuel gave a whoop of delight. Sweeping her into his arms, he kissed her hard on the mouth.

'I hope you like the ring,' he said, a few seconds later, opening the box to reveal a small solitaire diamond. His hands were shaking so much he could hardly steady them enough to slide the ring on to Alice's slender finger. 'I'm afraid it's the best I could afford on my stipend.'

'It's beautiful,' Alice whispered. 'Thank you.'

'Thank you,' Samuel said, kissing her again. 'I was thinking a spring wedding. My ordination is in May, so perhaps April? It's a pretty time of year.' He frowned. 'Would that give you enough time to get your trousseau in order and for your mother to make you a wedding gown?'

'Plenty of time,' Alice laughed. Her stomach flipped pleasantly. She was itching to show off her ring to her friends.

'Shall we go in and tell your parents the good news?' said Samuel, opening the garden gate.

'I'm sure they've already guessed,' smiled Alice. She held up her hand, admiring the way the diamond sparkled in the cold moonlight. 'But my mother will be impatient to see the ring.'

'Then let's not keep her waiting.' Samuel grabbed her hand and together they ran up the frosty path. Martha was watching from the window, lamplight spilling across the glistening lawn from the crack in the curtains.

'They're coming,' Alice heard her shout as the door flew open. Lily stood silhouetted in the doorway, smiling expectantly.

'Samuel has asked me to marry him,' Alice said, feeling suddenly self-conscious.

'Oh, darling, I'm so happy for you,' Lily cried, giving her a hug. 'Welcome to the family, Samuel,' she said, embracing him tearfully.

'Don't keep them standing in the cold, woman!' Alice's stepfather shouted, emerging from the parlour. 'And shut that door, before we all catch our death. Congratulations, my darling.' He held out his arms and Alice fell into them, breathing in his warm, familiar scent of pipe tobacco and the cologne he was so fond of. 'May I wish you every happiness, my dear. You deserve it.' He shook Samuel's hand. 'Congratulations, young man. You've got yourself a fine woman here.'

'Thank you, sir. I promise I shall look after Alice to the best of my ability.'

'Make sure you do,' replied James with mock severity. 'You'll have me to answer to if you don't.'

Lily shut and bolted the door and, as Martha and Violet crowded into the small hallway to congratulate the couple, there came the creak of bedsprings overhead, followed by the sound of running footsteps on the landing punctuated by loud whispering.

'All right,' James called up the stairs. 'You may come down for a moment to congratulate your sister.'

Amid much giggling, Jimmy and Caroline hurried down the stairs, half-carrying a sleepy Jonathan between them. For a moment pandemonium reigned until James said, in a voice loud enough to be heard above the ruckus, 'I think this calls for a glass of sherry,' and ushered everyone into the parlour where a large, decorated Christmas tree stood in pride of place beside a blazing fire.

'May I be bridesmaid?' Caroline asked a few minutes later. She was curled up in front of the roaring fire sipping a glass of warm milk. Johnny had fallen asleep on the hearth rug, his head resting on his sister's lap. Jimmy sat beside her, yawning, but determined not to give in and go to bed until everyone else did.

'I'm sure you can,' Alice smiled. 'And Martha too, if you'd like?'

'Yes, please,' Martha beamed.

'Have you set a date?' Violet asked, her grey eyes shining

with excitement. Despite never having married herself, she loved weddings and had made many a bridal gown over the years.

'We were thinking April,' answered Samuel.

'I suppose you'll want to be married in St John's,' James said. 'But have you thought where you'd like to hold the reception?'

'We haven't really discussed it yet, have we?' Alice replied, looking at Samuel who was perched on the edge of the sofa, sipping his glass of sherry.

'I'd thought we'd be married in St. Luke's,' Samuel frowned, running his fingers round the collar of his shirt, nervously. 'I'm sure Mrs Hurst wouldn't mind putting on a bit of a spread at the vicarage.'

'St. John's here in Hedge End is Alice's parish church,' James reminded Samuel mildly. 'And there will be a sizeable guest list which I doubt the vicarage could accommodate.'

'You've got plenty of time,' Lily interjected quickly as Samuel cleared his throat ready to object. She knew Samuel had no family and few friends, but she was also aware how much her husband had been looking forward to giving Alice a good wedding. 'You don't need to decide just yet.'

'We will have a lot to plan in the coming weeks,' agreed Alice, stifling a yawn. 'Sorry,' she apologized. 'I'm so tired all of a sudden.'

'I'm not surprised,' exclaimed Lily, throwing up her hands. 'It's gone one o'clock. Jimmy, Caroline, back to bed at once. James, would you carry Johnny up, please?' She turned to

Samuel. 'Are you sure I can't persuade you to spend the night? It would be no trouble to make a bed up for you down here.'

'Thank you, Mrs Russell, but I must get back. I shall need to be up early to prepare my sermon for tomorrow's service. It's downhill all the way and the moon is bright tonight.'

'But we shall see you for Christmas dinner tomorrow?'

'I wouldn't miss it for the world,' he grinned.

While Lily and Violet carried the dirty glasses to the kitchen, Alice walked Samuel to the door.

'It's too cold to linger,' he said, as he wound his thick scarf around his neck. 'So I shall say goodnight.' He kissed her tenderly. 'My beautiful fiancée,' he smiled. 'I'll see you tomorrow. We shall be quite a crowd round the dinner table.'

'The more the merrier,' smiled Alice. They exchanged one last kiss before Samuel got on his bicycle and peddled off down the street.

CHAPTER TWENTY-TWO

Waking that morning to the sound of church bells, Leah rose from her bed with a heavy heart.

'Merry Christmas, Leah,' Daisy sang, bounding out of bed and dancing out onto the landing. 'Merry Christmas, Mum,' she called down the stairs.

With still no news from Harry, she felt hollow inside and envied her sister's childlike exuberance. Pulling on her stockings, she took a deep breath and resolved to put her own misery aside and make an effort to be cheerful. She mustn't let her own unhappiness spoil the day for everyone else.

She had little appetite but forced down her breakfast, plastering a smile on her face as they exchanged their modest gifts, before hurrying to wash up and get ready for the morning service.

'It looks lovely,' whispered Daisy as they made their way down the aisle twenty minutes later. The altar was bedecked with holly branches. Fat, white candles burned on every available surface, their tiny flames casting flickering shadows up the grey stone walls. Pale, wintery sunlight shone through the stained-glass windows, sending rainbows of light dancing on the worn flagstones.

Sliding into the pew beside her sister, Leah picked up her hymn book and paged through it looking for the first hymn. It was 'Hark the Herald Angels', a particular favourite of Reverend Aldridge for, after all, Charles Wesley had written it to be sung on Christmas morning. She looked up as someone slid into the pew beside her.

'Merry Christmas, Dor,' she smiled, pleased to see her friend.

'Merry Christmas, Leah, Daisy.' Dora said. Leaning forward to look round Leah, she whispered, 'Merry Christmas, Aunty Hannah.'

'And to you, my love,' Hannah whispered in reply. 'How's your dad this morning?'

'He's in fine spirits,' Dora replied, somewhat dubiously. 'Mrs Gardener is sitting with him. As she has every day for the past week and a half,' she added to Leah in an undertone.

'Are they still as thick as thieves?' Leah asked as Dora rolled her eyes.

'I don't know what goes on when I'm at work, but she seems to be constantly at his side. I shouldn't grumble, I suppose,' Dora sighed. 'He's certainly in a better humour.' She glanced about her before adding, 'Alice would have a fit if she heard some of the things she tells Dad about her mum. I told him he's not to encourage her. Alice is our friend and what went on in the past is none of our concern. I said as much to him but, as far as he's concerned, Mrs Gardener is the bee's knees and he won't hear a word said against her.'

'It's got to be the money she's interested in, surely?' Leah said.

'Of course, it is,' Dora replied with a dismissive wave of her hand. 'She barely acknowledged him before Mr Lyle's visit. Nate said I mustn't trust her. That says something, doesn't it? What sort of person must you be for your own son not to trust you?'

'What are you going to do?' asked Leah, with a frown.

'What can I do except hope Dad comes to his senses before it's too late?'

'Shush now, here comes Nate,' Leah said. Dora nodded her understanding and, glancing over her shoulder, smiled at Nate as he made his way down the aisle.

'I just have a horrible feeling in my tummy about all this,' Dora murmured, making Leah recall to mind Pearl's warning that something dark and evil was about to unfold. 'I'm starting to wish I'd never heard of Benjamin Baker and his wretched money,' she whispered, swiftly replacing her frown with a smile as Nate slipped quietly into the pew beside her.

'Good morning, good morning,' Reverend Aldridge intoned from the pulpit, as he beamed down at his congregation. 'Merry Christmas to you all and welcome on this most holy of days. Before we sing our opening carol, I'd like to make an announcement. It is my happy pleasure to announce that our dear curate ... Stand up, Reverend, don't be shy.' There was a ripple of laughter amidst the rustling as

Samuel got to his feet. His flowing clerical robes did nothing to detract from his handsome features as he surveyed the congregation with a bashful smile.

'Our dear curate,' continued Walter Aldridge, 'has, on this very special morning, become betrothed to our lovely parish clerk, Miss Alice Russell.' He paused to let the murmurs die down. Dora nudged Leah in the ribs, her knowing look saying, 'I told you so.'

Leah fixed her gaze at the red poinsettias that adorned the base of the pulpit, and stopped listening to the vicar's effusive words of congratulations. She'd been expecting the news and she was happy for her friends. She really was. But she couldn't help feeling relieved that Alice wasn't in church that morning as she knew she'd find it hard to muster any elation for her friend while her own heartache was still so raw. Perhaps in a day or two, her words of congratulations might sound more convincing.

'Miss Russell is spending the day with her family today and so cannot be with us,' she heard the Reverend say. 'But I'm sure you'll all join me in a prayer of blessing over our happy couple. Shall we bow our heads?'

It was snowing again by the time they emerged from the church. Walking behind Hannah and Daisy, Leah listened idly to Dora and Nate's friendly banter. He seemed to be genuinely interested in what she had to say, inclining his head towards her whenever she opened her mouth to speak. *Was he was just being kind?* Leah mused. Much as she loved

Dora, her friend wasn't blessed with the sort of looks that would usually attract a man as devastatingly handsome as Nate Gardener. For Dora's sake, she hoped he had seen beyond her rather plain features to the warm-hearted girl within. She was grateful she was still so very much in love with Harry, or she might well have been attracted to Nate herself.

'Tell your dad we'll be around in about fifteen minutes,' Hannah told Dora as they came to a standstill outside the cottages. Mathew Turner was helping Beatrice up into a pony-drawn cart. Her veil had already frosted over and she used a thickly-gloved hand to brush snow from her face. Samuel stood beside the pony, waiting his turn to clamber aboard. Alice's grandparents were giving him a ride to her parents' home. He stamped his feet, blowing on his cold hands, a shapeless lump in his thick coat. The snow was falling heavily now, drifting against the cottage walls and all but obliterating the fields from view.

'Merry Christmas,' Mathew Turner called, his voice muffled by his thick scarf, as he took his place beside his wife. Samuel clambered up beside him and Mathew shook the reins, urging the sturdy pony forwards. The cart wheels churned on the slippery ground and the pony's hooves threw up clumps of freshly fallen snow in its wake.

'Godspeed,' Hannah called after them, fumbling with the latch.

'It'll be a blizzard before long,' Nate said, tugging his cap over his eyes as the swirling flakes stung his cheeks. 'Good job you don't have far to come for your dinner,' he joked to Hannah.

'I could do with a strong pair of hands to help carry some chairs next door,' she said, standing aside to let Leah and Daisy duck inside where they stamped their feet on the mat and shed their coats, before hurrying through to the kitchen.

'Sure, Mrs Hopwood,' Nate nodded, rubbing his frozen hands. 'Anything I can do.'

While Nate ferried the necessary items from Hannah's cottage to Dora's, Leah, Daisy and Hannah busied themselves preparing the food. The fat goose had been in the oven since early morning and the aroma of roasted meat permeated every nook and cranny of the cottage. Leah covered the roast potatoes, crisp and golden and cooked in goose fat, with a cloth, and packed them in the basket along with the vegetables and the Christmas pudding. Dora would be providing the custard and the brandy sauce. Hannah fetched the iced Christmas cake from the pantry along with a tin of mince pies.

'Right, I think that's everything,' she said, with a quick glance round the kitchen.

With Nate bearing the golden-brown goose on a platter, they trooped next door where Dora was putting the finishing touches to the table. With Nate's help they'd dragged the kitchen table into the parlour. With the two tables pushed together and the extra chairs, there was ample room for everyone around the table. Leah's eyes pricked with tears to see the effort her friend had made in trying to bring a bit of

Christmas cheer to the dingy little cottage. Paperchains were suspended between the beams and draped around a small fir tree which stood in a pot on the hearth.

'Nate fetched it for me,' she smiled, noticing Leah looking at it. 'Nate helped me make the paperchains, too. And fetched the holly.' She nodded to the wreath hanging on the wall, smiling at the memory of cosy evenings with the two of them hunched over the kitchen table.

'That's my boy,' Mrs Gardener crowed. She was balanced on a stool beside Stephen's bed. Her ruby-red dress was just that little bit too tight, the lace collar biting uncomfortably into her double chin. Despite her apparent discomfort, she appeared in a jolly mood, and seemed perfectly content to sit back and watch everyone else do the work.

'I'm a bit under the weather today,' she excused herself, consoling herself that she wasn't actually lying. The quantities of brandy she and Stephen had consumed the previous evening had resulted in a raging headache.

'You just sit and chat to Stephen,' said Hannah affably, as she unpacked the basket, setting out the platters of food. 'The girls and I will manage.'

Leah and Dora exchanged glances. The way Stephen was looking at Mrs Gardener like an adoring puppy hadn't gone unnoticed by any of them. Daisy caught Leah's eye and pulled a face. Leah scowled, and rolled her eyes at her friend.

'Like they say,' she whispered, following Dora into the kitchen to fetch a spoon for the vegetables. 'There was no fool like an old fool.'

214

'That's true,' Dora sighed, 'And dad is definitely that, if he thinks for one minute she cares a jot about him.'

'Is everything ready?' Stephen called from the front room. 'I'm starving.'

The meal passed pleasantly enough. Nate was good company and kept the conversation going. Propped up in bed, eating from a tray on his lap, Stephen was as cheerful and animated as any of them had ever seen him.

'Though it pains me to say it, Mrs Gardener does seems to be doing your dad good,' Leah whispered to Dora a while later as they carried the dirty plates in the scullery. 'He's almost like he was before he got ill.'

'That's what I'm afraid of,' Dora said, fetching the plum pudding from the pantry and handing Leah the jug of custard and the dish of brandy butter. 'What will he be like when it all ends?' She sighed. 'And it will end, I know it will. It's just a case of how long she can keep up the act. Nate told me this was how she caught his stepfather. Of course, she was younger then, and thinner.' She scowled. 'She probably sees Dad as an easy target because he's a cripple.'

Leah laid a comforting hand on Dora's quivering shoulder. 'Nate seems to like you,' she said, in an attempt to make Dora feel better.

'He's just being kind,' Dora said, dismissively. She poured a splash of brandy over the pudding and struck a match, the air immediately filled with its warm, comforting aroma.

'Lights,' she called, more cheerfully than she felt. Someone extinguished the lamp and she carried the flaming pudding into the front room to cheers and whistles of appreciation.

'Merry Christmas,' shouted Stephen, holding his glass aloft. 'This is one of the nicest Christmases we've had in a long while,' he announced, with a meaningful glance across at Barbie-Jean.

'Here's to many more,' she smiled back at him, batting her eyelashes coquettishly.

Around the table they raised their glasses, and tucked into the spicy, fruit pudding, as the wind howled outside. Snow was falling so thick and fast it was impossible to see anything out of the window except the raging blizzard. Leah shivered, glad that they were warm and safe indoors.

'I feel sorry for anyone out in that storm,' she said, as a particularly violent gust of wind rattled the roof tiles.

'It does sound dreadful,' her mother agreed. 'I hope Bea got to her daughter's in time. It wouldn't do to be caught out in this.'

It was late afternoon by the time the storm abated. Mrs Gardener was snoring loudly, slumped on the sagging sofa, her mouth hanging open unattractively. Stephen was on his third sherry, or was it his fourth? Dora had lost count. His cheeks glowed from the effects of the alcohol and the warmth of the fire. She reached down and grabbed the handle of the shovel, lifting it from the coals, and slid the roasted chestnuts onto a plate, breathing in their smoky aroma.

'I think I'll put the kettle on and make a start on the

supper,' Hannah said, rousing herself from her post-dinner stupor and peering out of the window. By the thin light of the moon, she could see that the wind had blown the snow into deep drifts on either side of the lane, leaving the lane itself relatively clear. Unsurprisingly, there wasn't a soul about. The moon was surrounded by a ghostly halo, a sure sign that more snow was on the way. She drew the curtains against the cold night, and hurried into the kitchen. Dora set the plate of chestnuts on the table and followed Hannah to the kitchen.

'I suppose we'd better help,' Daisy said, laying aside the copy of Jane Austen's *Sense and Sensibility* she'd received for Christmas and getting up. 'Come on, Leah,' she said shooting her sister a look over her shoulder. 'Don't be lazy.'

Leah didn't move. She knew she really should go and help, but she was so warm and comfortable on the sofa. A sort of lethargy had settled over her and she couldn't muster the energy required to get up.

'Do you fancy a game of Rummy, Mr Webb?' said Nate, picking up the deck of cards and shuffling them with the expert hand of someone who played often.

'Why not?' Stephen grinned. 'Pull up a chair, lad. Leah, will you play?'

Leah shook her head. She didn't have the energy for cards, either. She didn't know quite what ailed her. Her eyes felt hot, as if she were coming down with a fever, but she didn't feel ill, apart from the strange queasiness in her stomach. Perhaps she'd eaten too much?

She closed her eyes, letting the various sounds wash over her, the clatter of crockery and cutlery in the kitchen, the rise and fall of Nate and Mr Webb's voices, the splash of a glass being refilled, the hammering on the door . . .

Her eyes shot open. She looked at the door. Stephen and Nate both turned in surprise. The banging came again. Mrs Gardener woke with a snort.

'What's happening?' she squeaked, squinting in the lamplight.

'Who on earth . . . ?' Hannah exclaimed, appearing in the kitchen doorway, Dora and Daisy peering around her.

'Don't just sit there, Leah,' she said in exasperation. 'Open it.'

Stirred into action, Leah hurried to lift the latch. The door flew back, almost knocking her off her feet. For a moment she just stared at the shapeless lump weaving unsteadily on the doorstep. All she could see of the ice-encrusted figure was the eyes. They seemed to burn into her soul. She shrieked.

'Harry!' He lurched forward and would have crashed to the floor had Leah not caught him. Nate and Hannah hurried over to help. Each taking an arm, they helped him to the sofa while Leah quickly shut the door. Kneeling at his feet, she caught his gloved hand in hers.

'I can't believe you're here,' she murmured. 'Why didn't you tell me you were coming?'

Harry tried to speak, but seemed unable to summon the strength.

'Get his shoes and stockings off, Daisy,' Hannah ordered, unwinding Harry's frozen scarf. 'Nate, take his coat off. Dora, make some ginger tea.'

'Who is this?' Mrs Gardener demanded in a querulous voice. 'What's he doing here?'

'He's a friend of ours,' Dora replied, hurrying to the kitchen. She cast a worried look over her shoulder and frowned. Poor Harry. What on earth possessed him to be out and about in this weather. The poor man looked frozen stiff.

Hannah was rubbing Harry's bare feet. Now that he was inside, close to the fire, he began to shiver violently.

'Dora, where's that tea?' Hannah called, her words laced with concern.

'Coming.' Dora emerged from the kitchen with a steaming mug. The strong aroma of ginger filled the air. 'I've put plenty of sugar in for shock,' she said, ignoring her father's frown. He'd just have to go without sugar in his tea for a few days. Harry's need was greater.

'His feet aren't frostbitten,' Nate said, 'and his cheeks are red, not bloodless.' He grinned at Harry. 'I reckon you'll be all right once you've thawed out, mate. Nate Gardener,' he introduced himself. Harry nodded and tried to speak. His teeth were chattering so hard no one could make out what he said. He tried to raise his hand but it was too much effort and he let it fall back at his side.

'This is Harry Whitworth,' Dora did the introductions. She glanced at Leah. She was sitting beside Harry, her face pale, her hands clenched, a puzzled frown creasing her brow.

So many questions were racing around her head. She hadn't heard from Harry in almost two months.

'What are you doing here?' It was only when all eyes turned towards her that she realized she'd said the words out loud.

Harry's bloodless lips moved. The words were so faint, Leah had to lean forward to hear them.

'I had to come.'

CHAPTER TWENTY-THREE

'You walked? All the way from Southampton in this storm?' Hannah threw up her hands in horror. 'You're lucky you didn't end up frozen to death in a ditch,' she scolded.

Harry managed a weak smile. He was sitting close to the fire in the Webbs' parlour, his hands wrapped around the mug of hot, sweet ginger tea. The colour was slowly returning to his hands and feet and he had stopped shivering, apart from an occasional sudden, violent shudder.

'The train stopped running because of the snow,' Harry explained. His voice was rough, his words slightly slurred. 'Most of the passengers planned to spend the night in a hotel but,' he fixed his gaze on Leah and reached for her hand. 'I couldn't wait. I had to come. I had to know why you stopped answering my letters?'

Leah's mouth fell open and she stared at him in stunned surprise. 'What?' She blinked, confused. 'I've been writing every week, even though you never replied.'

'What do you mean?' Harry frowned. 'I've sent loads of

letters. I . . .' His words trailed away as realization dawned. His expression clouded. 'My mother,' he said, tightly. 'I should have suspected something was up when she tried to prevent me coming here.'

'Well,' Hannah said, breaking the silence that had fallen over the room. 'You must be hungry, Harry? Dora, Daisy, you can help me get some supper together. Nate, would you put some more coal on the fire.' She didn't bother to ask Mrs Gardener for help, knowing the woman was unlikely to comply. According to Dora, all she did all day was sit and make cow's eyes at Stephen. Hannah sighed as she fetched the remains of the Christmas goose from the pantry. There was no doubt the woman's friendship with Stephen allowed Dora more freedom, but Hannah couldn't help but wonder at her motives. She was inclined to agree with Dora, that it was Stephen's impending inheritance that was the attraction, rather than the man himself.

She wondered what Nate made of his mother's behaviour. He was a quiet lad, for all his size and maturity, and said little but, on occasion throughout the day, she'd caught the odd pursing of his lips, and the narrowing of his eyes, as he watched her with Stephen.

Nate came into the kitchen now, his dark eyes immediately seeking out Dora who was buttering thick slices of homemade bread. It was no secret that with the arrival of Nate and his mother, the Webbs' fortunes had improved significantly. Nate earned decent money and he often slipped Dora a little something extra to spend on herself, like the blue ribbon she wore in her hair. Dora looked up and Hannah caught the smile that passed between them. It was clear Dora was smitten with the lad. And no wonder. He was a good-looking boy. She just hoped he wouldn't play fast and loose with Dora's emotions. She didn't deserve to have her heart broken.

Wiping her greasy fingers on her apron, her thoughts turned to her own daughter. That was a turn-up for the books, Harry arriving unexpectedly, and on Christmas Day to boot. Hannah smiled. She'd have paid good money to see Frances Whitworth's face when her son had told her he was coming to see Leah. She wondered what Isaac had made of the fact his son would rather spend the day travelling rather than indulging in his family's lavish celebrations. Her first impression of the boy was certainly been proved correct. Harry was made of sterner stuff than his dad.

'I've made a bed for you beside the range,' Hannah said. They had left the Webbs shortly after six o'clock and now it was almost nine. 'I've put the warming pan under the covers.'

'Thank you, Mrs Hopwood.' Harry gave Hannah a grateful smile.

'Yes, thanks, Mum.' Sitting beside Harry on the sofa, Leah smiled at her mother. Ever since Harry had arrived, she'd felt as though she was walking on air. *Pearl and her silly predictions could go jump,* she thought, joyfully, rolling her eyes. Harry loved her. He'd said as much and he'd certainly proved it by coming all this way in such a terrible storm, and on Christmas Day to boot.

Hannah surveyed the warm parlour. 'Right, well, I'm off to bed,' she said.

'I won't be long behind you, Mum,' promised Leah. Daisy had gone up half an hour earlier.

'All right,' Hannah nodded. 'Though I'm sure you've got lots to talk about. Goodnight, then.'

'Goodnight, Mum. Sleep well.'

'Goodnight, Mrs Hopwood. And thanks again for everything.'

'Don't mention it.' Hannah waved his gratitude aside and went upstairs.

'I'm so glad you're here,' Leah said softly as the sound of Hannah's footsteps receded.

'I couldn't bear to be away from you another minute,' Harry said, staring into the glowing embers. 'I'm so angry with my mother. There's no other explanation as to why our letters to each other have gone astray. The odd one or two, perhaps, but all of them?' He made a face. He shook his head in disgust. 'Stupidly, I left them on the hall table, ready for the maid to post. I never thought to ask the girl whether she'd actually posted them. Mother must have destroyed them. And likewise, she must have kept your letters from me.' His voice shook with anger.

'Shush,' soothed Leah. 'It doesn't matter now. You're here.' She leaned her head against his shoulder. Harry squeezed her fingers. With his free hand he took something from his trouser pocket.

'This was my grandmother's,' he said, holding out his

hand. On the flat of his palm was a ring. It was white gold and set with a small diamond and surrounded by tiny emeralds.

'It's beautiful,' Leah said with a quick intake of breath.

'She gave it to me a few weeks before she died and told me it was a gift from her to my future wife.' He faced Leah, his eyes bright in the flickering lamplight. 'I want you to have it, Leah. I want you to say you'll be my wife.'

Leah swallowed. Her heart was beating so fast. She nodded, unable to speak.

'I know it's not a proper engagement ring but I think money's going to be a bit tight from now on so,' Harry said, with a rueful shrug.

'I don't need a proper engagement ring,' Leah said, breathlessly. 'It's perfect.' She picked it up, admiring the way the stones caught the light, and slipped it on to her finger. It was a perfect fit.

'You'd have liked my grandmother,' Harry said, with a grin. Leah held her hand up to the light, loving the feel of the cool metal against ger skin.

'I'm sure I would,' Leah replied, while thinking that if his grandmother was anything like his mother, it was doubtful.

'So, do I take it from your delight with the ring that you're consenting to marry me?' Harry asked, one eyebrow raised quizzically.

Leah laughed. 'Of course, I will marry you,' she said, giving him a quick kiss on the cheek. 'Thank you.'

'Can't you thank me better than that?' teased Harry, pulling her against him. Their kiss was long and passionate and they were both flushed and breathing hard when they drew apart.

'We can't marry without my father's permission until I'm twenty-one,' Harry said, clearing his throat, as he made an obvious effort to compose himself.

'That's only three years,' Leah replied. 'It will pass in no time and perhaps, by then, your parents might have come round to the idea.'

'I doubt it,' Harry snorted. 'Anyway, I'm done with all that. I'm going to see about taking a room at the Glyn Arms tomorrow. Perhaps Reuben will give me a job.' He grinned. 'My father's decision to put me to work in the fields has actually done me a favour. I'm quite used to manual labour. So, even if he makes good on his threat to disinherit me, I'll be all right.'

Leah flung her arms around his neck, wondering how she could ever have believed Harry didn't care. He was prepared to give up everything for her. It was an exhilarating thought.

The clock was striking ten by the time she finally made her way up to bed. Snores drifted from Hannah's room but Daisy stirred when Leah climbed beneath her covers.

'Well?' she asked, sleepily. 'Everything all right?'

'We're engaged,' Leah whispered, excitedly.

'What?' Wide awake now, Daisy sat up. 'Engaged? Never?'

'It's true,' Leah laughed softly. 'We're going to be married.'

'That's so romantic,' Daisy breathed. 'Oh, I'm never going to get back to sleep now.'

'I certainly don't think I'll be getting much sleep,' Leah replied. 'I'm far too excited.'

Harry's mother wasn't expecting to get much sleep that night, either. Her reflection stared back at her from the dressing table mirror. Her eyes glittered and her cheeks were red as she fingered the string of freshwater pearls around her throat.

'I have never been so humiliated in my life,' she said, as Isaac emerged from his dressing room. 'I invited the Beaumont-Smythes to luncheon with the express intention of introducing Henry to their daughter. Poor Araminta. She looked as mortified as I felt.'

'Darling, I'm sure Araminta will get over it,' Isaac said, moving behind her to unclasp her necklace. 'She seemed perfectly agreeable over dinner.'

'That's because she has a sense of propriety,' Frances seethed. 'Unlike our son.' She snatched the string of pearls from her husband's hand and dropped them in a little dish along with her pearl earrings.

She closed her eyes, massaging her forehead with her fingertips where the beginnings of a headache throbbed. Try as she might, she couldn't banish the memory from earlier.

She'd been welcoming the Beaumont-Smythes who had arrived only moments before. They'd been in the hall, admiring the large, tastefully decorated Christmas tree, and divesting themselves of their wraps when Henry came down the stairs, carrying a small valise.

'Henry?' Frances had frowned at her son.

'Merry Christmas, everyone,' Harry had said, politely. 'I'm sorry I shan't be joining you for dinner, but I have a previous engagement. I hope you all have a jolly time.'

'Henry, may I have a word?' Frances's tone was arctic. 'Mrs Peat,' she nodded to the housekeeper who was relieving the guests of their coats. 'Show the Beaumont-Smythes into the drawing room and ask Mr Whitworth to join me in the dining room, please.'

As the housekeeper had done as she was bid, Frances ushered her son into the dining room. The table was immaculate. A fire burned cheerfully in the grate. Candles flickered on every surface. The holly centrepiece, from Harrods' florist department, had been hand delivered late the previous night. The cut glass crystal goblets sparkled and the silver cutlery gleamed against the ruby red napkins that were a startling contrast to the starched white tablecloth.

'What are you doing?' she hissed, careful to keep her voice low so as not to be overheard.

'I'm going to Strawbridge,' Harry said firmly.

'It's Christmas Day!' Frances had stared at him, flabbergasted.

'That's why I'm going. I need to see Leah. I'm going out of mind with worry. I haven't heard from her in weeks.'

'Forget her, Henry,' she snapped, guilt causing her to speak sharper than she intended. 'She's obviously moved on. You need to do the same. Now, come on. The Beaumont-Smythes are keen to introduce you to their daughter. She's a lovely girl.'

'I'm sure she is, Mother,' Harry had said calmly. 'But I'm afraid I have a train to catch.' He picked up his valise and made to leave the room but his way was blocked by his father.

'What's going on?' Isaac had looked from his son to his wife. 'Frances?'

'Henry says he's leaving for Strawbridge,' Frances said, a note of hysteria creeping into her voice. 'You have to stop him.'

'Please don't forbid me, Father,' Harry said, looking Isaac in the eyes. 'I am determined to go.'

'Let him go,' Isaac told his wife. 'If that's what he wants.' He pursed his lips. 'Where will you stay?'

'He's not staying at Streawberige House,' Frances said frostily. 'Mrs Lamb is away visiting her brother over Christmas. There will be no one to attend you.'

'I plan to take a room at the Glyn Arms,' Harry said.

'You're staying in a public house!' Frances shrieked, forgetting, for a moment, the guests waiting in the drawing room. 'You can't stay there,' she insisted, more quietly.

Drawing himself to his full height, Harry looked his father straight in the eye. 'Father, my train leaves at five minutes past twelve. If I don't leave now, I shall not make it.' For a moment, it seemed Isaac was going to object but then, with a sigh, he stepped out of the way.

'Thank you, Father,' Harry said. 'Merry Christmas.' He thrust out his hand which, after a brief hesitation, Isaac took. But when he tried to kiss his mother goodbye, she turned her face away angrily. Harry looked at her sadly for a moment, before walking out the door.

Frances kept her gaze fixed on the beautifully arranged table settings, her fingers gripping the back of one of the chairs so tightly her knuckles whitened. She stayed that way until the front door banged shut. She felt Isaac's hand on her back, and tensed, her anger at Henry now directed towards his father.

'You should have made him stay,' she spat.

'Pull yourself together, Frances,' Isaac said, coolly. 'Our guests are waiting.'

Now, she opened her eyes to see Isaac watching her in the mirror.

'I blame you,' she said, her expression sullen. 'If you hadn't insisted Henry spend his summer working in the fields like a common labourer, he would never have met that wretched girl.' Her bottom lip trembled. 'Oh, Isaac, what if he never comes to his senses?' She turned her head, reaching for his hand. 'What if we've lost our son?'

'Give it time, my darling,' Isaac said, matter-of-factly. 'A couple of nights at the Glyn Arms and he'll soon be home with his tail between his legs. And anyway, who's to say that Hopwood girl wants to see him? He hasn't heard from her in weeks. Likely he'll get all the way there and realize he's on a fool's errand.'

'She did write,' Frances said softly.

'Sorry, darling. I didn't catch that.'

'She did write. Every few days, for weeks. I burned her letters, and the letters Henry wrote to her.'

'What?' Isaac's expression in the mirror was of puzzlement. 'But why?'

'Why do you think?' his wife snapped crossly. 'I hoped that if each of them assumed the other had stopped writing, the whole silly romance would fizzle out.' She snatched up her hairbrush and began to brush her hair.

'And what do you think will be the outcome when they discover that neither one of them ceased writing and that someone – and I'm sure it won't take Henry long to work out it must be either you or I – has been meddling in their affairs?'

Frances shrugged. Her cheeks were pale but for two bright spots of pink.

'Henry will never trust us again, Frances,' Isaac said, shaking his head sadly. 'Well, my dear. I'm afraid your little plan has backfired. He'll only be more determined to have this girl now.'

'He won't be of legal age for another three years,' Frances blurted out. 'He's bound to have come to his senses by then' She knew she was clutching at straws but she had to cling to something. He was her only son, her only child. She would die without him.

'There's always Gretna Green,' Isaac reminded her drily, getting in to bed. Frances swallowed. Her throat felt dry and her head was really pounding now.

'Would you mind awfully if you slept in your dressing room tonight, Isaac?' she said coldly. 'I've got a migraine coming on and I'll need absolute silence.'

She watched in the mirror as Isaac threw back the covers and pulled on his gown.

'Oh, and please ring down for Mrs Peat. I'll need some warm milk, or I'll never get to sleep.'

'Anything else?' Isaac glared at her reflection.

Yes, screamed a voice in her head. *You can get me back my son.*

Instead, she just shook her head.

'No, that's all,' she said quietly.

CHAPTER TWENTY-FOUR

'Dora, let me carry that.'

Dora put her basket down while she waited for Nate to catch up with her. She massaged her aching shoulder.

'Have you carried this all the way from Botley?' he asked, slightly out of breath after his brisk walk home from work.

Dora nodded. 'It's not that far.'

'Give me your list next time,' he said, 'I'll pick up whatever you need.' He frowned. 'Why aren't you at work?'

'The owner's mother-in-law died this morning so they closed the factory for half a day as a sign of respect,' she explained, burying her chin in the folds of her woollen scarf. It was bitterly cold. January had brought some of the worst weather seen for decades. Blizzards had raged on and off for days and, for almost a week, Strawbridge had been cut off from the outside world. It had been so cold in the cottage that ice had formed on the inside of the windowpane. Dora, Leah and Daisy had both been docked five days' wages, money they could ill afford to lose. Thankfully Dora had stocked up on coal and other basic necessities before the bad weather hit but she knew some families in the hamlet had had to resort to burning their furniture in order to keep warm.

She glanced up at the darkening sky. The worst of the weather seemed to be behind them, but it was still only January and spring seemed a long way off.

'How was your day?' Dora asked, breaking the companionable silence. Over the past months, Nate had become a good friend. With his mother and her father so enamoured with each other to the exclusion of their children, the two of them spent a lot of time on each other's company. Unable to bear his mother's simpering over Stephen, Nate spent much of his evenings in the kitchen, helping Dora with the chores.

We're like a married couple, Dora often mused as Nate dried the dishes while she washed up. The thought gave her a warm feeling in her chest. Much as she enjoyed Nate's company, she wasn't fool enough to believe that what he felt for her was anything other than friendship. And she was determined to keep her own feelings firmly under wraps. She didn't want to spoil what they had by letting him see how much she liked him.

'Not too bad,' he said, replying to her question. 'We had a new girl start today, in the office.'

'Oh,' Dora said, surprised at the twinge of jealousy in the pit of her stomach. 'What's she like?'

'She seems nice.' Nate shrugged. 'I only met her briefly. She's been to one of those new secretarial schools,' he added with admiration. Dora looked away. Nate was clearly impressed with this girl. She shivered as a gust of wind swept down the lane, rattling the twigs on the bare hedgerows.

'This wind goes right through you,' she complained.

'What my stepfather used to call a lazy wind,' Nate said.

'What was he like?' Dora had often wondered what sort of man would take on a woman like Nate's mother. One as besotted as her father, she answered herself sourly.

Nate smiled. 'He was a decent man. Too good for the likes of my mother. Not that I'm sorry she married him. My life before that was pretty grim. We lived in the basement of an old tenement house in Poplar. There was no heating and it never got any natural light so it was dank and damp all year round. I remember being cold just about all the time.' He paused, his eyes clouding at the memory. 'Young as I was,' he said with a slight bitter edge to his voice. 'I remember the men. There was a succession of them. One or two of them were all right, but most treated me with indifference.

'Mum worked nights in a pub, that's how she met them. The woman upstairs would pop down and check on me once or twice but for the most part I was left to fend for myself. I was about five, when she met my stepfather. He was comfortably well off. A widower, and lonely, which is probably what drew him to my mother in the first place. They married quite quickly, something I think my stepfather soon regretted but, no matter how bad things were between him and my mother, he always treated me well.'

'He sounds like a decent chap.'

'He was,' Nate agreed. 'One of the best.'

A shiver ran down Dora's spine but it wasn't from the bitter wind. Nate's story had merely served to confirm her suspicions that Barbie-Jean was only after her father's inheritance, and had no real feelings for him at all. And it wasn't like she could even discuss the matter with her father. The woman stuck to his side like a limpet. The only chance she might get was once Mrs Gardener had gone up to bed. Perhaps tonight, she resolved. She'd try to get her father to see sense. Please God, she had to succeed. The thought of the woman for a stepmother was enough to turn her stomach.

'About time,' Barbie-Jean said in her irritatingly high-pitched tone as Dora and Nate blew through the door. 'I'm parched. Put the kettle on, will you, Dora?'

'I'm sure you could have managed to make a pot of tea, Mum,' Nate said with disgust as he carried the basket into the other room. 'Dora isn't your slave.'

'No one's treating Dora like a slave,' Stephen said placatingly. 'Are we, love?' He looked at Dora for confirmation. Dora shook her head as she took off her coat.

'The terms of our tenancy include meals. That includes cups of tea.' Barbie-Jean smiled lazily.

'I'm sure you're right, my dear,' Stephen agreed, looking at the woman with such adoration, Dora could feel the bile rising in her throat. 'Now don't fret. My Dora knows her duty, don't you, love?'

Divesting herself of her scarf, hat and gloves, Dora escaped to the kitchen without answering. She found Nate unpacking the shopping. He raised his eyebrows, and she couldn't help smiling. Life always seemed that bit more bearable when Nate was about.

'Put the kettle on,' he whispered. 'I'll start peeling the potatoes for supper.'

'That's women's work,' Dora chided him, filling the big black kettle. 'How did you get to be so domesticated, anyway?' She struck a match and lit the hob. A gust of wind rattled the window frame. Only one of the chickens had ventured from the henhouse to scratch fruitlessly at the frozen earth, the wind ruffling its feathers.

'My stepfather worked long hours,' he said, his voice low. 'And Mum has never been very good with the whole childrearing thing. I was left to my own devices a lot of the time, so I hung around the kitchen getting under Mrs Meadow's feet. I think she felt sorry for me but she let me help with simple domestic chores and she taught me to cook. It was our secret and we had a good laugh, the two of us, when my stepfather complimented Mrs Meadows, or my mother, on a well-cooked meal, when all along I was the one who'd cooked it.'

'Why didn't you ever tell him it was you?' smiled Dora.

Nate shrugged. 'I think the secrecy made it all the more fun. It all came to an end when I went away to school.'

'You certainly haven't lost your skills,' Dora said, watching the way he peeled the potato. 'Your housekeeper taught you well.'

Their easy banter was interrupted by Barbie-Jean's screech. 'Is that tea ready yet?'

'The water's just coming to the boil,' Dora called back, grabbing a tea towel and lifting the steaming kettle from the hob. *Lazy cow*, she thought, as she left the tea to brew and busied herself fetching mugs from the dresser. Mrs Gardener never lifted a finger round the house, preferring to let Dora and Nate run around after her like a pair of skivvies. She even expected Dora to make her bed, though most days it remained unmade as she only surfaced long after Dora had left for work.

For the rest of the afternoon and early evening, Dora had been pondering how to get her father alone long enough to broach the subject of his relationship with Nate's mother. Her opportunity came when, just as the clock struck nine, the woman heaved herself out of her chair and, bidding them all a goodnight, lumbered up the stairs to bed.

Nate had already settled down for the night in front of the range. Dora could hear his steady breathing. She, too, would usually have been in bed long before now, but she hadn't wanted to miss the chance to talk to her father.

She laid aside the book she had only been pretending to read. It was a Charles Dickens that Alice had lent her from her stepfather's library and, though she was enjoying the story, she hadn't been able to concentrate, the words she wanted to say to her father whirling around her head in a jumbled mess. Overhead came the sound of Mrs Gardener using the chamber pot. She winced. The daily disposing of her lodger's bodily waste was a chore she despised above all others.

'Dad.' Leaving the warmth of her chair, Dora crossed to her father's bedside. Taking the chair recently vacated by Barbie-Jean, she sat down.

'Shouldn't you be heading to bed?' Stephen asked, yawning.

'I will in a minute.' Dora took his hand in hers. His warm skin was dry to the touch.

'Is something the matter?' he asked, frowning. Dora's insides quailed. Her father had been so cheerful of late and, while it irked her that Mrs Gardener was the reason for the improvement in his mood, she was loath to say anything that might plunge him back into the despair that had coloured his life for so long. She took a deep breath and said,

'What are your intentions towards Mrs Gardener, Father?'

'What business is that of yours?' Stephen exclaimed. His eyes narrowed suspiciously. 'Who've you been talking to?'

'No one,' Dora retorted, wounded. 'I just don't want to see you hurt.'

'It's that meddling Hannah, isn't it?' he snorted. 'Jealous, that's what she is. Her William was barely cold in his grave before she was sniffing around here, God rest him.'

'Father!' Dora stared at him, appalled. 'Aunty Hannah has only always done her best for us.'

'You might ask yourself why?' Stephen smirked. 'It's taken me a while but I've got the measure of her now.' Dora's mouth fell open in astonishment. Could her father really be so deluded as to imagine Leah's mother had designs on him? Was that the sort of rubbish Barbie-Jean was filling his head with?

'Anyway, not that it's any business of yours but I'm seriously thinking of asking Barbie-Jean to marry me.'

Dora blanched. She had suspected as much but to hear her father confirm it made her feel sick.

'You can wipe that sour look off your face, my girl,' Stephen muttered, pouting like a spoiled child. 'I've seen you and Nate cosying up in the kitchen.'

'Father! We're friends,' Dora protested, blushing. 'We've never behaved improperly.'

Stephen shrugged as if to say he didn't care either way.

'I'm entitled to a bit of happiness,' he said, 'and Barbie-Jean's such a selfless soul.'

He scowled as Dora sniffed in derision. 'She is selfless,' he insisted. 'I've told her that once my inheritance comes through, I'll employ a nurse but she insisted she wants to nurse me herself, of course . . .'

'I bet she did,' Dora muttered through gritted teeth.

'She did,' her father insisted. 'That's what I love about her. Heart of gold, she has. Not many women would be prepared to do what she does.'

'What? Sit around all day playing cards and chatting?'

'She keeps me company,' Stephen snarled. 'Which is more than you do. You're always swanning off with your friends, leaving me on my own. Well, I've got Barbie-Jean now, so you'll just have to lump it. We're going to be married, if she'll have me.'

'What's going on?' Nate stood in the doorway, his gaze moving from Dora to Stephen. 'Do you need a hand?'

Dora shook her head.

'I'm just setting Dora right about a few things, lad,' Stephen said, jovially. He was clearly keen to keep Mrs Gardener's son on his side.

'Are you all right, Dora?' Nate asked gently.

'Yes, thank you. I'm fine,' she said, her voice strained. 'It's late so I'll say goodnight.'

'Goodnight, Dora,' Nate said. She nodded and, picking up a lighted candle, made her way up to bed. As she neared the top of the stairs, she heard the creak of a floorboard, followed by the squeak of bedsprings. Had Mrs Gardener been listening? She wouldn't put it past her. The woman was a snake in the grass and, if it wasn't for Nate, she'd rue the day she'd ever said yes to Sally Shaw.

CHAPTER TWENTY-FIVE

'I don't know Mrs Gardner as well as you do, Dora, obviously,' Leah said the following evening after Dora had related her conversation with her father of the previous day. They were making their way home after a long twelve-hour shift. Leah's feet and back ached and her chest felt tight from inhaling chemicals all day in the poorly ventilated factory. 'But I honestly think your dad would be making a huge mistake. I mean, marriage? Surely, he can't be serious?'

'He certainly seems so to me,' Dora replied, mournfully.

'I know Mum isn't keen on her,' Leah said, bowing her head against the stiff wind that gusted around them. 'She didn't lift a finger to help on Christmas Day, did she? Lazy old cow.'

'She won't even use the privy in this cold snap,' Dora fumed. 'So guess who has to clean out her chamber pot? Not Madam.'

'I'd leave it, if I were you,' Leah said with a toss of her head. 'She'd empty it out soon enough, then.'

'Don't tempt me, Leah,' Dora laughed ruefully. 'I can just picture the look on her face if I told her she's got to empty her own waste.' She sighed. 'She'd only complain to Dad, though, and he thinks the sun and moon shine out of her bottom.'

'Well, I think you're a saint for putting up with her,' Leah said.

'Only cos she's paying me.' Dora grinned. 'Anyway, I don't need to ask how things are with you. You've been walking round like the cat that's got the cream ever since Christmas.'

Leah's eyes sparkled. 'I never imagined it was possible to feel this happy,' she said, her words slightly muffled by the scarf she had wound round her face to ward off the icy wind. And it was true. Since Harry's arrival late on Christmas Day, she felt like she'd been walking on air. Jewellery was forbidden in the factory so she wore Harry's ring on a string around her neck and day-dreamed of the day they could marry.

Harry had taken a room at the pub and was working odd jobs here and there. He was currently coppicing on a woodland estate just the other side of Botley. He had written to his parents in an attempt to build bridges but to the dismay of both him and Leah, the only reply had been a short, curt note from Isaac telling Harry not to contact them again until he'd come to his senses.

'Their loss,' Harry had said, his mouth a tight line as he'd crumpled the note up and tossed it into the fire. If it hadn't been for the fact that she knew Harry was hurt and upset by his parents' attitude, however much he tried to pretend otherwise, Leah couldn't have cared less. They were both earning enough at the moment to lay a little aside for their future.

'I've even started buying a few things for my bottom drawer,' Leah told Dora now as they reached her front door.

'My two dearest friends betrothed,' Dora said, slightly wistfully as they neared her front door. 'It's so exciting.'

'Your turn will come, Dor,' Leah told her. 'Gosh, I shall be glad to get in front of the fire. I'm frozen to the bone.' Her gloved fingers fumbled with the latch. 'I'll see you in the morning. Goodnight.'

'Goodnight, Leah.' Dora let herself into her front parlour. 'Hello, Dad, Mrs Gardener.' She glanced round the drab room with a flash of irritation. Would it kill the woman to put the supper on just once? 'I'll put the kettle on,' she said wearily. To her dismay, Mrs Gardner got up from her chair and followed her into the kitchen.

'Is Nate not home yet?' she asked, surprised not to find him in the kitchen. He, at least, wasn't averse to helping with the household chores and she'd often come home to find him peeling potatoes.

'He's working late,' replied Mrs Gardener. She leaned against the dresser, arms folded across her chest. 'I know you and I have had our differences, Dora.'

Dora's shoulders sagged. She was exhausted. She really didn't have the energy to cope with a confrontation right now.

'I'm sorry you feel that way,' she said evenly as she lit the stove and set the kettle to boil.

'Your father and I are very fond of each other, you know?'

'So I understand.' She turned round, wiping her hands on her apron.

'Dad's been through a lot,' she said, her voice loaded with meaning. 'I'd hate to see him hurt,' she said.

Mrs Gardener smiled slyly. 'Don't you worry about him,' she said, her blue eyes glittering with what? Malice? Goosebumps prickled Dora's skin and, despite the warmth of the kitchen, she shivered.

'I just think we should start afresh. After all, if I'm going to be your stepmother, we need to get on, don't we? For all our sakes.'

The way she emphasized the word 'stepmother' made Dora's skin crawl.

'Barbie-Jean,' Stephen called from his bed. 'Are you bringing that tea?'

'Just waiting for the kettle, pet,' she called over her shoulder.

'You go sit with him,' Dora said. 'I'll bring it through.'

'Thank you.' Mrs Gardener paused in the doorway. 'By the way, have you heard anything more from that Lyle bloke? About the money, I mean?' she added, when Dora looked blank.

'Why would I hear anything?' she replied, surprised. Mrs Gardener shrugged.

'Just wondered, as it's taking quite a long time, isn't it?'

'Mr Lyle did say it we shouldn't expect to hear anything until the end of February at the earliest, but don't forget that they may still find another beneficiary,' Dora reminded her archly, and was rewarded by the way the woman's florid cheeks drained of colour.

'Don't say that,' she hissed. 'You'll upset your father.'

'Perhaps you should prepare him for that possibility,' Dora suggested, smiling sweetly.

Mrs Gardener scowled as she squeezed her way through the narrow doorway and returned to her usual chair.

Dora was just pouring the tea when she heard her father bellow from the parlour. She sighed. What had that old witch said now?

'Coming.' She picked up the mugs and, bracing herself, she carried them into the parlour.

'What have you been saying to upset Barbie-Jean?' he spluttered. His clean-shaven face gleamed sallow in the lamplight. Lately he had started to shave himself, a huge step forward as far as Dora was concerned. There was no denying that he resembled his old self. It was just a pity Mrs Gardener was the one responsible for his on-going transformation.

'I don't know,' replied Dora calmly, her gaze settling on the woman slumped at her father's bedside, eyes glistened with tears. 'What have I said?'

'This woman is the most selfless person I've ever known,' Stephen said sternly. Reaching for Barbie-Jean's hand, he lifted it to his and kissed it. Dora's stomach churned but she kept her expression neutral. 'I told you that even though I've offered to pay for a nurse, she's insisting she wants to nurse me herself?' He turned to smile at the woman by his side. 'I won't allow that, of course. You're still young, Barbie-Jean.

You deserve a life, so I'm determined that you shall not become my full-time nurse.'

'Father, you have no idea how much Mr Baker's estate is worth, or even if you'll get the money. Mr Lyle did warn you that it isn't guaranteed. There may be another beneficiary.'

'Rubbish!' Stephen snapped. 'Why do you always have to be such a doom-monger? You're just like your mother. Her glass was always half-empty, too. She could never look on the bright side.'

'Dad!' Dora exclaimed in shock. In all his darkest days, her father had never criticized her mother's memory. 'You don't mean that.' Stephen turned his face away and Dora was gratified to see the flush of shame that stained his cheeks.

'Nevertheless, I think we can accept that the money is almost certainly mine,' he said after a moment. 'That Lyle fellow wouldn't have come to see me, otherwise. He wouldn't want to give false hope.'

Dora sighed. 'I'd better get on with the supper,' she said, wearily. 'It's getting late.'

'Just start treating Barbie-Jean with the respect she deserves,' Stephen called after her. Dora looked back over her shoulder to see Barbie-Jean's malicious smile. She turned away without replying.

Nate arrived some time later, just as Dora was dishing up. He came into the kitchen, smelling of coal fire and ink. He helped carry the plates into the parlour and then joined Dora at the kitchen table. He spoke enthusiastically about his work, and especially about the new girl, Rosie King.

Dora listened in miserable silence, the food turning to sawdust in her mouth. Nate seemed so in awe of Rosie's intelligence and her skill with the typewriter. *How must he see her?* Dora mused, catching sight of her hands, stained purple by the dyes she'd been working with that week. She bet Rosie King's hands were spotless.

I bet she's pretty too, she thought sourly, pushing a strand of hair from her face. Pearl's prediction flashed briefly into her head and she smiled ruefully. Nate was a tall, dark, handsome stranger, all right, but he clearly had no interest in her other than friendship.

CHAPTER TWENTY-SIX

Alice and Leah stared around the cold, dingy room in dismay. Leah had lived on the breadline most of her life but she had never seen such abject poverty as was evident in this tiny, one-roomed hovel.

Lit by a solitary candle, the room was dank, dark, and smelled strongly of unwashed bodies. When she and Alice had arrived, the three older children, all under five, had been dressed in what could only be described as rags and their bare feet had been blue with cold. All three of them had streaming noses and a hacking cough. The children, two girls and a boy, had wolfed down the bread and cheese Alice had brought, leaving not a single crumb uneaten, and were now tucked up in the bed. The bedding had been so cold as to feel damp and so Leah had fetched the warming pan from the buggy that Alice had used to keep their feet warm during the journey and placed it in the bed.

A bone-numbing draught wafted beneath the ill-fitting door. Seated on the filthy rug, the youngest child, a baby of barely a month old, slept fitfully in her arms, Alice shivered. The fire gave off little heat and the windowpane was crusted with ice.

'Shall I make some tea?' Tilly, the children's mother, asked in her soft Irish brogue, getting to her feet. She looked barely more than a child herself and Alice doubted she could be any older than she was. Alice and Leah exchanged glances.

'That's very kind but we're fine, thank you,' Leah said. Tilly nodded and sat back down.

'I am going to ask Reverend Roberts to apply to the poor board on your behalf,' Alice told Tilly, kindly.

'Thank you, miss,' Tilly whispered. 'I would do it myself, only I can't get into town, what with the little 'uns.'

'I understand,' Alice said, as Leah busied herself chopping vegetables to make soup. The children watched her with wide-eyed interest. 'I'll make a list of your most pressing needs,' Alice continued, peering up at Tilly through the dim light. 'Candles, coal, warm clothes for the children.'

'A few toys for the kiddies,' Leah added. Her sharp eyes had noticed that there wasn't a single toy in the sparsely furnished room.

'Of course,' agreed Alice, resolving to look out for some of the toys her siblings had outgrown and drop them round in the next few days. The poverty in which Tilly and her children were living was appalling. The tiny cottage was situated on the far edge of the hamlet and, bar the bed pushed up against the wall, a rickety table in the centre of the room, two straight-back chairs at angles to the fireplace, a wide window seat on which was propped two faded threadbare cushions, a small shelf that housed a few cooking utensils and a selection of mismatched crockery, there was nothing in the room.

'You'll need to confirm that you're not earning,' she told Tilly, glancing up from her list, pen poised.

'I'm not, miss,' Tilly shook her head vehemently, her eyes wide in innocence. Again, Alice and Leah exchanged glances. They were both very much aware of the rumours that Tilly had earned her living as a prostitute in the past and while they both felt only pity for the girl, Alice in particular could not condemn her for it. Who knew what any woman might be prepared to do to provide for her children? After all, hadn't her own mother considered just such a path when she'd found herself penniless on the streets of Poole after they'd escaped Alice's father? Alice shuddered. Thank goodness, Lily had found sanctuary at the Wesleyan Chapel. She hoped that the parish relief would have compassion on Tilly's situation and she'd be able to leave that life behind her for good. If anyone could persuade them, it would be her Samuel.

The knock at the door startled them all. Wiping her hands, Leah went to open it.

'Joshua!' she exclaimed in surprise.

'Leah!' Joshua exclaimed, mirroring her surprise. 'What are you doing here?' He frowned.

'Alice asked me to come.' Her eyes narrowed as she lowered her voice. 'You should be ashamed of yourself, Joshua Mullens. Tilly and the children are in appalling state.'

'Nan and me didn't even know she was back here until

yesterday,' Joshua replied, looking past Leah to where Tilly sat huddled on the bed with the two older children. 'I dropped a bit of stuff round last night and I've brought more now.'

'Will you let him in, Leah,' Alice said, over the wails of the baby. 'You're letting the heat out.'

Leah stood aside and Joshua stepped into the room. He carried a sack, which he dropped to the floor with a dull thud.

'What have you brought us?' Tilly asked, her weary gaze drawn to the sack.

'A couple of rabbits and a pheasant. That should keep you going for a few days.' He sniffed the air. 'Hmm, something smells good.'

'Miss Leah's making soup,' one of the children told him.

Joshua's smile turned onto a frown. 'Why aren't you kiddies wearing the stockings I gave you last night?' he asked, glaring at Tilly suspiciously. 'And where are their new shoes?'

'I'm sorry, Joshua,' Tilly said, her voice trembling. 'There was nothing I could do. Declan pawned them,' she mumbled, shamefaced. Joshua shook his head in disgust.

'Who's Declan?' Alice asked.

'My husband,' Tilly replied.

'Husband?' Joshua spat contemptuously. 'Your pimp, more like.'

'We'll get the children some more shoes and stockings,' Alice assured Tilly quickly. 'But,' she added sternly, 'you must tell your husband that he'll have the Parish Relief Committee to answer to if he pawns them again.' She turned to Joshua. 'I'm going to ask Samuel to apply for parish relief for Tilly,' she said.

Leah turned down the heat on the stove, letting the soup simmer gently as she watched Tilly unpack the sack of poached game. She was older than Leah, but they had known each other all their lives. Leah had been quite frightened of Tilly when she was growing up, for Tilly had had a reputation for being a being a 'handful' and a 'worry to her mother'. No one had been surprised when she'd found herself in the family way at just sixteen.

'Thanks, Alice, Leah.' Joshua said. 'Tilly, I'll chop some wood and get that fire going,' he said grimly. 'It's a wonder these little mites aren't dead from the cold.'

'We'll be going now, too,' Alice said, getting to her feet.

'Keep an eye on the soup, Tilly,' Leah said.

'We'll be back in the morning with some more provisions,' Alice promised. 'And I'll ask Reverend Roberts to go to the parish offices first thing to see about getting you some help.'

'Thank you, Miss Alice. Thank you, Miss Leah.' Tears filled Tilly's eyes as she walked them to the door. 'I'm ever so grateful.'

Joshua followed them out. Despite the bitter weather, he wore only a jacket over his thin shirt but, as always, he seemed impervious to the cold.

'Thank you, Alice,' he said. 'And thank the Reverend for me, won't you?'

'I will. Goodnight, Joshua, and thank you.'

Picking up the axe he'd left leaning against the wall, Joshua slung it over his shoulder and disappeared into the darkness.

'That man must have eyes like a cat, the way he finds his way about in the dark,' Alice remarked to Leah as they climbed up onto the trap. The pony pawed the frozen ground, impatient to be off.

'That Tilly is her own worst enemy,' Leah said, tucking the blanket around her legs. 'She lets Declan treat her like dirt. Everyone knows he pimps her out and takes all the money.'

'Is he really her husband?' Alice asked. She flicked the reins and the pony pranced forwards with a toss of it head, its breath frosting in the icy air.

'Common law,' Leah replied.

'And the children? Are they his?'

Leah shrugged. 'Who knows? I'm just glad we got there when we did. Those poor little kids. How did you know things were so bad?'

'Mr Whitworth's gamekeeper called at the vicarage. He'd bumped into Pearl on her way back from visiting Tilly. She said Declan had gone off and left them with barely any food or wood for the fire.'

'Well, they'll be glad of that soup, and what with the game Joshua brought, they should eat well for a while,' said Leah.

'I think we'll need to keep an eye on Tilly, though,' Alice said, biting her lip. 'Just check that she's coping all right.'

'Joshua will keep an eye on her,' Leah assured her. 'I reckon he'll be looking for Declan, too.'

'How can a man treat his family so badly?' Alice mused out loud. 'It's criminal.'

They rode in silence for a while, the pony's hooves clattering on the frigid ground, until they passed the wrought-iron gates of Streawberige House, the lantern light dancing on the frosty verge.

'How are your wedding plans coming along?' Leah asked, tucking the plaid rug tightly over her lap.

'Mother and I are seeing the proprietor of the Red Lion tomorrow to discuss the wedding breakfast,' Alice smiled. 'Samuel's meeting us there at half-past four. I just hope he's not late.'

CHAPTER TWENTY-SEVEN

The cold wind scoured Dora's cheeks as she emptied the dirty washing-up water over the grass. All around her there were signs of new life. The trees were in bud and clumps of daffodils and crocuses bloomed. The hens had begun to lay again and were clucking contentedly as they burrowed in the soil, protected from the brisk wind by the hedge. The air was alive with birdsong and the far-off bleating of lambs.

'Hello, Dora,' Leah called cheerfully, coming out of her cottage lugging a large basket of wet laundry.

'Morning, Leah.' Dora expelled a long breath of air and flexed her shoulders. She nodded at Leah's basket. 'I've just got to put mine through the mangle,' she said, turning to go back indoors.

'You'd better hurry up. Alice wants to leave by nine,' Leah said, putting the wicker laundry basket down and wiping her damp hands on her apron. 'I'm dead excited. I've never been a bridesmaid before and I reckon Alice's mum will make us lovely dresses.'

'I'm going as quick as I can,' Dora replied, resting the empty washing-up bowl on her hip. 'If I'm running behind you two will have to go on without me and I'll catch you up.'

'At least it'll get you away from her indoors for a bit,' Leah grinned.

'Yes, thank heavens,' Dora grinned back. 'She's becoming a proper thorn in my side. Goodness only knows what she'll be like once she and Dad are married.'

To Dora's dismay and the amusement of the hamlet, Stephen and Barbie-Jean had announced their engagement on St Valentine's Day. Barbie-Jean had hardly been able to contain herself, showing off her ring, which was as big and tasteless as she herself, to all and sundry. Dora could only wonder at how her father had afforded such a showy ring and had been utterly horrified to learn a few days later that Barbie-Jean had pawned Dora's mother's own engagement and wedding rings. Always believing her mother's jewellery would be hers one day, a huge argument had followed after which Stephen refused to speak to Dora for almost a week. It was only when her father fouled the bedsheets again, that he'd relented slightly. After all, Barbie-Jean couldn't be expected to change soiled bedlinen, he'd told Dora huffily. At least not until they were legally married.

'Perhaps we could have our dinner at the village cafe,' she suggested to Leah now. 'Make a day of it.'

'Good idea,' Leah replied, regarding her friend with sympathy. Though Dora might not admit it, she knew how much her friend had come to dread being at home. The soon-to-be

Mrs Webb made Dora feel like a stranger in her own home. Thank goodness, she had Nate. Dora was always telling Leah that he was the only thing that made her evenings bearable.

'I'd better get on then if I'm to be ready to leave by nine,' Dora said, going back indoors. As her eyes adjusted to the gloom after the bright sunshine, she hung the washing-up bowl on its peg and sat down beside the mangle. From the other room came the sound of voices: her father and Mrs Gardener's.

What do they find to talk about all day, every day? she wondered, picking up a dripping sheet and squeezing it through the mangle. Just a few minutes of Dora listening to the woman's simpering was enough to bring on a headache.

She wished Nate were here. They would have had a laugh together. Their friendship was certainly growing stronger with every passing day, yet sometimes she felt she couldn't fathom him at all.

So often his behaviour intimated that his feelings for her were moving beyond friendship, yet twice this week he had arrived home late from work with the distinct scent of perfume hanging around him. She tried not to mind. No promises had been made. He owed her nothing, but she couldn't help feeling betrayed and let down.

Perhaps he does just see me as a friend, after all, she mused morosely now, as she picked up another sheet, water dripping on to the cold flagstones. Or even a sister. After all, if his mother has her way, that is what we shall be soon enough. She wondered where Nate was now. He'd left early that morning, before Dora had got up. Had he gone to see Rosie King? The thought gave Dora a queer feeling in the pit of her stomach. She knew very little about the girl except that it was obvious Nate was quite taken by her. He spoke about her all the time.

She threaded the last sheet through the mangle and dumped it crossly in the laundry basket. Getting to her feet, she carried the heavy laundry basket outside where Leah was pegging out her second wash load.

'I meant to ask, has Harry found some more work?' Dora asked, reaching up to peg the first sheet on the line.

'Yes,' Leah replied, removing a clothes peg from her mouth. 'He's got work on a farm over at Boorley Green.'

'I don't expect he's heard anything from his parents?'

'Not a word.' Leah shook her head. 'Mum's a bit worried we might get evicted. She bumped into Mrs Lamb in the butcher's and, according to her, Mrs Whitworth is all for having us thrown off their land.'

'It won't come to that, surely?' Dora looked at her in alarm.

Leah shook her head. 'Harry's adamant his father wouldn't allow her to do such a thing. Besides, Mr Whitworth held my father in high regard. He would never evict his widow.'

'It must be hard for Harry, to be at such odds with his parents,' Dora said, bending down to retrieve another sheet.

'Well, you'd know all about that, wouldn't you,' Leah grinned. 'How are the two love birds?'

'Oh, don't.' Dora rolled her eyes. 'I can't help feeling it's all going to end in tears.' She shrugged. 'I'm really worried, Leah.' Lowering her voice, Dora moved closer to her friend.

'It's already March and we haven't heard a word from that Mr Lyle about the inheritance yet Dad and Mrs Gardener are buying things on tick everywhere. I'm scared we're going to end up in terrible debt. Dad just tells me I'm being a killjoy. He's convinced no news is good news but the longer it takes the more doubtful I am that we'll get anything.'

'Your dad's probably right,' Leah said, reassuringly. 'If they'd found another beneficiary you'd likely have known by now. Don't give up hope.'

'To be honest, I'd rather forego the inheritance if it means getting rid of her.' Dora gave a jerk of her head.

'I hope that's not me you're referring to, young lady?' At the sound of Barbie-Jean's voice on the other side of the bedsheets, both girls spun round, startled. Dora felt herself growing red.

'Would we ever, Mrs Gardener?' Leah said cheerfully, picking up her empty basket. 'Well, I'd better get on. I'll call for you at nine, Dor,' she said.

'Thanks,' Dora called after her. 'I'll try to be ready.'

'Off out, are you?' queried Barbie-Jean.

'I've got my dress fitting this morning,' Dora replied, watching her picking her way across the dew-damp grass to the privy. 'I did tell Dad.'

'Hmm, I think I recall that Lily had something of a rep-utation as a dressmaker.' Barbie-Jean opened the privy door, and smiled back at Dora. 'Perhaps she'll make my wedding gown.' She laughed. 'You might ask her,' she cackled, as she shut the privy door, slamming the bolts home.

A door banged and Dora smiled to see her neighbour Beatrice Turner emerge from her cottage. The silver threads in her auburn hair sparkled in the sun and, as always, she was well-dressed, the dark green fabric of her dress accentuating her eyes.

'Oh,' she said. 'The water closet's occupied.'

'I won't be a minute,' shouted Barbie-Jean

'Mrs Gardener's only just gone in,' Dora said as she and Beatrice exchanged amused glances. The length of time Barbie-Jean spent in the privy was a running joke among the tenants.

'Are you looking forward to your dress fittings?' Beatrice asked, leaning down to grab one of Dora's bedsheets and peg it on the line.

'I am,' Dora nodded. 'Alice must be so excited?'

'She is, bless her,' Beatrice said with a fond smile. 'And so am I. Poor Lily's had her work cut out making dresses for us all.'

They both heard the flush of the lavatory and a few seconds later the door opened slowly and Barbie-Jean squeezed herself through the door.

'All yours, Bea,' she smiled, straightening her skirts as she waddled down the path.

Alice studied her reflection in the mirror. Her lilac dress with its white collar and cuffs, hugged her neat figure and complemented her olive complexion. One of the benefits of having an accomplished dressmaker for a mother was that Alice had always been dressed fashionably. And now her mother was making her wedding dress. The thought sent a shiver of delicious anticipation down her spine. They were getting married in five weeks' time, on Easter Saturday. As Samuel had no family, it would be a relatively quiet affair, with only Alice's family and close friends in attendance. Along with her younger sisters, Martha and Caroline, Alice had asked Leah and Dora to be bridesmaids. Harry was to act as Samuel's best man. Despite their differences in background and upbringing, the two men had formed a close friendship since Christmas and often spent a pleasant half-hour playing dominoes in the snug of the Glyn Arms or chatting over a pint.

A gust of wind howled down the chimney, sending a flurry of sparks into the air. Alice glanced out the window. The clear blue sky and bright sunshine were misleading, for the trees were waving wildly and she could hear the wind shrieking under the eaves. It would be the perfect day to wear the soft kid gloves her grandmother had said she could have. Now, where did she say she kept them? She glanced round the room. Ah, yes, the sideboard. Kneeling on the floor, she slid out the bottom drawer. At once she was hit by the musty scent of mothballs. The drawer was where her grandmother kept her mementoes from her time in Africa. There were intricately woven bead tablemats and embroidered napkins, a few porcupine quills tucked down the side, some scarves and her assortment of gloves. As Alice lifted the napkins from the drawer, a small photograph slipped from between the folds, landing face down on her lap. She set the napkins on the floor and picked it up. It was a studio portrait of a small child. On the back was written

Ian, aged 3
12 August 1890
Pietermaritzburg

'My son.'

At the sound of her grandmother's voice, Alice jumped and dropped the photo. Beatrice stood in the doorway, her arms hanging loosely at her sides, her shoulders slumped.

'I'm sorry,' Alice found her voice. 'I wasn't prying. I was looking for those gloves you said I could have.' She picked up the photograph again and studied it. He was handsome boy, light hair and dark eyes, a cheeky smile. 'Your son?' she frowned. 'You've never mentioned him. Does my mother know she has a brother?'

Beatrice nodded and cleared her throat. She was clearly upset by Alice's discovery.

'Why have you never spoken of him?' Alice said, getting to her feet. 'Did ... did something happen?'

Beatrice walked over to the nearest easy chair and sat down. Contemplating her hands, she seemed momentarily lost in thought.

'Grandma?' Alice prompted her tentatively.

'That photograph was taken the last time I ever saw him,' she said finally. She smiled, but her eyes were sad. 'It was his third birthday. My husband ...'

'You were married?' exclaimed Alice in surprise. Beatrice seldom spoken about her past and there was so much, Alice realized now, that she didn't know about her grandmother's life in South Africa. She wondered how much her mother knew.

'I'll come back to that,' Bea said. 'I remember that it was a nice day, cool, it was winter after all, but pleasant and sunny. We'd gone into town for the day. Howard, my husband, had arranged for Ian to have his photograph taken. He gave me some money and sent me off to the market. I was to meet them at the hotel for dinner later. I arrived at the hotel promptly at midday. Howard was very strict about punctuality and I didn't want to annoy him and spoil such a rare day out.' Beatrice's expression clouded. She fixed her gaze on the flames flickering in the blackened grate. 'I waited in the lobby until a quarter to one. When I enquired at the desk, I was told that no luncheon booking had been made. At first I thought I'd made the mistake, that I'd misunderstood. I went to the photography studio where I was told by the proprietor that, as far as he was aware, Howard had been planning on heading straight home.' A sob caught in Beatrice's throat and Alice went to her side.

'Why would he do that?' she asked, appalled that someone could behave so callously. She laid her arm across her grandmother's shoulder. 'What happened?'

'Our farm was a good twelve miles out of town and it was mid-afternoon by the time I found a wagon heading that way. By the time I got home, Howard and Ian were gone.

Three weeks later that photograph arrived in the post with a brief note saying they were starting a new life without me and that I had a month to leave the property.'

'So, you lost your child and your home? Grandma, that's horrible. Why would your husband be so cruel?'

Beatrice shook her head. 'It was never a love match,' she said, with a mirthless laugh. 'He won me in a card game.'

'What?' Alice stared at her grandmother in shock.

'It was a different life out there. I was a paid companion to a sweet young woman. But my employer ran up huge gambling debts. He stood to lose everything. Howard was his biggest creditor. They agreed to one last game. I was the stake. My employer lost, of course, and I belonged to Howard.' Her cheeks suffused with colour as tears filled her eyes. 'I was his whore, his slave. It was a miserable existence, but then I had Ian and he made everything worthwhile. He was such a delightful, happy child. I dread to think what lies Howard told him after they left. He'd be twenty-seven this year and I still think about him every day.'

Alice swallowed the lump in her throat. 'Does my grand-father know?'

Beatrice shook her head. 'I know I should tell him, but I'm afraid. Howard and I were never legally married. He's accepted me having Lily out of wedlock, I suppose he under-stands that I was only a silly girl swept away on false promises of love, but to have another illegitimate child some ten years later, how can he justify that? He would despise me.'

'Grandma!' Alice exclaimed. 'Grandfather adores you.'

Beatrice smiled sadly. 'He doesn't really know me. I should have been truthful before our marriage. He's churchwarden, for goodness' sake.'

'Do you know where Ian is now?'

Beatrice shook her head.

'What about asking my Uncle Charlie to investigate?' suggested Alice. 'He could use the same firm of solicitors he used to find you. You'd want to make contact, surely?'

'Oh, I don't know, Alice, love,' Beatrice replied doubt-fully. 'It would open up old wounds, and I have no idea what Howard has told him about me. What if he doesn't want anything to do with me? I don't think I could stand the rejection.'

'Surely it's better to know?' Alice persisted, excited at the prospect of another uncle. 'I'm sure Mother would want to meet her half-brother, don't you think?'

'I'd have to tell Mathew,' her grandmother said, with a tremor in her voice.

'I'm certain he'd understand,' Alice assured her. 'You were alone in a strange country. What choice did you have?'

'I'll think about it,' Beatrice sighed. There was a knock on the door as, simultaneously, the clock chimed nine. 'Not another word now,' she said, putting a finger to her lips. She forced a smile. 'Let's go and get these wedding clothes sorted out.'

CHAPTER TWENTY-EIGHT

'Oh, Alice, you look beautiful!' exclaimed nine-year-old Caroline, clapping her hands in excitement.

'You do look lovely,' Dora agreed.

'Beautiful,' Leah sighed, with a twinge of envy. Much as she was pleased for her friend, she couldn't help wishing this was her dress-fitting and her wedding in five weeks' time. She gave herself a mental shake and scolded herself. Her time would come and she would have a dress as fine as the one Alice now wore.

'You look like a princess,' Caroline said, stroking the off-white silk with a tentative finger.

'Don't touch, Carrie,' Beatrice scolded gently.

'I feel like a princess,' Alice said, turning to grin at her little sister. She turned sideways, to admire the short train. The dress was from a pattern her aunt Eleanor had found in Harrods and sent down by post. The high neck was edged with lace and emphasized Alice's slender throat. The bust was comprised of a V-shaped lace panel between two panels of

267

ruffled silk, the three meeting in a silken band which showed off her slim waist. The sleeves were long, the lace-edged cuff reaching to her wrists. The hem of her silk skirt just brushed the tip of her shoes.

'Aunt Eleanor sent this,' Lily said. She folded back the flaps of the cardboard box sitting on the workbench and there was a collective gasp of admiration as she lifted out a delicate lace wedding veil. 'She wore it on her wedding day, and she wanted you to have it.'

'It's beautiful,' breathed Alice as her mother arranged the delicate folds carefully around her shoulders.

'You'll make a beautiful bride.' Lily's eyes glistened with tears as she met Alice's gaze in the mirror, her heart swelling with pride.

'Thank you, Mother,' Alice said, throwing her arms around her mother. 'I love it.'

'Mind you don't crumple the material,' warned Beatrice in alarm.

'It will be all right,' Lily laughed. Together with Leah and Dora, she helped Alice out of her dress. It fell to the floor in a shimmer of pearl-white silk.

'Who's next?' asked Lily, as she hung the wedding dress on its hanger.

'Me, me!' Caroline cried impatiently, hopping about from one foot to another in a half-finished dress of pale mauve, with an embroidery anglaise bodice. She and Martha were wearing identical dresses, which, although Martha had decried the dress as too young for her, suited them both very well. The two older girls would be wearing slightly less fancier versions of Alice's wedding dress in a darker shade of mauve.

The stove kept the workroom at an even temperature as the girls stripped down to their shifts while they waited to try on their dresses.

'I think the fit is perfect, Leah,' Lily said as she finished pinning the hem of Leah's dress and stood back to cast a critical eye over her handiwork. 'You've got a pretty figure and I think this pattern complements it nicely.'

'You all look lovely, Leah,' Beatrice said smiling round at the girls standing in various state of undress in the chaotic workroom.

'As there are so few alterations needed,' Lily said, helping Leah down from the stool, 'I should have them finished in plenty of time.'

'I'll make us some refreshments,' Beatrice said, heading for the kitchen. 'I'm sure you could all do with a drink.'

'I do hope you are blessed with good weather,' Dora said, pulling her dress over her head.

'We can only hope,' Lily said, briefly remembering her own wedding to Alice's father. It had been a bitter cold day, the church dank and dim – but then it had been a marriage of convenience, a drastic contrast to her marriage to James who, despite his sometimes serious demeanour was a warm, loving man, the total opposite to Jez.

'Whatever the weather, you will have a happy day, because you are marrying a good man,' she reminded Alice.

'I know, Mother,' smiled Alice. 'I'm very lucky.'

'I think Samuel's the lucky one,' declared Leah, to which everyone laughed.

'I'll go and help Mother with the refreshments while you girls finish getting dressed,' said Lily hurrying towards the door.

'I wish I was getting married,' Caroline said. Reluctant to take off her dress, she spun round on her heels, almost careering into one of Lily's dressmaker's dummies. Alice managed to right it just in time.

'Be careful. Take it off now, come on. You don't want to spoil it.'

'I'm never getting married,' declared Martha stoutly. 'I wish to have a career, and a woman can't have both.'

'Mother does,' Caroline argued, reluctantly allowing Alice to lift the dress over her head and hang it up.

'Mother works from home,' Martha replied. 'I want to train as a doctor and work in a hospital.'

'Good for you,' said Dora. 'I think you should make a very good doctor. Look how well you set your neighbour's cat's leg when she got kicked by that horse. She barely has a limp now.'

'Here we are,' Lily said, entering the workroom with a tray. 'This is the last of James's elderflower cordial. Do help yourselves. It's very refreshing.' Leah cleared a space on the workbench and Lily set the tray down. Beatrice followed with a plate of freshly baked biscuits which the girls fell upon eagerly.

*

'Grandma says she told you about Ian,' Lily said in an under-tone to Alice as the girls prepared to leave for the café.

'Yes. I didn't mean to pry,' Alice explained apologetically. 'I was looking for some gloves and I came across the photo-graph.' She glanced round to make sure they weren't being overheard. 'Grandfather doesn't know.'

'No.' Lily took Alice's arm and drew her into a corner of the room. 'She's too ashamed to tell him. She said you suggested asking Charlie to see if he can find out any infor-mation about him?'

Alice nodded. 'It would give Grandma such comfort to know he is well, and you'd like to know, too, surely? He is your half-brother.'

'Sometimes we don't always want to know our blood rela-tions,' Lily smiled, giving Alice a knowing look.

'If you mean Nate,' sniffed Alice, 'it's a different scenario all together. My father was a nasty piece of work. How do I know Nate hasn't inherited his evil streak?'

'While I have no time for Nate's mother . . .' Lily began quietly then paused. She cast a surreptitious glance in Dora's direction to be certain she wouldn't overhear but she was laughing over something Leah was saying, and appeared unaware of the conversation.

'From what Dora has said, I do feel Nathan is a decent enough boy. And after all, you're nothing like your father, so perhaps he isn't, either.'

'Dora is besotted with Nate,' Alice said disparagingly. 'And I don't blame her. He's a good-looking boy and with everything she's had to put up with, of course she'll become attached to the first person who shows her kindness, and he is good to her, I grant you. He helps her a lot but I don't want to see her hurt if he doesn't return her feelings.'

'You don't know that he doesn't,' Lily whispered. 'And if you want to have a friendship with Nate, I don't mind. Honestly, if you're harbouring these feelings of distrust and anger towards him because of how your father and Nate's mother treated me, there's no need. Barbie-Jean has no power over me. If anything, I feel sorry for her.'

'You're too forgiving,' said Alice kissing Lily's cheek. 'Are you sure you and Grandma won't join us for dinner?'

'No,' her mother replied firmly. 'You girls go and have some fun. You deserve it. You all work so hard.'

Chattering and laughing, the girls put on their hats and coats, and left in a flurry of goodbyes and some whining from Caroline who was annoyed that she couldn't join them.

'Another time, Carrie,' her mother told her sternly, one hand on the girl's shoulder as she saw the older girls off. 'You can give me a hand tidying up while Martha helps Grandma get the dinner on. Father and the boys will be back from the park soon and they'll be starving.'

Arm in arm, Alice, Leah and Dora made their way down the street. Despite the bitter cold wind, the high street was bustling. The brightly coloured striped awnings above the row of shops snapped and crackled in the stiff breeze and a smartly dressed man let out a cry of dismay as his bowler hat went flying down the street before coming to rest in the gutter. The wind tugged at their skirts and pulled their hair from its pins, and they were red-faced and laughing by the time they reached the quaint little tearoom. The bell jangled shrilly as they blew in on a squall of old leaves and dust, into its steamy warmth.

They found a recently vacated table close to the roaring fire and divested themselves of their wraps before sitting down.

The waitress bustled over with a tray. 'Let me clear this for you,' she said, pleasantly, handing them each a menu.

They ordered a pot of tea and soup, which arrived piping hot with a hunk of crusty bread.

'It's nice to catch up,' Leah said, blowing on the surface of her soup. 'I feel like all I do is work and sleep at the moment. I hardly ever see you anymore, Alice.'

'I feel the same,' agreed Dora, picking up her spoon. 'How are the wedding arrangements coming along?' she asked Alice.

'Everything is going to plan,' Alice replied. 'I'm so pleased my stepfather agreed to Samuel's wish to have our wedding ceremony at St. Luke's. I wasn't fussed either way, but I know it means a lot to Samuel for us to be married by Reverend Aldridge.' She paused to swallow a mouthful of soup. 'We've had another meeting with the manager of the Red Lion and finalized numbers. They've offered us the room at the back which, I believe, can accommodate up to forty people. We shan't be anywhere near that many, of course, but it is nice to have somewhere a bit private. My stepfather is being very generous.'

'That just shows his high regard for you,' said Leah, her gaze straying to the door as the bell jangled. She was about to ask Alice what menu she'd decided on for the wedding breakfast but the question died on her lips. She and Alice looked at each other, lips pursed. Seated with her back to the door, Dora looked up at her friends, suddenly realizing the conversation had ceased.

'What?' she asked, with a frown. Leah looked at Alice, at a loss as to what to say but inside she was seething. How could he do this to Dora? Alice had been right to be suspicious of him all along. The scoundrel!

Dora craned her neck in order to see what her friends were looking at, and the colour drained from her face. Quickly she faced forward, humiliation sending the colour flooding back into her cheeks so that they glowed crimson. Had she really seen what she thought she'd seen? Yes, her mind confirmed, she had, and she couldn't unsee it. Nate had come into the café with a young woman on his arm and she knew exactly who the pretty auburn-haired beauty must be.

'Rosie King,' she said dully, answering the unasked question in her friends' eyes as she pushed her bowl aside. Her appetite had deserted her.

'Do you know her?' Leah hissed, dabbing her lips with her napkin as she watched the couple across the busy café.

'No, but he's spoken about her enough. They work together.'

'What's he doing taking her out for dinner while allowing

you to believe he's interested in you?' Alice growled. 'The man's a cad!'

'He's never . . .' Dora began, the truth leaving a bitter taste in her mouth. 'Nothing has been said between us. I'd hoped, obviously . . .' Tears burned the back of her throat but she resolutely refused to cry in public. There would be time for tears later, when she was alone.

'Uh-oh,' Leah squeaked, feeling the heat rise in her cheeks. 'He's spotted us.'

'Oh, my goodness!' Alice hissed. 'He's coming over!'

Dora stiffened. It took all her self-control not to turn round. Over the bustle of the tea room, she couldn't hear his approaching footsteps but the prickle down her spine told her he was standing right behind her.

'Ladies, good afternoon.' Nate grinned round the table. 'What a pleasant surprise.'

Taking a deep breath, Dora finally allowed herself to face him.

'Hello, Nate,' she said politely. Her pride wouldn't allow her to show how hurt she was.

'How did the dress fitting go?' he asked, seemingly oblivious to the tension running round the table.

'Very well, thank you,' Dora replied, stiffly.

'Who is your friend?' Alice glared at him.

'My colleague, Miss King. I've been helping her run some personal errands and she insisted on treating me to dinner.' He turned and grinned at the attractive, auburn-haired woman watching them from across the room. She fluttered her gloved fingers in a semblance of a wave and smiled lazily. She looked to Dora like the cat who'd got the cream. Dora glanced away quickly, before her face could betray her.

Still seemingly oblivious to the undercurrent of awkwardness his presence had caused, Nate continued to make conversation for several minutes and, although he was careful to include all three of them in his conversation, it was obvious to Leah how his gaze kept settling on Dora. She wondered if Alice had noticed. Probably not, she decided, seeing as how she was glowering at him over the rim of her tea cup.

Alice swallowed and set her cup down. It rattled against the saucer and she realized her fingers were trembling. Swiftly she tucked her hands on to her lap, out of sight, hoping her flushed cheeks would be put down the tea shop's steamy warmth, rather than the flustered feeling that always came over her when in close proximity to her half-brother.

Part of her longed to know him, her blood relative on her father's side, yet, out of loyalty to her mother, she couldn't bring herself to be anything but hostile to him. Her mother's words from earlier had resonated deep within her. She wanted to believe that Nate, like herself, had not inherited her father's callous nature, but she had been blessed with good role models: her mother, grandmother, her stepfather, James, her Uncle Charlie, and Aunt Eleanor. All good people of strong moral character. Nate had been brought up by a woman of dubious morals who felt nothing of using her charms to further her own ends. Having heard how the woman was playing Dora's father curdled Alice's stomach and she couldn't help but feel Nate was doing the same with her sweet, biddable friend. He was clearly stringing her along while all the time carrying on with this King girl.

'I believe Miss King is growing impatient,' Dora said quietly, nodding in the other woman's direction. Nate glanced back over his shoulder. Rosie King raised a questioning eyebrow.

'I'm afraid I'm neglecting her. If I'd known you were going to be here, I'd have suggested we dine together. I'm sure you'd find Miss King's company very entertaining. She's an enterprising young woman.'

'I'm sure she is,' Dora muttered under her breath.

Nate's smile faltered. 'Pardon?' he asked, his eyes clouding slightly.

'Our soup is growing cold,' Alice said, pointedly.

'Of course. I'm sorry to have interrupted your meal, Ladies. Do excuse me.' Nate gave a little bow, and turned away. Dora didn't dare follow his progress back to Miss King. She couldn't bear it.

CHAPTER TWENTY-NINE

'At least the wind's dropped,' Leah remarked, as the three girls walked back towards Strawbridge.

'Yes,' Alice agreed. 'It's not as fresh as it was.'

'I can't wait for summer,' Leah sighed. 'To be back in the fields with the sun on my face instead of slaving in that horrible factory. I had to scrub my hands for a good ten minutes on Thursday before that red dye came off. And I've got a permanent tickle in my throat. It can't be good for us, can it, Dora?'

'Hmm?' Dora looked up blankly. 'I beg your pardon. What did you say?'

'Are you all right, Dor?' Leah asked kindly. 'You've been quiet ever since we left the tearooms.'

'I'm perfectly all right,' Dora lied, mustering a smile. She couldn't banish the image of Nate hanging on to Rosie King's every word. She'd been aware that Rosie was a well-educated young woman with a quick wit. What Nate hadn't told her was just how beautiful Miss King was. Well, now she'd seen for herself. Pretty and clever. How could she, a plain Jane with only a basic education, compete with someone like that? She couldn't, clearly. Disappointment burned the back of her throat.

'Don't be upset about Nate,' said Alice, tucking her arm through Dora's. 'He's not worth it. He'll turn out a scoundrel like my father, you mark my words.'

'You don't know that!' Dora snapped, yanking her arm free. 'You're just assuming he's like your father because you're jealous!'

'Jealous?' Alice whirled round to face Dora, her brows almost to her hairline. 'Jealous of whom?'

'You're jealous because deep down you crave a good relationship with your brother, but you're too proud to admit it.' Dora paused to draw breath. Leah watched the two girls in amazement. Dora seldom lost her temper and certainly not with her friends.

'I understand you don't want to upset your mother but, from what Nate has told me, she has been quite amiable on the few occasions they've happened to meet. He's a good person, Alice. I just wish . . .' She broke off, unable to restrain the tears any longer.

'Oh, Dora. I'm sorry.' Alice flung her arms round Dora and hugged her tight. 'I'm so, so sorry. I didn't mean to upset you. I know how you feel about Nate.' She drew back, and rested her hands on Dora's shoulders. Holding her at arms' length, she looked into her tear-filled eyes. 'But surely his behaviour today proves the sort of person he is? He can't be ignorant of your regard for him, yet he blatantly sat there laughing with that King girl, knowing how it would upset you.'

Dora shook her head. 'It's my own fault,' she sniffed. Ferreting in her coat pocket for her handkerchief, she blew her nose. 'I shall be all right.'

'Look,' Leah interrupted. 'Smoke.' She looked between her two friends anxiously. 'Has Isaac Whitworth returned from London early?'

They had passed the gates to Streawberige House and the Glyn Arms pub a while back, and were walking down a long stretch of lane that was devoid of cottages. A blackbird hopped in the thicket and the breeze sighed through the newly budding trees. Streawberige House was visible through the spiky hedge, smoke curling from its tall chimney stacks.

'Not that I've heard,' replied Alice. 'I'm sure Samuel would have mentioned it. Has Harry not said anything?'

Leah frowned. 'No, nothing at all. How odd. Mr Whitworth doesn't usually return until just before the strawberry harvest.'

They were interrupted by the heavy plod of horse's hooves and turned to see Joshua coming along behind them, leading his pony by the reins. She was laden with bundles, tossing her head from side to side.

'Joshua, hello,' Alice called with a wave of her gloved hand. 'How are Tilly and the children?' she asked once he'd caught up with them. She and Leah had visited Tilly at her little cottage several times over the past few weeks and had been pleased to see that the children were looking better nourished and, thanks to Lily, at least had some warm clothing.

'They're faring well,' Joshua replied. 'I've been taking in plenty of fresh meat but that might come to an end soon. I'm up before the magistrate next week.'

'Oh, Joshua, no!' Leah exclaimed in dismay. 'For poaching?'

Joshua swept a hand through his thick, black hair. 'Yep. Old Cuthbert Ryall finally caught me red-handed,' he grinned ruefully.

'That's so unfair,' said Leah. 'You've seen him helping himself to game. He's a hypocrite.'

Joshua shrugged. 'It's my word against his.'

'Will you be sent to prison?' Dora asked, her pale eyes anxious.

'Who knows. It depends who's on the bench.' His expression grew serious. 'If I do get sent down, you'll look out for my Nan, won't you? And Tilly and the little 'uns?'

'Of course,' Leah assured him, soberly.

'Perhaps Harry might have a word with his father?' Dora suggested. 'Mr Whitworth could be persuaded to drop the charges.'

'Would Harry do that for me?' asked Joshua, with a sceptical raise of his brows. 'We don't exactly see eye to eye, him and me.'

'That's not Harry's fault, is it?' Leah retorted archly. 'But I'm sure he will do what he can. He bears you no malice.'

Joshua gave a good-natured shrug. 'Speaking of Mr Whitworth, I just saw him pull up outside the Glyn Arms.'

'What?' Leah's brows rose in surprise. 'He must have come to see Harry?' She spun round, biting her lip in consternation. 'I wonder if that's good or bad.' She started pacing, her skirts swirling. 'He's either here to persuade him to break off our engagement, or to build bridges.' She threw her arms up in despair. 'He's here to change Harry's mind, isn't he?'

'Oh, Leah,' Alice soothed. 'You don't know that.'

'Oh, yes, I do!' Leah rounded on her. 'I knew things were going too well. Something always has to come along and throw a spanner in the works, doesn't it?'

'Leah.' Dora grabbed her arm. 'Look at me.'

'What?' Leah pouted, her eyes sparkling crossly.

'Harry isn't the man he was last summer. He's grown up. He's used to standing on his own two feet now. He's not going to let his father bully him.'

'Dora's right,' Alice agreed. 'Harry's his own man and he knows his own mind. He won't be swayed.'

'I hope you're right,' Leah sighed wretchedly. 'I wish you'd never told me,' she grumbled to Joshua.

As they continued down the lane in silence, Alice was the only one whose thoughts weren't in turmoil.

Harry was playing a game of dominoes in the Glyn Arms' cosy snug. A fire roared in the grate and the smoky air carried the smell of stale beer and the underlaying scent of beeswax polish.

'Not long to go, now, Reverend,' he said, studying the dominoes on the table in front of him. 'Five weeks, is it?'

'Exactly.' Samuel replied with a grin, lifting up his pint.

'Nervous?'

'A little,' replied Samuel, licking foam from his upper lip. 'I just hope I can live up to her expectations. I want to be the best husband I can be.'

'And so you shall,' Harry nodded, placing his domino at the end of the row. 'You and Alice are so well suited.'

'We do have a lot in common,' agreed Samuel as he perused his dominoes. 'She's the ideal vicar's wife, actually. Walter is besotted with her, bless him. I reckon if he was twenty years younger I'd have a serious rival on my hands,' he laughed.

'She's a very attractive young woman,' Harry began, glancing out the window as the sound of carriage wheels drew his attention. 'Oh, what's he doing here?' He swore under his breath, his eyes narrowing suspiciously.

'Who?' frowned Samuel, following his friend's gaze.

Harry sat back in his seat. 'My father,' he replied, folding his arms across his chest in a gesture of defiance.

The two men watched as Isaac emerged from the carriage, looking very suave in a grey morning coat and hat, which he tipped at his coachman, before disappearing from view, to appear a few moments later in the doorway of the snug.

'Henry, my boy. Good to see you.' Hat in hand, he strode towards Harry, his free hand outstretched. The two younger men rose swiftly to their feet.

'Father,' Harry responded coolly, giving his father's hand a brief shake.

'Mr Whitworth.' Samuel nodded, shaking Isaac by the hand.

'Good afternoon, Reverend. May I?' Isaac indicated the upholstered bench along the opposite wall.

'Please,' Harry said, sitting down at the small card table, their game abandoned.

'I have to be going,' Samuel said, assuming correctly that Isaac would like some time alone with his son. He laid a hand on Harry's shoulder. 'I'll see you at church tomorrow?'

'Of course,' Harry replied, his distrustful gaze leaving his father's face only long enough to give Samuel a friendly grin. 'See you then.'

'Church?' Isaac said, once Samuel had left them. He raised an eyebrow.

'Leah's mother likes me to attend,' Harry replied, sullenly. Isaac nodded.

'You're looking well.'

'Why are you here, Father?' Harry asked, draining his pint.

'I have some business with Ryall,' Isaac said. 'And I wanted to see you.' He sighed and leaned back in his seat, regarding Harry with an amused air. 'Don't you think it's time you stopped playing silly beggars and came home? Ah, Reuben.' He broke off to address the landlord. 'Another pint of ale and a glass of port, if you please.' Reuben cast Harry a wary glance. Having Isaac Whitworth's son boarding in his pub didn't sit comfortably with him. Hopefully there wasn't going to be any trouble, he mused, wiping his hands on his greasy apron and heading back to the bar.

'I am quite happy where I am, thank you, Father. I certainly have no intention of returning to London.'

'I'm not asking you to return to London,' Isaac retorted with an exasperated sigh. 'Look, the truth is, your mother is beside herself. I have no problem with you making your own way in the world. Good for you, I say.' He rested one arm along the back of the bench. He fell silent, appearing to study the blackened stone around the hearth. Harry waited. From the main bar came the sound of men's voices and the clink of glasses.

'I take it you're still seeing that Hopwood girl?' Isaac said, finally breaking the silence.

'Yes, and I'll thank you to call her by her name. We are betrothed.'

'Betrothed?' Isaac snorted. 'The girl's what? Sixteen, seventeen?'

'She will be seventeen in May,'

Isaac shook his head. Reuben appeared in the doorway, his dog at his heels.

'Here you go, sir,' he said, placing the drinks on the table.

'Thank you, Reuben. Put it on the slate, will you?'

Reuben nodded. 'Yes, sir.'

Isaac watched him go, the dog padding silently behind him. 'Here's to your engagement, I suppose,' he said mockingly, lifting his glass. 'You know you can't marry without my permission until you are twenty-one?' he said.

'So you keep reminding me,' Harry scowled. 'We are pre-pared to wait. Of course, Leah is too young now but by the time I am of age she will be nineteen. Her mother will have no objection to her marrying then, I'm sure.' He gulped a mouthful of ale and leaned forward in his seat. 'Father, what is the purpose of your visit?'

Isaac sighed. 'You mother is insisting you stay at the house.'

'I thought she was determined I wasn't to put Mrs Lamb to any trouble?'

His father shrugged. 'That was her initial stance, yes. I believe she thought a few days at the Glyn Arms would bring you to your senses. However, as her plan clearly hasn't worked, I believe she now finds it rather humiliating admitting to our acquaintances that our only son is living in a public house.'

Harry shook his head. 'I'm happy here. I've made friends. I can be myself here. I'm not "Isaac Whitworth's son", I'm just plain old Harry.'

Isaac regarded his son wistfully. 'I admire your guts, Henry, I really do. This Hopwood girl . . . all right, all right!' He held up his hands in a placatory gesture. 'I apologize. *Leah* is a fortunate girl indeed.' He downed the last of his port. 'I'd like you to work for me again this summer,' he said, getting to his feet.

'I'd prefer to stay where I am,' Harry replied, standing up.

'I see.' Isaac nodded as he held out his hand. 'Of course, you realize your mother blames me entirely for this situation.'

'I don't doubt it, sir,' Harry grinned as they shook hands warmly.

'Look, I'm staying at the house tonight. Why don't you and Leah come for supper? Perhaps it's time I got to know the girl a little better.'

'Oh, well, thank you,' Harry spluttered, taken aback by his father's invitation. 'I wouldn't want to put Mrs Lamb out.'

'Nonsense.' Isaac waved away his concern. 'She always cooks far too much, as I'm sure you remember. And she'd love to see you. Shall we say eight o'clock?'

'Very well, as long as Leah is agreeable, we'll see you at eight.'

Leah was hopeful they could build bridges with his parents, he mused as he walked his father outside, so perhaps she'd welcome the invitation. His father was much easier to get along with. He certainly couldn't imagine his mother bonding with Leah over a cup of Earl Grey.

CHAPTER THIRTY

'Heavens to Betsy, Leah,' Hannah exclaimed, looking up from the stocking she was darning. 'Will you find something to do? You're trying my patience.'

'I can't concentrate on anything, Mum,' Leah wailed. 'It's been ages since Mr Whitworth arrived at the pub. It's over an hour since we saw Reverend Roberts go by.' She paused to look out of the window but saw no sign of Harry, or anyone else for that matter. The lane was quite deserted. 'Perhaps I should go along to the pub and see if he's still there,' she suggested, turning round.

'You are not going to a public house, my girl,' Hannah said sternly, biting off a piece of thread. 'Your father would turn in his grave.'

'But I'm going out of my mind,' she cried, flouncing across the room to collapse into a chair.

'Oh, don't be so melodramatic,' scoffed Daisy. 'Harry's having a pint with his father. Where's the harm in that?'

'The fact that his father is Isaac Whitworth does put a

slightly different slant on things, don't you think?' Snapped Leah. 'I mean, he'd say and do anything to get Harry to change his mind about me.'

'I think Harry's proved himself not to be so fickle,' Daisy said in a kinder tone. 'Hasn't he, Mum?' She looked to her mother for confirmation.

'Of course he has,' Hannah agreed, getting up to light the lamp. 'And any lad who's so easily swayed isn't worth his salt, as far as I'm concerned.'

'I hope you're right,' Leah sighed. She'd had a sick feeling in the pit of her stomach ever since Joshua had told her of Isaac's visit. Much as she trusted Harry, she couldn't help the niggling fear that he might be persuaded that she wasn't good enough for him. She would certainly never be good enough for Isaac and Frances Whitworth.

'Well, you can stop worrying,' Daisy said, nodding towards the window. 'Because here he comes now.'

Leah wrenched open the door and met Harry in the lane.

'Joshua saw your father going into the Glyn Arms. Is everything all right?' Her smile wavered uncertainly.

'Perfectly,' Harry grinned. 'My father has invited us to dine with him this evening.'

'What?' Leah exclaimed, her initial relief giving way to panic as she stood aside to let him in.

'Good afternoon, Mrs H. Daisy, good afternoon.' Harry said, as Leah stared after him.

'I'm so glad you're here, Harry,' grinned Daisy. 'Leah's been in a right state.'

'I have not,' retorted Leah, crossly.

'Daisy,' Hannah said mildly, barely able to hide her smile. 'Put the kettle on. I'm sure Harry would like a cup of tea?'

'Thank you, yes.' Harry took Leah's hand. Her blue eyes were anxious and he gently brushed a strand of hair from her face.

'And bring the cake tin,' Hannah told Daisy. Turning to Harry and Leah she added, 'You'll need something to tide you over if you're only eating at eight.' She busied herself tidying her sewing basket, her back half-turned away from Leah and Harry to afford them a little privacy.

'This invitation to supper ...' Leah said slowly. 'What does it mean?'

'I believe my father may be coming round to the idea of us. Once he gets to know you properly, I'm sure he will approve and will, in turn, persuade my mother to accept you. I hope so, anyway.'

Leah's smile felt forced. She couldn't see Harry's mother ever warming towards her. But no matter, she tossed her head. They didn't need the Whitworth money. Harry had proved he was more than capable of earning a living. As long as they had each other, they would be happy, whatever their prospects.

Her train of thought was interrupted by the arrival of Daisy with the tea tray.

'Thanks, love,' said Hannah, lifting half a fruit cake from the tin. 'How's work going, Harry?' she asked, picking up a knife to slice the cake.

'Very well, thank you, Mrs H,' Harry replied politely. 'Ah,

thank you, Daisy,' he said, accepting his cup of tea with a grin. 'Farmer Doyle has assured me I'll have a job for as long as I want it.' He turned to Leah, seated next to him on the sofa. 'I know it's a long way off,' he said with excitement. 'but there might even be a cottage going, once we're married.'

'That sounds . . . wonderful,' Leah breathed. A farm cottage of her own. She could already imagine herself making her own cheese and butter while Harry worked on the land. It was just over two years until Harry turned twenty-one and they would be free to marry. She couldn't wait.

'That sounds very promising,' Hannah said, handing round slices of rich fruit cake. 'And Mr Doyle is a fair man. I went to school with one of his daughters.'

'I get on well with him,' Harry said, taking a bite of fruit cake. 'This is delicious, Mrs H.'

'Daisy deserves the credit,' Hannah smiled. 'She made it.'

'It's very tasty, Daisy.'

'Thank you,' Daisy said, grinning at the compliment.

Only half-listening to the conversation flowing around her, Leah forced herself to swallow a mouthful of cake. The prospect of supper with Harry's father had turned her stomach into a jumble of nerves. She inhaled deeply, determined to accept Isaac's olive branch and take the opportunity to build bridges. Despite Harry's determination to make his own way in the world, she was aware that the estrangement wounded him deeply. In spite of their faults, he loved his parents and Leah was prepared to do her part in bringing about a reconciliation. She took a sip of her tea to wash down the cake and smiled at Harry, who was in the middle of telling her mother and Daisy about a childhood visit to Regent's Park Zoo.

'I've never been to London,' Daisy said wistfully.

'Nor have I,' said Leah, slightly embarrassed by the fact that she had never travelled further than Southampton.

'I went once,' Hannah said, getting up to refill the tea pot. 'It was before I married your father. A group of us went up on the train for the day.'

'You would enjoy it,' Harry said, 'Perhaps we could go up at Christmas? The tree in Trafalgar Square is something to behold and the windows in Harrods are spectacular.'

'Maybe we should?' agreed Leah. 'Alice said her aunt has issued an open invitation. We're welcome to stay with her any time. Why don't we plan something? I'll speak to her about it.' Her face fell. 'I'm not sure Dora would be able to afford it.'

'She will when Mr Webb's inheritance comes through,' Daisy pointed out.

'Once he's married to Barbie-Jean, poor Dora won't get a look-in,' Leah scoffed. 'That woman will have the lot.'

'Let's hope Stephen comes to his senses before then,' her mother remarked drily. 'Have they still not heard anything about the money?'

Leah shook her head. 'Dora's convinced they've lost it.'

'Unfair of that chap to get their hopes up before he had firm proof it belonged to Mr Webb,' Daisy added.

'Well, it's the first week of March. They should hear soon,'

Hannah said, sounding unconvinced. She picked up the tea pot. 'More tea, Harry?'

Holding the lantern aloft, Harry gripped Leah's hand tightly as they traversed the winding gravel driveway up to Streawberige House. It was a clear, cold night, their breath billowing in front of their faces. The dew-wet lawn sparkled in the moonlight and the sky was studded with stars.

'Nervous?' Harry asked as they approached the front of the house, their footsteps sounding eerily loud in the stillness.

'Yes,' Leah whispered. 'Are you?'

Harry gave an anxious laugh and cleared his throat. 'Very.' He squeezed her gloved hand. 'It will be fine,' he said slowly, but Leah couldn't help but wonder whether he was trying to convince himself as much as her.

Light spilled across the gravel from the downstairs windows. Taking a deep breath, her heart thumping wildly in her chest and gripping Harry's hand tightly, she climbed the steps. Harry rang the bell.

The door was opened almost immediately, flooding the steps with light.

'Good evening, Mrs Lamb,' Harry said politely. 'Leah, this is Mrs Lamb, our housekeeper. Mrs Lamb, my fiancée, Miss Leah Hopwood.'

Mrs Lamb was a squat, stern-looking woman with greying brown hair worn in a bun and dark, disapproving eyes that seemed to appraise Leah for an inordinately length of time.

'Good evening, Miss Hopwood,' she said, her tone

bordering on mockery. 'Good evening, Master Henry. Your father is awaiting you in the drawing room.'

'Thank you, Mrs Lamb.' Harry sniffed the air appreciatively. 'Something smells delicious.'

If he intended to appeal to the housekeeper's with flattery, he failed dismally. Choosing to ignore the compliment, she simply stood aside to allow them into the brightly lit hall.

Leah blinked, the light blazing from the wall sconces making her eyes water, and took a quick look round as Mrs Lamb ushered them towards what she assumed to be the drawing room. There was a grand staircase leading up to a galleried landing on which hung several portraits of a rather sombre-looking man.

'My grandfather,' Harry whispered as Mrs Lamb opened a door to their left and announced their arrival.

'Thank you, Mrs Lamb,' Leah heard Isaac Whitworth say over the rustle of a newspaper. 'Show them in.'

The housekeeper stood back to allow them into a tastefully furnished drawing room. Leah made to thank her but at the woman's dark, censorious glare, the words died on her lips and she clutched Harry's hand all the harder as she followed him into the room.

'Good evening, Henry. Miss Hopwood. A pleasure to see you again,' Isaac said as he rose from a ruby-red wingback chair and strode towards them, hand outstretched.

'Good evening, Father.' Henry shook his father's hand.

'Have a seat,' said Isaac, indicating the red velvet

Chesterfield sofa. 'Supper will be a few minutes, yet.' He went over to an elaborately carved wooden cabinet, the polished walnut gleaming in the lamplight. 'A glass of port?' he asked, opening it to reveal an assortment of glassware and several bottles.

'Thank you,' Leah croaked nervously. It was warm in the drawing room and she could feel herself perspiring under her corset. The room, decorated in red velvet and dark walnut, with heavy red and gold brocade floor length curtains, was dominated by an ornate black and white marble fireplace above which hung an oil painting of Isaac and Frances.

'I commissioned that for Frances' twenty-sixth birthday,' Isaac said, following Leah's gaze as he handed her a glass of port.

'It's lovely,' Leah said, taking a quick swig of her drink in an effort to lubricate her dry throat.

'It's always been one of my favourite paintings of the two of you,' remarked Harry. Settling back on the sofa, he casually laid his arm along the backrest, his hand resting lightly on Leah's shoulder. 'I believe it used to hang in the drawing room in Richmond, am I right, Father?'

'Yes.' Isaac replied shortly. 'I'm afraid Frances finds it hard to look at which is why I arranged to have it moved down here,' he explained, giving Leah a wry smile. 'I should burn it, I suppose, but I can't quite bring myself to get rid of it.' There was a lengthy silence while all three studied the painting. It depicted Isaac and Frances sitting on a wooden bench, Streawberige House in the background. Their faces were slightly turned towards each other, and they were holding hands and smiling. They were clearly a couple very much in love and excited about the future ahead of them.

Frances' other hand, Leah noticed, was resting gently on her stomach. *Had she been expecting little Celestia then?* she wondered. The baby girl who'd lived barely a week?

'I dare say you keep it because it reminds you of happier times,' Harry said, breaking the silence in which the only sounds were the crackle of the flames and the melodious tick of the grandfather clock.

'I reckon you're right,' Isaac agreed, as the sound of approaching footsteps heralded the arrival of Mrs Lamb.

'Supper is served, sir.'

'Thank you, Mrs Lamb.' Isaac stood up. 'Shall we?' he said to Leah, offering her his arm. She hesitated, looking to Harry for guidance. He gave her an almost imperceptible nod. Her stomach clenching with nerves, she got to her feet. Taking Isaac's arm, she allowed him to escort her into the dining room.

The long table was laid for three and dominated by an elaborate floral centrepiece, despite it being too early in the year for most blooms. A large candelabra hung from the baroque ceiling, sending a diamond-effect pattern of light dancing up the walls and across the white tablecloth.

The walls were off-white and the curtains a soft, buttery yellow. A fire burned in the grate, above which hung a por-trait of Queen Victoria.

Isaac took the head of the table, of course, with Leah on

his right. Taking his place opposite her, Harry winked. Leah smiled, taking courage from his presence.

The meal was delicious: celery soup followed by steak and mushrooms and Valentia pudding. Leah was relieved she didn't seem to be expected to contribute much to the conversation, simply nodding and smiling whenever she deemed it appropriate, as most of the talk appeared to be about estate matters. She tried to pay attention though, as one day, if she were indeed mistress of Streawberige House and its surrounding land, she would need to know how to best support Harry in his duties. Her first task as mistress, she reflected mischievously, would be to get rid of the sour-faced housekeeper.

Her expression and mannerisms left Leah in no doubt that the woman disapproved of her relationship with Harry. Isaac, on the other hand was playing the perfect host. Despite most of the conversation going over her head, he did make an effort to include Leah in as much as he could and so, it came as something of a shock when, after sending Harry down to the cellar to fetch another bottle of red wine, Isaac turned to Leah and said, 'I'm prepared to pay you fifty pounds to stay away from my son.'

Leah's smile froze on her face. 'I beg your pardon?' She frowned, unable to comprehend what her ears had heard.

'I'm sure you heard me, Miss Hopwood.' Isaac smiled but where, a few moments before his expression had been open and amiable, his eyes were now cold and his smile brittle. 'I will pay you the sum of fifty pounds tonight if you break off your relationship with Henry.'

Leah's mouth fell open. Was she hearing right? Harry's father was offering to buy her off?

'It's a vast sum of money,' Isaac continued. 'You will be able to leave Strawbridge. Grief, child, you could buy yourself a house. Make a better life for your mother and sister.'

'But we love each other,' blurted Leah.

Isaac shook his head. 'Henry believes himself to be in love with you, and why wouldn't he? You're a very pretty girl. But you're what, nearly seventeen?' Leah nodded, anguish rendering her mute. 'Too young to know your own mind. And as for Henry, well, he'll tire of you soon enough. I'm sorry, my dear, but I must be blunt. It's not unusual for a young man in Henry's position to rebel a little. It's natural. I was the same at his age. However, when all is said and done, Henry is a Whitworth and it is his duty to marry well and produce an heir.'

Leah swallowed. Her food churned alarmingly in her stomach and for one awful moment, she thought she might be sick all over the beautiful snow-white damask tablecloth. Taking a deep breath, she pushed her shoulders back and said, in a shaky voice,

'I'm sorry, Mr Whitworth, but I'm afraid I cannot accept your bribe.'

'I wouldn't call it a bribe, as such,' laughed Isaac with a wave of his hand. 'More an inducement.'

'Nevertheless,' Leah said, forcing herself to remain calm. It was all she could do not to run from the room in tears. 'I will not be paid off. If Harry wishes to end our relationship, he can tell me so himself.'

To her immense relief, footsteps sounded in the hall, alerting them to Harry's return.

'Sorry I took so long,' he grinned, brandishing a bottle. 'I had a devil of a job finding the right one. You've got quite the collection down there, father.' As if sensing the atmosphere, the smile slipped from his face, his gaze darting between his father and Leah. 'What's happened?' he asked, his eyes narrowing suspiciously. 'Leah, what has he said?'

'As you are incapable of behaving in a responsible manner and fulfilling your duty as a Whitworth,' Isaac said slowly. 'I attempted to get Miss Hopwood to see sense and release you from whatever rash promises you have made to her.'

'He offered me fifty pounds to leave you,' Leah said, defiantly, her eyes glittering dangerously. Now that the shock was wearing off, she felt like her anger might choke her.

'Is that true, Father?' Anger rose like a red tide up Harry's cheeks. 'You led me to believe you were ready to offer an olive branch and accept Leah into our family as my future wife?'

'Poppycock!' Isaac banged his fist on the table making the tableware and Leah jump. 'For pity's sake, Henry! See sense, will you? She's our tenant. You'll be a laughing stock. Your mother and I will be a laughing stock. How will we hold our heads up in polite society? And you,' Isaac nodded at Leah. 'You'll only show yourself up with your lack of breeding. Can you really see yourself as mistress of this house? You'd be so out of your depth it would be laughable if it wasn't so tragic.'

'Leah, come on.' Harry pulled back her chair. 'We're leaving.' Leah needed no second bidding.

'Don't be a fool, Henry!' Isaac blustered angrily. 'You walk out now and you'll burn your last bridge. That will be it. You'll be dead to your mother and I.'

'So be it, Father,' Harry said, with all the dignity he could muster. 'Give Mother my fondest regards when you see her.'

'Did you hear a word I said, boy?' Isaac bellowed after them. He got up from the table so quickly his chair fell to the ground with a crash, bringing Mrs Lamb hurrying from the kitchen.

'What's going on?' she asked, perplexed to find Leah and Harry in the hall pulling on their wraps.

'You're not welcome in this house anymore!' Isaac shouted. Standing in the doorway of the dining room, Leah thought he looked like someone demented. And perhaps he was – demented with grief at the loss of his only son. But she couldn't find it in her heart to feel sorry for him. He had only himself to blame.

'You should be ashamed of yourself,' Mrs Lamb hissed, as Harry wrenched open the heavy door. 'And as for you.' The look she gave Leah dripped pure venom. 'You're no better than you should be, I shouldn't wonder.'

'I'll thank you not to use that tone with my fiancée,' said Harry coldly. He glanced over to where Isaac was leaning against the doorframe, shoulders slumped, looking deflated.

'Goodbye, Father,' Harry said crisply. 'I doubt we'll speak

again.' Pulling Leah out in to the cold night, he let the heavy door bang shut behind them. It was only when they were halfway down the driveway that Leah allowed the tears she had been keeping at bay to fall.

CHAPTER THIRTY-ONE

Nate was waiting for Dora as she and Leah left work the following Tuesday evening.

'Have you got time for a cup of tea?' he asked, pushing himself off the lamppost against which he'd been leaning.

Dora hesitated, puzzled by his unexpected appearance. She'd been avoiding him at home as much as was possible given that they lived in the same cottage. 'Not really. Father will be wanting his supper.'

'He'll be fine,' Nate said. 'My lazy mother's quite capable of warming up a bowl of stew. Please,' he continued earnestly when Dora didn't reply. 'I really need to talk to you away from our parents.' Dora looked at Leah.

'I'll let your dad know you'll be late,' she offered.

'All right.' Dora shrugged. 'But I can't be long. I'm exhausted.'

'This won't take long,' promised Nate. As they said good-bye to Leah and walked down the road, Dora was acutely aware of her red-stained fingers and the chemical smell that clung to her clothes and hair and she wondered what the immaculately turned out Miss King would think about Nate inviting her for a cup of tea.

They walked in silence, turning the corner into Princes Street. It had been raining off and on all day and the wet pavements shimmered in the light of the streetlamps. At the far end of the road light spilled from the steamed-up windows of a small café. Frequented by sailors and factory workers it had a reputation for serving hearty, wholesome food.

The handful of customers occupying the tables looked up at the jangle of the bell but gave Dora and Nate no more than a cursory glance.

'I'll be with you in a minute,' Katy, the proprietor, called cheerfully from behind the counter as they sat down at an out-of-the-way table in the corner. The warm, damp air reeked of tobacco smoke and fish. From behind a dirty screen came the clatter of pan lids and the babble of voices. The walls were decorated with postcards depicting exotic, faraway places and, in a large cage on the counter, a colourful Macaw kept a watchful eye on the proceedings.

'Is Miss King well?' Dora asked coolly once Katy had taken their order for a pot of tea and fish stew.

'Yes, I believe so.' Nate raised his eyebrows in surprise. 'Why do you ask?'

Dora shrugged. 'No reason. I just assumed she must be under the weather as you've chosen to spend your evening out with me.'

Nate's frown deepened and he fiddled with the cuff of his

white shirt. 'I believe Rosie, Miss King, is dining with her in-laws this evening.'

'She's married?' exclaimed Dora, scandalized.

'Yes.' Nate looked at her, perplexed. 'Her husband is a merchant seaman. He's away at sea a lot.'

Dora's eyes narrowed. 'I see,' she said, pursing her lips in disapproval. She would never have imagined Nate to be the sort to dally with a married woman.

'Anyway, I'd rather not discuss Miss King's marital status this evening, if you don't mind.'

'I've no doubt,' responded Dora drily, ignoring his apparent confusion.

'May I ask why you've been so cold towards me the past few days?' he asked.

'I'm sure I didn't mean to be,' Dora said as their food arrived. 'Thank you,' she smiled as Katy set the bowl of steaming hot fish stew on the table.

'You're welcome,' Katy beamed. 'Enjoy.'

Nate regarded Dora quizzically through the haze of swirling steam. 'I thought we were friends,' he said, picking up his spoon. 'But since the weekend you've been treating me like a stranger.' He put his spoon down again and leaned back in his chair, arms folded across his chest. 'So, come on, Dor. Tell me what's going on? What have I done to upset you?'

'I thought we were friends, too,' Dora replied, pouring milk into their cups.

'Then what is it?' Nate persisted as Dora poured the tea. Her haunted expression cut him to the quick and, more than anything, he wanted to take her in his arms and kiss away all the pain and hurt, whatever was causing it.

'It's just ...' She looked away, feeling the heat rising in her cheeks. The café was bustling. Voices ebbed and flowed. The bell jangled as the door opened to admit three swarthy-skinned sailors. They were laughing and joking as they took a table by the steamed-up window.

'Evening, boys,' Katy beamed, hurrying over to take their order.

'What, Dora?' Nate said softly. 'You can tell me anything, you know that? Is it Mum? You know you really should stand up to her. I hate the way she treats you like a skivvy. It makes my blood boil, it really does.'

Dora sighed. 'Look, Nate, it's none of my business what you get up to,' she said, keeping her gaze fixed on her bowl. 'If you wish to see a married woman behind her husband's back, then do so. It's just, I thought, well ... It's not your fault you don't feel the same.' The colour rushed into her cheeks, humiliation suffusing her whole face with colour. Discomfort pricked her spine and her stomach clenched.

'What?' Nate looked at her, incredulous. 'You think I'm having an affair with Rosie? That's preposterous.' His face clouded. 'And frankly, I'm shocked you could even think that of me.'

'But the other day in the cafe,' Dora blinked in confusion. 'You and Miss King ... or I assume it's Mrs King, is it?'

'She uses her maiden name at work.' Nate smiled. 'I've been helping her find somewhere for her and her husband to live when he comes home on shore leave next month. She had a few bad experiences with prospective landlords and asked if I'd accompany her. That's all.'

'Oh.' Dora lowered her gaze. She could feel her cheeks burning.

'Are you jealous of Miss King?' Nate asked teasingly. 'So, does this mean, you like me?' he went when she didn't reply, his voice soft. 'As more than a friend?' Not daring to raise her eyes, Dora simply nodded. Her embarrassment was so acute she wished the ground would open up and swallow her. How would she ever be able to look Nate in the eye again after this?

'Dora,' he reached across the table and took her hand in his. She tensed, aware of how rough her discoloured fingers must feel. Sensing her unease, Nate let go and sat back.

'Look at me, Dor,' he said gently.

She slowly lifted her head, her cheeks aflame.

'Oh, you silly goose,' he said so quietly she had to strain her ears to hear him over the noise of the café. 'Don't you know I practically fell in love with you the day we moved in?'

Dora stared at him in disbelief. Surely, she hadn't heard right? Nate was in love with her? Her eyes narrowed suspiciously. Was this some elaborate joke at her expense?

'Don't tease me, Nate,' she said.

'I'm not,' Nate retorted, sounding wounded that she could believe he could be so callous. 'I didn't think you were interested in me, which is why I was content to be your friend.'

Looking at his earnest expression, she wanted so much to believe him.

Nate squeezed her fingers. 'So, do you feel the same way about me?' Dora pretended to study him thoughtfully. Nate's sixteenth birthday had passed relatively uncelebrated in February. Dora would be seventeen in October. She was older than him by four months, yet Nate's height and maturity gave lie to the fact that he was the younger of the two. He could easily have passed for eighteen any day of the week.

'Honestly?' she smiled, abandoning the pretence. 'I think I was attracted to you from the start, too. Although, I never imagined for one minute you'd fall for someone like me?'

'What do you mean?' frowned Nate.

'Well,' Dora flushed beetroot red. 'You're so good looking and I'm, well, a bit plain.'

'Plain?' Dora smiled at Nate's look of astonishment. 'How can you possibly consider yourself to be plain?' he asked, genuinely puzzled. 'You're beautiful.'

As they left the café sometime later, a warm glow lingered in her stomach that had nothing to do with the hearty stew.

'Alice lent me her bicycle,' Nate said as they rounded the corner. 'I left it across the road from where you work.'

'Oh,' said Dora, who hadn't been looking forward to the long, cold, walk home.

With Dora balancing on the handle bars, Nate peddled the bicycle home. They arrived at the cottages just as the church clock was chiming eight.

'That's one of the most hair-raising journeys I've ever had,' she laughed, jumping down.

'Nonsense,' grinned Nate. 'You'll always be perfectly safe with me.'

Still laughing, Dora lifted the latch and pushed open the door. Stepping over the threshold she knew at once that something was wrong.

'Father?' she cried, shocked by the sight of him slumped dejectedly in the bed. 'What has happened?' She glanced around the room. 'Where is Mrs Gardener?' Afraid something untoward had happened to Nate's mother, she shot him a quick glance. When Stephen made no move to answer, Nate strode across the room.

'Mother?' he shouted, taking the stairs two at a time.

'Dad, what has happened?' Dora knelt at Stephen's side. His breathing was ragged, and his skin pale and waxy. For a frightening moment, Dora thought he might be suffering another stroke. She lifted his hand to her cheek. Raised voices sounded overhead and she frowned. 'Have you and Mrs Gardener had a falling out?'

'It's over,' Stephen whispered hoarsely without raising his eyes.

'What's over?' asked Dora as her father continued to stare into the fire. 'Dad, what has happened?'

Stephen shook his head, his eyes swimming with tears.

'It came this morning.' With a shaking hand he pointed to something lying on the table.

'What is it?' Dora asked, getting to her feet. From upstairs came the sound of a drawer being slammed shut and more shouting but the words were indistinct and Dora couldn't hear what was being said. At the sight of the letter lying on the table she was filled with a sense of foreboding. With surprisingly steady hands, she picked it up. Behind her, her father started to sob.

'It's from Mr Lyle,' she read, her heart sinking. 'They've found another will. There's another sole beneficiary.' She read it through several times, feeling the disappointment rising as the news slowly sank in. Despite her philosophical approach to the money, and not wanting to count her chickens, it was still something of a blo. Her heart ached for her father. He had been so convinced the money was his.

'Oh, Dad,' she said sorrowfully, turning towards him. 'I'm so sorry.' The sight of him sobbing pitifully into his hands broke her heart and she hurried to his side. 'It's all right, Dad,' she tried to comfort him. 'We'll be all right. We always have been. I've got my job and in another couple of months the strawberry harvest will start again. We'll be all right, you'll see.'

Stephen shook his head. Rocking from side to side, he keened wildly, his garbled sentences making no sense.

'I can't tell what you're saying,' Dora said gently, leaning closer.

'She's leaving me,' he heaved, almost choking on the words.

'Who's leaving? Mrs Gardener?' Dora's question was answered by the heavy tread of footsteps on the landing. Nate descended the stairs at breakneck speed, his face red, his eyes glittering angrily.

'Dora, I'm so sorry.' He crossed the gap between them and took her in his arms. 'Mr Webb, I'm sorry for the way my mother has treated you.' His eyes flashed. 'I'm ashamed of her.'

'Who are you to be ashamed of your own mother, you little upstart?' Barbie-Jean hollered, from the landing, her large suitcase banging against the banister as she dragged it down the stairs.

Dora leaned against Nate, grateful for his arm around her shoulder. 'You're leaving?'

'Of course I'm leaving,' Barbie-Jean sneered, breathing hard. 'Do you think I really wanted to tie myself to a snivelling cripple?' She gave a shrill laugh. 'It was the money I was interested in,' she snapped, giving Stephen a filthy look. 'You led me to believe it was a dead cert. Well, we're not sticking around. Come on, Nate. We'll spend the night at the pub and take the train back to London tomorrow.'

'No,' Nate said. 'I told you, I'm not going with you.'

'You'll do as I say, my boy.' Barbie-Jean rounded on him angrily. 'Or I'll box your ears.'

'You can try,' Nate sneered with a mirthless grin. He was at least two inches taller than his mother. Visibly shocked that her son would dare to defy her, Barbie-Jean started to cry.

'Oh, don't try the waterworks with me, Mum,' Nate said. He shrugged his shoulders. 'Look, you want to go back to London, go. I think it's best under the circumstances, don't you? I'll come with you for now. I'm sure Mr Webb won't want me hanging about tonight, but I'm not leaving

Strawbridge. I'm not giving up my job.' He turned his face towards Dora and his expression softened. 'And I'm not leaving Dora.'

'Oh, do what you want,' Barbie-Jean snapped angrily, her tears drying as quickly as they'd come. 'I'm better off without you anyway. You can carry my suitcase, though, or are you going to force your poor mum to lug it all the way up the road?'

'I'll carry it,' Nate sighed as Barbie-Jean made for the door.

'Barbie-Jean,' Stephen said, his gaze pleading. 'Don't go. Please?'

'Dad, don't.'

Barbie-Jean shot Stephen a contemptuous glare and, lifting the latch, stepped out into the lane.

'Nate?' Dora said, her eyes wide and anxious.

'I'll stay at the pub,' he said. 'I can't stay here. Not after what she's done.' He glanced at Stephen, who was crying pitifully. 'I'll see you tomorrow, after work.' Giving her hand a quick squeeze, he followed his mother out into the night.

Shoulders drooping, Dora hurried to her father's side, but he pushed her away.

'Go away,' he sobbed. 'Just leave me alone.'

'I'm not leaving you like this,' Dora told him sadly. Fetching a blanket from her bed upstairs, she settled herself in the chair, dozing fitfully on and off until dawn.

CHAPTER THIRTY-TWO

'It's nice to see you happier, Dora' Leah said as the girls made their way up the lane.

'I honestly thought it would take Dad ages to get over Mrs Gardener,' Dora replied. 'But he's been remarkably cheerful these last couple of days.'

'He was obviously not as fond of her as he thought,' offered Alice, wheeling her bicycle alongside them.

'Apparently not,' Dora replied, gaily. 'In fact, as I was leaving this morning, he asked for a bowl of water and his razor.'

'That's a good sign,' Leah said. 'At least he's making an effort with his hygiene again.

'It's certainly lifted my spirits,' agreed Dora.

In the first few days since Barbie-Jean had upped and left Dora's father had sunk into a melancholy so deep, she'd been afraid he'd never come out of it. Not even Hannah had been able to rouse him. Alternating between grief and violent bouts of anger, Dora had found him almost unmanageable. Several times during his violent outbursts, she had to run to fetch Mathew Turner. Thankfully, Stephen still retained a little self-respect and pride and had calmed down, clearly ashamed that the churchwarden, and old friend, would see him behaving so appallingly.

Over the past two days, however, his behaviour had undergone a remarkable change. He'd been polite and amiable, even going so far as to invite Nate to join him and Dora for supper. Both Dora and Nate had been on edge, expecting recriminations over Barbie-Jean's behaviour but, except to enquire over whether she had arrived in London safely, Stephen hadn't mentioned the woman's name again.

'And how are things with you and Nate?' asked Alice nonchalantly. She still couldn't bring herself to approve of Nate and his mother's latest shenanigans had done nothing to improve her opinion of him.

'Good,' replied Dora, blushing. 'Really good. We're taking things slowly. He's barely even held my hand but, like he says, we've our whole life ahead of us.'

'I can't wait to marry Harry,' Leah sighed. 'It's just such a shame we have to wait.'

'There's no chance of a reconciliation between Harry and Mr Whitworth, then?' asked Alice.

'No, not after the things he said. Harry can barely bring himself to mention his name. I'm glad he's gone back to London. Goodness knows how it will be when he's back for the strawberry harvest, though Harry believes he may not bother to come down at all.'

'But Mr Whitworth always spends the summer here,' Dora pointed out. 'He won't change his habit, surely?'

Leah shrugged. 'Who knows? Harry wants nothing to do with him.' She stopped talking as all three girls came to a halt, their gaze drawn to the three cottages up ahead. A horse and buggy was tethered outside Dora's cottage and a small crowd had formed outside.

'Oh, no!' Dora cried in alarm. 'What's he done now?' Picking up her skirts, she broke into a run.

With Alice still pushing her bicycle, she and Leah ran after her. She wasn't surprised to see her mother amongst the onlookers. Hannah was always first on hand when Stephen Webb needed help. Only this time, Leah noticed with a growing sense of alarm, her mother didn't look like someone who had control of the situation.

'Oh, Dora!' Hannah cried, her face ashen, as she stepped forward to prevent Dora from entering.

'Sweetheart, don't go inside,' she said gently.

'What's happened?' Dora shrieked, terror etching her voice up several notches. She made to push past Hannah, but the older woman grabbed her arm. 'Let me through,' she screamed, terror rendering her hoarse. Through the half-open doorway, she caught a glimpse of Mathew Turner. He was grim faced and appeared to be talking to someone.

'Dad!' Dora called, struggling frantically against Hannah's grip. 'Dad! Let me go. I need to see my dad.'

'Dora, no, you mustn't.' Beatrice cried as Leah and Alice exchanged shocked glances.

'Dora, sweetheart.' Putting her arm around Dora's quivering shoulders, Hannah gently drew her to one side. 'I'm afraid I've got some bad news for you.' Dora shook her head.

'No,' she murmured. 'No. No. No!' Her cries grew louder with every utterance. With a sudden, violent movement, she shoved Hannah aside and ran back to the cottage, reaching the door just as Nate was coming out.

'Don't go in, Dora,' he said, putting out his arm to stop her. Ignoring him, she pushed her way past him and into the house where she stopped short, her shocked mind unable to comprehend what her eyes were seeing. The walls, the bed, the floor, were all bright crimson. It took her bewildered mind a moment to realize that it was blood. So much blood. She could taste its metallic scent on her lips and smell it in the air. Trembling, she took in the scene, her gaze coming to rest on the figure on the blood-soaked bed. Dora screamed.

'Get her out of here, for pity's sake!' shouted a man she'd never seen before but whom she later learned was a doctor from Botley.

Her knees buckled and it took Nate and Hannah together to bustle Dora out of the house. She collapsed in the lane, where she rocked back and forth, moaning and shivering violently.

'What's happened, Mum?' Leah asked Hannah, wide-eyed with shock and fear.

'Stephen's done away with himself,' her mother whispered.

'Help me get Dora inside away from this gawping lot. Daisy, stick the kettle on. Oh, thank God. Here comes Reverend Aldridge and Samuel.'

'... slit his own throat ...' The words, softly whispered but still loud enough to reach Dora's as ears caused her to retch painfully.

'Come on, Dor,' said Leah softly, slipping her arm around her friend's shoulders. 'Let's get you inside.' With Nate's help, she half-dragged Dora into the warm parlour and onto the sofa where she immediately curled up into a ball, sobbing quietly into the cushions.

'Is it all right if I stay?' Nate asked. He was perched on the arm of the sofa, gently stroking Dora's hair.

'Of course, you can, love,' Hannah said, bustling in with a mug of tea. She handed it to Nate. 'See if you can get her to drink this, will you?'

Wrapping her mother's shawl around her shoulders, Leah went and stood in the doorway. She could hear the onlookers murmuring amongst themselves. Strawbridge would be buzzing with the news for days. She spotted Alice talking to Samuel.

'Poor Dora,' Alice was saying. 'She'll be devastated.'

Samuel placed a comforting hand on her arm. 'She'll be all right with Leah's family. You and your grandmother go home,' he said. 'Walter and I will help Mathew take care of things in there.'

'The place will need washing down,' Beatrice said tearfully.

'There's time enough for all of that tomorrow,' Samuel said kindly, ushering her towards her own cottage. 'Dora won't be going back home for a few days at least.'

Leah shivered. She couldn't imagine ever wanting to stay in a house where such a terrible tragedy had taken place.

'At least the poor man is at peace now,' said Samuel.

'I don't understand, though,' Leah said, stepping into the lane. 'Dora was only just saying how much happier he'd seemed this past day or so'

'We shall never understand the torturous thoughts which drives a person to such lengths,' Samuel said. 'Now, if you'll excuse me, I must go and see what use I can be inside.'

'Give Dora my love, won't you,' said Alice as Leah made to go indoors. 'And tell her if there's anything I can do ...'

Leah nodded and patted her friend's arm. 'Of course, I will.'

'It's a terrible business,' Hannah said several hours later as she showed Nate out. She had given Dora one of Pearl's sleeping draughts in warm milk and put her to bed. She'd left Leah lying in the bed next to her, arms wrapped around her friend while she sobbed herself to sleep.

Nate nodded. 'What will she do now?' he asked. 'Will she be able to keep the cottage?'

Hannah shrugged. 'She's managed the rent by herself since Stephen had his accident so there's no reason why not.' She shuddered. 'I'm not sure she'll want to go back there. Would you?' She pulled her shawl tighter around her shoulders. 'I know I wouldn't.'

'Probably not right away,' Nate agreed.

'Well, she's welcome to stay with us as long as likes.' She gave the cottage next door a sideways glance. It was dark and silent. Everyone had left over an hour ago once Stephen's body had been taken away. 'I wonder if there'll be a funeral. Poor man. He deserves to be laid to rest alongside his late wife, though I doubt all folks will see it that way.'

'Reverend Aldridge is a reasonable man,' Nate said. 'Surely he'll make an exception?'

'I hope so. Anyway, lad,' Hannah said, looking up at the dark sky. 'You get yourself home before the heavens open. I'll see you tomorrow.'

'Goodbye, Mrs H, and thank you.'

'You're welcome, love. She's like a daughter to me, is Dora. I'll see she's all right, don't you fret.'

Dora took the next three days off work on compassionate grounds. She could ill afford the loss of wages but Nate had offered to make up the shortfall in her rent.

Her father's death was the talk of the tiny hamlet and it was inevitable that the news would reach the ears of Isaac Whitfield. On the Friday, three days after Stephen's death, and the day of his funeral, a telegram arrived for Dora offering Isaac and Frances' condolences and informing her she had until the end of the following week to vacate the cottage. Though notice of her eviction didn't surprise her, coming on the day of her father's funeral left a bitter taste in her mouth.

'You know you'll always have a home here with us, don't

you?' Hannah told her as they got ready upstairs. Dora nodded. She looked very pale in her black dress and hat. Her eyes were red-rimmed from crying. Nate was waiting downstairs with Daisy and Leah, looking very dapper in the dark suit he'd borrowed from Mathew Turner.

The funeral would be a small affair. Despite Walter's entreaties to the Bishop, Stephen would not be allowed to spend his eternal rest beside his beloved wife. He was to be buried on the north side of the church with very little ceremony. There would be no service or sermon. Reverend Aldridge would utter a few words at the graveside. That was all.

Clinging to Nate's arm, Dora could barely swallow for the huge lump in her throat as she followed her father's coffin down the cinder path around the side of the church. Rooks cawed in the belfry and the bell tolled mournfully as they made their way across the dew-damp grass to the freshly dug grave on the very edge of the churchyard.

They were a small group. Alice and Samuel, Beatrice and Mathew Turner, the Hopwoods and Harry, Nate and herself. Reverend Aldridge said a brief prayer and Stephen's coffin was lowered into the ground. Despite her resolve to behave in a dignified manner, Dora dissolved into tears. She buried her face against Nate's chest and he gently stroked her hair as he led her away.

They went back to Hannah's for tea and cake but even Daisy's fruit cake tasted like sawdust in Dora's mouth. She was exhausted. She wandered into the garden, desperate for some fresh air. The weather had turned warmer and dryer. Fluffy white clouds scudded across a pale blue sky and the fresh air was filled with the scent of spring flowers. The hens were laying again and the vegetable garden was tilled and ready for the spring planting.

She leaned against the coal bunker and tilted her face towards the sun. Before his accident, her father had loved being out of doors and it pained her that in the five years since he had never been outside once. Fresh tears of regret welled in her eyes. *If only she'd made more of an effort*, she thought, as she was flooded with feelings of guilt and shame.

'Here you are.' At the sound of Nate's voice, she turned. He had taken off his jacket and tie and rolled up his sleeves. He gave her a sad smile. 'How are you feeling?'

Dora gave a wan smile. 'Awful. I wish I'd done more to help him,' she said. 'I should have been kinder. Whenever I think of all those times I lost my patience with him, I . . .' Her voice cracked and she looked away.

'It's not your fault,' Nate said, coming towards her. 'If anyone is to blame, it's my mother. You did everything you could for your father, Dora. I know he wasn't the easiest man to get along with, but he did love you, and he appreciated all that you did for him. He told me so.'

'Did he?'

'Yes. He was a very unhappy man, Dora. He's at peace now. That should give you some measure of comfort, at least.'

'I'm going to miss him so much,' she sobbed, pressing her face into his suit jacket.

'I know.' Nate put an arm around her. 'But I'm here. You'll always have me. All right?'

Dora nodded, and wiped her eyes.

'Good.' He kissed her softly on the forehead. 'Come on. Let's go back inside.' He took her hand and led her into the kitchen where Alice was wrapping the leftover sandwiches in brown paper. She looked up as they entered.

'Dora, how are you bearing up?' she asked, her brow creased with concern.

'I'm coping,' Dora said, managing a weak smile.

'Mrs Hopwood was looking for you. Mr and Mrs Merrifield have come to pay their respects.'

'That's very kind of them,' said Dora, visibly touched. 'My father wasn't much of a drinker but he used to enjoy the odd pint in the Glyn Arms before ... Well, I must go and say hello.' She smiled at Nate. 'Will you excuse me?'

'Of course,' he smiled back. 'I'll give my sister a hand.'

At his use of the word 'sister' Alice stiffened but if Nate noticed, he gave no sign.

'Shall I take this sponge cake and offer it round?' he asked, picking up a slightly lopsided Victoria sponge that Leah had made.

'No thank you,' Alice replied a trifle frostily. 'I'll do it.'

Nate looked at her in surprise. 'I don't mind.'

'I said I'll do it,' Alice snapped.

'Look Alice,' Nate said, lowering his voice. 'I know you don't like me, but do you have to make it so obvious?' He was grinning which only served to infuriate Alice all the more.

'I don't know what you mean.'

'Could we at least try and get along? Instead of making things awkward for Dora?'

'Speaking of Dora,' Alice hissed, lowering her voice. 'Just what are your intentions towards her? The poor girl's just lost her father and ... I don't want her hurt any more,' she ended lamely.

'I'm not my father, Alice,' Nate said firmly. 'I'm very fond of Dora. Indeed, I'd go as far as to say I'm in love with her.'

Alice eyed him suspiciously.

'Look, I know what you're thinking. With a mother like mine and a father like Jez Elkin, there's no way I could possibly be a decent human being, right?'

Alice's crimson cheeks told him he'd hit the nail on the head.

'I was lucky,' he continued. 'My stepfather was a good man. He brought me up well.' He looked at Alice's stony expression and sighed. 'I'd really like to get to know you better, if you'd give me a chance. Apart from my mother, you're my only living blood relative.' He looked at her hopefully.

Alice didn't answer. Instead, she picked up the bucket and went outside to the pump. She worked the lever, filling the bucket, her heart and head warring within her. She'd wanted to embrace Nate as her brother for so long, yet something had always held her back. Was it fear? Was she afraid that if she let him into her life, he'd let her down like her father? Or worse, was she frightened that she would begin to see traces of her father in herself?

'Let me carry that for you.' She looked over her shoulder as he came up behind her. For the first time she seemed to see him clearly and it was like looking in a mirror. He had her features as well as her colouring, the same rich, dark chestnut-brown hair, the same dark brown eyes and olive skin. 'Please?'

Suddenly, she could fight it no longer and her resistance crumbled. She smiled, feeling as though a heavy yoke had been lifted from her shoulder.

'All right,' she said, stepping away from the bucket. 'Thank you.' As she made to pass him by, she stopped, her hand on his arm. 'In a fortnight or so, once Dora's feeling more herself, come round for supper. I can tell you what little I know of our father.'

'Thank you.' Nate nodded. 'I'd like that.'

CHAPTER THIRTY-THREE

Holy Saturday dawned fine and sunny. The dew was still on the ground when Beatrice let herself in to St. Luke's, her arms laden with golden daffodils. She always enjoyed being alone in the church. She liked the quiet stillness. She paused for a moment to admire the way the stained-glass windows cast their rainbows of colour over the freshly polished pews. The chime of the church clock made her jump. *No time for dillydallying today,* she mused with a smile, hurrying up the aisle, her footsteps sounding loudly on the stone slabs as dust motes moved lazily through the disturbed air.

Grandmother of the bride. The mere words sent a ripple of pride through her body. There had been a time when she didn't even know she had a granddaughter, and now here she was, preparing for her wedding. The thought sent a thrill down her spine. Her beaded ivory chiffon dress, one of her daughter Lily's creations, was hanging in her wardrobe. Lily had been working almost non-stop over the past couple of months to get all the dresses made in time. Beatrice smiled as she imagined the expression on Samuel's face when he saw Alice walking up the aisle in her wedding dress.

As she arranged the bright yellow flowers on the altar, she pondered on how well suited the young couple were. They both had a heart for the destitute and down-at-heel, and a willingness to serve their community. It was two weeks until Samuel's ordination at Winchester Cathedral and, as far as Beatrice was concerned, Alice would make the perfect vicar's wife.

Flowers done, she slipped into the front pew where, uttering a quick prayer for blessings over the soon-to-be married couple, her thoughts turned to Ian. Unable to bear the pain of loss a second time, she had tried to close her heart to the little boy, but in her darkest, loneliest moments he still came to her. In her mind's eye he was still that chubby, rosy-cheeked three-year-old, but he would be a man now. She tried to imagine what he might look like. As a child he had favoured her. Did he still look like her, or had he grown to be more like his father? These were the thoughts that tortured her when she lay awake in bed, listening to Mathew's gentle snoring. She sighed. Her husband was a good man, a decent man. How would he react when he learned the darker secrets of her past?

Her thoughts were interrupted by the creak of the heavy oak door and, as if conjured up by her thoughts, Mathew came striding up the aisle, his face a wreath of smiles.

'Well, isn't this a joyful day,' he said, rubbing his hands in glee. 'Happy the bride the sun shines upon.'

'It is a beautiful day,' Beatrice agreed.

'You've done a good job with the flowers,' Mathew said, nodding at the altar. Following his gaze, Beatrice smiled. After the austerity of Lent, the daffodils, combined with the sunlight streaming in through the stained-glass windows, lent the grey-stone building the touch of brightness it needed.

'Nervous?' he asked, slipping into the pew beside her.

'Excited,' she replied after a moment's thought. 'I know Alice and Samuel will be very happy together.'

'I don't believe I've ever seen a pair so well suited,' Mathew agreed, unconsciously echoing his wife's thoughts as he took her hand in his. 'I'm happy for them both.'

Beatrice opened her mouth. It was on the tip of her tongue to say something about Ian, but before she could utter a word, the door creaked open again to admit Reverend Aldridge. He was wearing a pair of brown trousers and an old fawn cardigan over a checked brown and white shirt.

'Good morning, Mathew, Mrs Turner,' he said jovially. 'What a glorious day for a wedding. Please excuse my attire. I've been catching up on a spot of weeding. It helps me gather my thoughts. Lovely arrangement, Mrs Turner. Now, Mathew, is there anything I need to be aware of, any last-minute hitches?'

'Not as far as I know, Reverend,' grinned Mathew, standing up.

'The groom was a bundle of nerves at breakfast this morning,' Walter laughed, 'But no sign of cold feet.'

'He'd better not get cold feet,' remarked Beatrice drily. 'I'm trusting you to get him to the church on time, Reverend.'

'Oh, he'll be here, Mrs Turner, don't you worry. Nerves notwithstanding, I doubt wild horses could keep him away.' He glanced at his pocket watch. 'Right, if there's nothing else, I'll see you both at eleven o'clock.'

'I'd better get on and prepare the marriage register, Bea,' Mathew said, giving Beatrice's cheek a quick kiss. 'I'll see you at home in a while.'

He hurried off to the vestry, leaving Beatrice alone again with her thoughts. The joy of today went some way to erasing the pain of the past. She had lost so many years with Lily, yet she had been blessed with the joy of seeing Alice and her other grandchildren grow up. She loved all her grandchildren, but Alice held an extra special place in her heart and she was overjoyed that she would get to celebrate this special day with her.

'You look so beautiful,' Lily breathed, wiping a tear from her eye.

'I feel beautiful,' laughed Alice, fingering the delicate lace sleeves.

'Reverend Roberts is a very lucky man,' said Leah, looking ravishing in dark mauve, a circlet of spring flowers in her dark blonde hair.

'You do look very lovely, Alice,' said Dora, slightly subdued. It was less than a month since her father's death and the pain was still raw but she forced a smile, determined not to spoil her friend's big day.

She was sitting on Alice's bed in her rose-sprigged bedroom in her parents' house. She sat up straighter, careful not to crease her gown. Her new mauve shoes pinched her feet slightly and she eased them off. Caroline, looking a picture in her pretty light mauve dress, was almost bouncing off the walls with excitement. Martha, too, could barely contain herself but, as a mature almost-12-year-old, she was desperately trying to conceal it.

'What a bevy of beauties,' Lily's friend, Violet exclaimed, coming into the room in a flurry of perfume and rustling duck-egg-blue silk. 'Oh, Alice,' she murmured, her bottom lip trembling with emotion. 'You look absolutely stunning. Lily, how can you be so calm? I'm almost in bits myself, and I'm only the honorary aunt.'

'Oh, the tears keep coming,' laughed Lily. 'Have Eleanor and Arthur arrived yet?'

'That's what I came to tell you,' Violet replied. 'They've gone ahead to the church and taken Jimmy and Johnny with them.'

'Oh, that's good of them,' Lily said with a sigh of relief. 'They were getting very boisterous and I'd hate them to mess their suits. How is James bearing up?'

'He's been out in the garden for the past half an hour practising his Father of the Bride speech,' Violet chuckled.

'Well,' Lily said, adjusting Alice's veil and stepping back to admire the full effect in the mirror. 'I think we're just about ready.' She glanced at the small clock on the nightstand. 'We'll have to leave for the church shortly, ladies.'

'Yipee!' shouted Caroline, dancing across the pale pink carpet and almost upsetting the tea tray.

'Do be careful, Carrie,' her mother admonished her. 'If you spill tea on your dress you'll have to forgo being a bridesmaid.' The threat of missing out on her big moment did the trick and she calmed down immediately.

'Right, come on, girls, it's time to go.' Lily gave Alice a hug. 'I'll see you at the church, my darling.'

'Thank you, Mother.' Alice's lip wobbled. 'For everything.' The words spoke volumes and for a moment, as the two women looked into each others eyes, it was as if they were alone in the room. 'You always did your best for me, Mother, and I'm so grateful.'

'You're my daughter and I love you,' whispered Lily. 'I could do nothing less, as you'll discover when you are blessed with children of your own.' They drew apart and Lily handed Alice her bouquet of spring flowers. Each of the bridesmaids had a similar bouquet, albeit slightly smaller, the stems tied with mauve ribbon.

Alice gave a shaky laugh. 'Would you mind if I had a few minutes with Leah and Dora before you leave?'

'Of course not,' Lily smiled. 'We have a few minutes to spare, girls.' She and Violet ushered the two younger girls out of the room, leaving the three friends together.

'I just want to thank you both,' Alice said in a tremulous voice. 'Over the past two and a bit years you two have been the best friends I could have wished for and I'm so happy that I'll have you both at my side today.' Her expression clouded. 'I'm especially grateful to you Dora. I know it can't be easy for you.'

'I wouldn't miss this for the world,' replied Dora, with genuine warmth.

'Nor I,' grinned Leah. 'I just hope you'll still have time for us once you're Mrs Samuel Roberts.'

'Of course,' Alice grinned back. 'Friends forever, that's us. Now, at the risk of creasing our dresses, give me a hug.' The three girls hugged warmly then, giggling like giddy schoolgirls, made their way carefully down the stairs. James was waiting for them in the hall, looking very handsome in his grey morning suit and top hat. Leah thought the expression on his face priceless as he watched Alice coming down the stairs.

'You are a vision of loveliness,' he said, stepping forward to take her hand. 'I shall be so proud and honoured to walk you down the aisle, my dear.' Blushing, Alice offered her cheek to accept his kiss.

'The carriage is waiting, my dear,' he said, turning to Lily. 'We shall be a few minutes behind you.' He turned back to Alice, saying with a grin. 'It doesn't do to appear too eager. Got to keep the young man on his toes.'

'Not too far behind, please,' relied Lily, giving Alice's hand a final squeeze.

They left in a flurry of silk and clattering of hooves, and Alice was left alone with her stepfather.

'Well, here we are,' said James, looking suddenly awkward as he cleared his throat and checked his appearance in the hall mirror. He smiled. 'Excited?'

Alice nodded. 'Yes.'

'Then let's go.'

They stepped out into the warm spring sunshine where the carriage was waiting, the pretty white horse pawing the ground impatiently.

'Thank you,' Alice said, smiling at the young coachman who leapt down to open the door. James helped her into the carriage, waiting while she arranged her skirts, before joining her on the plush seat. The coachman shut the door and within minutes they were off, the horse setting a jaunty pace.

'I have to admit,' James said, taking Alice's right hand in both of his, 'that when you announced your engagement, I thought it was too soon. After all, you haven't even known Samuel a year. I did think you were rushing into marriage.'

'Marry in haste, repent at leisure?' Alice smiled.

'Something like that,' James nodded, a small smile playing on his lips.

'And now?'

They were trotting down a leafy lane, dappled sunlight shining through the carriage windows. The air was filled with birdsong and the rush of the carriage wheels on the smooth ground.

'I am confident that Samuel will make you happy. He's a good man. To my mind, one of the best. I am assured that you will both be very happy together.'

'Thank you. Your blessing means a lot to me.'

'There was a time I hoped you might make a career for yourself.'

'Secretarial school,' Alice smiled. 'I probably would have enjoyed that, had my life taken a different path.'

'Had you not met a devastatingly handsome young curate,' her stepfather grinned.

'Well, quite.' Alice grinned back. She could hear the church bells ringing out in the clear air and she was touched to see how many residents had come out of their cottages to wave and wish her well.

'God bless you, Miss Alice,' called Tilly, standing outside her mean cottage, holding her baby in her arms, the older children clustered around her legs, waving handkerchiefs.

'Thank you so much,' she called, leaning out of the window and waving back.

The carriage rolled to a halt behind several others that lined the verge outside the church and she waved to Leah, Dora, Martha and Caroline who were waiting by the lychgate.

'I wish you all the best, miss,' the coachman said, opening the door to help Alice out of the carriage. She thanked him and waited impatiently while her bridesmaids adjusted her veil and took their place behind her. Reverend Aldridge appeared in the doorway, and Alice's heart began to race. *This is it*, she thought. *I'm about to become Samuel's wife.* James came to stand beside her and take her arm.

'Ready?' he whispered, giving her an encouraging smile. Alice nodded.

She heard the organist start to play and, taking a deep breath, they walked into the church.

Alice and Samuel emerged forty minutes later, hand in hand, to a shower of confetti.

'You look beautiful, my darling,' Samuel whispered as they accepted the congratulations of their family and friends before hurrying down the path to the carriage.

Having no family, Samuel had invited a handful of fellow curates he knew from theological college to the reception at the Red Lion. Eleanor and her family were there, of course, and Violet. Harry and Nate, both looking very smart, and Hannah and Daisy. Reverend Aldridge, Mrs Hurst, and Alice's grandparents, as well as a number of old school friends.

The food was delicious but Alice found she was too excited to eat. Samuel kept looking at her as if he couldn't quite believe that this lovely creature was actually his wife. Both his and James's speeches were witty and had everyone in stitches.

'You've got a good one there,' Violet whispered to Lily under her breath, both of them wiping their eyes as James sat down to a round of appreciative applause. Samuel raised the toast to the bridesmaids and his new in-laws, and then it was time for them to catch their train. They were honeymooning in Bournemouth.

'Our friends and family have done us proud today,' Samuel said as the carriage pulled away amid a flurry of cheers and good wishes. 'But it's so nice to be alone with you at last. What do you say, Mrs Roberts?'

'I agree wholeheartedly,' smiled Alice, as Samuel took her in his arms and kissed her.

CHAPTER THIRTY-FOUR

'So, how are you finding married life?' asked Leah, leaning back on the wooden bench and tilting her face to the sun. It was a week later and she and Alice were sitting in the vicarage garden. Reverend Aldridge had moved out three days previously and was staying with his sister in Botley until he officially retired in May.

'Wonderful,' Alice grinned mischievously. It was the first time she'd seen Leah since returning from honeymoon.

'You look like the cat that's got the cream,' Leah smiled, sipping her tea. 'He hasn't got any annoying habits then? He doesn't snore too loudly?'

'Samuel does snore,' Alice laughed. 'But not so loud that I can't bear it.'

'Just as well,' said Leah. 'As you're stuck with him now.'

'And what about Mrs Hurst?' Leah said, lowering her voice and glancing round to make sure the housekeeper wasn't nearby.

'She's perfectly amiable towards me,' Alice said. 'Though I think she misses Reverend Aldridge a lot.'

'You're so lucky having a housekeeper,' sighed Leah, cradling her mug.

'If Harry gets his rightful inheritance, then you'll have an army of servants,' scoffed Alice.

Leah shrugged. 'We'll see.'

'Still no word from the Whitworths?'

Leah shook her head. 'No. I know it pains Harry. He pretends he doesn't care but he does.'

'It's a shame,' agreed Alice. The gate between the churchyard and the vicarage squeaked as it opened. 'Oh, that'll be Joshua Mullens,' she said, getting up. 'He's going to be looking after the garden for us. Neither Samuel nor I are green-fingered and I can't bear the thought of Reverend Aldridge's beloved garden going to rack and ruin through lack of care.'

'Morning, Joshua,' she called, raising her hand to wave at him as he rounded a stone statue of a water nymph half-covered in lichen and ivy.

'Mrs Roberts,' he said, with a nod as Alice smiled. She still felt a thrill inside every time someone addressed her by her married name. 'Leah.' Joshua inclined his head towards her.

'Hello, Joshua. How's Pearl?'

'She's doing well,' replied Joshua. 'Especially now the weather's warming up. The cold and damp play merry hell with her bones.'

'It can't be good for her living in that caravan all through winter,' Alice said. 'Tea?' she asked, holding up the tea pot. Joshua shook his head.

'Thank you, no. The only way Nan'll leave that caravan is feet first.' He shoved his hands in his trouser pockets. 'Where do you want me to start?' he asked, surveying the neat, well-tended garden.

'Whatever you feel needs doing,' replied Alice. 'I'll leave it up to you.'

'I might tidy up the beds a bit then,' he said.

'Splendid. Let me know how much we owe you at the end of the week,' said Alice, sitting back down. Thanks to Isaac Whitworth's intervention, Joshua's arrest for poaching had led to an unusually short prison sentence, but his time inside had hardened him. He was still poaching, though he claimed to be more careful now.

But Samuel, with his strong belief that everyone deserved a chance in life and, being fond of Joshua, was quite happy employing him to tend the garden.

Bees hummed in the wisteria that clung to the old stone walls and flittered amongst the pots of pansies and tulips that were dotted about the flagstones.

'How is Dora?' Alice asked, refilling their tea cups. Leah frowned.

'She still cries herself to sleep sometimes and I think she's finding it hard now there's a new family in her old cottage. They do seem nice though.'

'Yes, they do. Samuel and I met them yesterday.'

'I thought it was nice gesture, you putting your wedding bouquet on Dora's dad's grave. She was very touched.'

'It seemed the right thing to do,' said Alice.

'I put mine on my family's grave, too,' said Leah. 'Dora asked me how long it took for me to get over losing my dad. I couldn't really remember. I was a lot younger, though.'

Alice sipped her tea. 'It's bound to take her a while to get over it.'

Leah nodded. 'Thank goodness she's got Nate. He's a godsend, Alice, he really is. She brightens up no end when he's around. How are you getting on with him now? He said you were making progress.'

Alice grinned. 'Yes, I know. I can be pig-headed at times. I haven't seen much of him since he came to supper that evening at my grandparents, what with the wedding and everything, but I think we broke the ice that night. I told him as much as I could about our father and Grandma added her tuppence worth, an account she'd obviously heard from my mother. None of which painted him in a good light, of course.'

'Yes, Nate relayed some of Jez's past to us. He wasn't gossiping,' Leah added quickly, in case Alice might take offence, but her friend just smiled.

'I think my father's character was thoroughly destroyed by the press at the time of his trial and again after his death, so I hardly think Nate was breaking a confidence. Where are they this afternoon, Dora and Nate?'

'They've gone to a concert with that Miss King and her husband.'

'It's odd, isn't it,' Alice said with a frown. 'Keeping your maiden name. Very modern. I don't think Samuel would appreciate it if I insisted on still being known as Miss Russell.'

'Well, you've had quite a few names in your time,' laughed Leah. 'I'm surprised you can remember who you are.'

'That's true, that's true,' admitted Alice, thinking back over all the names she'd been known as. There had been her given name, Elkin, and then she'd been known as Brown when she and her mother were on the run from her father. After Jez's death, her mother had reverted to her maiden name of Hayter, the name by which Alice had been known until James officially adopted her. 'At least Roberts will be for keeps.'

'I still can't get used to you being a married woman,' Leah said, a trifle wistfully.

'To be truthful, it took me a while,' grinned Alice. 'I know it's early days yet, but I'm so blissfully happy, I can't help thinking something's bound to go wrong soon.'

'Don't be silly,' chided Leah scornfully. 'You and Samuel are the perfect example of wedded bliss. I only hope Harry and I will be the same.'

Once Leah had gone, Alice made her way through the churchyard to her grandparents' cottage.

'Anyone home?' she called, rounding the side of the cottage to find her grandmother on her knees tending her seedlings.

'Ah, Alice,' she said, getting stiffly to her feet. 'This is a nice surprise.'

'Hello, Grandma.' Alice kissed her on the cheek.

'Are you all settled in at the vicarage now?' asked Beatrice, dusting soil from her hands.

'I've still got a couple of boxes to unpack but I'm just about there.'

'Would you like some tea?' her grandmother asked, leading the way indoors.

'A glass of water, please. Is my grandfather here?'

'No, he's helping Samuel prepare for his ordination.'

'Oh, yes, of course. Samuel's been shut up in his study most of the morning.' Alice leaned against the dresser, watching Beatrice slip a couple of homemade biscuits on a plate. 'The thing is, Grandma, I received a letter from Uncle Charlie this week. He was wishing me well for my wedding. He sent a postal order for five pounds.'

'That's very generous of him,' Beatrice said, raising an eyebrow. 'How is his little girl?'

'Baby Jane is thriving well. She'll be, what? Almost four months now.'

'Give him my regards when you reply, won't you?'

'Well, that's what I wanted to talk to you about. Would you like me to ask him if he can discover any information on Ian's whereabouts? Have you mentioned anything to Grandfather about him?'

'I haven't,' sighed Beatrice, leaning against the table and folding her arms. She pursed her lips in consternation. 'I would like you to ask Charlie if there's anything he can do. I'm just dreading what Mathew will say.'

'I'm sure it won't be as bad as you imagine. Grandfather is a kind man. I'm sure he'll understand you had no choice.'

'He was shocked when I told him about your mother,'

Beatrice reminded her granddaughter wryly. 'Nice girls don't get themselves into trouble.'

'Grandma, you made a mistake. It happens. Grandfather Copperfield was to blame more than you. He seduced you.'

'I wasn't exactly unwilling,' said Beatrice with a rueful smile. Her smile faded. 'I shall speak to Mathew. When were you planning on replying?'

'Tomorrow. Then I can post it on Monday.'

Beatrice nodded, her green eyes anxious. 'Very well. I shall speak to Mathew this evening.'

CHAPTER THIRTY-FIVE

Beatrice's opportunity came late that afternoon. She was sitting in the window seat working on her crocheting when Mathew came in from tending to some business in the church.

'It's such a pleasant afternoon,' he said, standing in the doorway. 'Shall we take a walk?'

'I'll get my coat.' Beatrice said, setting aside her work basket.

'How is young Samuel coming along?' she asked as they strolled arm in arm. A cool breeze swept the hedgerows. Within a few weeks the strawberry fields beyond would be teeming with workers, but now just a handful of men were working to spread bundles of straw around the young plants.

'He's doing well. I think he'll make an excellent vicar. Walter has high hopes for him.'

'I wonder how he'll enjoy his retirement,' Beatrice smiled.

'As long as his sister allows him free rein over her garden, he'll relish every minute of it,' Mathew joked, patting his wife's hand.

Beatrice sighed, anxiety churning her insides. It was so peaceful in the lane. She was dreading spoiling the pleasant walk with her revelation. Twice she opened her mouth to speak but the words died on her lips.

'You're very pensive,' Mathew said at length after they'd walked some way without speaking. 'Is there something on your mind?'

Beatrice stopped walking and, turning to face her husband, she took a deep breath.

'There's something I need to tell you.'

'All right,' Mathew said slowly. 'It sounds serious. Shall we find somewhere to sit down?'

Beatrice shook her head. 'I'd rather keep walking, if you don't mind?'

'You're not ill, are you?' The concern in Mathew's eyes brought tears to her own.

'No, it's not that.'

'The children?' he said, in alarm.

'No, everyone is quite well. It's just that, I have another child, a son.' There she'd said it. She held her breath as a myriad of expressions flitted across Mathew's face as he stared at her in stunned silence.

'His name is Ian,' she continued, walking on. Mathew kept pace with her but remained silent. 'And I haven't seen him since the day of his third birthday.'

'Go on,' Mathew said, quietly.

Beatrice cleared her throat. 'After I gave Lily up, Reverend Redfern found me a position as a companion to a young lady.

343

The family emigrated to the Cape Colony and I went with them. The next few years were good. I was happy, well as happy as I could be. Content, I suppose is a better term to describe how I felt.

'After I'd been working for the family for about five years, my employer ran up huge gambling debts. His creditor offered him a way out. I was the prize. My employer lost, inevitably. He was a fool. He never knew when the stakes were too high or when the cards were stacked against him. From that moment I belonged to Howard Foster.

'We were never legally married.' Beatrice stopped walking, the pain of what she was about to reveal causing her to double over in physical agony.

'Bea?' Mathew took her arm.

'I'm all right,' she wheezed, straightening up. 'He offered me to his friends,' she said hoarsely. Mathew recoiled in horror, sending a sharp pain straight to her heart. The tears were flowing freely now.

'There was nothing I could do,' she cried, wiping her nose on the back of her hand. 'We lived in the middle of nowhere. I knew nobody and, anyway, who would dare interfere? What went on between a man and his wife was nobody's business but their own.'

Mathew handed her his handkerchief and she paused long enough to wipe her face and blow her nose.

'Thank you,' she whispered, grateful for that small offer of kindness. 'I eventually gave birth to a son. Whether Howard is the father – your guess is as good as mine – but he accepted the child as his. It stopped then, the ... well, you know. He kept me a virtual prisoner in the house until Ian was born. He was such a beautiful baby,' Beatrice said, smiling through her tears. 'I was truly happy or the first time in years. I believed Ian was my redemption child. I finally felt God had forgiven me for abandoning my Lily all those years before.'

The tears came thick and fast as she told him how heartbroken she'd been when Howard had taken the child without any warning, how she had prostituted herself just to survive.

'I was getting my life back on track when Charlie found me.' She finally found the courage to look Mathew in the face. His expression was inscrutable. 'Say something,' she whispered. 'Please.'

'I ...' Mathew's mouth opened and closed. He looked dazed. He coughed, and cleared his throat. 'I need some time, Bea,' he said roughly. 'You go on home. I'm going to take a walk. I need to clear my head.'

Beatrice nodded. Head bowed, she slowly walked back the way they'd come. She didn't dare look back.

She sat in her rocking chair, gazing into the dying embers. It was dark but Beatrice had neither the inclination nor the energy required to light the lamp or throw more wood on the fire. She pulled her shawl tighter around her shoulders and wondered where Mathew was. He'd been gone ages. Perhaps he wasn't coming back at all. The thought brought a lump to her throat. She loved him. She'd never believed she'd have another chance at love at her age, yet he'd come along. Kind, loving, reliable Mathew. She wouldn't be able to bear it if he left her.

She must have dozed for when she woke the fire had gone out completely and she was freezing. The parlour was pitch black. She heard the latch being lifted and sat up, her head jerking in the direction of the door.

'It's freezing in here, woman,' Mathew said, stumbling into the room. Something rattled as he fumbled to find the matches. Striking one, he lit the lamp, brightening the room with its pale, yellow light. Rubbing his hands together, he took in Beatrice's white, tear-stained face.

'Come here,' he said, holding out his arms.

Choking back a cry, Beatrice got out of the rocking chair and stumbled into his waiting arms.

He smelled of tobacco, wood smoke and beer. He'd obviously popped into the Glyn Arms for a few, but Beatrice didn't care. He was home, and he still wanted her.

'None of what happened is down to you, Bea,' he said softly, stroking her hair as she cried tears of relief into his chest. 'I realize that. You're a good woman and I love you. I always will.'

She drew back, blinking in the lamplight. 'I love you, too, Mathew Turner.'

'There's something else I need to tell you,' Beatrice said softly a while later. Mathew had got the fire going and they were sitting on the sofa together, fingers entwined like young lovers. 'I've asked Alice to ask her uncle Charlie to look into finding out Ian's whereabouts. Do you mind?'

Mathew didn't answer immediately. They both stared into the fire, listening to the crackle and pop of the wood. He picked up her hand, playing with her fingers. 'My wife and I never had any children,' he said at last. 'Much as we wanted them, we were never blessed. I'd have liked a son to carry on the family name.' He stroked Beatrice's cheek. 'If you want to find your boy, I shan't stop you.'

'Thank you,' Beatrice said, kissing him. 'I must have done something right in my life to deserve a man like you.'

CHAPTER THIRTY-SIX

Winchester Cathedral was filled to capacity. Leah glanced about her nervously, feeling totally out of place amongst the impressive stone pillars and the high, vaulted ceiling. Beside her, Dora fanned her flushed face with her hymn book. Nate smiled and took her hand, running the fingers of his other hand around the collar of his shirt. The weather had turned unseasonably warm for late April and many in the congregation appeared to be sweltering in their finery. Leah could only feel sympathy for the assembled clergy in their heavy robes.

Seated as they were towards the back of the vast nave, she could see little over the sea of bobbing hats. Occasionally, if she craned her neck, she would catch a glimpse of Alice's navy-blue hat set at a jaunty angle on her dark hair. Samuel sat somewhere off to the side with the rest of the nervous-looking ordinands. Walter had one of the seats reserved for the clergy near the front, though not in an exalted position like the Bishops, who occupied the seats behind the altar.

A hauntingly beautiful hymn drifted from the choir stalls.

The hymn came to an end and the Bishop of Winchester rose to address the congregation. Of medium height, with neatly trimmed grey hair, he placed his hands on the pulpit and gazed out over the congregation. He cleared his throat, pushing his wire-rimmed spectacles up his long nose with his forefinger, and began to speak.

'Good morning and welcome to this ordination service.' He went on to welcome local dignitaries and the visiting bishops, before announcing the first hymn.

Bishop Talbot spoke eloquently, stroking his beard in a contemplative manner as he delivered his sermon, before it was time for the ordinands to move towards the altar to make their vows.

'There's Samuel,' Dora whispered to Leah behind her hand as he followed his fellow ordinands up the carpeted steps.

Seated on her other side, Harry shifted uncomfortably in his seat. Sitting still for any length of time had never been his strong point and his mind began to wander. He'd heard just the previous evening that his father was set to return to Strawbridge in five days' time and Harry wondered if he would make any attempt to build bridges with his son. There had been no communication between him and his parents since the evening he and Leah dined at Streawberige House almost two months earlier. How would his father react to Harry working for him again? He'd already signed on with Mathew Turner for the summer. Much as he'd enjoyed working on the farm over at Boorley Green, he'd felt compelled to come back home for the strawberry harvest. Farmer Doyle had told him he'd always have a job, should he change his mind.

Harry thrived on manual labour and he enjoyed the comradery of the other men. He and Samuel had become good friends, and he had a feeling that, given time, he and Nate would too, but he had a definite affinity with the other strawberry pickers. Even once they'd realized that he was heir to the Whitworth estate, the majority of the men had accepted him without question and treated him as their equal.

A sharp nudge in his side from Leah brought his musings to an abrupt end as he realized the congregation were getting to their feet. Giving Leah a sheepish smile, he stood up in time to watch the bishops, clergy and newly ordained vicars progress down the aisle.

It took a while for the congregation to filter out behind them in to the sunshine. As soon as they were outside, Leah, Dora, Nate and Harry hurried to find Alice and Samuel. They were standing with Lily, James and Reverend Aldridge on the sun-dappled grass beneath the canopy of a mighty oak tree, two quarrelsome magpies squabbling above their heads.

'Congratulations,' said Harry, thrusting out his hand.

'Thanks,' grinned Samuel as the two men shook hands.

'He did us proud,' Reverend Aldridge said.

'You must have heard how nervous I was,' Samuel said ruefully.

'Your voice was definitely a few octaves higher than usual,' grinned Nate, shaking Samuel's hand. 'Well done, mate.'

'I'm very proud of you,' said Alice, giving her husband's hand a surreptitious squeeze. He smiled at her.

'Have you seen your grandparents?' asked Lily, trying to spot them in the milling crowds.

'Over there,' James said. 'Talking to one of the vicars.' He waved, in the hope of attracting his mother-in-law's attention. Beatrice saw him, and waved back, mouthing that they would join them shortly.

'We're going into town for a meal,' Samuel told Walter. 'Will you join us?'

'Thank you,' Reverend Aldridge shook his head. 'I'm afraid I've got to attend a rather stuffy luncheon with the bishops and other members of the clergy.' He clapped Samuel on the back. 'Enjoy yourself, lad. Ladies, Mr Russell, Mr Gardener, I must bid you good day.'

Mathew and Beatrice came over as Walter was leaving. They spoke for a few minutes then the Reverend took his leave.

'It was a good service,' Mathew said, as they made their way down the street. 'Very moving.'

The Cathedral Inn was nestled in the heart of the city in The Square. Its small paned windows glinted in the sunlight while its black and white frontage was a stark contrast to the red-brick buildings on either side.

Careful not to hit their heads on the low beams, they followed the pretty waitress to their table. It was close to a large fireplace, the blackened brickwork decorated with horse brasses. A tapestry fire screen, depicting the cathedral, stood in front of the empty hearth.

'Nice place,' Mathew said, approvingly.

'I came here with some friends once,' said Samuel. 'The food is excellent. I can highly recommend the game pie.'

'I may have to try it,' Mathew said, picking up his menu.

'The soup sounds good,' remarked Lily. 'Oh, by the way, my sister Eleanor sends her fondest congratulations. I received a telegram from her this morning.'

'Thank you. I shall be sure to write and thank her.'

'Any news from Aunty Violet?' asked Alice, once the waitress had taken their orders. 'Has she recovered from her cold?'

'I got a letter from her on Thursday,' Lily replied. 'She's much better and hoping to come down for a visit in a week or two.'

'Hopefully, we'll have finished working in the city by then,' said Leah, gazing ruefully at her hands. The skin between her fingers was flaky and sore from the effects of the dyes.

'I can't wait to get back out in the fields,' agreed Dora. 'No more long walks in the dark and cold.'

'No more standing over steaming hot vats of dye breathing in those horrible fumes,' added Leah.

'Oh, roll on summer,' sighed Dora, sitting back in her chair as the waitress arrived with her soup.

'I do like it when all the pickers are out in the fields,' admitted Beatrice. 'Strawbridge seems more alive, somehow.'

'It's because we're all so spread out,' said Leah. 'You hardly see anyone during the winter months, especially as we're scattered all over the place for work.'

'How's your job going, Nate?' James asked, tucking into his pork chop.

'Very well, thank you,' Nate replied, wiping his mouth with his napkin. 'There's talk of me being transferred to Southampton which would mean a promotion and more money. I'd be able to save a lot more.' He smiled at Dora. She blushed as Leah and Alice exchanged amused glances. Despite Alice's initial reservations about Nate, both she and Leah were pleased Dora had finally found some happiness. Though she was still mourning her father, her relationship with Nate went a long way to assuaging her grief.

'Good lad,' James nodded approvingly. 'Always try and put a little by.'

As the conversation flowed, Alice was pleased to notice that her grandfather was as attentive to her grandmother as ever. She knew how frightened Beatrice had been about revealing the less savoury details of her past and she was pleased her instincts had been proved right. Mathew Turner was a good man.

Lily, James, Beatrice and Mathew caught the early after-noon train back to Southampton but Leah, Harry, Dora, Nate, Alice and Samuel had elected to spend the afternoon exploring the city.

'Has Nate heard anything from his mother?' Alice asked

Dora as they wandered beneath the soaring Purbeck marble columns and Gothic pointed archways of the Great Hall. The three men had wandered off to look at the round table, which had supposedly been used by King Arthur and his knights.

'No, nothing,' Dora replied, tucking a strand of hair beneath her hat as they strolled towards Queen Eleanor's Gardens. 'Do you believe there's much truth in the rumour that this is where Camelot was situated?' she asked as they wandered through the scented herb beds and fragrant flowers and shrubs.

'It certainly has the air of myth and legend about it,' replied Leah, as they settled themselves on a bench in a sunny corner of the pretty garden. 'So, I suppose it could be true.'

The three men emerged into the sunlight. 'We're just going to explore the underground passages,' called Harry with a wave of his hand. 'Will you three ladies be all right for a little while?'

'Yes, of course,' replied Leah. 'Go and explore. We're quite happy enjoying the sunshine, aren't we, girls?'

'Indeed,' replied Alice, closing her eyes and tilting her face to the sun. Water splashed musically in a nearby fountain and birds warbled in the surrounding shrubs, or cooed from the battlements.

Dora watched as Nate followed Samuel and Harry into a shady arbour. He turned to wave and she blew him a kiss. As he disappeared from view, she sighed contentedly. She still found it hard to believe that someone as handsome as Nate had chosen her. Sometimes she still felt the urge to pinch herself, just to convince herself that it wasn't a dream. She was still grieving her father. She missed him more than she could have ever imagined, and she missed the cottage. Nice enough as the new neighbours seemed, she couldn't get used to seeing strange faces at the windows, or strangers tending what used to be her garden. If it hadn't been for Nate, she didn't know how she would have coped. Hannah was wonderful, of course, as were Leah and Daisy. They'd taken her into their home without question or hesitation and she would always be grateful, but knowing how Nate felt about her made her life that little bit more special.

'How is Tilly doing these days?' asked Dora, after a few moments of contemplative silence.

'She's all right,' Alice replied with a sigh. 'She struggled a bit when Joshua was in prison but Samuel and I did what we could. That Declan is as feckless as ever. Every time he leaves, she says it's the last time and she not going to take him back, but she always does. I just hope she doesn't get herself in the family way again.'

'The parish relief board won't look favourably toward her if she does,' pointed out Leah.

'I've suggested she put her name down for the strawberry harvest,' said Alice. 'But she didn't seem keen.'

'I shouldn't think she would be,' Leah sniffed with disdain. 'She'd lose her relief money.'

'It would be perfect for her, though,' insisted Dora. 'She could bring the kiddies along.'

'Well,' shrugged Alice. 'Like I said, I made the suggestion. It's up to her.'

'I heard Pearl hasn't been too well,' Dora remarked, brushing a speck of lint from her maroon-coloured skirt.

'Joshua said she's a little better.'

'She's getting on a bit, though,' said Leah. 'It can't be good for her, spending the winter in that old caravan.'

'It must be terribly damp,' Dora said. 'She must be well into her eighties.'

'Must be,' agreed Leah. 'She seemed ancient even when we were little.'

Dora grinned. 'She probably wasn't really that old then. She just looked it.'

A group of sightseers ambled by them, chatting amiably, followed by the clatter of footsteps on the stone as Harry, Samuel and Nate emerged from the underground sally port.

'That was jolly interesting,' Harry said as they joined the three girls.

'And jolly damp and chilly,' added Samuel, rubbing his hands together. 'We've got a bit of time before we need to catch our train. Do you fancy a quick wander in the Long Gallery?'

'Yes, please,' answered Alice, getting to her feet and taking Samuel's arm. 'Grandfather said it's worth a visit.'

'All right, then,' said Leah. 'As long as we've time to stop at the market on the way to the station. I really must buy some ribbon for my new hat.'

CHAPTER THIRTY-NINE

Beatrice wiped her hands on her apron and gazed across the fields. It was a gloriously sunny day with only a hint of a breeze. A plaintive cry drew her eyes upwards to where a pair of buzzards circled lazily in a cloudless sky. It was the end of May and the strawberry harvest was in full swing.

She glanced over to where Mathew was stacking crates of ripe fruit onto the back of a waiting cart. His sleeves were rolled up to the elbow, displaying taut, tanned forearms. He paused to run a hand through his greying dark hair and wipe sweat from his brow. Catching her watching him, he grinned, and waved. She waved back, the letter in her apron pocket rustling. She slipped her hand into the pocket, relishing the feel of the envelope against her fingers, her heart racing.

Alice had brought the letter round just after breakfast, appearing at the back door just as Beatrice was heating the water to wash the breakfast dishes.

'It's from my Uncle Charlie.'

357

With trembling hands and a rapidly beating heart, Beatrice slit the envelope with a hairpin and unfolded the single sheet of writing paper within.

Dear Beatrice

I trust this letter finds you and Mathew well?

On receiving your letter last Monday, I immediately engaged the services of Mr Armstrong's firm in locating your son. I can tell you that Howard Foster passed away in 1910. So far, the whereabouts of Ian Foster remain unknown. Rest assured that as soon as I have any information, I shall forward it on to you.

Yours affectionately,

Charlie.

The news that Howard was dead caused her neither grief nor joy. She wondered if Ian was alone in the world or whether he had brothers and sisters, a stepmother, perhaps. He would be almost twenty-six now, perhaps even married with children of his own. The thought that she might have other grandchildren she had never met filled her with sadness and she regretted not trying to find Ian sooner.

She took a deep breath, savouring the scent of the warm, dry earth. She must be patient, she told herself sternly. She knew Mathew was worried she would end up hurt. If Ian could not be found or, if he was, that he might not want anything to do with her. She would be a stranger to him, after all. But that was a bridge she would cross if and when the matter arose.

Shielding her eyes against the sun's glare, she looked over to where Leah and Dora were working on the far side of the field. Leah had taken off her hat and her dark blonde hair gleamed in the sunlight. *They were good girls, those two,* she mused. Alice was lucky to be able to call them her friends. Although since her marriage, she didn't see as much of Leah and Dora as she would like, they remained close. It was fortunate the three men got on so well, too.

Ah, well, she chided herself. She mustn't stand here idling when there was work to be done. Picking up her empty basket, she picked her way over the uneven ground to where Hannah was working.

'Hello, Bea,' Hannah said, looking up, her plump cheeks pink and glistening. 'It's a warm one today.'

'It is that,' agreed Beatrice, crouching down beside her friend. 'I received a letter from Lily's brother this morning,' she said, plucking a fat, juicy strawberry from the plant.

'Oh,' Hannah replied with interest. 'Did he say anything about your son?'

Beatrice showed Hannah the letter and they fell into a companionable silence, working their way slowly along the row.

'I thought I would wear my bridesmaid's dress for the ball this year,' Dora said to Leah, brushing a strand of hair from her face. 'As long as you aren't planning on wearing yours, of course. We can't both wear the same thing.'

Leah laughed. 'No, you're all right, Dor. I've found an

old ball gown of Mum's she said I could have. It's a bit old-fashioned but with a few alterations it should be fine. I'm going to work on it on the evenings when Harry's off with Samuel.'

'I'm actually looking forward to the ball this year for the first time,' Dora said, sitting back on her heels. 'I still miss Dad, of course. Some days I feel almost overwhelmed with guilt but I'm finding it easier and I've got my dear Nate to thank for that.'

'I'm really happy for you, Dor.' Leah touched her lightly on the arm. 'If anyone deserves to be happy, it's you.'

'At least Pearl's prediction over my life came true,' she laughed, foraging beneath the leaves until her fingers closed on a large, ruby-red strawberry. 'Nate is certainly tall, dark and handsome.'

'I bet that's the line she uses to all her customers,' Leah grinned. 'I'm more convinced than ever that most of what she says is nonsense. Look at me and Harry. We couldn't be happier. I have a feeling this is going to be a wonderful year, for all of us.'

CHAPTER THIRTY-EIGHT

It did seem to Leah that 1914 was turning out to be an idyllic year. The warm, sunny weather continued through May and into June. The three couples often spent the long, balmy evenings together, picnicking along the stream or walking as far as Botley to have tea in their favourite tea room. Occasionally, they would take the train into the city to see a concert or a play and, on one memorable Sunday afternoon, they took the ferry over to the Isle of Wight and spent a pleasant couple of hours exploring the streets of East Cowes and eating fried fish on the quayside, the salty breeze ruffling their hair and seagulls screaming above their heads.

It was now the third Saturday in June, the day of the Pickers' Ball, and the past week had been spent in a flurry of activity as last-minute alterations were made and hairstyles experimented with. A huge pig had been delivered early that morning and the mouth-watering aroma of roasting pork had been wafting from the direction of the church hall for much of the afternoon.

As she braced herself against the bedstead so Daisy could lace up her corset, Leah pondered whether Isaac would make an appearance. She knew Harry was hoping he might. Several times over the past few weeks, he'd approached his father in the field, when he'd come over to speak to Mathew Turner, but each time his overtures had been rebuffed, Isaac making it abundantly clear that until Harry was prepared to relinquish Leah, he would be treated as an employee, and nothing more.

For herself, Leah couldn't care less but she knew how hurt Harry was, even though he tried hard not to show it. When she'd broached the subject with her mother several days earlier, Hannah had been very matter-of-fact about it.

'I wouldn't worry about it, if I were Harry,' she'd said. She'd been rolling pastry at the time, her hands covered in flour, the pan of last autumn's dried apples rehydrating on the stove filling the kitchen with the warm scent of cinnamon.

'Just remember the one thing Isaac Whitworth wants more than anything is an heir. Once you and Harry are married and the babies start coming along, it will take a heart a lot harder than his not to welcome you both with open arms. I doubt even that cold fish Frances will be able to resist her own grandchild.' She'd given Leah an encouraging smile. 'It will turn out all right in the end, you'll see.'

Leah hoped she was right, for Harry's sake. It did make sense. Isaac had a sister but she had married late in life and had never had children. She had also suffered with poor health for many years and, in all probability, was not expected to outlive her brother. As far as Harry was aware, after him and his aunt, next in line to inherit was a distant cousin who lived somewhere on the continent and, as far as anyone knew, hadn't stepped foot in England for at least two decades. So, Leah consoled herself, Isaac was unlikely to bequeath his hard-earned estate to someone who may, in all likelihood, simply sell off the properties and use the proceeds to fund his lavish foreign lifestyle.

Staring at her reflection in the full-length mirror, she wondered how she might react should Isaac make an appearance. She'd be polite, of course. He was her employer and landlord, after all, but his manner towards her at their last meeting still rankled. If Isaac was not prepared to build bridges with Harry, then their only option would be to leave Strawbridge for good. Thankfully, Harry had the option of returning to the farm over in Boorley Wood once the strawberry season ended. She smiled as she imagined how the sour-faced Frances Whitworth must feel knowing that her Eton-educated son was working as a farm labourer.

'Will you stand still, Leah?' sighed Daisy. 'I can't do up your stays if you keep moving about.'

'Oh, that will do.' Leah smoothed her hands down her slender waist. 'Any tighter and I'm likely to expire halfway through the dancing.' She reached up for the dark pink gown with golden trim hanging on the back of the door. With some assistance from Alice's mother, Leah had spent several evenings working on the alterations and it now fitted her like a glove. She slid it over her head, relishing the feel of the delicate material slithering down her body.

'Do me up, will you, Daisy?' She faced the mirror, turning this way and that as she admired the way the dress hugged her slender frame.

'You look very nice,' Daisy said, her nimble fingers working the buttons. 'Harry will be proud.' She came to stand beside her sister, her arm around Leah's waist. She was fifteen now, and as curvy as Leah was slender. She'd spent an uncomfortable night with her hair trussed up in rags but, admiring the way the pretty ringlets framed her face, she decided the discomfort had been well worth it.

'You look very nice, too,' replied Leah, smiling at their reflection. 'That colour suits you.'

'Thank you.' Daisy ran her hand down the wine-coloured material of her regency-style gown. 'Let's hope Sidney appreciates it,' she said.

'Are you intent on working your way through all five of the Merrifield brothers?' asked Dora, leaning down to fasten her shoes.

'Certainly not,' Daisy retorted acerbically, as Leah joined Dora on the bed, grinning over at her. 'Seth's all right but Percy and George are far too old.'

'And they're courting,' Dora added as she straightened up, smoothing down her skirts.

'What happened to Leonard anyway?' Leah asked, rolling up her stockings. 'Didn't he ask you this year?'

'Yes, but Sidney asked me first.' She twirled around,

craning her neck to admire her dress from behind. 'I prefer him, anyway. At least you can have a decent conversation with Sid. Leonard doesn't have much to say for himself, bless him.'

'Are you almost ready, girls?' called Hannah, coming up the stairs and pushing open the door. 'Well,' she said as the three girls formed a row next to the bed. 'What a bevy of beauties. You all look lovely.' Her eyes sparkling with a private memory as she gently fingered Leah's dress. 'You've done a good job with this. I hardly recognize it as my old gown. Well done.'

'Mrs Russell helped me quite a bit,' Leah admitted.

'Nevertheless, you spent a lot of time on it and your hard work has paid off. No one would ever guess it wasn't brand new off the peg from some fancy department store.'

'Now I know you're teasing me,' laughed Leah. The sound of voices drifted up from the lane and she glanced out of the open window. 'People are heading over to the hall already.' She leaned her head out to wave at Alice and Samuel who had come to call for Beatrice and Mathew Turner.

'We'll see you there,' Alice called up. She was looking very elegant in her rich, midnight blue, Leah thought, with a twinge of envy. Even wearing a plain work-dress with her arms elbow deep in the laundry, Alice always managed to look elegant and sophisticated.

'Harry and Nate are on their way,' Samuel added with a grin.

Alice's grandparents emerged from their house and the two couples set off up the lane.

'We're ready to leave as soon as the boys get here,' Leah said, turning back to face the room. 'Is Sid calling for you, Daisy, or are you meeting him there?'

'I'm meeting him outside the pub,' she said. 'Don't worry, Mum,' she went on quickly, catching the steely glint in her mother's eye. 'I shan't be tempted to go inside.' She gave her Hannah a hug. 'Did I tell you how lovely you look, by the way?'

'Thank you, dear.' Hannah laughed, adjusting the cuffs of her dove-grey dress with its red-sprigged pattern. 'I think this is probably about the sixth ball I've worn it to.' She smiled ruefully. 'And about the third time I've had to let out the waist.'

'Then next year you should treat yourself to a new gown,' announced Leah. 'I insist.'

'Oh, do you, miss?' laughed Hannah. 'I'm sure this old dress had got a few more years left in it yet, even if I do have to keep letting out the seams.'

There was a loud knocking on the front door.

'That'll be them,' Leah grinned. 'Lift the latch and come on in,' she called to Harry and Nate, from the open window. 'We'll be right down.'

The evening sunshine shone through the trees as the three couples and Hannah walked up the lane towards the church hall. The sky was streaked with colour and the air was balmy and filled with the scents of summer. They could hear the music halfway up the lane and by the time they reached the hall several couples were dancing to the string quartet.

Couples sat perched on bales of hay, or sprawled on blankets spread out on the sweet-smelling meadow grass. Groups of men stood about, talking loudly and clutching pints of cider. Several unattached ladies huddled together on the hay bales, primped and preened in an effort to attract the attention of any unattached male.

'Goodness,' exclaimed Hannah, throwing up her hands. 'They're serving all ready. I'd better get inside and help,' she said, unrolling her apron as she hurried across the grass towards the hall's broad doorway.

'There's Alice,' Dora said to Leah as they hovered on the periphery of the gathering. Alice and Samuel were standing near the entrance to the hall talking to Mrs Lamb.

'Excuse me a moment,' Harry said, gently removing Leah's hand from his arm. 'I must go and give my regards to my housekeeper.'

'I wonder if Mr Whitworth is here?' Dora whispered.

'If he comes, he'll come later' Leah whispered back. 'He likes to make an entrance.' She watched as Harry approached the small group. Alice looked at him and smiled, as did Samuel. Mrs Lamb's expression, however, remained cold and unyielding. Harry said only a few words before, nodding to Alice and Samuel, he turned on his heels and marched back to where the others waited under a magnificent red-leaved copper beech, his cheeks glowing.

'What's happened?' asked Leah, taking his arm.

Harry shook his head. 'My father has returned to London. Mrs Lamb had the front to tell me, in front of my friends, that I am a disgrace to the Whitworth name and if it was up to her she'd cut me dead.'

'The old cow!' Leah snorted. 'How dare she?'

'Take no notice, Harry,' Dora said soothingly. 'I'm sure your father's absence has nothing to do with you. He probably had some business to attend to.'

Harry and Leah looked at her. 'That's kind, Dora,' he said with a wry smile. 'But we all know that once my father arrives in Strawbridge for the summer, wild horses wouldn't drag him away.' He ran his hand through his fair hair. 'No, I'm afraid my father is punishing me.' Leah squeezed his arm. His muscles were taut with suppressed anger.

'Come on, mate,' Nate said, slapping Harry between the shoulder blades. 'Let's get a drink. Ladies?'

'Just a lemonade for me,' Leah said, knowing her mother would have her guts for garters if she tried anything alcoholic.

'I'll have the same, thanks,' said Dora.

'Nothing for us, thanks,' Daisy grinned, tugging Sid by the hand. 'We're going to dance.'

As Daisy and her large, big-boned beau joined the other dancing couples, Leah and Dora found an empty hay bale and sat down.

'Harry looked really upset,' Dora said, her voice low. Though the music was so loud she doubted they would be overheard.

'It certainly isn't Mrs Lamb's place to offer an opinion

368

either way,' fumed Leah. 'She's staff, for goodness' sake. How is she any better than us?'

'Don't let her spoil your evening,' Dora said. 'Harry will be all right. Nate will cheer him up. Look, Samuel's gone after them, too. They'll cheer him up.'

Leah followed Dora's gaze to see Samuel bounding up the steps into the hall where plates of succulent pork were being served. She smiled at Alice who was hurrying towards them.

'That woman!' she said, rolling her eyes as she sat down next to Dora. 'It's not her place to speak to Harry like that. I'm afraid Samuel was rather stern with her. She's gone off in a bit of a huff.'

'Serves her right,' muttered Leah. 'Miserable old bag.'

'Ah,' Alice nudged Leah's elbow. 'They're coming back.'

'Harry does look a lot cheerier,' Leah said in relief. That was what she loved about him. Nothing kept Harry down for long.

'Let's have a toast,' he said, raising his glass as Samuel and Nate handed round the drinks. 'To friendship. May it last until we're old and grey.'

The others laughed and raised their glasses, echoing his heartfelt words.

The evening wore on as twilight crept slowly across the fields. Someone had placed lighted lanterns in the boughs of the surrounding trees and the damp grass was dappled with yellow light. The musicians were playing some ragtime.

'Shall we, Mrs Roberts?' Samuel said, holding out his hand.

'Thank you, Reverend,' Alice smiled, taking Samuel's hand and letting him draw her to her feet. 'I should love to dance.'

Harry and Leah, and Dora and Nate, were already dancing. Daisy and Sid had barely taken time to draw breath, never mind sit down. They whirled passed now, Daisy's head thrown back as she laughed. Ankles kicking, arms waving, she was clearly having a whale of a time.

Even Hannah had ventured on to the dance floor a couple of times, dancing first with Beatrice and then with Mathew. Now she was leaning against the hall's grey stone wall, her cheeks suffused pink, enjoying watching the dancers.

'I'm having such a great time,' Dora panted, as the three couples took a short break from the dancing to quench their thirst and sample some of the delicious desserts.

'Me, too,' laughed Leah. 'I don't know when I've ever enjoyed a ball more.'

'My feet are going to be killing me in the morning,' Alice said ruefully, easing off her shoe and gently massaging her throbbing foot. 'Daisy and Sidney seem to be getting along very well,' she remarked as the couple whirled passed them. They were both pink-cheeked and breathing heavily. 'They haven't sat down once, have they?'

'Not that I've noticed,' Leah said, shaking her head in amusement.

'Everyone seems to be having such a wonderful time.' Dora leaned back on her hands. The moon had come out and the plum-coloured sky glittered with a million stars.

'And it's such a perfect night.' She sat up with a jerk. 'Look, a shooting star. Quick, make a wish!'

'I wish we could stay as happy as we are now, forever.' Said Leah, quickly, closing her eyes as the meteor disappeared from view.

'Here, here,' yawned Alice. 'Just think of me while you two are having a lie-in tomorrow morning,' she said. 'I've got to be up for morning prayers by eight.'

'Are you saying being a vicar's wife isn't all it's cracked up to be?' grinned Leah.

'I enjoy being a vicar's wife just fine,' Alice grinned back. 'And it's no hardship getting up early on a Sunday. Bless him, Samuel always gets up and brings me a cup of tea while I get dressed and Mrs Hurst cooks the breakfast while we're at prayers, so it really isn't that bad. It's just that I would like a lie-in on a Sunday, once in a while.'

'I hope when Harry and I marry we will be as happy as you and Samuel.'

'You will be,' insisted Alice. 'And so will you and Nate.' She reached out and squeezed Dora's fingers. 'I'm sorry I was such a silly about him. He's a good man and the more I'm getting to know him, the more I admire him. He's got a clever head on him, Dor. He'll go far, you mark my words. In that respect he is like the man who fathered us. He had an excellent business brain. It's just a shame he used it for bad instead of good.'

'Come on, ladies, how about another turn on the dance floor before the band winds down?' called Samuel, wending his way through the crowd towards the three girls. He was joined by Nate and Harry and the three couples were laughing and joking as they made their way on to the dance floor.

CHAPTER THIRTY-NINE

'It sounds like you had a good time last night,' Lily said to Alice the following afternoon as they strolled along the path through the woods on the outskirts of the village. The trees formed a leafy canopy overhead, providing much needed relief from the afternoon heat. The children had run on ahead, their delighted shouts and squeals echoing through the thick foliage. Ferns brushed Alice's skirt and squirrels scampered overhead, rustling the leaves. A symphony of birdsong rang out in the shadowy tranquillity.

'It was a lovely evening,' Alice replied. 'One of those times you wish would last forever, you know? I feel a bit deflated today.'

'I know what you mean,' her mother replied. 'But I have some news that may cheer you up. I didn't want to mention anything in front of the children but yesterday I received a letter from your Uncle Charlie.'

'Did he say anything about Ian?' Alice asked eagerly. 'Has he found him?'

'Well,' Lily held up her hand. 'That's just it. It would appear that Ian came to England shortly after his father's death.'

'He's in England?' Alice couldn't keep the excitement from her voice. 'But that's wonderful news. It should make it so much easier to find him.'

Lily nodded. 'In theory, yes, though it isn't always that straightforward. Charlie has suggested I ask Eleanor to engage our father's old solicitors and see if they are able to trace him. I believe Mr Jessop retired some years ago but the firm is still operating.'

'I'm sure they'll be able to find your brother,' Alice said, lifting her skirt as she stepped over a decaying branch. 'They found Grandma, after all.'

'If he's able to be found, then I'm sure they will,' agreed Lily. She gave a small laugh. 'It's funny to think I have a half-brother. I mean, Uncle Charlie will always be my brother. Even though we're not related by blood. I couldn't love him any more than I do but, the idea of having a brother who shares my blood, well, it is exciting.'

'It's like me and Nate,' Alice remarked. 'What a very complicated family we are,' she laughed.

'Aren't we just?' Lily smiled, taking her daughter's arm. 'How are things between you and Nate now?'

'We're getting on well. I know he isn't like my father, nor, thank goodness, does he seem anything like his mother.'

'Thankfully people can rise above their circumstances. It helps if you have someone who believes in you. I was fortu-nate enough to have Aunty Violet. If it hadn't been for her faith in me, I don't know where I might have ended up, and Nate, thankfully, had his stepfather's steadying influence to guide him.'

'We've spoken a little about Jez. Of course, I only know what you've told me, and Nate never knew him at all.'

'I'm afraid Jez had no redeeming features. He was bad through and through.' Lily smiled up at her daughter. 'Thankfully, you are nothing like him and neither is Nate.'

They walked on in companionable silence. The woodland floor was carpeted in wildflowers and nodding ferns. The drone of insects flitting here and there mingled with the birdsong and chatter of magpies.

'It's so peaceful here,' Alice sighed. They had arrived at a small clearing. The children were playing games among the trees. A large, fallen trunk, the victim of a long-ago lightning strike, lay to one side. Brushing away the moss and the odd woodlouse, Alice and Lily sat down.

'I've always enjoyed walking in these woods,' her mother remarked, leaning her lace-edged parasol beside her and adjusting her hat. 'Do you remember when we first moved here and James brought us here for a picnic? And I thought you'd got lost?'

'We were playing hide and seek,' remembered Alice. 'And it took you so long to find me, I fell asleep.'

'You were so well hidden and so quiet.' Lily gave a shaky laugh. 'It was starting to get dark. I was beside myself and James was ready to get up a search party. If that man hadn't come along with his dog . . .'

'It was quite a shock being woken up by a huge, smelly dog licking my face. I thought it was a wolf and it was going to eat me.'

The two women laughed as Lily reached for Alice's hand. 'We've had some good times,' she said.

'We have, Mother.' Alice smiled back. 'One day, God willing, I shall bring my children here,' she said, watching as Caroline and Johnny emerged from behind a thick oak tree in their quest to find Martha and Jimmy. At twelve, Martha was a dab hand at hiding, something which annoyed her younger siblings as it always took them so long to find her.

'The babies will be along soon enough,' Lily smiled. 'Take the time to enjoy being a couple,' she counselled. 'Once the children arrive, you'll be so busy you won't know yourself.'

'Thank goodness for Mrs Hurst,' Alice said. 'I'm already so busy helping Samuel that I have no time for household chores, as it is.'

'How is your Lady's Aid group coming along?'

'Very well,' Alice replied with a hint of pride. 'There are five of us so far. I'm hoping more ladies will join as word spreads. We're planning a summer fayre for the August bank holiday weekend, and a Christmas party for the children. I'm hoping Mr Whitworth will donate something towards it. There are so many children in our parish who will not have a warm meal on Christmas Day, never mind a gift.'

'Remind me and I shall look out some of our old toys.' Lily sighed. 'Much as I'd like to stay here all afternoon, we should start back. James and Samuel will be wanting their tea soon.' She stood up, brushing bits of twigs and moss from the skirt of her peach-floral skirt. 'Children, come along. It's time to go.'

There were the usual half-hearted grumbles and complaints but within a few minutes they were heading back the way they'd come.

'Shall I let Grandma know what Uncle Charlie said?' asked Alice as they emerged from the shady woods into brilliant late afternoon sunshine.

'Please do,' replied Lily, unfurling her parasol. 'You'll see her before I will.'

Beatrice was in her garden talking to Hannah when Alice rounded the side of the cottage.

'Afternoon, Mrs Hopwood, Grandma.' Alice kissed Beatrice on the cheek.

'Did you have a nice afternoon with your family?' Hannah asked.

'Thank you, yes.'

'Leah's off somewhere with Harry,' Hannah told her. 'I'm not sure where Daisy's got to. Off with that Merrifield boy, I shouldn't wonder. She seems quite smitten with him.'

'He seems a nice lad, from what I can tell,' said Beatrice.

'They're all well brought up boys, those Merrifields. Their mother has made sure of that.'

'Well, I mustn't stand about chatting all day,' Hannah said, obviously realizing that Alice had something she wished to discuss with her grandmother. 'I'll see you tomorrow, Bea.'

'See you later, Hannah,' Beatrice said, picking up the two empty mugs. 'Are you all right, love?' she asked as Alice followed her down the steps into the kitchen. 'What's on your mind?'

'Mother got a letter from Uncle Charlie,' she said without preamble, taking the mugs from Beatrice and placing them in the washing-up bowl. 'It's possible that Ian might be in England,' she said, rolling up her sleeves.

'In England?' Beatrice pulled out a chair and sat down heavily. 'Does he know where?'

Alice shook her head. 'No. They know only that he left the Cape shortly after his father died.' She washed the mugs and set them on the side to drain. Drying her hands, she said, 'I expect he landed at Southampton.' She heard her grandmother's intake of breath.

'So close,' Beatrice murmured.

'If only we'd known ...' said Alice, taking the chair opposite. 'Mother is going to ask Aunty Eleanor to instruct Grandfather Copperfield's solicitors to investigate. I'm sure Southampton is the first place they will concentrate their enquiries but ...' she shrugged her shoulders. 'He could be anywhere by now.'

'He may have travelled on somewhere. America maybe,' Beatrice pointed out, sounding dejected.

'Then there will be records,' Alice said brightly. 'Don't lose hope. For all we know he could be just down the road.'

'Wouldn't that be something?' Beatrice said with a weak smile.

They were interrupted by the arrival of Mathew. He strode in the back door in his shirtsleeves, his jacket over one arm.

'Hello, Alice, hello, sweetheart.' He kissed his wife's cheek. 'Gosh, it's a warm one.' He slung his jacket over the back of a nearby chair and sat down to take off his shoes. Sensing the tension, he raised his head, and regarded his wife and granddaughter quizzically. 'Everything all right?'

Beatrice cleared her throat. 'I've had some news.'

'Oh, yes?' Mathew queried, straightening up.

'About Ian.' Beatrice's lip trembled and Mathew made to get up.

'Not bad news?'

She shook her head. 'He sailed for England four years ago.'

'He's here?' Mathew turned to Alice.

'We don't know his whereabouts,' admitted Alice. 'I'm hoping Grandfather Copperfield's solicitors might be able to trace him.'

'I have contacts at Customs House,' Mathew said, stroking his beard thoughtfully. 'I could ask them to look back through their records. There might be a clue as to where he might have been headed.'

'It's worth a try,' nodded Beatrice.

'I'll call in when I'm next over that way,' Mathew said. He reached for his wife's hand. 'Well, this is a turn up, isn't it? Let's hope you find him very soon.'

I hope so,' Beatrice smiled. 'I really do hope so.'

CHAPTER FORTY

'It shouldn't affect us, will it, sir?' Mrs Lamb asked, glancing at the newspaper headlines as she dished up Isaac's breakfast kippers and mushrooms.

It was the end of July and Austria-Hungary had just declared war on Serbia.

'It's complicated,' replied Isaac, lowering the paper. 'Hard to understand and even harder to explain.' He folded the newspaper and laid it aside. 'Tensions have been brewing in Europe for some time and I believe the assassination of the Archduke is just the excuse they needed. So, yes, Mrs Lamb, I do believe it will affect us.'

'But those things that's happened,' she said, looking perplexed. 'It's all so far away. Most people round here have never even heard of this Sarajevo place.'

'That's as may be, Mrs Lamb,' Isaac said patiently. 'But I'm afraid Europe is a massive powder keg at the moment and the fuse has been lit.'

'Will there be a war?' Mrs Lamb's bottom lip trembled.

'I am almost certain there will be,' replied Isaac. He picked up his knife and fork, then laid them down again. The smell of the kippers turned his stomach. 'Thank you, Mrs Lamb,' he said, dismissing her.

She nodded and left the room leaving Isaac staring into space.

What would war mean for Henry? he wondered. Should England declare war on Germany, there would be a recruitment drive, of that he had no doubt and Henry, being Henry, would be one of the first to enlist. *War could be the making of the boy*, he thought, reaching for his cup of coffee. And, even better, it would get him away from the Hopwood girl. He glanced at his pocket watch. The best place for him right now was London. If war broke out, he needed assurance that Henry would enlist as an officer. He forked up some of the mushrooms and rang the bell. Mrs Lamb appeared a few moments later, the pink flush on her cheeks telling him she'd hurried up from the kitchen.

'Mrs Lamb,' Isaac said, wiping his lips with his napkin. 'Run over to Mathew Turner and tell him I shall need him to take me to the station in time for the 10.45 train. Then pack my valise. I shall be gone a few days, a week at most.'

'Yes, sir.' Mrs Lamb hurried from the room. Leaving his breakfast largely untouched, Isaac got up from the table and, taking the newspaper with him, shut himself away in his study where he remained until Mrs Lamb knocked on the door to tell him Mathew Turner had arrived with the pony and trap.

*

The impending war was the talk of the strawberry fields during the last few days of July. The weather had been gloriously hot and the strawberry plants continued to yield a bumper crop. The schools had broken up for the summer and more children had joined their parents in the fields.

Alice and her Lady's Aid members, now numbering eight, had been kept busy organising the summer fayre due to be held on the bank holiday Monday, less than a week away. Leah had found her looking very flustered when she'd popped round to the vicarage the previous evening to drop off some knitted doilies for the craft stall. Now, as the midday whistle blew, Leah caught sight of Alice hurrying towards her, one hand holding on to her hat.

'I wonder what she wants?' said Dora, squinting into the sun as she got to her feet.

'I hope nothing's wrong,' Leah replied, waving. 'What's the matter?' she asked as their friend reached them.

'Nothing's the matter, as such,' Alice replied. 'I just needed a break from all the fayre activity and wondered if you'd like to join me for dinner? It's such a glorious day I thought we might eat in the garden.'

'Sounds wonderful,' Leah said, looking at Dora for confirmation. She nodded.

'I'd love to.'

'What do you think of all this talk of war?' Alice said with a sigh as they walked back towards the vicarage. 'Samuel's hoping we won't get involved but Grandfather seems to think it's inevitable.'

'Harry says the same.'

'Perhaps it will all blow over,' said Dora.

'Grandfather drove Mr Whitworth to the station yesterday. He's gone to London to see if he can find out what's going on. He is convinced we shall be at war within weeks.'

'I still don't understand why a squabble between some foreign countries I've never heard of should affect us,' Dora mused. 'I doubt I'd be able to find them on the map.'

'I shouldn't worry too much,' Leah said, pushing open the gate to the vicarage grounds. 'Harry says that even if we do go to war, it will all be over very quickly.'

'It might not even happen,' Alice said optimistically. 'And it's too lovely a day to spoil it with doom and gloom.'

They spent a pleasant forty-five minutes in Alice's garden. Now that the strawberry harvest was under way, Joshua didn't have the time to spend taking care of it as much as he had but, even so, it was a pretty garden. The flower beds were a riot of colour and swarming with bees. The rose bushes were beginning to shed, scattering the lawn with their delicate petals.

Mrs Hurst had prepared a luncheon of cold meat and bread which she brought out on a tray along with a jug of Reverend Aldridge's homemade elderflower cordial.

'There are several bottles left in the pantry,' Alice laughed, pouring them each a glass. 'So we shall be drinking it for some time to come.'

'It's very refreshing,' Dora remarked, taking a long swallow to wash away the field dust from her throat.

'A lot more successful than his attempt at making elder-flower beer,' Alice chuckled. 'It wasn't long after Samuel first arrived. The Reverend was brewing a batch of beer in the cellar and he'd obviously left it to ferment for too long. One evening as they were preparing for bed, they heard what sounded like an explosion and shattering glass coming from the cellar. They both ran down to find the bottles of elderflower beer had exploded. The cellar floor was littered with broken glass and beer. It took them ages to clear it all up and the cellar stank for weeks.'

'That happened to my dad when he tried making his own beer,' Leah smiled. 'Only we don't have a cellar so he stored it in the pantry. It made such a mess. Mum was livid. She didn't speak to him for two days.'

Dora smiled, and wondered if she would ever be able to think of her father with laughter instead of tears. It had only been four months, after all, and she had the added guilt over her father's suicide to fuel her grief. Her sombre thoughts were interrupted by Alice.

'Are you two still all right to help man a stall on Monday?' she asked.

'Of course,' replied Dora. Leah nodded with her mouth full.

'Thank you.' Alice smiled in relief. 'I'll need all the help I can get. Pearl has offered to tell fortunes.'

'She wasn't very accurate with mine, was she?' Leah laughed.

'I must say I'm slightly more inclined to believe her than I was,' Dora smiled.

'Well, it'll just be a bit of fun, nothing too serious. Samuel wasn't keen on the idea but I think I've managed to persuade him. Pearl does bring in a fair amount of money and it's all for a good cause.' She consulted her sheet of paper. 'Joshua is giving pony rides and there will be a coconut shy and other games for the children. Leah, your mum and my grandmother are running the tea tent. With you two helping on the stalls, we should manage perfectly well. We should get a good turnout. I've put posters up in the post offices in Hedge End and Botley, and one or two of the ladies who come in from Southampton every day have taken a few to put up in their local shops so, with luck, we should get people from further afield.'

'You've done a brilliant job, Alice,' Leah said. 'Well done.'

'Let's not congratulate ourselves too soon,' she said, biting her lip doubtfully. 'But I am hopeful it will go well, and we shall raise a decent amount of money. Oh, by the way, Mr Whitworth is the guest of honour.' She smiled sheepishly. 'I mean, we could hardly hold it in his grounds without asking him, could we? Do you think Harry will mind?'

Leah shrugged. 'I'm sure he'll be fine with it. It might give them a chance to talk.'

'That's what I thought,' Alice said, sounding relieved. 'He's going to judge the vegetables and cake competitions, as well as handing out the prizes. There will be prizes for the children's games, too. I think we're just about organised.'

'I beg your pardon, Mrs Roberts,' Mrs Hurst said, appearing in the doorway, drying her hands on a tea towel. 'It's almost time for the whistle.'

'Oh, thank you, Mrs Hurst.' Leah got to her feet. 'I completely lost track of time.'

'Me too,' said Dora. She drained her cup. 'I could sit in your lovely garden all afternoon.'

'You know our door is always open,' said Alice getting up to walk her friends out. 'You're welcome whenever you like. You don't need an invitation, for goodness' sake.'

'Wouldn't Samuel mind?' asked Leah, lifting the catch on the gate.

'Of course not,' replied Alice. 'He's usually got something to do in his study, or he's out visiting a parishioner. I miss your company in the week, so whenever you want to join me for dinner, feel free. You can come every day if you like.'

'We'll probably take you up on that,' Leah grinned. 'Ooh, there's the whistle. We'd better hurry.' She gave Alice a quick hug. 'See you tomorrow.'

'Hurry now,' Alice urged them. 'You don't want to be late.'

'We won't,' laughed Dora. Picking up their skirts, both girls started to run.

CHAPTER FORTY-ONE

The success of the bank holiday fayre was looking to exceed Alice's expectations. The day had dawned hot and sunny, drawing the crowds. The gates of Streawberige House were bedecked with bunting and when Cuthbert Ryall unlocked them at ten o'clock, the visitors came flocking up the driveway.

The men of the hamlet had spent the previous afternoon erecting two large tents, one for the serving of teas, the other for the exhibits, and putting up the numerous stalls that were dotted about the lawn. The grounds had the air of a carnival about them, as if, with the prospect of war being declared imminently, the people of Strawbridge and the surrounding villages were determined to make the most of the bank holiday. Just before midday, Isaac Whitworth emerged from the French windows. Leah watched as he stood on the patio, fastening his cufflinks as he scanned the crowds.

She was in charge of the tombola, and was glad of the

shade the awning afforded her, but there was no relief from the heat and she could feel the dampness beneath her clothing. Shielding her eyes against the sun's glare, she watched Isaac mingle with the crowds. Despite his easy laughter, she thought he looked strained. She stiffened as he made a beeline for Harry who was recruiting participants for the tug of war later. Her stomach muscles clenched anxiously. From the expressions on both men's faces, it was evident that the conversation was serious. At that moment, her attention was drawn away from the pair by a surge of children wishing to try their luck. When she looked over again some five minutes later, Isaac was walking away, his back stiff and erect, his head high, Harry staring after him, red-faced and angry.

'Can you cover for me?' she called to Dora who was manning the button stall next door.

Dora nodded. Waving her thanks, Leah hurried across the lawn to where Harry appeared in deep conversation with Samuel.

'Leah.' Samuel greeted her with a bright smile. 'How's the tombola doing?'

'Very well,' Leah replied. 'We've still got plenty of prizes left.'

'Excellent.' Samuel pulled his handkerchief from his pocket and mopped his brow. He was sweating in his clerical robes. He clapped Harry on the back. 'I'll see you at three for the tug-of-war,' he promised. Tipping his hat at Leah, he hurried off in the direction of the tea tent.

'People seem to be enjoying themselves,' Harry said, taking Leah's hand. 'Alice should be very proud.'

'Yes, Alice can be very proud of herself,' agreed Leah. Lowering her voice, she asked, 'What were you and your father talking about?'

Harry sighed and drew her to one side. 'Father is convinced we'll be at war by tomorrow.'

Leah sucked in a lungful of air. She knew Isaac had contacts in the government. If he was convinced that war was imminent, he was unlikely to be wrong.

'He's arranged to get me a commission.'

'A commission?' Leah frowned. 'Harry, you're not still entertaining that silly notion of enlisting, are you?'

His expression confirmed her worst fears.

'Oh, Harry, why? You're not a soldier.'

'Me and the lads have been talking,' Harry said, playing with her fingers, his gaze fixed somewhere in the distance. 'In fact, it's all we've talked about since that Duke fellow got himself assassinated. We don't have enough soldiers to fight a war, Leah. They're going to be crying out for men like us. We're all agreed. We're going to enlist together.'

'No, Harry. You can't.' Leah grabbed at his arm. 'Listen to me. You mustn't go, please. I need you here.' She could see the determination in his eyes and it sent a dart of fear into her heart.

'It'll be over in a few weeks,' he said, his tone reassuring. 'A couple of months at most. I doubt I'll even get to leave England, but I've got to do my duty. We've discussed this. You know how I feel.'

'I thought I'd spoken some sense into you,' Leah replied sullenly.

'Don't be like that, Leah,' he said, pulling her towards him. She resisted at first, then allowed him to hold her close. He kissed her hair, his arms circling her waist. She pulled back, searching his face.

'If you are adamant about joining up, then you must accept your father's offer of a commission.'

'What?' Harry pulled a face. 'Certainly not. I shall say to you what I said to him. I intend enlisting up with my friends. I don't want to be above them. We're equals. I don't want to have to give them orders or be responsible for disciplining them.'

Leah wandered over to a small bench beneath a blossoming magnolia tree. Harry followed, sitting down beside her. They sat in silence, Leah watching the crowds. There was a lengthy queue outside Pearl's tent. Children ran about shouting and laughing. Several were waiting in line for the pony rides. Joshua looked up and met her gaze. She smiled and he nodded, before lifting the child next in line on to the broad back of the sturdy little pony.

'It's such a beautiful day,' she said at length. 'Everyone seems so happy.'

'But you can feel the tension,' Harry said. 'Everyone knows that any day now our lives could change irrevocably.'

'It's so unfair,' Leah said, twisting her handkerchief in agitation. 'Alice and Dora are so lucky. At least they won't have to say goodbye to the man they love.' When Harry remained silent, she gave him a sideways glance.

'Samuel's not thinking of enlisting, is he?'

Harry looked away.

'Does Alice know?'

'He's planning to talk to her tonight. Don't say anything to her,' he warned, seeing the angry gleam in her eyes. 'It's not your place.'

'She's my friend,' Leah pouted. 'It's only fair I warn her.'

'Don't,' Harry said sternly. 'I've already betrayed Samuel's confidence by telling you. He's holding an all-night prayer vigil tonight in the church. I thought I might go along. Praying's not really my thing but in light of current events ...'

'I'll come with you,' Leah said. 'I expect mum will want to come too. I won't stay all night though. I've got to be up at four.'

'I don't think I fancy their chances,' said Alice, as she joined Dora and Leah in the shade of a large oak to watch the tug-of-war. 'The other team look much stronger.'

'Oh, I don't know,' mused Dora. 'We've got the five Merrifield boys, as well as our three lads. They're all pretty sturdy.'

'I'm not sure Grandfather should be taking part, though,' Alice frowned.

'Oh, it's just a laugh,' Leah said. Though she flashed Alice a smile, she couldn't help noticing her friend appeared a little distracted.

'It was nice to see your family here, Alice,' Dora said. 'Johnny was ever so chuffed when his carrots won third prize.'

'Bless him, yes. He was so proud.'

'Have they gone then?' Leah asked, blinking as she glanced round as though she'd just woken up.

'Yes. They've gone home to pack. They're going to London to spend a few days with my Aunt Eleanor. They leave first thing tomorrow.'

'It's nice to see Tilly here as well,' Dora said, nodding to where the young woman stood at the forefront of the crowd of onlookers, cuddling her baby while her other children sat at her feet, eagerly awaiting the start of the tug-of-war.

'The children look so much healthier,' Leah remarked, her gaze travelling down the line of waiting men until it settled on Harry, second from the back. He saw her looking and grinned. She gave him a tight smile in return. She wasn't quite ready to forgive him just yet.

'Declan's gone back to Ireland apparently,' Alice said, lowering her voice.

'Good riddance, I say,' said Dora with uncharacteristic venom. 'He'd only make her pawn all the things you got them from the church charity barrel.'

'Well, let's hope he stays away,' Alice said. 'Oh, look, they're about to start.' At the sound of the whistle, she cupped her hands around her mouth and yelled, 'Come on, Reverend.' Hearing her, Samuel glanced her way, grinning, and promptly lost his footing. A mixture of cheers and groans rippled through the crowd as the opposing team gained the advantage. By sheer determination, the Strawbridge men managed to claw back a few inches, to the delight of the crowd, before finally making it over the line to be declared the winners.

Alice gave a whoop of delight and, hoisting up her skirts, ran to fling her arms around Samuel's neck.

'Well done, my love,' she said, kissing him firmly on the mouth.

'I'm not sure this sort of behaviour is befitting a vicar's wife,' Samuel whispered as he swung Alice round. 'But I'm not complaining.' He kissed her back. He smelled of sweat and dust. Running his hand through his hair, he turned to slap Harry and Nate between the shoulder blades. 'Well done, lads!'

'I honestly didn't think you'd win,' Leah grinned, hanging on to Harry's arm. He was breathing heavily and his cheeks were pink from the exertion.

'They were the stronger team,' Nate said, reaching over to shake the hand of one of their opponents. 'But I think we won by sheer tenacity.'

'I'm very proud of you all,' declared Dora, straightening her hat.

'We're all heading over to the Glyn Arms to celebrate,' Harry said, wiping his face with his shirt. He kissed Leah's cheek. 'We'll be back in a bit to help dismantle the tents.'

The three girls watched them walk away, laughing and jostling each other, as they were joined by the rest of their team.

The crowds were dwindling though there was still queue outside Pearl's tent.

'She's done a roaring trade,' Dora remarked, as a young woman emerged from the tent smiling.

'Probably everyone wanting to know what's going to happen,' Leah said morosely.

'I think Samuel warned her to keep it all light-hearted and fun,' Alice said. 'No dire predictions of doom and gloom.' Pausing in folding a large white table cloth that had covered the tombola stall, she turned to Leah.

'Is everything all right, Leah? You seem a bit out of sorts.'

'Harry's joining up,' she blurted out.

'Oh, sweetheart.' Alice put an arm round her friend's shoulders. 'Of course, he will. So will most of the young men around the country. It's the patriotic thing to do.'

'I'm just glad Nate's too young to enlist,' Dora said, her eyes full of sympathy for Leah. 'It will have all blown over by the time he's eighteen.'

'Samuel reckons the expeditionary forces will likely sort it out before any new recruits get to leave England,' Alice said in an effort to console Leah.

'Samuel's planning on joining up, too,' Leah blurted before she could stop herself. 'I'm sorry,' she muttered in the face of Alice's shocked expression. 'Harry made me promise not to tell.'

'But Samuel is needed here,' Alice said. 'He must see that? If we're at war, people will need spiritual comfort more than ever. What is he thinking? And why hasn't he mentioned anything to me?'

Leah shrugged. 'Harry said he was going to talk to you later.'

'I just wish he'd said something to me first,' she said, looking troubled. The three girls carried on with their task but in a much more subdued manner, the joy of the day completely spoiled by the dark clouds of war hovering on the horizon.

CHAPTER FORTY-TWO

'I bumped into my sister coming back from Botley,' Mrs Hurst said, handing Alice a much-needed cup of tea. 'They've been to Weymouth for the day and she said they had a right job getting home. All the trains were full of soldiers that had been recalled.' The older woman's lip trembled. 'Oh, Mrs Roberts. I think it's happening. We're going to war, aren't we?'

'I do believe it's inevitable, Mrs Hurst,' replied Alice distractedly. She was waiting for Samuel to get home so she could confront him. She hadn't said anything while they were tidying up after the fayre. It wasn't something she wished to discuss in public but she could tell by Samuel's worried frown that he realized something was amiss. Several times over the course of the last hour he'd asked her what the matter was but she had refused to tell him.

She glanced at the parlour clock. Samuel had planned his vigil in the church to begin at eight. It was just gone six. She could hear Mrs Hurst in the kitchen preparing a supper of cold chicken leftover from yesterday's roast, and salad vegetables fresh from the garden. Rabbits had wreaked havoc amongst the lettuces lately and Alice made a mental note to ask Joshua to rig up some sort of netting to keep them out.

She heard the clang of the metal gate in the hedge between the vicarage and the churchyard, and took a deep breath. Straightening her shoulders, she tucked her feet under her skirt and folded her hands in her lap to wait.

'Sweetheart, I'm sorry I was so long. We had a job getting the tents on to the back of the wagon,' he apologized, leaning down to kiss her. 'I'll just wash up. I'm filthy.'

'You can do that in a minute,' Alice said with a firmness that clearly startled her husband.

'All right,' he frowned. 'Am I in trouble?' he joked, perching on the edge of his favourite armchair and resting his elbows on his knees.

'It depends,' Alice said soberly. 'I believe you intend to enlist?'

Samuel's shoulders sagged. 'Harry told you?'

'Leah did, but that's beside the point. Why didn't you tell me yourself?'

'I was going to,' Samuel said seriously. 'I had planned to speak to you now, as it happens. I wanted to make sure I was certain in my own mind that it is the right thing to do?'

'And is it?'

'I believe so, yes.'

'Why? Is it because Harry's going? Is that it? You feel

left out? Like you're missing out on some jolly *Boy's Own* adventure?'

'Alice,' Samuel protested mildly, regarding his wife with a reproachful stare. 'It's all the lads have been talking about for weeks but that's not why I want to join up. I've prayed about it extensively and I believe it's what I'm meant to do. I plan to enlist as a chaplain. If the worst happens, the lads will need someone like me.'

Alice was silent for a moment, considering Samuel's reasoning. 'But what about your parishioners here? You can't just abandon them.'

Samuel cleared his throat. 'I spoke to Walter this afternoon and he's happy to come out of retirement to help out.'

'You're a married man. Grandfather's sure they won't expect married men to enlist.'

'But they won't turn me down, either,' Samuel said. He smiled. 'Don't look so worried. If the reports from Westminster are to be believed, it will likely all be over in a month or so.'

'Then why not wait and see?'

'Alice, these men are my friends. I have to go with them, don't you see?'

Alice fell silent, unable to think of a response. She should have known this would happen. Her husband was not the sort of man who would allow others to go off and do what he wasn't prepared to do himself.

Samuel rubbed his hand across his face, stifling a yawn. 'Isaac Whitworth has been saying for a while now that the country will need to recruit thousands of men. I want to be one of them.'

They were interrupted by a gentle cough and she looked up to see Mrs Hurst standing in the doorway.

'Pardon me, but will you be dining in the dining room or would you prefer the garden?'

'I think the garden, please, Mrs Hurst,' replied Alice. 'It's a shame to waste such a beautiful evening.' *Especially as we don't know what the future will bring*, she thought, getting to her feet. She held out her hand to Samuel. 'I don't understand your reasoning, Samuel, but I shall support your decision. Shall we?'

He stood up and took her hand. Bringing it to his mouth, he kissed it. 'My precious Alice,' he said. 'You know I would never willingly do anything to vex you, but I believe that this is a cause worth fighting for.'

'As I said,' Alice repeated. 'You have my full support.'

'Thank you, my dear. That means everything.' He kissed her warmly on the lips and led her out into the garden.

Alice was unable to sleep. She'd spent an hour in the church as part of the night-long vigil. She'd been surprised by the number of parishioners who'd turned up. Mothers with their sleeping babies, young children, bleary-eyed with sleep, troubled young men, determined to do their duty to King and country, yet terrified about what that might mean.

She rolled on to her side. She was wide awake and she didn't doubt that she was the only one finding sleep elusive that night. With a sigh, she threw back the sheets and padded to the window. The church windows flickered with candlelight. She perched on the window seat and leaned her forehead against the cool glass. The open window brought little relief from the sultry heat.

She wasn't expecting Samuel back until sunrise so she was surprised to see a shadowy figure fumbling with the gate. She heard the squeak of its rusty hinges and saw the figure glance upwards, the face obscured by the darkness and she felt a stirring of trepidation as it disappeared out of view.

Moments later, the doorbell chimed. Heart thumping, Alice grabbed her gown and hurried downstairs to open the door.

'Leah?' she whispered, relief flooding her veins. 'What are you doing here?' she asked, standing aside to let her friend in.

'I reckoned you'd be awake,' Leah said, taking off her cloak, her face white in the lamplight. 'I knew Samuel would be at church all night.'

'I haven't slept a wink,' Alice admitted, closing the door and sliding the bolt across. 'Shall I make some cocoa?' she asked, leading the way to the large kitchen. 'I'm sure Mrs Hurst has a fruit cake stashed away in the pantry somewhere.'

'Cocoa would be lovely,' Leah said, pulling out a chair at the big, scrubbed pine kitchen table while Alice lit the stove and set about heating the milk.

'I don't think anyone's getting much sleep tonight,' she said.

'I heard Mum tossing and turning,' Leah agreed. 'And

there were lights on in all the cottages I passed on my way here.'

'It's the not knowing, isn't it?' Alice said, blowing out the match. 'We know going to war is inevitable but we're not sure what that means exactly, for any of us.'

'Frightening times,' Leah murmured.

'They are indeed,' sighed Alice. She was keeping a close eye on the milk so it didn't catch her unawares and boil over. 'Samuel told me about his plans to enlist,' she said, her back to Leah as she spooned cocoa powder into the waiting mugs.

'And?' Leah cocked her head.

'I support him, obviously,' she said. Pouring the warm milk into mugs, she turned to face Leah, leaning against the worktop as she stirred vigorously. 'I'd rather he remained here, but it's his decision and, I'm proud of him actually. Despite what they all seem to think, it's not going to be a jolly boys' outing.'

'That's what I keep telling Harry,' Leah grumbled. 'Thanks.' She took the mug Alice handed her and wrapped her fingers round it. Despite the warm night, she felt cold. She breathed in the warm, chocolatey aroma and sighed. 'I'm proud of Harry, too, of course I am. That goes without saying but it doesn't stop me being worried sick.'

Alice sat down at the table and reached for her hand. 'I'm just praying their predictions are right and it will be over by Christmas. If that's true it's unlikely our chaps will see any action at all.'

'Let's hope that proves to be the case,' said Leah, sipping her cocoa.

'I wish Dora were here,' Alice said.

'She's at the church. I said if I wasn't back in ten minutes it meant you were up and for her to come over when she was done.'

'Oh, good. It feels fitting, somehow, that the three of us see this night through together.'

The words had barely left her mouth when they heard the chime of the doorbell.

'That'll be her now.' Leah looked at Alice and grinned.

'Get another mug, will you, while I let her in.'

'Hello, Alice. I'm glad you're up. Leah said you would be.' Dora followed Alice into the kitchen. 'Hello, Leah.'

'Hello, Dor,' replied Leah, setting a third mug of cocoa on the table. 'Are there many there still?'

'About twenty or so,' Dora replied, pulling out a chair. 'Some have come from other parishes. Apparently, ours is the only church that's open tonight. I spoke to two women whose sons are part of the expeditionary forces. They'll be among the first to be sent off to France. One of them lost her brother in the Boer War, so you can imagine how she's feeling about her son going off to war.'

'Poor woman,' said Alice, sitting down.

'Well, there's going to be plenty more like her over the coming months,' said Leah glumly.

'I'm really warm,' said Alice suddenly. 'Shall we take our cocoa outside?'

'Good idea,' agreed Dora. 'It's so pleasant out.'

The garden was bathed in pale moonlight. The soft strains of an old hymn drifted from the church and the sky twinkled with a million stars.

'Do you realize,' said Leah as they settled themselves on the old wooden bench against the side of the house, 'after tonight our lives will never be the same again?'

'It's a sobering thought,' nodded Dora, hugging her mug of cocoa to her chest.

'However the next few weeks and months play out,' said Alice softly. 'At least we'll always be here for each other.'

'I should hope so,' Leah exclaimed. 'Crikey, I couldn't imagine Harry being gone for a day if I didn't have you two to cry and moan to.'

'Likewise,' said Alice. 'We're going to rely on each other a lot more over the coming months.'

'We won't have time to brood,' Leah said with a wry smile. 'If all the men are off fighting, there'll be loads more work to do round here. I quite fancy driving the carts. Maybe you could put a word in for me with your grandad, Alice.'

'Joking aside, I reckon that's exactly what's going to happen. We'll be expected to muck in and do all sorts.'

'As long as we're paid a fair wage, I'll turn my hand to anything,' Dora said, draining her mug and licking the residue from her lips.

'I think we deserve another slice of cake,' Alice said, getting up. 'And I think there might be a box of chocolates in Samuel's study. I'll fetch them.'

Leah and Dora chatted quietly about nothing in particular until Alice returned a few minutes later with the cake and chocolates.

'Ooh, mint creams,' Dora grinned. 'My favourite.'

They sat under the moonlit sky finishing off the chocolates and Mrs Hurst's rich fruit cake and talking until dawn.

CHAPTER FORTY-THREE

The following day felt as if everyone was holding their breath. All anyone could talk about was when the announcement might come.

'We could already be at war,' Dora remarked, picking up her basket of strawberries. 'We wouldn't know, would we?'

'Mr Whitworth has gone to the *Echo*'s offices to await the news so we'll know as soon as he gets back,' one of the pickers told her.

'Well, I hope it's soon,' grumbled Leah. 'The not knowing is killing me.'

'Hey, Leah,' called Harry, coming towards her, his basket laden with ripe fruit. 'How's the prettiest girl in the strawberry fields?' he whispered, putting his basket down so he could wrap his hands around her waist.

'I'm not bad,' Leah grinned, tilting her face to his kiss. 'Did you know your father has gone into town to wait for news?'

'Yes,' Harry nodded. 'Mathew told me. He drove him to

the station. Let's hope the news comes soon. It's the sole topic of conversation. They were talking about it at breakfast in the pub this morning and it's all I've heard all day out here, too.'

'The waiting is the worst,' said Leah. 'We know it's inevitable so why not put us out of our misery and get on with it?'

'I expect we'll know soon enough,' Harry said. He kissed her quickly and released her.

'Would you like to come for tea tonight?' she called after him as he started to walk away. He turned, grinning. 'Nate's coming.'

'Thanks,' grinned Harry. 'Shall we say six? Unless we get news in the meantime.'

'Six will be fine,' replied Leah. She smiled. 'I'll see you later, then.'

Night fell with no word from London. Lamps were lit but curtains were left open. Samuel had promised to ring the church bell as soon as Isaac returned with news but as the night wore on and still the bells remained silent, the residents of Strawbridge took themselves wearily off to bed.

The crowd outside the offices of the *Southampton Echo* had been growing since mid-morning. Isaac had enjoyed a fine luncheon at a pub just around the corner and had dined, just after seven o'clock, with the editor, a personal friend of his, at an upmarket hotel, the editor having left strict instructions with his staff to be fetched immediately should there be an announcement.

Now, at just gone eleven o'clock there was a tension in the air. A sense of expectation rippled through the crowd. Isaac, sitting in a pub across the street and watching from the window, could see the sudden, frantic activity in the lighted window one storey up. Draining his pint, he picked up his jacket and hat, and hurried out into the street.

He set his hat on his head and fought his way through the crowd.

'What's happening?' he asked a bystander. 'Any news?'

'Not yet,' the man responded, not taking his gaze off the upstairs window.

Isaac glanced up. As soon as war was declared, he planned to telegraph an old acquaintance in the ministry and get a commission for his boy. He knew Frances was against him enlisting altogether, but Isaac wasn't as naïve as some. He'd had word from someone in the know and, contrary to the common predictions, the war was unlikely to be over in six months. Eventually they would need to bring in conscription and it would be better for Henry if he enlisted rather than waited to be called up.

He sighed. He was proud of his boy, even if he didn't show it. He'd showed a grit and determination Isaac had lacked all those years ago when faced with a similar dilemma. Isaac had chosen duty to his family, Henry had chosen love and, misguided as he thought his son's choice might be, he couldn't help but admire the boy. He shivered suddenly, the hairs on his arms standing to attention as an icy finger seemed to run down his spine. He shook his head and shrugged his shoulders in an effort to compose himself. The feeling passed but it left him feeling on edge for the rest of the night.

The doors to the newspaper offices finally opened at quarter past eleven. The crowd fell silent as the editor emerged to stand at the top of the steps, his expression sombre.

'Ladies and gentlemen,' he said, his words clear and precise in the humid air. 'It is my unpleasant task to announce that, as of eleven o'clock this evening, Britain is at war.'

Isaac had missed the last train home so by the time he'd arranged a carriage to drive him back, it was gone one in the morning before he arrived in Strawbridge. He went straight to the vicarage where he roused Samuel from his bed. They spoke in hushed tones, Samuel's wife hovering nervously in the background. As soon as Isaac had left, Samuel hurried over to the church. At a quarter to two on the morning of Wednesday 5th August, the residents of Strawbridge were woken by the tolling of a single bell, ringing out in the darkness.

'That's it then,' Dora whispered to Leah and Daisy, as they sat up in bed. 'We're at war.'

'Yes,' Hannah said grimly, hurrying from her room next door. 'God help us all.'

In the cottage next door Beatrice and Mathew stood arm in arm at the window listening to the mournful tolling of the bell. Only that morning Beatrice had received a letter from the solicitors in London informing her that the man they believed to be her son, Ian Foster, was working as a wheelwright in Mere, a small village in Wiltshire. He was a young man, twenty-six years of age. Would he join up? Would she ever now get to meet him? And what of dear Samuel, whom Alice had told her was adamant he was enlisting, and young Harry? What would become of all the hamlet's young men and boys?

In the Glyn Arms, Reuben Merrifield and his five sons cheered as they drank a toast to the King while Reuben's wife, Florence, quietly wept.

And in the moonlit vicarage kitchen, Alice sat dry-eyed and alone at the table listening to the bell, her heart a leaden lump in her chest. After weeks of speculation, the cold hard fact of war seemed so much harder to stomach. She had to face the truth. Samuel would be going away. She swallowed the lump in her throat. She was determined to be cheerful and brave and so, when the bell fell silent, and Samuel came into the kitchen, his eyes sorrowful, she took hold of his hand and led him up the stairs to bed.

CHAPTER FORTY-FOUR

The next day the strawberry fields were buzzing with the news. Isaac had arranged for copies of the *Echo* to be delivered to every one of the sixteen homes that made up the hamlet of Strawbridge. Over the days that followed, posters appeared in every shop window or were plastered on every available wall space. Soon the news that recruitment offices were opening up all over the country filtered through to the villages and hamlets, and the roads and lanes to cities and towns teemed with men and boys heeding the cry of Lord Kitchener to take the king's shilling.

Saturday morning dawned bright and sunny. Alice stood at her bedroom window looking out over the fields. The only men now working there were those too old or too young to join up. They had started streaming up the lane just after dawn. Draping a shawl about her shoulders to ward off the early morning chill, Alice walked with Samuel as far as the pub where a large crowd had gathered. Reuben, in shirt sleeves, his braces flapping against his thighs, was dispensing frothing mugs of ale.

'Dutch courage,' a woman's voice muttered amidst the laughing and joking of the men. Florence Merrifield stood to one side, Leonard, too young to enlist, at her side, his expression mutinous.

Many of the women had left the fields to come and wave them off. Leah and Dora wandered over to stand with Alice.

'Everyone's so patriotic all of a sudden,' remarked Leah drily, as two women walked past them waving small union flags.

'I've been thinking the same thing,' said Alice. 'I got a letter from my mother yesterday. My stepfather and Uncle Arthur were in Trafalgar Square when the news was announced and they said everyone was cheering and throwing their hats in the air. No wonder all the young chaps are so eager to join up.'

'Well, I'm hoping Harry will get turned down,' Leah admitted quietly, smiling over at him. He was laughing at something Samuel had said. The pair clinked their glasses, foam sloshing on to their hands and drank deep.

'Has he got flat feet?' asked Dora. 'You can't march with flat feet, apparently.'

'I doubt it,' she sighed. 'I mean, look at him. He's the picture of health.' She smiled at her friends. 'I am proud of him, of course I am. I wouldn't want him to be a coward but that doesn't make it any easier.'

'Of course not,' Alice assured her. 'We're all proud of our boys. Grandfather doesn't think they'll get called up for a while yet, anyway and they'll certainly not leave England for months.'

'I'm just glad my Nate's too young to enlist,' said Dora. 'I think that's why Leonard Merrifield looks so disgruntled.'

'It must be difficult being the youngest of five boys,' Alice said, glancing over to where Leonard was clearly receiving a stern talking to from his mother. 'It's natural he'll feel a bit left out.'

'Right, come on lads,' called George, the eldest of the Merrifield boys. He was twenty-four, and well-built with a shock of dark hair. 'Drink up. We need to get going.' A loud cheer went up as the men, some looking barely old enough to shave, drained their pints. Reuben and Florence went round collecting the empty glasses as the crowd surged into the lane.

It seemed to Leah that there was something of a carnival atmosphere as they waved the men off. Men and boys, they were singing and laughing as they marched away.

'I bet this is the most exciting thing most of them have ever done, isn't it?' one of the women said, staring after them.

Leah, Dora and Alice followed as far as the church. Harry and Samuel turned to wave their hats as they rounded the bend. The three friends leaned against the gate, waving at the men filing past.

'Well, there they go,' Alice exhaled as they listened to the singing fading away. 'When they come back, they'll be soldiers.'

It was a sobering thought and Leah and Dora were quiet making their way back to the fields. Now that the initial excitement had dissipated, the day felt like an anti-climax. The women weren't as chatty as usual and as the day wore on the pickers became more subdued. Leah heard one of the older woman remark; 'Now they're joining up, it makes it all seem so much more real.'

The day grew hotter as the sun reached its zenith but by mid-afternoon dark clouds were billowing across the sky and the heavens opened. The women hurried to take shelter under trees until the cloudburst was over and, inevitably, the conversation revolved around Lord Kitchener's call for half a million recruits.

'I told my Bert if he doesn't join up, I don't want to see him anymore,' said a young blonde woman.

'They're joining up in their thousands,' said another. 'My sister works near the recruitment office in Northam Road and the queue's been down the road all day. They had to stay open an hour later yesterday, they had so many men wanting to enlist.'

'Well, my Bert had better get on down there today,' the blonde said, pouting. 'Both my brothers have enlisted. I won't have him showing me up.'

'My lad's only sixteen,' piped up a thin, mousy-looking woman. 'It'll all be over by the time he's old enough to go, thank God.'

'I think the rain's stopping,' Dora said, holding out her hand. Patches of blue sky had appeared amongst the grey and the damp air smelled fresh as they made their way over the now muddy field to continue working.

'I wonder what time they'll be back?' Leah murmured, gazing down the empty lane.

It was late afternoon by the time the sound of many voices and marching feet could be heard drifting up the lane. Dusting soil from her hands, Leah straightened up, shading her eyes from the sun's glare. All around her other women were rising to their feet, some even cheering as the men came into view. Children ran about shouting and waving and there was a carnival feel to the air with fathers swinging their children onto their shoulders and men embracing their wives and sweethearts.

'You've done it, then?' Leah murmured into Harry's chest as he pulled her close.

'I have,' he said, his face glowing with pride. Leah's smile didn't reach her eyes and she wondered if the other women felt a hollowness inside, like she did.

'Nate? What are you doing here? You haven't joined up?' Dora said, her voice trembling. Nate's sheepish expression told her all she needed to know. 'But you can't,' she wailed in disbelief. 'You're too young.'

'Listen, Dora,' Nate said, putting his hands firmly on her shoulders and forcing her to look him in the eye. 'I couldn't watch my mates going off to serve their country while I stayed at home and did nothing, could I?'

'But you're not old enough,' Dora persisted, blinking back tears.

'The recruiting officer didn't even ask my age,' Nate said

with a shrug. 'Please don't be angry, Dora. It'll all be over by the time I'm old enough and I'll have missed my chance,' he insisted, his dark eyes begging her see things his way. 'They've promised that we'll all be in the same regiment.'

'Why didn't you stop him?' she rounded on Harry.

'Samuel and I tried to talk him out of it,' replied Harry with a shrug of his shoulders.

'You obviously didn't try very hard. Why didn't you warn me?' she demanded of Nate.

'To be honest, it was a spur of the moment decision. I was on my way to work when they caught up with me. At first, I got swept along in the excitement, I suppose but once we got to Southampton and I saw the queues, I knew I had to be a part of it. Some of the lads in the line were talking about mates of theirs who were under eighteen who'd managed to enlist. If you look old enough, they don't always ask.'

'I'm so angry with you,' Dora said, using the cuff of her sleeve to wipe away a stray tear.

'I know. And I'm sorry, Dor,' Nate said, genuinely remorseful for causing her pain. 'But I'm going. Please understand.'

'I'll never understand, but I shall just have to accept your decision. I don't have a choice.' She laid her head against his chest and sighed. She felt someone groping for her hand and turned to see Leah's wistful smile.

'I'm in the same boat as the rest of you now, then,' she managed to say. The lump in her throat made more conversation impossible.

'Well done, lads!' Reuben Merrifield shouted, emerging from the Glyn Arms with a tray laden with mugs of ale. 'Get these down your neck. You've done your country proud, boys.' The crowd erupted into loud cheering and Reuben nodded. 'You've done us all proud, lads,' he reiterated, looking tearful as he disappeared back inside the pub to replenish his tray.

'When do you leave?' Dora asked, as she and Nate slipped away from the crowd.

'I should receive my papers in a few days' time,' Nate said as they walked towards the pond. 'I expect I shall be leaving within the next week or so.'

'That soon?'

'It won't be for long,' Nate assured her, kissing her softly on the mouth. 'And when I come home, we'll start saving to get married.'

'Is that a proposal?' Dora asked, with a shaky smile.

'Indeed, it is, Miss Webb.' Nate grinned at her. 'I know we haven't been courting very long but I knew the moment I first saw you that you were the only girl for me. So, what do you say? Will you marry me one day?'

'Yes.' Dora's smile was stronger now. 'Yes,' she said again, blinking back tears as she reflected on the bittersweet moment. 'Yes, Nathan Gardener. Of course, I will marry you.'

'Henry! Henry, wait!' At the sound of his father's voice, Harry froze. Holding fast to his hand, Leah's heart sank at the sight of Isaac Whitworth making his way towards them. She was surprised at how haggard and drawn he looked, as though he'd barely slept. Ignoring Leah, he pushed his face into Harry's so that they were almost nose to nose, his expression grim.

'You've done it then?' he barked. 'You've enlisted?' Harry took a step backwards, and squared his shoulders.

'Yes, Father, I have.'

'You fool.' Isaac's sharp reply caused several heads to turn towards them. 'You stupid, bloody fool,' he blustered. 'If you'd waited I could have got you a commission. You'd be joining up as an officer.'

'I believe we've already had this conversation, Father,' Harry said stiffly. 'I've joined the same regiment as my friends.' He grinned. 'We shall be the Strawbridge Chums,' he said proudly.

'The Strawbridge Chums?' Isaac sneered. 'You're breaking your mother's heart, you know,' he said. 'First you demonstrate a total disregard for your duty.' He glared at Leah. She felt herself colour but held his gaze, determined not to be cowed by him.

Isaac snorted in disgust. 'And now this, deliberately shunning my help and advice. Well, that's it, Henry. You're on your own. I wash my hands of you.' Turning on his heel, he stalked away, leaving Harry staring after him, impassively.

'Good for you, Harry,' one of the men slapped him on the back. His sentiments were echoed amongst the crowd.

'Yeah, well done, mate.'

'Good for you.'

Harry smiled ruefully. 'Thanks, lads.' He accepted a pint of ale and drank heartily. As the attention drifted away from him, Harry drew Leah aside. 'If you don't mind, I shall go up to London tomorrow,' he said, licking froth from his lip. 'I need to at least try and make peace with my mother before I leave.'

'Of course,' Leah replied, nodding her head in understanding.

'I shall stay only one night, two at the most. It's likely I'll be posted very soon and I'd like to spend as much time with you as I can.'

Leah leaned her head on Harry's broad shoulder. 'We'll have to make the most of whatever time we have left,' she said softly, turning her face away so he wouldn't notice her tears.

Around her grandparents' supper table, the conversation seemed stilted, Samuel's imminent departure hanging like a dark cloud over the room. Alice's appetite had deserted her and, although her grandmother's food was delicious as always, she had to force down every mouthful.

'Your parents return tomorrow, do they?' asked her grand-father, tearing off a hunk of bread and mopping up his gravy.

'Yes.' Alice put down her knife and fork and reached for her water glass. 'I'm pleased they will get to see Samuel before he leaves.'

'What will your duties be as a chaplain?' Mathew asked, directing his question to Samuel.

'Moral support, mostly, I expect. Leading services on Sundays and,' he pulled a face, 'perhaps performing the odd funeral.'

'Do the army not already have chaplains?' queried Beatrice. 'I'm still not clear why you felt the need to enlist. I'm sure you could be just as useful to the war effort if you were to remain here.'

'That is true,' Samuel nodded. 'However, with new recruits joining up in their thousands, there will hardly be enough chaplains to fulfil all the roles. And how much more of a comfort to our lads, to have a chaplain that they already know.' He grinned. 'And I know Walter is champing at the bit to get back to preaching. I'm sure he'll do perfectly well in my absence.'

'Let's hope it is of short duration,' remarked Beatrice. 'You've a young wife here who needs you at home.'

'Grandmother-in-law,' Samuel smiled at Beatrice across the table. 'I have every confidence that I shall be home by Christmas.'

'I doubt it will be over that quickly,' said Mathew, raising his glass. 'But I'll certainly drink to victory, and may it come quickly.'

'Victory,' whispered Alice, looking at Samuel. He squeezed her fingers and winked.

'You two stay put,' Beatrice said, getting up to clear the table. 'Mathew can help me with the dishes just this once.'

With her grandparents out of earshot, Samuel laid his hand on Alice's flat belly.

'Maybe you'll soon have some happy tidings to share. That would give me something to look forward to.'

Alice smiled shyly. 'Only time will tell,' she replied coyly. She pressed her hand on his. She didn't want to get his hopes up, but she was certain that she was expecting. Her monthlies were due in less than a week and so far, she hadn't experienced any of the familiar niggling cramps that warned her of their imminent arrival.

'That was a splendid supper,' Samuel said, patting his own stomach as Beatrice and Mathew returned to the dining room.

'Will you stay for a couple?' Mathew asked, holding up a bottle of sherry and glancing at the clock. 'It's early yet.'

'Of course,' Samuel agreed. 'And perhaps you might agree to play your fiddle for us. It may be some time before I hear such music again.'

'My pleasure,' Mathew grinned. Setting the bottle and glasses on the table, he fetched the fiddle from its case and began to play. Alice and Samuel took their glasses of sherry over to the sofa and sat down. Pushing all thoughts of war from her mind, Alice nestled against her husband and closed her eyes, concentrating on nothing but the haunting notes of her grandfather's fiddle.

CHAPTER FORTY-SEVEN

The call-up papers came two days later.

'They were waiting for me at the pub when I got back from London this morning,' Harry said. 'I'm to be at Botley station by twenty-past nine on Thursday morning.'

'Thursday!' lamented Leah. 'That's in three days.'

'I expect Nate will have received the same? Did you not see him this morning?' Dora said, rocking back on her haunches. A warm breeze ruffled the strawberry plants and tugged at the tendrils of her hair that had escaped its pins.

Harry nodded. 'No, he must have been busy in the office when my train got in. I'll see him later. His papers are bound to be waiting for him at the pub. All the lads seem to have received theirs today.'

'They have,' confirmed Leah. 'I overheard some of the women talking about it earlier. At least it sounds like you're all going to the same place. Where is it they're sending you, again?'

'Some training camp in Dorset,' he replied, his eyes

scanning the letter. 'From what I can gather from the other lads, it seems they've kept their promise to keep us together.'

'Three days,' Dora sighed. 'It's not long, is it?'

'It's nothing,' Leah replied, dejectedly. 'And today's almost over so we've only got tomorrow and Wednesday, really.' She picked up her basket of strawberries. 'This is just about ready for emptying,' she said to Harry. 'Will you walk with me?'

They walked slowly along the row, sidestepping other pickers.

'I missed you just while you were up in London,' she smiled. 'How will I cope when you're away for weeks on end?'

'You'll manage,' Harry replied, his fingers brushing against hers.

'How did your visit go?'

He shrugged. 'We've managed a truce of sorts. Mother ranted a bit about me enlisting. At least her worry over me going to war has taken her mind off my relationship with you.'

'What a shame,' Leah said, pulling a face. 'I quite enjoyed being the cause of your mother's sleepless nights.'

'Now, now,' Harry chided her, but he was grinning. 'I know Mother is inclined to be difficult. Perhaps all that's going on in the world will put things in perspective for her and she'll change her point of view.'

'I hope you're right, for your sake.' Leah kissed him on the cheek. 'I'll meet you after work. Maybe we could take a walk to the pond?'

'I don't mind where we go, as long as I'm with you,' replied Harry. With one quick kiss, they parted ways. Leah watched him loping across the field and sighed. She was going to miss her Harry so much.

Thursday morning arrived all too quickly. The small platform at Botley station was bustling with men ranging in age from sixteen to mid-twenties. They milled about, smoking cigarettes, and cracking jokes, the inevitable nerves hidden behind an air of bravado.

Those with wives, mothers or sweethearts stood in family groups, doing their best to be brave and send their loved ones off with a smile and a wave as the advertising posters commanded them, rather than with a tear and a sigh.

'I've never seen the station so busy,' Leah said. She was clinging on to Harry's hand as though she would never let go. They had sat up until the early hours just talking but neither of them felt tired. She glanced across at Dora's pale face. Beside her, Nate stood tall and calm, his hand resting gently on the small of her back. He had written to a few old friends of his mother's back in London, asking if any of them knew her whereabouts but had received no reply. Not that he was bothered, he told Dora. He just wanted to let her know he'd joined up as a courtesy.

'Leah, Dora.' Alice pushed her way through the throng, Samuel following behind her. 'Gosh! I thought we were going to miss the train,' she panted, straightening her hat which had become dislodged in the crush. 'Mrs Hurst tidied

Samuel's study in readiness for Reverend Aldridge's arrival and misplaced Samuel's call-up papers. We've been in a right tizz all morning trying to find them.'

'She'd put them inside a book,' Samuel said with a grimace. 'Thankfully they happened to fall out when I knocked it off the shelf.' He grinned. 'It wouldn't do to fall foul of the sergeant major on my first day.'

'Certainly not if it's one of those chaps over there,' Leah said, inclining her head to where three stocky-looking army officers were chatting beside an empty train carriage. All three had broad shoulders and thick necks, their caps pulled low over their eyes. One sported an impressive moustache and continually slapped his thick thigh with what looked like a small riding crop.

'They do look rather intimidating,' Samuel commented.

'As long as we do as we're told, we'll be just fine,' Nate said, flicking a glance in the officers' direction. 'I'm quite looking forward to learning to march and handle a gun.'

Joshua shouldered his way passed. He nodded at Samuel and Nate. 'Harry.'

'Joshua.'

'Has Pearl not come to see you off?' asked Leah. Joshua shook his head. He took a long final drag on his cigarette and dropped it on the ground, grinding it with the heel of his boot.

'I told her not to bother. I'm not one for emotional good-byes.' He grinned. 'Well, this is going to be an adventure and a half, isn't it? I always wanted to see the world.' Leah noticed that behind his genial expression he looked a little pale, and his smile didn't quite meet his eyes. She wondered what, if anything, Pearl had said before he left. She must have read her great-grandson's leaves out of natural curiosity. Suddenly she felt a cold hand clutch at her own heart as Pearl's predictions from the previous summer came back to haunt her. She turned to Harry, wanting to say something, anything, that would change his mind but, of course, it was far too late. He'd accepted the king's shilling. There was no going back now, even if he'd wanted to.

A shrill whistle sounded, instantly silencing the crowds as the three officers waved their clipboards aloft and shouted for the men to get in line.

'Well, this is it, sweetheart,' Samuel said, hugging Alice as tight as he dared, given that they were both hopeful that there might be new life growing inside her. 'I'll write as soon as we arrive at the camp.' He kissed her hard on the mouth. 'I love you, Mrs Roberts.'

'I love you, Reverend Roberts.'

Leah clung to Harry, unable to shake the sense of foreboding that had fallen over her like a heavy cloak. 'Stay safe,' she whispered. 'Come back to me, please.'

'I promise,' Harry murmured into her hair. 'I love you. Always remember that.'

Tears brimmed in her eyes as she choked back a sob. Her fingers slipped from his arm and he was gone, swallowed up by the crowd of young men surging for the train.

'Goodbye, Nate,' Dora said stoically. 'I will miss you.'

'I'll miss you like crazy,' Nate said, hugging her tight. Dora slipped her arms around his neck. 'I'll be waiting when you get back,' she said softly, gazing into his dark eyes.

Unable to speak, Nate just lowered his head and kissed her.

'Come on lads, say your goodbyes and get in line,' bellowed the officer with the moustache. 'Ladies, it's time to let your menfolk go.'

'I must go.' Gently, Nate eased himself free of Dora's embrace and started to push his way forwards. A hand gripped his arm tight and he found himself looking into a face so similar to his own. 'Alice.'

'Stay safe, Nate,' she said, her chestnut-brown eyes swimming with tears.

'I will.' Nate nodded. For a long moment their gaze lingered on each other. The whistle blew again, breaking the spell. 'Write to me?' Nate called over his shoulder as he was swept forward. Dora nodded. She half raised her hand to wave, but Nate was already gone.

The three girls huddled together amid the throng of women. Some were openly crying. Steam hissed and swirled around them as doors clanged and whistles blew. It seemed to take an age to get all the men on board but finally only woman and children and older gentlemen remained on the platform. The new recruits crowded at the train windows, each one eager for a final glimpse of their loved one's face. Leah stood on tiptoes, craning her neck in her attempts to catch sight of Harry. She searched the crowded windows in vain. She had no idea which carriage he was even in.

'Do you see them?' Dora asked, frantically scanning the faces leaning out the open windows.

'No,' wailed Alice. 'You'd think Samuel would be easy to spot. He's the only one wearing a dog collar, after all.'

Leah gave a shriek. 'There! Look.' She pointed to a carriage halfway along the platform. 'I can see Nate, look. And there's Harry next to him. Harry!' she shouted, waving madly. 'Harry!' The worried frown on Harry's face was instantly replaced by a grin as he spotted her. He edged over slightly and Samuel's head appeared next to him. Leah gripped Alice's hand tightly. 'I'm so glad they're going to stay together,' she whispered. 'That gives me such comfort.'

With a hiss of steam and screech of metal, the train gave a shrill whistle and began to roll forwards. The three girls clutched each other's arms and held their breath. Leah could hardly see through her tears. She waved, dragging Alice and Dora along as they followed the crowd of women running along the platform. She could no longer make out Harry, or Nate, or Samuel, in the blur of faces and waving hands, but still she waved. They followed the train for the length of the platform, stopping only when there was nowhere left to go yet still they stood, watching as the train disappeared from view, enveloped in a swirling cloud of steam.

A heavy silence fell over the station, broken only by the occasional sob and the distant whistle of the departed train.

'What do we do now?' said Dora, shakily as she wiped her eyes.

Alice took a ragged breath. 'It's going to be hard,' she

said, blowing her nose. 'None of us know how long they'll be away for but if what everyone is saying is true, and it is all over by Christmas, they'll be back before we know it.' Slipping her hands through Dora and Leah's arms, she gave a brittle laugh. 'Until then, we'll always have each other. Reverend Aldridge arrives tomorrow so I shall be moving back in with my grandparents. We shall be neighbours again.'

'Are we going to be all right, do you think?' Leah asked in a small voice.

'Of course, we are,' replied Alice stoutly, blinking back the tears. 'Like I said, we still have each other. Through thick and thin, come what may.' Forcing down the lump in her throat, she pasted on a bright smile and said, 'We need something to cheer us up before we go back to work. Who fancies a cup of tea and a toasted muffin at Joyce's tea shop? Aunt Eleanor sent me some money for my birthday, so it will be my treat.'

'Well, if you're happy to treat us, how can I refuse?' Leah smiled, swallowing down her tears.

'Me too,' said Dora. 'Thank you.'

'No thanks needed,' said Alice, steering them towards the exit. 'After all, that's what friends are for,' she added as, arm in arm, they hurried down the steps and out into the morning sunshine.

Discover more from Karen Dickson ...

The Dressmaker's Secret

Dorset, 1876. Born out of wedlock and given up by her birth mother, Lily is taken in by a kindly couple as a baby. But when, at the age of nine, Lily loses her adopted parents, she is forced to live with her awful Aunt Doris and cousin Jez, who treat her no better than a slave. She can only find solace in her dream of one day escaping her aunt and becoming a seamstress.

Five years later, now aged fourteen, Lily makes a startling discovery: that her birth father is none other than local aristocrat Sir Frederick Copperfield. Lily is stunned. And when she gets the chance to work for the Copperfields, she can't pass up the opportunity to get to know her half-sister Eleanor.

But will Eleanor ever really get to know her, or will Lily's true identity forever remain a secret?

'A compelling saga that will hold you fast from the first page to the last. Loved it' **Val Wood**

AVAILABLE NOW IN PAPERBACK, EBOOK AND EAUDIO

SIMON & SCHUSTER

The Shop Girl's Soldier

'An exciting, fresh and talented new voice –
a five-star read!' **Carol Rivers**

Southampton, 1905. Ellie-May and Jack
have been inseparable since birth. But when
Jack and his mother fall on hard times they
are thrown into the workhouse, and he and
Ellie-May are forced to say goodbye.

Four years later, now aged sixteen, Jack returns
to Southampton and is reunited with Ellie-
May. Quickly they both realize that their
feelings for each other go beyond friendship.
But when WWI approaches, Jack's duty to his
country is hard to ignore, and when he enlists
to fight, they are once again torn apart.

**Will Ellie-May and Jack find their way
back to each other before it's too late?**

**AVAILABLE NOW IN PAPERBACK
AND EBOOK**

**SIMON &
SCHUSTER**

A Songbird in Wartime

Shaftesbury, 1936. Mansfield House Hotel has been a refuge for Emily ever since she was orphaned at the age of 16. Not only did they give her employment as a chambermaid, but it's also where she met her fiancé Tom.

When theatre agent Roland stays at the hotel and hears Emily singing, he is determined to take her away to Bristol and make her a star. But knowing she'd never leave her fiancé, he hatches a plan to get Emily away from Tom.

Six years later, Emily has made a name for herself as 'The Bristol Songbird'. Her love for Tom is still as strong as ever, but she's not heard from him since that fateful night so long ago. And with the world enveloped in a war, it seems unlikely the two will ever meet again.

Will Emily and Tom ever find their way back to one another? Or will the war – and Roland – succeed in keeping them apart?

AVAILABLE NOW IN PAPERBACK AND EBOOK

**SIMON &
SCHUSTER**